I0891637

PRAISE FOR DEBRA WEBB

Deeper Than the Dead

"Expertly plotted and whip smart, *Deeper Than the Dead* is an exceedingly clever crime thriller filled with secrets, betrayals, and complex characters. Webb manages to hit that sweet spot between family drama and police procedural. This one is sure to be a hit in the crime-thriller genre. A wild and massively entertaining ride."

—Christina McDonald, *USA Today* bestselling author

The Last Lie Told

"A complex case fraught with angst and danger ends with surprising revelations."

—*Kirkus Reviews*

"Debra Webb writes the kind of thrillers I love to read. Sure, there is a murder or more. Yes, there's a twisted mystery to be solved. Once again, in *The Last Lie Told*, her characters are fully rendered and reveal themselves authentically as her novel unfolds and careens to its stunning conclusion. *The Last Lie Told* is her best yet. Webb is the queen of smart suspense."

—Gregg Olsen, #1 *New York Times* bestselling author

Can't Go Back

"A complex, exciting mystery."

—*Kirkus Reviews*

"Police procedural fans will be sorry to see the last of Kerri and Luke."

—*Publishers Weekly*

"Threats, violence, and a dramatic climax . . . good for procedural readers."

—*Library Journal*

Gone Too Far

"An intriguing, fast-paced combination of police procedural and thriller."

—*Kirkus Reviews*

"Those who like a lot of family drama in their police procedurals will be satisfied."

—*Publishers Weekly*

Trust No One

"*Trust No One* is Debra Webb at her finest. Political intrigue and dark family secrets will keep readers feverishly turning pages to uncover all the twists in this stunning thriller."

—Melinda Leigh, #1 *Wall Street Journal* bestselling author of *Cross Her Heart*

"A wild, twisting crime thriller filled with secrets, betrayals, and complex characters that will keep you up until you reach the last darkly satisfying page. A five-star beginning to Debra Webb's explosive series!"

—Allison Brennan, *New York Times* bestselling author

"Debra Webb once again delivers with *Trust No One*, a twisty and gritty page-turning procedural with a cast of complex characters and a compelling cop heroine in Detective Kerri Devlin. I look forward to seeing more of Detectives Devlin and Falco."

—Loreth Anne White, *Washington Post* bestselling author of *In the Deep*

"*Trust No One* is a gritty and exciting ride. Webb skillfully weaves together a mystery filled with twists and turns. I was riveted as each layer of the past peeled away, revealing dark secrets. An intriguing cast of complicated characters, led by the compelling Detective Kerri Devlin, had me holding my breath until the last page."

—Brianna Labuskes, *Washington Post* bestselling author of *Girls of Glass*

"Debra Webb's name says it all."

—Karen Rose, *New York Times* bestselling author

THE FATAL CONFIDANT

OTHER TITLES BY DEBRA WEBB

Vera Boyett

Deeper Than the Dead

Closer Than You Know

Secrets You Can't Keep

Finley O'Sullivan

The Last Lie Told

The Nature of Secrets

All the Little Truths

Devlin & Falco

Trust No One

Gone Too Far

Can't Go Back

Standalones

The Devoted Game

The Ten Year Lie

Deep Dark Truth

The Drowning Season

Lost in the Dark

What Goes Around

THE FATAL CONFIDANT

DEBRA WEBB

THOMAS & MERCER

This is a work of fiction. Names, characters, organizations, places, events, and incidents are either products of the author's imagination or are used fictitiously. Otherwise, any resemblance to actual persons, living or dead, is purely coincidental.

Published by Thomas & Mercer, Seattle

www.apub.com

EU product safety contact:
Amazon Media EU S. à r.l.
38, avenue John F. Kennedy, L-1855 Luxembourg
amazonpublishing-gpsr@amazon.com

ISBN-13: 9781662534478 (paperback)
ISBN-13: 9781662534461 (digital)

Cover design by Faceout Studio, Molly von Borstel
Cover image: © Grand Warszawski / Getty; © wavebreakmedia, © caesart, © Kriengsuk Prasroetsung, © PETER A WOMER / Shutterstock

Printed in the United States of America

There are some characters who simply write themselves. I'll be in the middle of a story and realize that a certain character very nearly outshines the main protagonists. In this story there is a character like that. A character whose wit, charm, and straight-shooting ways snap you up and sweep you more deeply into the story. The character Kim Schaffer is the type of honest, hardworking member of law enforcement who makes us proud. Lucky for me, Kim is also very real and one of my friends. Kim, her brilliant son, Jonathan, and sweetheart of a husband, Jim, are amazing people. This book is dedicated to the one and only Kim Schaffer.

1

Sunday, September 5, 9:40 p.m.
Mountain Brook, Alabama

She clicked off the flashlight then froze.

Didn't dare move.

Didn't even breathe.

She listened intently beyond the frantic pounding in her chest and the roar of blood in her ears. She'd heard something. Anticipation fired through her veins.

The rustling of leaves. An animal? Maybe. These woods were full of wildlife.

Ten . . . twenty seconds passed with the breeze whispering through the trees. Her heart rate slowed. Nothing. Not another distinguishable noise beyond the night sounds. The consuming darkness continued pressing in on her, engulfing her—and the unsavory business to which she had no choice but to attend.

She had to do this and get out of here.

Now!

Slowly, the panic drained away. Urgency took its place. She was still alone. Hadn't been caught. Thank God. But she had to hurry.

Reaching for the courage that had momentarily deserted her, she drew in a ragged breath and forced herself to return to the task. With a flex of her thumb, she slid the flashlight's switch back into the on position and put it on the ground to illuminate her efforts. The narrow beam sliced across her arms as she continued digging, clawing at the soft earth with the shovel. Deeper. A shiver rushed over her skin. She had to hurry. Getting caught would not be good.

Not good at all.

Her respiration grew labored as that reality shrouded her as surely as the darkness had. Dig! Harder. Deeper. Faster. Get done and get the hell out of there!

She had to hide this mess . . . *all of it.* This part, the most important part, had to be here, where no one would think to look. Not now, after all these years. On the off chance someone did, the evidence would only do what it had done all along . . . point in the wrong direction.

Good enough. She stopped, lowered the shovel to the ground, and sat back on her haunches to scrutinize the hole she'd carved out. Yes. This was sufficient.

Twisting her torso, careful not to make the slightest noise, she reached into the bag she'd carried from her borrowed car parked half a mile away. The plastic bag felt heavy though the contents weighed hardly anything at all.

Two gold bands. Symbols of love and commitment, the precious circles stained with blood after being tugged from cold, lifeless fingers.

Goose bumps spilled across her skin as that scenario played out in her head. She banished the images, dropped the rings into the Beanee Weenee can, then crushed the opened end as tightly together as her strength would allow before placing it in the small grave she'd burrowed. If anyone happened to dig around in this spot, they would merely ignore what was presumed to be trash. Campers and hikers buried their trash all the time.

Satisfied, she carefully returned the excavated soil into its rightful resting place. She smoothed and patted the surface, then spread fallen leaves across it.

There.

No one would ever suspect that barely a foot beneath the seemingly undisturbed spot lay the final pieces of a puzzle that to this day, fifteen years later, had not been solved. She shivered.

Grabbing the shovel and flashlight, she pushed to her feet. The past wasn't important right now. What mattered was the present. And the future. Protection, survival, those were the key elements.

She had learned from experience that survival was the only thing that really counted.

She intended to survive.

Cautiously retracing her steps through the trees and dense underbrush, she reached the side road where she'd left the car. After scanning carefully for any sign of approaching headlights, she moved more quickly.

She was almost home free.

Just one last detail to take care of and this bothersome night would be behind her.

The tools grasped firmly under one arm, she dug the key fob from the pocket of her jeans and opened the trunk. The accessory light flickered once then steadied, filling the trunk with a dim, eerie glow. She tossed the shovel and flashlight inside and should have closed the lid then. That would have been the smart thing to do. But she didn't.

Instead, she stared at the one remaining obstacle in this monumental mess that required her immediate attention.

The body.

She had to figure out what to do with the body.

2

Tuesday, September 7, 3:00 p.m.
Birmingham, Alabama
Criminal Justice Center

Death was too good for the son of a bitch.

Silence choked the remainder of the air out of the interview room, making it impossible for Carson Tanner to draw a breath. The traumatic seconds expanded into a full minute that felt like an hour.

Misery sat like a cold, hard stone in his gut. He had waited fifteen long years, had bucked the very system to which he'd devoted his entire adult life just to be present today and hear what the shackled animal seated at the table across from him had to say.

Joseph Stokes. The psychotic killer who had murdered Carson's family. A serial offender who had eluded justice for far too long.

District Attorney Donald Wainwright and Aidan Moore, the court appointed attorney assigned to Stokes's case, were seated next to Carson. One of Jefferson County's finest stood nearby, his right hand resting on the butt of his holstered weapon.

The entire tristate area, first and foremost the city of Birmingham, had been watching this drama unfold in the media . . . praying that Stokes would get what was coming to him for his heinous deeds. A single move of aggression and Stokes might not exit the room alive, leaving the world home to one less homicidal maniac.

The mere thought had anticipation exploding in Carson's chest. But as gratifying as that resolution would be, it would not give him closure. He had unanswered questions. One in particular he wanted—no, he needed.

"This is a one-time offer, Stokes," Wainwright reminded him. "Back out now and it's over. I'll have you scheduled for lethal injection so fast you'll think you're in the express lane at the Walmart."

"I told you," Stokes maintained with a haughtiness that made Carson sick to his stomach, "I ain't signing nothing till you give me your word I can have my say."

The legal document awaiting endorsement by Stokes offered him one thing, just one. *Life.* He'd murdered at least a dozen people. He wasn't worthy of another second on this earth. But death would be far too simple a penalty to pay.

Carson wanted him to live. A long, long time. In a five-by-nine maximum security cell until the day he dragged in his last pathetic gasp of oxygen. He wanted him in the worst prison in Alabama, getting what he deserved day in and day out from the cellblocks full of inmates who despised those who included the abuse or murder of children in their inventory of evil deeds.

"Mr. Stokes." Moore took a moment to adjust his standard, black-framed eyeglasses. "I have a legal obligation to advise you against additional comments at this critical juncture. As the district attorney said, we should move forward with the reason we're here."

Stokes smirked. "You don't understand, counselor. I had a dream last night. Made me remember things like it was yesterday. This one part was so vivid." He looked straight at Carson with glee in his repugnant eyes. "I really need to tell *someone*."

Carson's jaw clenched. He steeled himself despite the probability that whatever the revelation, it couldn't be worse than what he'd witnessed with his own eyes that day . . . fifteen years ago. So much blood . . .

"No more stalling." Wainwright folded his arms over his chest. "Sign the contract, then you can say what you have to say. Otherwise this meeting is over."

Carson felt those old haunting fears nip at his resolve. No second thoughts. He had to hear this . . . had to know.

Smug with victory, Stokes picked up the pen. "In that case, it'd be my pleasure, Mr. DA." The lowlife scrawled his name, then tossed the pen aside. "Satisfied?"

Moore studied the document briefly then passed it to Wainwright, who glanced at the signature before dropping both the contract and the pen into his briefcase. He leveled a cold, hard stare on Stokes. "Get it over with. But"—he pointed a finger at the piece of shit who'd just signed away his right to trial by a jury of his peers—"you tread carefully."

Stokes lounged in his chair, not the slightest bit intimidated. "You see," he said carefully, "things didn't happen exactly the way the official reports said." He inhaled a deep, gratifying breath. "The little girl." He turned his attention fully on Carson. "She didn't die right away."

Agony pierced Carson, twisting his insides into writhing knots. The little girl. *My sister, Katie.*

"Don't go down that path," Wainwright warned.

"Let him talk," Carson overruled.

After a decade and a half of wondering—of obsessing over the possibilities—Carson at last knew the name and the face of the man who had shattered his world.

Now he wanted to know why.

"We played those last few minutes." Stokes snickered, the vile, grating noise irreverent. "She kept crying, *Mommy,* but . . . Mommy was already dead."

"That's enough!" Wainwright cautioned.

Carson lifted a hand to quiet the objection even as murder burgeoned in his heart. "I want to hear what he has to say."

"Don't allow this, Carson," Wainwright urged. "It won't give you the closure you're looking for."

"What's the matter?" Stokes cocked his head, clearly excited about the tension he generated, even shackled as he was. "You got a problem with hearing the *real* story, Mr. DA?" The bastard snorted. "Well, you shouldda thought of that before. I sorta like seeing you bastards sweat."

Moore started to object but his client cut him off. "Besides, you don't gotta listen. What I have to say is personal. Between me and Carson Tanner." A sadistic grin spread across his loathsome face. "We should be alone for that."

Carson didn't flinch. "That's a reasonable request."

"Absolutely not going to—"

"Five minutes," Carson argued, interrupting Wainwright, his mentor, the man he admired and respected above all others.

The district attorney's gaze held Carson's for a beat, then two. He exhaled a heavy breath. "If you're sure that's what you want." Wainwright picked up his briefcase and stood. "You watch yourself, Stokes, this isn't over until *I* say it's over," he warned. "Five minutes. Not a second longer."

Moore rose from his chair, wordlessly announcing his concurrence. He'd done his job. Represented a killer to the best of his ability as required by law.

Wainwright nodded to the deputy standing by, and the three exited the room.

That suffocating heaviness crowded in once more.

Stokes settled his attention on Carson. After an endless moment of probing silence, he spoke. "Well, well, the lone survivor. Looks like you did pretty good for yourself, a deputy district attorney and all." Stokes leaned forward. "A regular hotshot, ain't you, boy? Newspapers call you the Avenger or some such shit. A chip off the old block." He made a disparaging sound. "'Course your daddy wasn't so big and powerful when he was on his knees begging for mercy."

Fury burned low and deep, but Carson wasn't going to waste this opportunity being baited by the son of a bitch. "I have one question."

Stokes eased forward a little more, putting his face only inches from Carson's. "I touched her," he whispered. "That little sister of yours. Could've been all up in that tight little pussy, but time was short and I still had your daddy to gut."

Carson's fingers curled into fists of restraint. "My sister wasn't raped. My mother, either." *Stay cool just a few minutes more.* "None of your victims were sexually assaulted." Stokes wanted Carson angry. Wanted him to react. Not today. He needed that one answer. "Your file says you're impotent so don't try your perverted strategy with me."

The bastard had the unmitigated gall to snigger. "That doesn't mean I didn't touch 'em." He growled with sick pleasure. "Felt *good.* Their skin was so smooth and soft. Their blood so hot, it scorched my hands. Made that old cock of mine stand at attention."

Carson swallowed back the rising bile of disgust. This one question had burned in his brain, twisted in his gut all those years. He had to know. "Why *my* family?"

Menace danced in the madman's eyes. "I watched them for days," he murmured, his voice thick with something like longing. "Waited for just the right moment."

"You didn't answer the question." Carson refused to let him see for a damned second that he was hanging on to control by a single unraveling thread. "Why?"

Stokes sprang to his feet, testing his margin of freedom. His shackles rattled. "Because I could," he snarled.

Carson took a moment, let those words permeate him, igniting the sheer determination necessary to see this through without yielding to his baser instincts. He pushed back his chair and stood slowly to put himself at eye level with the bastard once more.

"And there wasn't a damned thing you or anybody else could do to stop me," Stokes taunted.

The faintest glimmer of what had earned Carson the nickname *Avenger* awakened. Adrenalized him. "There wasn't a single link discovered between you and any member of my family."

Therein lay the rub, the part of this that gave Carson pause no matter that the scumbag had confessed. He hadn't been able to get past that discrepancy when considered with the other glaring deviation from Stokes's usual MO: the missing personal effects. Stokes never took so much as a lock of hair from his victims. Only their dignities and their lives—in that order. And why take items from two of the victims and not the third? Nothing of Katie's had been missing. Something was wrong with that scenario.

"With every other case linked to you," Carson continued, "that connection to the victims was present."

Stokes didn't answer, merely stared at Carson with demented amusement.

"I'll ask you again," Carson reiterated far more patiently than he had any obligation to given the blitz of emotions whipping inside him. "Why?"

"You think you got me all figured out"—Stokes jerked at his manacles, causing the chains to rattle forebodingly yet again—"that you're better than me, don't you? But you're not. You're just like me." His gaze narrowed with accusation. "The newspapers said you had their blood all over you. Felt good, didn't it?"

"You don't know me." Carson's wrath seethed dangerously close to the surface, the intensity increasing with each second, each breath. "Just like you didn't know my family. So answer the damned question. Why . . . *my* . . . family?"

"I could tell you something that would turn your fancy world upside down all over again." Stokes reared his shoulders back, full of himself. "*Guaranteed.* But I think I'll let you wonder. Keep that juicy little tidbit to myself for another decade or so."

Panic hurtled through Carson, overpowering all else before he could quell the reaction. What could this monster know beyond what he had confessed? Nothing. *Nothing.* Just more of his baiting. Had to be.

Didn't matter. Carson needed an answer. He couldn't let Stokes go off on one of his power trips. There was only one way to prevent that—withdraw the significance. "Then I guess we have nothing else to talk about."

When Carson would have turned away, the scumbag spoke again. "Wait, wait. You can't really say for sure I did or didn't have contact with your precious little family. That's not even what's bothering you." Stokes laughed softly, revoltingly. "It's the rings, ain't it?"

Pain detonated along Carson's nerve endings as more images burned his retinas. He blinked them away, snatched back his sinking authority. "You aren't the first to include a new step or to skip one," he countered, playing devil's advocate with his own doubts as well as Stokes's assertion. "Killers far more clever than you have deviated from their patterns on occasion."

Stokes inclined his head left then right as if evaluating the implication. "Or maybe," he proposed, "I just wanted something so I could remember your family. After all, they were so special. Way more than all the others. Especially that little sister of yours."

Carson snapped. He went for the scumbag's throat. His fingers gripped that disgusting flesh and instinctively locked like a vise.

Stokes grabbed Carson's shirtfront, pulling him in rather than pushing him away. "Do it, you coward," he dared. "Show 'em what you're really made of!"

Carson's brutal grasp tightened with anticipation. A surge of power rushed through him as the color of oxygen deprivation claimed Stokes's pale complexion. *Die, you bastard!*

The door flew open, banged against the wall. "Mr. Tanner, step away from the prisoner," the deputy ordered.

Carson couldn't stop. He couldn't let Stokes live. He'd thought he could. He'd intended to. But he couldn't. He had to stop him . . . to feel that throbbing pulse beneath his fingers slow to a dead stop before the scumbag slumped to the floor.

"Carson, back off!"

Wainwright's command barely trickled past the cloak of retribution . . . wasn't nearly enough to stop Carson from doing what had to be done.

Hands were suddenly on his arms, peeling his fingers back, pulling him away from Stokes. Stokes gasped for air. Coughed. Too bad he didn't choke to death.

"Get him out of here," Wainwright shouted to the deputy.

The fury still roiled inside Carson, making him want to grab for Stokes again even as the deputy unlocked the tether securing the shackles to the floor and another rushed in to assist with the prisoner's transport.

Stokes was going to Holman, the worst of the worst facilities in the state of Alabama, perhaps even the country. Carson had done his research; Stokes would spend the rest of his life wishing he were dead. He would never again have the opportunity to hurt another family.

And he would pay. How he would pay.

As Stokes was led past Carson, he stalled, refused to go a step farther. That detestable gaze locked with Carson's. "Follow your instincts, Tanner. You know something ain't right." His lips screwed into that insane expression that bore no resemblance to a smile. "Ask yourself if you'll ever really know what happened."

"Get him out of here!" Wainwright commanded.

"Maybe you're just like the others!" Stokes shouted as he fought to slow his removal from the room. "Tell me, Tanner, when did *you* stop caring about the truth?"

Carson stared after the bastard, his heart threatening its confines. The *truth.* He had that now, didn't he? But . . . what if there was more? That same old doubt and uncertainty weighed down on his shoulders, tightened like a band around his chest.

"He's toying with you, Carson," Wainwright insisted, his tone, his expression laden with regret. "You know he likes to watch his prey twitch. Don't let him get to you."

Carson nodded, the solitary action stiff and jerky.

"Let it go," Wainwright urged. "We both know his MO."

Yes, Carson knew. But that didn't change the fact that in this instance Stokes was right. Carson would never know with any degree of confidence what really happened.

There had been no witnesses . . . no conclusive evidence . . . just death. And questions.

Questions that remained unanswered.

3

7:15 p.m.
Birmingham
Jazz Factory

What the hell was he doing here?

Carson propped his forearms on the counter and leaned against the bar without bothering to slide onto a stool. He should be elated. The Stokes file was closed; the Tanner investigation resolved. Justice had been served and a killer was on his way to life in prison without the possibility of parole. By eleven o'clock tomorrow morning Stokes would be processed into Holman, the Alabama state penitentiary in Atmore, where his own personal hell on earth waited.

He was finally going to pay.

Ask yourself if you'll ever really know what happened.

Carson blinked, shattering Stokes's disturbing words. It was over. Done. Sifting through the details and the what-ifs wasn't going to change the facts. They had their killer, if not the answer Carson wanted so desperately. End of story.

But . . . what if Stokes wasn't the one?

Carson inhaled a deep breath, then blew it out.

The bastard confessed. The rest was nothing but bullshit. Enough with the doubts already.

The bartender tilted his head in question, drawing Carson's attention. "Sparkling water with lime."

Alcohol was off limits. Despite his inability to keep his emotions in check today, control was essential to Carson. He didn't like losing it . . . for any reason. Once in a lifetime was enough . . . and that one time had cost him everything.

"Check out the brunette at nine o'clock." Scotch in hand, Keller Luttrell, friend and colleague, perched on the stool next to Carson with his back to the bar to facilitate his babe-watching. Besides being a highly skilled strategist in the courtroom, the man was an expert marksman when it came to spotting hot chicks at maximum range.

Carson glanced over his shoulder to take a look at the target currently in his colleague's crosshairs and dutifully performed the expected appraisal. "Yeah. She's great." Hence the rarity of these sorts of male-bonding occasions. Unlike his friend, who appeared to do his best trial groundwork in this atmosphere, Carson had neither the time nor the inclination.

"I could fall in love with that." Luttrell tracked the brunette's movements with the same expertise he used to monitor and analyze a jury's subtlest reaction.

Carson should be at home working. He had a briefcase packed with work lying on the passenger seat of his BMW. "I'm having this drink and then I'm going home with my briefcase," Carson reminded his pal. That had been their bargain. One drink. An hour tops.

"Come on," Luttrell urged. "Snap out of it. Celebrate. The past is finally buried. You can move on. Hell, man, take a freaking vacation. I can handle most of your caseload." He shrugged. "The others will pitch in. You need a real break. I can't remember the last time you took a day off, much less a week."

Carson had never taken a vacation. He wouldn't now. "Yeah, right." He shot his friend a look that underscored the statement. "And let you suck up to Wainwright while I'm gone? No way."

"Oh ho." Luttrell belted out a laugh. "I'm good, but I'm not *that* good. You're Wainwright's favorite and everybody knows it. Nothing short of your going off the deep end will change that."

Carson cringed inwardly.

Luttrell just kept talking, like the Energizer-frigging-Bunny, without a clue he'd hit a nerve. "But we also know that you're the star for a reason," he waxed on before knocking back a slug of Scotch. "You're the best, buddy. There's no denying it."

His sincerity couldn't completely disguise the slightest hint of envy. Carson had gotten used to that long ago and understood that it wasn't actually personal. Came with the territory. It was lonely at the top for a reason.

"But we're not here to talk about work," his colleague went on. He stared pointedly at Carson's profile. "When's the last time you did anything spontaneous that didn't involve your briefcase?"

"Fuck off," Carson muttered. He wasn't looking for personal advice from his skirt-chasing buddy.

"Listen, man." Luttrell set aside the drink he'd been nursing since their arrival. "I know this excavating of the past has been tough on you." He paused, as lawyers do when allowing the jury's anticipation to build to a pivotal moment. "But you've got to stop spending every second focused on work. Real life is calling and you're ignoring the summons." He leaned closer. "Seriously, when's the last time you got laid?"

Carson should have seen that one coming. "That"—he took a swallow of his for-appearances-sake-only drink—"is none of your business." Luttrell had just dropped several notches on Carson's opinion scale, from confidant to asshole. Only an asshole would ask a man that question when he already knew the answer.

"We've all noticed how stressed you are," Luttrell had the balls to add. "There's a damned short fuse on your temper these days. You need to work off some of that tension. Going months without sex just isn't natural, man."

This conversation was officially over. Carson leveled a steady stare on Luttrell. "We are not analyzing my sex life."

Luttrell held up his hands. "Just calling it like I see it. You need sex, Carson. Look around you." He waved magnanimously, not about to give up without a closing argument. "This place is full of beautiful women. Let yourself go. Talk to someone, for Christ's sake. Share a drink. See where it goes. Sunday's your birthday, man. You've gotta live a little before you're too old."

His birthday. Thirty-one. Carson had almost succeeded in forgetting that insignificant date. "You know how I feel about birthdays." He looked his friend straight in the eye. "Do you understand me?" If anyone, *anyone,* had any ideas about a birthday party, Carson intended to quash that little scheme here and now. He hadn't celebrated a birthday since . . . he'd turned sixteen. More of the past tried elbowing its way into his head, but he crammed it back into that dark place he refused to visit.

"Yeah. Yeah." Luttrell jerked his head toward the clutch of patrons on his right. "Check it out. Forget the brunette. That lady in the red dress is seriously hot, bro. She's looked your way at least twice. Make a move." He leaned close again. "It's that easy. All you have to be is willing."

Carson shook his head. "I find it absolutely fascinating that you can read minds." He picked up his drink but paused short of setting the glass to his lips. "Must come in handy when speculating how a jury's leaning."

Luttrell rolled his eyes. "You won't let me throw you a birthday bash, at least let me get you off on the right foot tonight. I've pointed out two gorgeous ladies. Take your pick. You should celebrate putting the past to rest."

"Back off or I'm out of here." Maybe ten minutes more and Carson was gone anyway.

"All right, all right." Luttrell frowned. He reached into the pocket of his trousers and withdrew his cell phone. After checking the text message on the screen, he puffed out a bothered breath. "Dammit. Gotta go. Opposing counsel on one of my cases wants to have drinks." He tossed a couple of bills onto the counter. "Remember what I said, Carson. I didn't strong-arm you into coming here for nothing. Let go. Just this once. It'll make a new man out of you."

Carson didn't acknowledge his final remarks, just let him go. Instead, he stared into his glass, his mind wandering back to Stokes and the deal Wainwright had made in exchange for his confession. Two unsolved high-profile murder cases, including Carson's family, were now closed. They had their man.

Ask yourself if you'll ever really know what happened.

Carson banished the echo. He shouldn't have let the bastard get to him. It was over. No more questions.

"Drinking alone is never a good sign."

Carson turned to the woman who had moved up beside him. Long blond hair. Wide blue eyes. Lush lips. Before he could stop the move, his attention wandered lower. A great body packaged in a skin-tight red dress.

Wasn't this one of the women Luttrell had pointed out just minutes ago? The lady was definitely hot, and he couldn't deny an immediate attraction. But that wasn't going to stop Carson from going home alone.

"You're right," he said in response to her allegation, "drinking alone isn't a good sign." *Even when it's only sparkling water,* he didn't qualify. "That's why I always call it a night while it's still early enough to accomplish something meaningful." Like reading briefs and reviewing cases.

The lady smiled, somehow managing to hold on to the attention he'd fully intended to withdraw. "You look like the kind of man who searches for meaning in all that he does." She flashed that wickedly alluring smile for the bartender as he paused for her order. "Vodka. Straight up."

While Carson found himself watching her every move, the bartender poured her drink. She picked up her glass and tapped it against Carson's.

"Cheers."

Maybe he'd allowed Luttrell's comments to get under his skin. Had to be the reason his fixation with her profile and watching her sip the vodka persisted. All five senses abruptly yawned and stretched, making him keenly aware of the music, the cool glass in his hand, and her unique and stirringly subtle scent.

Six months. No sex in six months. Too long. The power of suggestion was undermining his self-discipline. He'd written the book on using that very tactic in the courtroom. Where was his ruthless willpower now?

She turned fully toward him then. "So." She steadily contemplated Carson, amping up the tension working its way through his body. "What deeper meaning are you searching for tonight?"

Just go.

Carson opened his mouth to bid her good night, but the words vanished somewhere between his brain and his tongue. Possibly due to the way she looked at his mouth in anticipation of his reply or just maybe because his own gaze kept venturing to *her* mouth.

Those voluptuous lips slid into another smile. “Oh, I see. You’re here for *that*.”

Shit. Had she seen something in his eyes? Noted some flash of interest on his face? He really was slipping here.

Time for polite regrets and a prompt exit.

“As stimulating as this conversation is”—he snagged some cash from his pocket and tossed it on the counter—“I have to be going.” He didn’t do relationships or one-night stands. He did work.

“Your friend said it was your birthday or something?” she asked before he could make his escape. “Did your party run out of steam already?”

Now Carson was beginning to get the picture. Damn Keller Luttrell. “Birthday parties are vastly overrated.”

Her mouth puckered into a sexy pout. “You’ve never had a birthday party?”

He hesitated, silently chastised himself for continuing the conversation considering Luttrell had likely scripted the scene line by line. “Not since I was sixteen.” He closed out the bittersweet memories that instantly took advantage of that line of questioning. *Just go.* He needed work to forget about the past . . . and birthdays. And sexy ladies in fuck-me red dresses.

“At least you had one.”

The unexpected vulnerability in her voice reeled him back in for more . . . shouldn’t have, but it did. “You never had a birthday party?” Now why the hell had he asked her that? He was supposed to wrap this up and walk.

She moved her head slowly side-to-side. “Not one.” The remembered pain in her eyes, the kind that was all too familiar to him, put another hell of a crack in his willpower.

“When you’re all alone at the end of the day it’s difficult to celebrate much of anything.”

She couldn't have guessed that about him. Had to be Luttrell. "Look." He held her wistful gaze with a firm, let's-get-this-straight one of his own. "I think I know what's going on here, and my friend can be overly ambitious in his machinations. You shouldn't trust anything he says." Luttrell was going to be sorry he'd hatched up this outrageous hoax.

The lady weighed his assertions before opening her clutch once more. Rather than making the exit he had planned, Carson watched with more of that inexplicable interest. He was making this way too easy for his friend.

The lady withdrew a key card and placed it on the counter. "I'm in room three fifteen at the Tutwiler. If *that* is what you're looking for, I'll be there all night."

She started to turn away but didn't; instead she tilted her lips close to his ear, and whispered, "No one should be alone on a night like this."

Then she walked away, her hips swaying in blatant invitation.

Had he just been propositioned?

Carson shook his head.

Luttrell would do anything to prove his point.

Carson wasn't falling for it. He was going home with his briefcase. His mistress, as Luttrell would say.

Yet his gaze lingered on the last place he'd seen *her* before she'd disappeared in the crowd. Temptation nudged him.

The whole idea was absurd.

No one should be alone on a night like this.

He couldn't do *that. That* was way out of bounds.

Carson didn't operate on impulse. He went with the facts, with instinct.

Stick with the plan. Go home. Work.

But then . . . Carson would never know what his friend was actually up to. And she had left her key lying right here on the bar. Before reason could sink past the undeniable taste of lust still making his mouth water, Carson picked up the key card and walked out of the club.

He was definitely crazy.

The question was, just how crazy.

The Tutwiler stood directly across the street. The 1914 building with its grand balconies and intricate architectural details loomed against the night. A Birmingham landmark. In the event his friend had gone momentarily stupid and sprung for the real thing, Carson wondered how the city would feel about a high-class call girl using the historic property for a base of operation. Or a county-paid employee arranging the rendezvous.

Carson entered the elegant hotel lobby, bypassed the bank of elevators, and went straight for the stairs. He would return the lady's key and give her a succinct message to pass along to his dickhead of a friend.

On the third floor Carson located room 315 but hesitated before knocking. He listened. No television noise, no whispering voices. Maybe music; too low to distinguish.

One quick rap of his knuckles and movement stirred inside the room. The door opened and those unforgettable blue eyes tangled with his. More of that startlingly keen interest swirled low in his belly. Oh yeah, he'd neglected his needs far too long.

"I see you've made up your mind." A half-empty short glass hung from the fingers of her right hand.

No one else appeared. No shouts of *Surprise!* Just the soft whisper of music floating on the air. This was not what he'd anticipated finding . . . this was apparently an actual proposition. *Maybe.* The jury was still out.

"I think"—Carson offered the key card—"there's been a miscommunication."

She accepted the card with her free hand. "That's regrettable."

His respiration quickened. "Well. Good night then." He turned to go.

"You're wondering . . ."

He shouldn't have paused as she spoke, but he did.

" . . . who paid me to try and seduce you."

Carson turned his head, looked directly at her to examine her expression, her eyes, for some indication of precisely what the lady was up to. To spot the deception.

"Or"—she lifted her shoulders in the barest of shrugs—"you're wondering just how much a night with a woman like me would cost.

And if it would be worth the price." The challenge in her voice, in her eyes, coerced him into once more abandoning his plan to just walk away. Experience told him he would regret that flaw in his personality. He never could resist a challenge.

"Prostitution is illegal in this state," he reminded her, though he suspected this woman was no hooker. She had an objective. She wanted to play. With him. The only remaining issue was the source of her motivation.

"I'm aware that prostitution is illegal." She inclined her head and studied his face a long moment before wetting those luxurious lips with the tip of her tongue. "Are you in law enforcement?"

"It so happens I am." The urge to loosen his tie an inch was overwhelming. If she knew who he was, she was damned good at not letting it show.

Would Luttrell go that far?

"Well," she offered, "perhaps you should investigate." She turned her back to him and disappeared into the room, leaving the door open for him to follow.

Carson glanced right, then left: The corridor was deserted. There was no one to watch, to witness him crossing the line she had drawn in the sand. *This is a mistake.*

He had work.

He should go.

Now.

And still he followed her inside. He closed the door and, despite mounting evidence that this was indeed a setup, waited to see what she would do next.

She lounged against the French doors that opened to the balcony and looked directly at him, her gaze resolute. He braced for the battle of wills, for anything she could possibly conceive to throw his way.

"Take off your clothes," she ordered.

Anything except that.

4

Carson choked out a laugh.

Then he frowned.

The lady was serious.

As intrigued as he was, it was time to cut to the chase. This whole clandestine rendezvous had gone far enough.

Tomorrow Keller Luttrell was getting his ass kicked.

Carson took control of the encounter by taking a step away from the door, in her direction. "Let's back this up just a little bit." Pushing aside the lapels of his jacket, he slid his hands into his trouser pockets. "Is this a business transaction or a social encounter?"

First, he would give her a chance to save face.

"This is not a business transaction." She moved a step toward him, calling his bluff. "This is about birthdays, celebrations, and physical attraction."

Her confidence ignited a new kind of anticipation before he could check the reaction. Whoever had given her cues had known all the right buttons to push. Carson hated celebrating birthdays and holidays alone . . . that was why he didn't do either anymore. Further, there was nothing he liked more than a challenge. No one knew that better than Luttrell.

"I like what I see and I'm certain the feeling is mutual," she added frankly as she took a long, slow survey from the classic cut of his hair to his polished oxfords. Unhurriedly, she retraced her path until her gaze collided with his once more. “Have I misjudged what I see?” She glanced pointedly at his crotch.

Heat ignited beneath his skin. The gauntlet was definitely on the ground. She wasn’t cracking without a battle. This was a woman accustomed to having her way with men.

A battle it would be. “Do you pick up men in this manner often?” Another step disappeared between them, this one his. Matching her maneuver, his gaze traveled down those long legs, all the way to the devil-red polish glinting on her toenails and over the strappy stilettos in the same sizzling color. Another blast of tension tightened below his belt, fueling the fire her words had kindled far too quickly.

“Often is relative, don’t you think?” She removed her dangly earrings and tossed them onto the closest table. “For some, there aren’t enough days in the week. For others, waiting is the best aphrodisiac of all.”

The muscle in his jaw tightened. *You need sex, Carson.* But not like this. He acquired the next step, decided to up the ante. Put her on the defensive. “So, this isn’t the first time you’ve lured a stranger to your hotel room.”

She abided the roundabout insult without a flinch. Instead of telling him to go to hell or slapping his face, she blatantly and deliberately assessed him a second time.

Another of the smiles that mesmerized him so easily glided across her sleek lips. “If I confess my sins, will you be afraid to play with me?”

Excitement shot through him. He dismissed it, refused to allow his baser instincts that kind of leverage twice in one day. He hadn’t run out of angles just yet.

Make it personal. “I assume you have a name.”

She moved closer, one more step then a second. “For tonight, why don’t we pretend we’re anyone but who we are?”

Temptation nudged him harder. Made him hesitate, but not for long. He gave his head a shake. “I’m afraid you’ve picked the wrong man.” He didn’t take risks outside the boundaries of a case; didn’t play these kinds of meaningless games. He was done.

"I see." Impervious, she claimed the final step between them. A subtle whiff of her perfume teased his senses. Made him long to be closer still . . . close enough to taste her.

Stupid, Carson. Incredibly stupid.

He drew in a breath, wished he hadn't. The fragrance that had tickled his senses now permeated his lungs, renewed his forbidden desire. It was either get the hell out of there or risk passing the point of no return. "I should go now." He hesitated before following through. "Tell my friend that payback is hell."

When he would have acted on his intent, she reached for his tie and dragged her fingers down its length. "You believe your friend had something to do with this?" Slowly, she inched her fingers upward again and worked loose the silk knot at his throat. "A birthday gift, maybe?"

Well, there was his answer. Luttrell would so regret this. "My friend has a predilection for skirting the fringes of ethics. Usually mine."

Her palms skimmed his chest. Already tense muscles hardened. "You should relax. I'll bet you don't do that often."

Before he could decide whether to counter her statement or simply walk out the door, she pulled away and crossed to the bar. She picked up the bottle of liquor waiting there. *Bacardi.* Memories bombarded him, set off an alarm. He hadn't tasted rum in fifteen years. Hadn't imbibed any alcohol.

Had to be a coincidence. She couldn't know that about him. Even Luttrell didn't know his onetime drink of choice.

"Do you prefer it straight or mixed?"

His mouth parched as if fifteen years had not elapsed since his last topple into that particular temptation. "Thank you. I'll pass." He told himself to go. To leave now as he'd planned. "You have your key," he explained for her benefit as well as his own. "That's why I came." Even as he said the words he understood he was lying to himself.

It had been way too long since he'd had sex. His gaze roved her slender curves as she filled the glass despite his veto. He started to remind her that he wasn't staying, but then she lifted the drink and swallowed deeply. Watching her do so inexplicably rendered him mute. The delicate muscles of her throat worked, welcoming the warming liquid. She made an appreciative sound as she moved in his direction and offered him the glass. "One drink. No strings. If you still want to go . . . I won't try and persuade you to stay."

The glass settled against his palm. Her fingers closed around his. Electricity crackled where their skin touched.

"One drink." The flavor of rum was on his tongue before he fully realized he had made the decision to taste it, much less said the words.

He didn't drink.

Never allowed his guard to fail this way.

And still he could not resist. She intrigued him on every level. Made him want her with a desperation he hadn't felt in years.

No one should be alone on a night like this. Maybe she was right. He emptied the glass. Felt the burn. His tongue slid across his bottom lip to taste the last drop.

She was watching. "One dance?" She took the glass from his hand and pulled him toward the center of the room, her actions slow and teasing like the music. "Just one."

Just one.

He watched her place the empty glass on the bar, walk back over to him. Felt her palms glide up his chest and her fingers lace behind his neck. She started to sway and, again, he didn't resist. His body fell into rhythm with hers. She leaned in. His arms instinctively went around her waist, pulled her closer. He thought of all the reasons he should have left already . . .

. . . and then he closed his eyes and stopped thinking at all.

Her forehead rested against his chin, and he relished the feel of her skin. The smell of her hair.

She pressed her body against him more fully and the battle of wills was over.

Whether it was his prolonged abstinence or the one drink or both, he needed . . . *this.*

He drew back, pushed the dress off her shoulders, exposing her bare breasts. He wanted to touch her. He needed to have sex. Here. Now. With her. There was no more denying it.

Her fingers tangled with his buttons, swiftly freeing each one. Together they dragged off his tie . . . his jacket and shirt. She ushered her dress past her hips, allowing it to float to the carpet.

In one sweep she was in his arms, then on the bed. His shoes and socks, his trousers, and then his boxers landed on the floor. He ripped the delicate panties from her hips and would have driven straight into her but the last brain cell still functioning with any semblance of intelligence sent a warning.

Condom.

As if she had read his mind, she reached beneath the pillow and withdrew a shiny package. She ripped it open and sheathed him in one smooth motion.

He thrust inside her without a moment's foreplay or the slightest inkling of finesse. She wrapped herself around him and met each flex of his hips. The heels of her stilettos scraped his thighs, urged him on.

And then she kissed him. Not slow. Not soft. She kissed the way she fucked: hard, furious, and without pretension. Her fingers rammed into his hair and pulled him deeper into the kiss. "More," she murmured against his lips, undulating her hips provocatively.

He gave it to her.

At some point he told himself this was crazy . . . over the top. But that didn't stop him . . . didn't even slow him down. The single viable idea remaining in his head was to have all of her.

5

9:55 p.m.
5900 Leeds Road, Birmingham
Wainwright Estate

Donald Wainwright prepared himself a double of the Kentucky bourbon he preferred and settled on the sofa to savor the burn. Lately, though, even his favorite whiskey seemed bland.

Life at home was bland.

His wife had already drunk herself into oblivion and gone to bed as she did every night. Claimed it was the only way she could endure being married to him.

He'd almost gotten used to her cutting remarks, had thought that nothing else she could say or do would get to him. But he'd been wrong. This evening she had announced that she planned to have an affair. With the mailman, of all people. How cliché was that?

For God's sake, why had she felt compelled to tell him?

There hadn't been much to say after that. He had mentioned, however, that discretion would be in her best interest if she had any aspirations of making it to the governor's mansion alongside him.

But then he hadn't really needed to point that out. The bitch wasn't going to screw up her chance to be first lady of Alabama. She liked the notoriety far too much to allow anything to get in the way.

Funny. The first twenty years of their marriage had been perfect. Perfect wife, beautiful and intelligent; perfect kids who grew up to be a doctor and an engineer. His own career had not once stagnated. What more could anyone ask for?

Then, twelve years ago, things had changed. Maybe he worked too much, maybe she drank too much. Whatever the case, they had slowly drifted apart.

He downed a generous gulp of bourbon. His work would just have to continue to make up for the lack of affection his wife showed him. For him, an affair was out of the question. He'd watched too many of his friends fall into that trap and pay the staggering price.

He would simply do what he always did . . . work.

Today had gone well. Stokes had gotten what he deserved, and the city could rest easy knowing that two of the most heinous crimes in its history were now solved. Stokes would never harm an innocent victim again.

It was done.

The past that haunted Carson Tanner was behind him now. He could focus on the future and stop rehashing old details.

If he would. Don had to see to it that he did. Some things were better left in the past. He'd groomed Carson to replace him in the position of Jefferson County District Attorney. Don owed Carson's father that much. Don blinked, forced those painful memories away.

The past wasn't the point. Carson was by far the best man for the job . . . if that damned past didn't get in his way.

Don didn't have to worry. Carson would not let him down.

He could count on that. Everything was finally falling into place. Nothing was going to get in the way of his bid for the governorship.

His cell phone rang, the sound mocking, as if to refute his closing argument.

His wife would call it intuition; he simply called it waning odds. Things had gone far too smoothly for far too long for his luck to continue.

His instincts hummed with dread as he accepted the call. "Wainwright."

"The situation we anticipated has been set in motion."

Don's insides cramped. That was not what he'd wanted to hear. There had to be some mistake. Even so, surely it wasn't too late to salvage the situation. Not like last time. "I could—"

"You understand what has to be done. An accident would be preferable, of course."

Don sat immobilized for five seconds before he dredged up the necessary response to the irrevocable order. Desperation screamed at him to challenge the verdict. But he knew. Once the decision was made, there was no stopping the momentum.

He cleared his throat. "I understand."

The call ended.

There was nothing he could do now.

It was done.

6

Wednesday, September 8, 8:00 a.m.

There was something he needed to do.

Carson slowly opened his eyes.

Sunlight filled the room.

He groaned. Closed his eyes against the brightness. Why had he left the blinds open?

He started to get up, but something stopped him. Something sweet. He inhaled deeply and tried to identify the scent.

Flowers . . . female.

He scratched his balls through the sheet.

Images filtered into his groggy consciousness. Sleek blond hair. Long, toned legs. Lush pink lips.

Sex.

The woman from the bar.

He bolted upright and looked around.

The Tutwiler.

Damn.

The stranger.

More of those images flooded his brain. Those slender legs entwining his body. Her blood-red nails clawing his skin.

What the hell had he been thinking?

That was the trouble, he hadn't been thinking.

"Shit."

Kicking the sheet aside, he sat up. Where was *she*?

He dropped his feet to the floor and fumbled for his boxers. Dragging them on, he walked unsteadily to the bathroom. Deserted. No toiletries other than the ones provided by the hotel. He checked the closet. No clothes. Just empty hangers, one swinging back and forth from the violent way he'd jerked open the door.

The only evidence that he hadn't imagined the whole event was the bottle of rum on the bar.

She was gone.

Luttrell. Carson was going to kick the shit of the guy.

Dread swelled in his chest.

What time is it?

His gaze veered to the bedside table and the digital clock waiting there, taunting him with its glaring numbers.

8:04.

"Damn it!"

He was late.

He tugged on his trousers. Fumbled around for his shirt, socks, and shoes. No time for a shower or to go home for a change of clothes.

After one last survey of the room, he grabbed his tie, shouldered into his jacket, and headed for the lobby. He hadn't drunk enough for a hangover, but he still felt like death warmed over. Side effects from the regret and the guilt sitting like an elephant on his shoulders.

How the hell had he let this happen?

Outside on the sidewalk, he took a moment to gain his bearings. He'd parked near the bar. Across the street and a block to the right.

Not far, but nothing was going to change the fact that he was late.

He stepped off the curb.

The roar of an engine bristled the hair on the back of his neck.

He swung his gaze left.

Car.

His heart launched into his throat.

He stumbled back. The vehicle whizzed past, the fender brushing the crease in his trousers.

What the hell?

Half a dozen seconds passed with him struggling to recapture his equilibrium. He sucked in a breath. Tires squealing, the black sedan with its heavily tinted windows disappeared around the corner at the next block.

"Close, Carson." He exhaled the air that had trapped in his lungs. "Damned close."

Careful to monitor both ways first, he darted across the street. By the time he reached the driver's side door and slid behind the wheel of his BMW, his head was spinning with the work he was behind on already . . . and he hadn't even gotten to the office.

Traffic was a bitch at this hour. The few blocks he needed to drive were congested with morning commuters. Sweat beaded on his forehead. Dammit. Dammit. He was an idiot. A complete and utter idiot.

He banged the steering wheel with his fist as he parked in the lower-level garage of the Criminal Justice Center.

Fool.

If Luttrell had set him up . . . if there were pictures . . .

Fury thundered inside Carson. It wouldn't be easy, but he would find a way to get even with his *friend.*

Once inside, Carson reached deep for calm, putting Luttrell and the near miss with the black sedan out of his mind. He nodded to the deputy on duty as he approached the line for the security checkpoint. Forty-five minutes ago there wouldn't have been a line.

But he was late.

For the first time in his adult life . . . the man who never missed a deadline or meeting, who was always on time for court, was officially late. He flashed his ID and opened his briefcase for the deputy.

"Running a little behind this morning, aren't we, Mr. Tanner?"

Carson managed a tight smile. "Traffic was murder."

The bottom of his feet tingled at the idea that he could be on his way to the ER or the morgue had his reflexes failed him. Too bad his instincts hadn't fared better last night. And if he was lucky, no one would ever know just how temporarily stupid he had gone.

The deputy shot him a wink. "Yeah, it can be that way some days."

Carson grabbed his briefcase and headed for the bank of elevators. There was no way anyone could know why he was late, yet it felt as if everyone he encountered did. Felt as if the whole world knew that Carson Tanner had finally screwed up, after so many years on the straight and narrow. He'd held it together all this time just to come undone as he sat poised to achieve the first major milestone of his career—running for Jefferson County DA. Not to mention after finally learning the truth.

Ask yourself if you'll ever really know what happened.

Stokes was on his way to Holman prison. The investigation into the murder of Carson's family was closed. Maybe there were a few details he would never know, but he couldn't change that. No more than he could retract last night.

He pushed both out of his head and stepped off the elevator onto the fourth floor.

Time to put it all behind him.

"Good morning, Anita." He passed the receptionist's desk, grabbing his messages as he went.

Anita Taggart smiled at him as she answered a phone call with the practiced greeting, "Good morning, District Attorney's Office."

The familiar sounds and environment set Carson at ease. He exchanged the usual pleasantries with colleagues as he made the journey to his office on the west end of the building. The most prized location on the floor besides Wainwright's suite of offices.

This was who he was.

This was what he did.

He placed his briefcase on his desk and shuffled through the messages. None were urgent. He would return most that afternoon when he'd done some serious catching up. For now, he wanted to review the files in his briefcase. The ones he should have reviewed last night.

Setting the messages aside, he took a mental step back. The truth was, he hadn't had sex in six months. If he really looked long and hard at the situation, he would have to confess that he'd likely needed to get the pent-up frustration out of his system. Just as Luttrell had suggested.

Carson shook his head. Seemed as good a way as any to assuage his conscience. But he would be damned if he would give Luttrell any credit for accurately assessing his needs.

Recharged with determination, Carson lifted the files from his briefcase—then hesitated. There was one thing he needed to do first. His attention shifted to the left where in the offices of his colleagues there would be a wall of pride. But Carson had opted for a different use of that valuable space. A whiteboard stretched from floor to ceiling and corner to corner. He kept a running timeline on his open cases on half the expanse, while the other half was covered with the details of the Stokes case.

Carson stared at the painstakingly collected facts related to his slain family. A sour taste churned in his stomach, resurrecting the burn of the rum he wished he hadn't drunk last night. He'd kept up with every piece of evidence, every known or suspected detail, clipped and saved every newspaper article from fifteen years ago. Sounded morbid but he had held one goal firmly in front of him. Find the truth.

The pictures of his sister . . . his father . . . and his mother stared at him from amid the data he'd collected. Carson had looked at those pictures a thousand times. Made the same promise each time. Begged for forgiveness.

You don't mean that, Carson . . . I know you don't.

Agony pierced him as his mother's voice resonated through his soul. For years the last words he and his mother had exchanged had tormented him. Even now he would give anything to take back that one moment. But there was no way to strike his arrogant, adolescent stupidity from the record.

I hate you! Do you hear me, Mother? I hate you!

A knock at his closed door jarred Carson to the present.

"Better late than never," Luttrell announced as he barged into the room without bothering with a second knock or waiting for consent.

Annoyance flared, chasing away the troubling memories. *Asshole.* "I don't have time for a postmortem about last night." Carson infused the remark with more vehemence than he'd intended.

Luttrell grinned. "What about last night?" He crossed the office and stepped squarely into Carson's personal space, his curiosity roused. "Did something happen I should hear about?"

Carson's gaze narrowed. The bastard had the nerve to come into his office trawling for details. "You left the bar. I left the bar. What's to know?"

Luttrell performed a slow, thorough survey of Carson's attire, then leaned in closer and sniffed. "You smell like sex, man. Did you take my advice and go home with someone last night?"

Another burst of tension stiffened Carson's spine. "Fuck off." He turned to his desk and reached for a file. "I don't have time to placate your deviant nature, Luttrell. Don't you have court this morning?"

Luttrell straightened his gold tie with an I'm-the-man panache. "I do. It's going to be a slam dunk. The defense won't know what hit them."

Carson nodded vaguely in the hope that Luttrell would get the hell out of his office. It almost worked, but then his *former* friend paused at the door.

"By the way, did you hear about Zac Holderfield?"

Carson frowned, shifted his attention to Luttrell. "What about him?"

Dr. Dwight Holderfield's son. Zac was a couple of years older than Carson; they didn't travel in the same circles, but he knew him well enough. Rumor was that Zac had spent his time at Auburn developing his skills as a drug connection. And Carson wasn't talking about his pharmaceutical science training.

"He went missing over the holiday weekend," Luttrell explained. "No one's seen him since Sunday."

"That's too bad." Though not exactly surprising, Carson hated to hear that news.

"Oh yeah." Luttrell hesitated once more. "Wainwright was looking for you this morning."

Carson's gut clenched. "When?"

Luttrell glanced into the corridor as if to ensure no one overheard. "Maybe half an hour ago. He's in a meeting right now." His cocky gaze intersected with Carson's, and the grin spread back into full form. "You know there's no point in keeping secrets. I will find out about last night. In time," he warned.

Jaw clenched, Carson waited until the door was closed behind the prick before picking up the receiver and entering the extension for Geneva Mitchell, Wainwright's assistant. "Good morning, Geneva. Is he in?" A line of perspiration formed on Carson's brow at the idea that the first time he was late the boss came looking for him. Dammit.

As Luttrell had said, Wainwright was in a meeting, and Geneva assured Carson she would let him know when the boss was free. She had no clue why Wainwright had sought out Carson that morning.

Perfect. Carson thanked her and dropped the receiver back into its cradle. He collapsed into his chair and allowed his gaze to rest on the timeline detailing the gruesome murder of his family. That ugly part of his history was at last resolved and now his present was going to hell.

All because of a stranger.

No. That wasn't right. Last night had been his mistake.

Too bad his first blunder in so long had to have been such a colossal one.

Pushing the disturbing thoughts aside, Carson grabbed a breath mint from his middle desk drawer, popped it into his mouth, then plunged into work mode. Before he'd gotten good and immersed, his door opened once more, again with no preamble. Not even a knock.

"Don't get up," Wainwright insisted as he entered the office with his usual fervor, a thick case file tucked beneath his left arm. He closed the door and made himself at home in one of the upholstered chairs flanking Carson's desk. His full attention rested on Carson then, his eyes glittering with anticipation, firing the same rush in Carson's veins.

"I'm about to give you," Wainwright began, "the case that will assure both of us our goals."

Carson closed the file on his desk. The anticipation morphed into searing adrenaline. "Excellent." Maybe this day was salvageable after all. "You're well aware that I'm prepared to do whatever's necessary to make that happen."

As the new DA of Jefferson County, it would be more than a little beneficial to have the governor in his corner. The next few months were going to be the most crucial of Carson's career. Pleasing the boss and the public was paramount. Wild, frantic sex acts flickered in front of his eyes. He could not take another risk like that. Could not allow his focus to be divided. His career had always come first. Now was not the time to allow that rigid discipline to falter.

"As *you* are well aware," Wainwright said, using Carson's words and relaxing more fully into the chair, "we've had our eye on Otis Fleming for two decades."

Otis Fleming. Carson sat up a little straighter. Fleming had long been considered Jefferson County's connection to organized crime, but no one had ever been able to prove it. No one got close to Fleming and lived to rat him out. Few tried.

"New evidence has come to light?" Carson eased back into his chair, matching his boss's posture, but he was by no means relaxed at this point. Wainwright was correct. A high-profile case like this could put them both where they wanted to be career-wise.

Wainwright placed the heavy folder on Carson's desk, then pounded it with the side of his fist. "Even better. We've found a weak link amid his faithful soldiers."

Carson took a moment to absorb that information. "Is the witness in protective custody already?" If not, he probably wouldn't be alive for long.

Wainwright shook his head. "This witness isn't ours just yet. That's where you come in."

Ah, the insider hadn't been flipped. Interesting. "Do we have enough leverage to do the job?" In these situations, leverage was everything. His heart ushered into a faster rhythm at the prospect of taking on this challenge.

"We have a start." Wainwright slid the file toward Carson. "Study what we have. Dig up every speck of dirt you can find. Don't stop until we have what we need to get *everything* we want." Wainwright pushed to his feet. "We can discuss your initial conclusions in my five o'clock with Senator Drake. You know how long he's wanted to nail Fleming. I want you"—Wainwright pointed at Carson—"to show him how we're going to make that happen."

Carson stood, gave a resolute nod. "I'll be prepared." When Wainwright was gone Carson opened the file. Years of reports and compiled data on Otis Fleming filled page after page. If only 1 percent of the suspected criminal activities were proven, the man would be going up the river for a very, very long time.

Carson reached the dossier on the suspected weak link. Annette Baxter. Thirty, an associate as well as personal friend of Fleming. Carson didn't recall having heard her name before. In fact, he was surprised to find Fleming's weak link was a female. All of his known, close associates were male.

Curiosity hastened Carson through the initial read of the facts on the insider. He turned the page and found the first of several eight-by-ten surveillance photos.

He stared at the vivid image. Denial detonated in his brain. "Impossible," he muttered.

Seconds turned into a minute with him staring at the photo, staring from every angle to be sure there was no mistake.

And there wasn't.

Annette Baxter was the *woman* . . . the stranger with whom he'd just spent the night having hot, dirty sex.

7

5:00 p.m.
Birmingham
Criminal Justice Center

Carson waited in the small lobby of District Attorney Wainwright's office. Hesitation. Another first in what appeared to be the domino effect. One misstep led to another . . . to cover one's ass.

He'd worked with his mentor for five years, and never once had he experienced dread or uncertainty.

But he was damned sure feeling both right now.

The entire day had expired with him digging as deeply into Annette Baxter's background as possible without leaving the sanctuary of his office.

There was not a doubt in his mind that he could get the job done. He was the Avenger. He never failed. But what had happened last night was exactly the sort of unethical behavior that could complicate matters.

Could ruin his career plans.

Yes, he was single, unattached, but this wouldn't be about morals. This would be about the law. If he considered nothing else save for his own ambition and the certainty that he was the best man for the job, he could not—under any circumstances—recuse himself from this case. Yet his own actions had left him biased. That undeniable truth could come back to haunt him as well as the case in a major way. Could reflect badly on the entire office.

But to pass on the case would show Wainwright that Carson was capable of failure, of weakness. The man who filled the district attorney's shoes could be neither weak nor a failure, professionally or personally.

"You don't need to wait, Mr. Tanner."

Carson stiffened at the unexpected intrusion. He propped a smile into place and turned to face Wainwright's assistant, who'd reentered the small lobby and caught him off guard. Hesitation was not the norm for him. "I was just gathering my thoughts."

Geneva nodded, her expression understanding. "Senator Drake has that effect on people." She winked. "Nice to see you're not completely immune to the qualms the rest of us suffer on a regular basis."

A chuckle strained from Carson's dry throat. "I'll try and take that as a compliment."

She patted him on the shoulder. "I've watched thirty years' worth of cocky young attorneys come through this office and I'm here to tell you, that *is* a compliment."

But it wasn't.

Not to Carson.

"Thanks." He squared his shoulders and opened the door. The only way to get this done was to do it.

Carson entered the room and both Wainwright and Drake shifted their attention to him. But it was the person who didn't bother to look his way who stole Carson's immediate, exclusive interest. *Elizabeth Drake.*

As if he'd spoken the thought aloud, she turned to him and smiled. Looked exactly the same. Long dark hair, vivid green eyes.

Senator Drake stood and extended his hand, drawing Carson's reluctant attention to him. "How's our future DA this evening?"

No pressure there.

Carson took the man's hand and gave it a firm, brisk shake. "Outstanding, sir. And you?"

"Can't complain," Drake said as he resumed his seat. He waved a hand toward his daughter. "The mayor thought it would be good if Elizabeth joined us."

Carson turned to her. "Unquestionably."

Elizabeth rose from her chair with all the grace and poise three years at the very best boarding school and then the top private women's university could bestow.

"Carson." Instead of offering her hand, she hugged him politely. "It's good to see you." She drew away but took a moment to give him a thorough once-over. "You're looking well."

He told himself her choice in words had no hidden meaning. *Maybe that boy's like his uncle.* Carson exiled the voice. "Thanks. It's a pleasure having you join us. And you"—he gave Elizabeth a nod of approval—"you look amazing." Their statements sounded so mundane, considering the history between them.

Ancient history.

But not so antiquated that he didn't feel things. Like the tightening in his gut at merely being in the same room with her. Or the pressure banded around his chest just remembering all they had shared. Sweet whispers, frantic touches . . .

Wainwright ushered the meeting to order, prompting Carson and Elizabeth to take their seats. He recapped the long-alleged suspicions regarding Fleming's activities. The lengthy overview allowed Carson's mind to wander.

Elizabeth Drake served as Birmingham's deputy mayor. The city loved her. Her name or face was constantly in the media. She was Birmingham's princess. Carson had run into her from time to time since her return two years ago, but that was about the extent of it. Avoiding her was easier than facing the parts of the past that just seeing her resurrected. He wondered, though, if she ever thought about how things might have been if his life hadn't taken such a sharp detour.

Doubtful.

Elizabeth was the only woman he'd ever loved. She, Carson, and her brother Dane had been inseparable. They'd gone to school together as kids, lived within a mile of each other, and shared every crazy moment of coming of age.

Until that day changed everything.

He'd lost the girl. He'd lost everything.

Ask yourself if you'll ever really know what happened.

"Carson?"

He snapped to attention, cleared his throat, and mentally grappled to catch up with the conversation. What had Wainwright asked him?

"We're all anxious to hear what you've deduced so far as to the viability of this investigation," Wainwright restated, displeasure scoring his brow.

Concentrate. Randolph Drake and Donald Wainwright were the two most pivotal players in his future. Carson had to get his shit together. That Elizabeth had discreetly checked her phone a couple of times indicated he wasn't the only one capable of being distracted during such a critical meeting. But then, this meeting was about his conclusions. His distraction was unacceptable.

"Annette Baxter." Even as Carson said the name, pornographic images from the night before cluttered his vision. "Born in Knoxville, Tennessee. She spent the first ten years of her life in extreme poverty. Spent the next six in foster care." The scenarios that had materialized in his head as he'd read her file twisted in his gut even now.

Poverty had been the least of Annette Baxter's problems. The reports from her adolescent years were filled with claims of sexual and physical abuse.

"Baxter," he went on, "eventually found her way to Nashville. Lived on the streets, doing anything necessary to survive. Until she was nineteen." He paused to allow his audience to process those details. "That's when Fleming discovered her. He brought her to Birmingham and took her under his wing. The exact nature of their personal relationship is somewhat undefined." Since Fleming was more than thirty years her senior, the prospect that they might very well be lovers was more than repulsive.

"She's garnered quite a name for herself as a fundraising organizer," Elizabeth noted. "I've seen her from time to time at the larger functions."

Carson was getting to that part. But Elizabeth's confirmation that he was, in fact, the only one in the room unaware of Annette Baxter's existence before today amazed him. Apparently his all-work-and-no-play lifestyle had isolated him from Birmingham society far more than he'd realized.

"My theory," he continued, "is that her fundraising work not only provides her with a legitimate cover but also gives her diplomatic contact with the power in the city. The most advantageous aspect of cultivating those connections would be to provide access and/or information for Fleming's activities. Ultimately, I believe she operates as a fixer, of sorts."

"A fixer?" Drake echoed.

"Someone who sets up situations to manipulate an outcome or to resolve a problem," Carson clarified. "According to Special Agent Kim Schaffer's reports and surveillance logs, whenever trouble surfaces in an activity Fleming is suspected of facilitating, Baxter shows up for a meeting and then the problem disappears." The Bureau's cooperation comprised a single, brief report that provided little information but did speculate as to Baxter's business arrangement with Fleming.

"Schaffer?" Wainwright looked confused.

Carson nodded. "She's my Bureau contact."

"I thought SAC Talley was handling this personally." Wainwright was clearly put off by the news.

"Special Agent in Charge Talley directed me to Schaffer." Carson had surmised that she was the agent most up to speed on Fleming. "Is that an issue?"

Wainwright gestured vaguely. "Considering the high-profile nature of this case, I assumed Talley would jump at the opportunity." He glanced at Drake and laughed, but the sound held little amusement. "I suppose we should be grateful they're cooperating at all."

"You're convinced Baxter can be turned?" Elizabeth asked, her question directed at Carson. She would want to give the mayor a sense of whether or not the end result was attainable.

"Yes." Carson didn't hesitate. "She's close to Fleming. Close enough that she unquestionably recognizes the potential for getting burned if he goes down. With the right incentive, she'll see the prudence in saving herself."

"The upshot," Wainwright declared, "is that we need to sever our city's ties to any and all organized crime links. Baxter is our first promising opportunity to get to Fleming."

"That will make the mayor a very happy man," Elizabeth chimed in. "I'm sure we all comprehend"—she looked from Wainwright to Carson and then to her father—"that organized crime is one of the most pressing global issues. An issue that needs to be addressed with the same urgency as terrorism since organized crime in fact fuels terrorism."

"A most valid point," Wainwright seconded. "It's men like Fleming who fund the very terrorists our troops risk their lives to stop. From gunrunning to drugs, that cash flow ultimately ends up in the hands of terrorists or their supporters. Stopping the flow is the least we can do not only for our city, but for our country as well."

"Hear, hear." Drake shifted in his chair to face Carson. "We're counting on your unbreakable determination to accomplish what others have tried and failed."

"You can count on me, sir," Carson guaranteed. Having the senator personally involved allowed Carson the opportunity to reiterate to him that he had made the right choice fifteen years ago.

I hate you! Do you hear me, Mother? I hate you! Carson's heart reacted as those painful words haunted him a second time today. Words he could never take back, could never make right. Mad as hell, he'd barged into his mother's office, caught her midsession with a patient, and said things no son should say. That patient had been only too happy to recount the whole ugly scene to the police, initially making Carson the primary suspect in the slaughter of his family.

Drake had staunchly stood behind Carson, even when he had doubted himself.

For fifteen years Carson had worked hard to prove his worth. That he somehow deserved to be alive . . . *the lone survivor* . . . when he knew in his gut that it should have been him who died. Wished a million times that it had been.

But Carson hadn't been home that night. Because of that he had spent every day of this undeserved gift trying his best to earn it. An impossible task, but one he would continue to strive toward for the rest of his days.

No matter the mistake Carson had made last night, he would not fall down on the job a second time.

Every living, breathing human had his or her breaking point. Had a weakness of one kind or another that could be exploited to attain cooperation. Annette Baxter would be no different.

All Carson had to do was pinpoint that spot.

8

6:50 p.m.
Five Points South, Birmingham
Java Joe's

Her brother had to be out of his mind. Thoughtless. Selfish! She wanted to scream! Didn't he care how hard she had worked to achieve her goals? He was risking everything!

He'd called her in the middle of a meeting, for God's sake! Twice!

Restraining her anger, Elizabeth stared at Dane, attempting to convey with her eyes the gravity of the situation. If she yelled at him, he'd just get up and walk out. She had to know everything. To be sure exactly what she was up against. "Do you understand how serious this situation is?"

He peered into his untouched cup of coffee as if it somehow held the answers he needed to escape this uncomfortable position. Since no excuse apparently surfaced, he ignored her.

Why did she even ask? He sat across the expanse of Formica from her, slumped in the booth as if he hadn't a care in the world. His eyes were sunken and red from lack of sleep and overindulgence in his latest drug of choice. He'd lost more weight, and she doubted he'd had a bath in days. His dark hair was stringy and far too long.

She closed her eyes a moment, trying to see her brother the way he'd been years ago. Tall, athletic, smart. Now—she opened her eyes—he barely existed. A college dropout, a drug addict . . . and that was only the beginning.

"Answer me, Dane," she demanded, unable to keep her anger subdued any longer. She had no time for this. What was she supposed to do with him? He wouldn't stay out of trouble. If their mother found out . . . or, God forbid, their father . . .

She didn't even want to think about that.

Dane's bleary-eyed gaze finally met hers. "What difference does it make?" He dropped his head back on the seat. "Nothing matters anymore."

"I don't understand," she said with amazing calm. "What's happened to set you off like this? You've done so well for the past few months." At least for Dane it was relatively positive behavior.

His gaze lifted to hers. "You should know. You're in on it, too."

Her patience thinned. "Explain what you mean, Dane."

"You cut me off, just like they did." His lips curled into a hateful sneer. "Left me with nothing. What was I supposed to do?"

There it was. He was unhappy because the family had stopped financing his bad habits. Well, tough. They had put up with enough. He needed to pull his life together.

"Dane."

He refused to look at her now.

Dammit.

He was going to ruin everything. *For her.* Fury tightened her lips. She couldn't let him do that. "If Father even suspects—"

Dane's head shot up. "Screw him. I'm not listening to him anymore."

Elizabeth took a steadying breath. She had to get her brother back under control. "Everything Father has ever done, he's done to protect us. You can't let him down like this."

Dane leaned forward and put his face close to hers, his breath as foul as his attitude. "I . . . don't . . . care." Then he flopped back once more.

Of course he didn't care. She shouldn't be surprised. "And what about me?" He at least looked at her then. "Do you care what happens to me?"

His silence was answer enough.

Elizabeth felt that familiar tranquility envelop her, dissolving the anger and frustration. There was only one way to handle this. "Let's put this behind us. It's done. I'll take care of everything the way I always do." She reached across the table in invitation. He stared at her hand . . . the one he'd held so many times when they'd sneaked through the woods to Carson's house or hidden together in fear. But not today. Today he refused to touch her.

"Very well." She drew her hand back, curled her fingers tightly against the emptiness. "If that's the way you want it to be . . ."

His continued silence reverberated in her ears. Elizabeth scooted from the booth and walked out of the coffee shop. There was nothing more she could say.

No one, *no one*, would stop her from having what she deserved this time. She had waited fifteen long years due to the actions of others.

Not this time. This time she was going to do what she should've done all along.

9

7:35 p.m.
Criminal Justice Center, Birmingham

Carson stared at the surveillance photos spread across his desk. Twelve different shots. A dozen different times and locations.

Annette Baxter met with Otis Fleming randomly.

There appeared to be no correlation to Fleming's alleged activities other than the idea that any problems rumored to have arisen seemed to disappear rather quickly after their meetings.

And yet not a single connection to the activities Fleming was accused of facilitating could be made to her—or the old man, for that matter.

Carson scanned his copious notes. The only piece of evidence, and it was damned thin, to indicate Annette Baxter might be involved in Fleming's illegal dealings was an August 15 audio recording provided by the FBI. And even that evidence was vague, circumstantial at best. As were the photos, since it wasn't illegal to visit a person.

Carson pushed play and listened to the taped conversation again.

"You know this requires great finesse." *Fleming.*

"I understand." *Annette Baxter.* "I know how to handle him."

"There can be no mistakes," Fleming prompted in that gravelly voice that spoke of years of smoking magnified by frequent alcohol consumption. And age. Too bad he was like a damned Timex: He just kept on ticking.

"Have I ever let you down?" Baxter's tone reflected her exasperation. But that emotion was tempered by patience and a reverence that confounded Carson.

Did she love this old man?

Had to be about the money.

Fleming couldn't have had sex with her the way Carson had.

What the hell kind of proclamation was that? Carson turned his back on the file and stared out at the glittering night view of the city he loved. That alone was the most compelling reason a wise man would step down and allow another, one not personally involved on any level, to proceed with this investigation.

Yet that was the one thing he couldn't do.

Wainwright was counting on him. Drake was counting on him.

And the truth was, as arrogant as it sounded, Carson was the best man for the job. He would not stop until he had the truth . . . until he uncovered the motivation to prompt her cooperation.

If hanging her was what it took, he would do it and feel absolutely no remorse. She was a criminal. A former prostitute, a drug mule. She deserved whatever she got.

The image of a young girl, ten or twelve years old, fighting off a brute of a foster father loomed in Carson's head. He banished it. There was no room for sympathy in this investigation.

However hard her childhood, Annette Baxter was a grown woman who made independent choices. She had chosen to be what she was now.

The thud of a door slamming had him wheeling around. It was almost eight. Everyone else on the floor had gone home hours ago. He glanced at the papers on his desk. The concept that he was working on a high-profile case involving a very powerful man wasn't lost on him. Taking extra precautions was necessary.

He walked out of his office, checked the corridor. It was empty. Closing his door behind him out of habit, he took a walk around the floor. The other offices were locked, lights out. Emptiness resonated around him. He was alone.

Sound carried in the silence. The thudding noise he'd heard could have come from the floor below this one or the one above it. He gave himself a mental boot in the ass. He wasn't generally so jumpy. Had to be the caffeine. And the case. And just maybe a guilty conscience.

It was late. He needed to gather up the file and head home. The change in scenery might give him a new perspective.

He entered his office. Closed the door. Froze.

He wasn't alone.

"Your photographer should learn to be a bit more creative."

Annette Baxter.

Surprise converted into fury before he could grab back the control he rarely lost. Until recently.

She waved one of his notes. "And the name of my second foster father is misspelled." The tight, dim smile she exhibited didn't hold a candle to the one she'd flaunted last night. "Of course, he's dead so I guess it doesn't really matter."

"Step away from my desk, Ms. Baxter." The order rushed from Carson's throat as if he'd exhaled a blast of fire.

Annette stilled. Well, well, Mr. Carson Tanner wasn't so happy to see her. A vast turnaround from last night's primal reaction.

Nothing she hadn't expected. Dropping the note and lifting her hands in mock surrender, she retreated two paces. "You caught me red-handed."

For several seconds he stared at her, probably hoping her appearance was just a bad dream. He might as well get used to the idea that the two of them were involved, because she wasn't backing off. She needed him.

As if she'd telegraphed that thought, his gaze raked her body. He liked what he saw. Good. From the twist she'd arranged her hair into to the shrink-wrapped black sheath she wore, all had been carefully selected for him. That was the one lesson she had learned on the street:

Dress to impress. A john was far more likely to be generous if he liked what he saw and thought what he was paying for was worth the price.

She smiled as she paid him back in spades. Same shirt and trousers as last night—both a little rumpled, but the look was good on him. The tie hung loosely, and the top two buttons of his shirt were undone. She imagined that showing up for work unshowered and unshaven, wearing yesterday's clothes, was far from the norm for this uptight deputy DA.

His gaze locked with hers. "I don't know what kind of game you're playing, but what you did last night is called entrapment. You broke the law." He crossed the room and stepped between her and his desk, shuffling the photos and reports into a stack, his anger visibly expanding with each movement.

"Did I?" The innocence she was able to impart in her tone surprised even her and did exactly what she intended.

He did a one-eighty, pinning her with his fury. "You knew who I was when you approached me at the bar. Don't bother denying it. I don't know how you discovered I would be assigned this case and I don't care, but your games aren't going to work."

The next logical step would be to call security. She had to act fast. "They're setting me up." The line wasn't exactly original, but it was all too accurate.

"Security will see you out."

Men. They were so easy to read. She had her hand on his before he could reach the receiver. "Give me five minutes," she urged, the desperation in the words frighteningly real. Too real. He was the only chance she had of stopping this thing before it went too far.

"Five minutes," she repeated when he didn't immediately reject her suggestion.

For a moment she thought he might just give in; then his expression hardened. "I'm certain you're aware, Ms. Baxter, that I cannot discuss any aspect of the case with you." He held up both hands to ward her off. "In fact, I can't be in the same room alone with you."

Damn. She sank her teeth into her bottom lip before she could stop the old habit. She hadn't done that in years . . . hadn't permitted that slithering insecurity to make her feel . . . afraid. She snatched back her courage. No fear. Play on his sympathy. Men were suckers for a woman in jeopardy.

"I need your help." If he refused to listen, she still had options, however unappealing. "This"—she indicated the file on his desk—"is a conspiracy. The very men you hold in great esteem are railroading me to cover their own crimes." That was a vast understatement.

Fury raged in his eyes, etched into the granite of his jaw. She wasn't getting through. "I'm telling you the truth." She had to make him see. "I have no reason to lie to you, *Mr. Tanner.*"

"Really?" He planted his hands on his hips. "You follow me to a bar. Come up with that wild proposition and then show up here like this—on the same day I'm assigned to investigate your activities." He shook his head, his disgust crystal clear. "I don't know, but that sounds a little manufactured to me."

"I knew you'd get the case," she confessed. "You're the best." Selecting a distant memory, she used it to summon tears. "I didn't know what else to do. I was scared." She searched his eyes for a glimmer of compassion. "I made a mistake." That was a lie, but he couldn't prove it. "You're the only person who can help me.".

"You don't know me."

"I know all about you, Carson Tanner." His anger seemed to abate the tiniest bit. "You're the Avenger. The man who never loses. The deputy district attorney poised to succeed Wainwright." Such a handsome man for a prosecutor, too. Dark hair, equally dark eyes. Classic jawline, nice lips. The whole package. Just a little too trusting. But he would learn that trust was vastly overrated.

"Get out." The words were as ruthlessly relayed as the glare he now aimed at her.

Any compassion she'd hoped for vanished in that same instant. Oh well. There was always plan B. She walked around him, his gaze tracking her every move, and scooted onto the edge of the desk. The hem of her dress slid to the tops of her thighs. His attention went straight there as if he had no authority over his own eyes. So very predictable. She crossed one meticulously toned leg over the other. He swallowed with difficulty.

Whatever it takes.

"All I want is justice," she implored, tracing with one red-nailed finger down the deep neckline that exposed her cleavage. His gaze followed the path of that finger.

As if he'd just snapped from a trance, his expression darkened with fury once more. "I sincerely doubt that you know a whole hell of a lot about justice, lady."

"I know many things, Mr. Tanner." His remark should have pissed her off, but she'd expected that and worse. "Don't mistake what I do for what I know."

"I'm asking you to leave." He stepped directly into her personal space. "It'll be considerably easier if you leave of your own volition rather than forcing me to call security."

"You're the defender of the underdog, the champion of truth," she insisted, taking the statement word for word from recent headlines. "Don't you want to hear my truth?" He wasn't fooled for a second. She read the derision on his face as easily as scanning the latest issue of *Cosmopolitan* at the checkout counter.

"That's what they say," he said, those straight white teeth practically clenched. "I'm sure you'll be able to see for yourself over the course of the next few months while I'm dragging you through legal proceedings." He wrapped the fingers of his right hand around her arm, careful not to apply excessive pressure. "Let me show you to the door."

Time to play hardball. "Where's the passion I felt last night?" she challenged. "A man with that much passion surely can't stand idly by and watch an innocent person destroyed." She toyed with his tie, the same one he'd worn last night, no doubt reminding him of those hours. His nostrils flared. "That would be a travesty, wouldn't it?"

"Back off."

Nice roar, but it would take more than that to scare her off. She reached out, molded her hand to the front of his trousers, squeezed his hard cock. "I know you want me."

"That's it." Carson had to get her out of here. Even as the thought formed in his brain she uncrossed her legs and spread them wide apart. His gaze zeroed in on the juncture between her thighs.

He blinked. Told himself to breathe. Didn't happen.

She wasn't wearing panties. Soft, blond pubes gleamed against her tanned skin.

Security. He should call now. Get her out of here.

"Perhaps"—she licked her lips—"I mistook desperation for passion."

Fury jolted him. His grip tightened in anticipation of hauling her out the door. "I'm not going to cross that line with you again. Now go." The term *assault and battery* abruptly dampened the fiery rage. He released her. Dropped his hands to his sides and ordered himself to keep them there.

"I know you want me." She glanced at the front of his trousers. "It's not like you haven't done it already."

He reached for the phone again. She diverted his hand, pressed it between her thighs. Want pumped through his arteries.

"Feel that." She moaned. "That's all for you."

Reason almost deserted him for a second time since finding her in his office. He grabbed it back, wrenched his hand away from her body. "I . . . don't . . . want . . . *you,*" he growled even as his erection strained against his fly.

"Yes . . . *you* . . . do." She grabbed him by the waist, pulled him closer, and wrenched open his trousers just enough to reach inside. She stroked him, squeezed and tugged.

He groaned. Couldn't help himself.

He was out of his damned mind.

"Get out now," he demanded, backing away and wrestling with his trousers. His hands shook with need. He couldn't think. It was insane.

She stared at him. Didn't make a move to go, didn't allow a single emotion to slip past her flawless composure. "If you won't do the job, I'll just do it myself."

Before he could fathom her intent, she reclined fully on his desk, heedless of the papers and photos there. Her slender fingers caressed that intimate dampness, tunneled inside. She whimpered as if this wasn't the first time she'd had to indulge herself. As if she knew just how to do it.

The oxygen evacuated his lungs. If he called security now, and they saw her here like this . . . damn it!

Her body writhed sensually. His mouth went dry. Just walk out. But sensitive files were here . . . *beneath* her. Her moans grew frenzied. His cock throbbed with need.

She cried out. Locked the heels of her stilettos on the edge of his desk as her movements became more frantic.

No more.

He stepped between her spread thighs, leaned in, and grabbed her by the shoulders to yank her upright. Bad decision. For several seconds he couldn't move. Immobilized in that erotic position, overwhelmed by the scent of her body . . . by the need to stab into her.

She fisted her fingers in his shirtfront. "I knew you couldn't resist."

Fury ignited. His fingers bit into her arms with the need to shake the hell out of her. "It . . . will . . . not . . . happen . . . again."

She stared at him, her expression cold even as she smiled in triumph. "Yes, it will."

Confusion, frustration, another burst of anger—it all bombarded him along with the adrenaline-charged lust. "Just go." He closed his eyes and told himself to release her and back away. But he couldn't move.

The door opened.

"Hey, man, I—"

Keller Luttrell stared at Carson, then at the woman sprawled on his desk in front of him. "Sorry, man." Luttrell executed an about-face and cleared the room before Carson could utter a word. The door banged shut.

Carson released her, frantically righted his clothes.

She draped her legs over the edge of the desk, lifted into a sitting position, then hopped off. "I suppose that was my cue to go."

"Don't approach me again without an official invitation," he warned. Too many violent emotions to label roiled inside him. He was a damned idiot! "If you do, I'll file charges."

She straightened her dress and stared at him, cool, utterly collected. "You'll change your mind."

He twisted his belt into place, struggling with the need to kick his own ass. "Whatever you think you're doing," he advised, "is over. If I have to step aside on this one, I will."

She laughed softly, brushed a wisp of hair back from her cheek. "Like that's going to happen." She skirted the chairs in front of his desk and walked deliberately toward the door, her hips swaying provocatively.

Idiocy seized first chair in his brain. "Whatever there is to find on you," he threatened, "I *will* find it. And then you'll talk or you'll do the time."

She paused at the door and turned back to him, that unreadable smile still in place. "I'm sure you'll try. But keep in mind, I know things that could bring down this entire office. You walk away and I'll do just that. I want *you* on this case."

Lies. All of it. If she had anything on this office, she would have used it to stop this investigation before it started. "Get out."

"Just one question."

"We have nothing else to discuss, Ms. Baxter."

"Tell me, Tanner, when did *you* stop caring about the truth?"

She didn't wait for an answer.

She left.

Her question delayed the action he knew he had to take next. He had to square this with Luttrell. Yet . . . what she'd said nagged at him. Hadn't Stokes made a similar statement? *Tell me, Tanner, when did you stop caring about the truth?*

Instinct nudged him. Dread trickled. How could she have known?

He'd worry about that later. For now, damage control was his top priority. Carson found his friend in the supply room at the copy machine.

"Look," Carson said, his head bowed a moment before meeting his colleague's eyes, "I want to apologize for what you walked in on. It wasn't—"

Luttrell waved his hands in front of him as if erasing the whole matter. "Hey, you don't have to apologize to me. I'm just glad you're finally getting some."

Uncertainty gave Carson an instant's pause. Shit. Luttrell did think the worst. Baxter being in his office was bad enough. "You don't understand. She was—"

"I didn't get a look at her face." Luttrell shrugged. "But judging by those gorgeous legs and what I saw of her fine ass, I'd say you have yourself a hot one on your hands." He growled like a horny beast. "I haven't banged a chick in that position in weeks."

Carson took a deep breath for the first time in about ten minutes. He would never convince his colleague that he hadn't been going at it. The good news was that Luttrell hadn't identified her. "Well." Carson cleared his throat. "There's a time and place for everything. I fell down in both categories."

Luttrell clapped him on the back. "Pussy's pussy, man. Take it when and where you can. We won't be young and single forever."

A laugh choked out of Carson's throat. "There is that."

"You had dinner yet?" Luttrell grabbed his original documents and the copies he'd made. "I was out with a client, but we never got around to dinner. I had to run back here and pick up a file." He shoved the documents into the briefcase lying next to the copy machine. "You want to get a bite?"

Carson grappled to regain some semblance of composure. "Sure."

Luttrell talked enough for the two of them as they stopped by Carson's office to lock up, then exited the building. For once Carson didn't care. He was just thankful that his colleague had no clue the woman caught in such a compromising position with him was Annette Baxter.

Carson had never really believed in luck. He'd always insisted he made his own with intelligence, preparation and persistence.

But tonight, it seemed luck had taken pity on him because he damned sure hadn't been capable of generating his own.

10:30 p.m.
2402 Altadena Road, Vestavia
Tanner Residence

Carson had almost put the incident behind him by the time he reached home. That a car sat in his driveway surprised him. He almost never had company. Unless it was Luttrell—and it wouldn't be. He didn't recognize the silver Camry. Someone sat silhouetted on the front porch steps just out of the overhead light's reach.

Female?

His heart prematurely contracted.

Couldn't be Baxter. She drove a Lexus. At least that was the vehicle registered in her name.

He let go a big breath as he turned into the drive, braked next to the Camry, and put his BMW into park. His visitor rose from the step. The light fell across her, giving him a glimpse of her face.

Elizabeth?

A dozen questions ran through his mind as he emerged, briefcase in hand. The last of his raging emotions and the accompanying tension drained away.

"Hey." She glanced across the yard to the quiet street before meeting his eyes. "I hope you don't mind my stopping by unannounced."

Carson closed the car door. "You're always welcome here, Elizabeth." A genuine smile tugged at his lips. How long had it been since he'd come home and found her waiting for him like this? Fifteen years? But back then home had been *home.* Not the place where his family had died. Not a hollow house that stood empty except for when he showered and slept.

That old but too-familiar pain squeezed his chest.

So much had changed after that day.

Elizabeth moved down a step. "Reminds me of old times."

No kidding. He followed the sidewalk to where she waited. "Very old times."

"It was good to see you today." She descended the final step. "I can't believe I've been home for two years and we've hardly bumped into each other."

"Work keeps me busy." That part was accurate if not the reason he had avoided running into her. Seeing her reminded him too acutely of all that he had lost. Of all that might have been if fate hadn't royally screwed him.

She surveyed his house. The automatic exterior lights included in the landscaping highlighted the daring, modern architecture. "I approve." Her gaze met his once more. "You did every single thing you said you would, including achieving the high-profile career."

High-end house in the exclusive neighborhood. Flashy car. Fast-tracked career. He'd dreamed of having it all. Including Elizabeth. But thanks to Stokes she was the one thing, in addition to his family, he would never have.

Going there was pointless. "You're one to talk." He sat his briefcase on the lowest step, took off his jacket one arm at a time before draping it over the banister, then loosened his tie. "A graduate of Wellesley. Deputy mayor of this thriving metropolis." He gave her the nod, the one that said how much he admired her accomplishments. "Two years back home and you're Birmingham's princess. The whole city loves you."

Elizabeth set a new standard for involvement in the community. Her fundraising work was unparalleled. Carson fully expected that when her father retired from the Senate in a few years, she would step up to the plate and win his seat. No one was more deserving.

She waved off his praise. "You can't put any stock in all that media hoopla, Carson. Here today, gone tomorrow."

"Now you're being modest." The idea that they were still standing outside hit him square on the forehead. Jesus, what was wrong with him? "Hey, why don't you come inside and we'll have coffee . . . or something."

"I should go." Elizabeth hugged her arms around her waist. "It's late. I was just thinking of you and thought I'd look you up. It was a little spur-of-the-moment. I didn't really plan on stopping . . . or staying." She gestured to his briefcase. "I'm sure you have a lot to catch up on."

He looked from the briefcase to her. "It can wait a few minutes."

For ten or so seconds she contemplated his invitation before allowing him to see regret in her eyes. "I have an early meeting tomorrow." She reached up and hugged him. "Next time," she whispered near his ear.

He watched her walk away, part of him wishing he could say something to make her stay. They needed to talk, to catch up on all the years yawning between them. But she was right, it was late. Far too late for them. And starting down that path would only resurrect too much hurt . . . too many memories.

"Hey!"

He shook off the troubling thoughts and met her gaze. "Did you forget something?"

She backed the final steps to her car. "I got a dog." Her smile widened to a grin. "Finally."

He frowned, tried to think how that was significant.

"Remember," she went on, her hand fumbling behind her for her door, "I could never keep a pet because of Mother's allergies."

Wait . . . yes, he did remember. The family had tried several pets, and they'd each eventually had to go. Elizabeth and Dane had been devastated each time.

"That's great. What breed?"

"A Lab." She opened her car door. "My favorite. I've always wanted a big old chocolate Lab. I have my own place now, there was nothing stopping me."

With all that was going on in his life, he had to laugh at the idea of discussing a new pet with Elizabeth. She sent a look of confusion in his direction.

"Are you laughing at me, Carson Tanner?"

He shook his head. "Absolutely not." He choked back the mirth but couldn't drag the goofy grin off his face.

"Just for that you can accompany me to the Newton Ball on Sunday night."

All signs of amusement evaporated. Did he hear her correctly? "Do what?"

She was the one grinning now. "Be my escort. The fundraiser for the Museum of Art. Sunday night, eight o'clock. You can pick me up at seven-thirty. Don't be late."

Elizabeth got into her car, wiggled her fingers at him, and then drove away. Carson waved, watching as her taillights disappeared into the night.

Sunday night. He and Elizabeth.

Whoa.

Another smile pulled at his lips.

It had been years since he'd given much if any thought to a personal life. Maybe it was time for that to change.

All the more reason for him to get his act together.

Whatever game Annette Baxter was playing with him, it wasn't going to work.

He would not fall for her manipulative ploys again.

He was going to nail her hot little ass straight to the proverbial wall.

His determination renewed, he grabbed his briefcase and jacket, climbed the steps, and crossed the porch. Hell yeah, he was back on track now. No more screwing around. He jammed the key into the lock and opened the door.

Carson Tanner was on the case.

The Avenger . . .

His hand hovered at the light switch.

Instinct fired a warning, making him hesitate.

What was that smell?

He took a deep breath, analyzed the noxious odor.

Gas?

What the . . . ?

The briefcase slipped from his fingers. Plopped onto the floor. The jacket followed.

Moving with extreme caution, he headed for the kitchen. Only two possible sources—gas heating system, gas stove.

As he entered the dark kitchen he raised his forearm to protect his nose. The foul smell was much stronger here. He blinked at the sting. Heard the faint rush of gas escaping.

Carson reached out, touched the first knob on the commercial grade cook top. Straight up in the off position. Next one, same thing. Next one . . .

Shit.

Set on high. No flame, just the rush of raw gas.

Carson shut off the flow then quickly raised windows to ventilate the dangerous fumes.

When the air inside was tolerable, he relaxed and turned on the lights.

He hadn't cooked that morning. Hadn't even been home.

How the hell . . . ?

The near brush with the black sedan . . . now this?

His heart rate reacted to a surge of adrenaline.

Coincidence? Maybe.

Then again, Otis Fleming was a powerful man. Maybe he was sending Carson a warning . . . or two.

Let him give it his best shot.

Carson wasn't backing off. Not today, not tomorrow. He was going to bring Otis Fleming down.

And Annette Baxter was going to help him.

10

10:50 p.m.

From his carefully chosen surveillance position, Lieutenant William Lynch watched Elizabeth Drake drive away from Carson Tanner's residence.

Nostalgic, to see the two together again. Bill sighed. Tanner had done well for himself. Elizabeth had, too. Though their lives had certainly taken different routes, in many ways the final destination had been the same.

Too bad a new course was taking shape . . . one that would surely lead to a bad end for the both of them. Again.

Tragic.

Bill shook his head as he started the engine of his Charger then rolled out of the driveway of the empty house just two doors east of Tanner's.

As a highly trained officer of the law, Bill had taken every precaution when selecting his surveillance position this evening. The house he'd chosen was empty; the owners had abruptly moved to Dallas, leaving the home in the hands of a reputable real estate agent. This late in the evening most folks were tucked in for the night. A vehicle parked in the drive of an empty house went unnoticed.

He glanced one last time at Carson Tanner's home, then drove away. Bill had been a homicide investigator for better than half his life, and he'd pretty much seen it all. No amount of experience changed how it felt to watch someone pulled under for the second time.

For fifteen years he'd kept up with that boy. Cut him a break every chance he got. Seemed like the only right thing to do considering. Some folks just needed more help than others. Couldn't catch a break on their own.

But then, that was the problem with helping folks out. Once you got involved, it never ended.

Unfortunately, Carson Tanner had no idea what he'd gotten himself into.

This time he just might not survive.

11

Thursday, September 9, 9:00 a.m.
31st Street, Birmingham
Fleming Estate

He wouldn't be happy to see her.

Annette Baxter entered the code at the gate to the twelve-foot wall shielding the Fleming estate from public access. With excruciating slowness the gate slid aside for her to enter.

It didn't matter whether Otis wanted to see her right now or not. She had to talk to him. She could trust no one else.

She accelerated, rolled through the entrance, then sped up the curving drive. Once she passed the halfway mark, the zoom lens tracking her every move from the two-story home across the street wouldn't be able to see her. For weeks now she had ignored the prying eyes of the federal agents as well as the occasional cop when they bothered, eluding surveillance only when necessary.

But now everything was different.

Now she understood that this wasn't about Otis.

It was about her. And what she knew.

Evidently with the decision of one powerful client to turn on her, others had scratched up the courage to join the mutiny. Or perhaps they had been prompted. At this point there was no way for her to know who was an ally or who was an enemy. But the identity of the *one* who had started this domino effect was obvious. Stopping him might just be impossible.

No. Annette climbed out of her Lexus. She was not beaten yet. She took a moment to adjust her slim-fitting jacket. She'd worn a black skirt that hit midthigh with a skintight, lace-trimmed black camisole. A leopard-print push-up bra showed just enough to intrigue; last were her matching black four-inch heels. Even her hair was styled in a flawless chignon.

Otis liked her to look a certain way. He had taught her to use her mercilessly toned body to her advantage at every opportunity. Her no-good parents hadn't given her much, but she couldn't attribute most aspects of her looks to anything but genetics. At least her parents had been good for something before they deserted her, forcing her to survive on her own. And she had survived, by wit and sheer force of will.

Pretty or not, socially acceptable or not. Legal or not.

She strode toward the front of the grand Georgian mansion. As she did she considered that Otis had taught her how to dress, how to wear her hair and makeup, and just about every damned thing else she knew. She had learned her lessons well.

Independently wealthy, highly sought-after skills, and the fear, if not the respect, of everyone who was anyone in Birmingham. Otis Fleming had schooled her in how to survive. For nearly a decade no one had dared cross her . . . until now.

Strangely enough, the sole reason she was in this predicament was because she'd done her job. Exactly what was required despite the extreme risk to her position, professionally and personally. Was *he* thankful? Fury set her teeth on edge. Not one damned bit.

All she had worked for, her entire world was poised on the brink of crashing down around her . . . and there appeared to be nothing she could do to stop the inevitable plunge toward certain destruction.

He had the power to do that.

Her lips trembled but she squelched the outward display of weakness. She would not be afraid. She was not ten years old anymore.

Annette stilled, closed her eyes, and fought the surge of memories. She had gotten her period. Her mother had been at work on her assigned street corner. But her mother's boyfriend, Reggie, well, of course he'd been home. He was always home. And always drunk. He'd shown her exactly what to do . . . and then he'd raped her. The first of many personal violations.

Deep breaths. Slow, really slow, deep, deeper. Annette forced the ugly past behind her. She was not that little girl anymore. She squared her shoulders. She was a powerful woman. One who could meet any challenge and survive.

This one would prove no different. One way or another she would regain control. *He* had no idea how very resourceful she could be when necessary. The real question was, could she bring him down before he brought her down?

It was all in the timing.

At the intricately adorned double doors Annette steeled herself for the encounter. Though she trusted Otis explicitly, he was the one person who possessed the power to intimidate her with a single glance.

Otis owned her as he did so many other powerful people in Birmingham.

Annette didn't bother knocking or ringing the bell. She opened the door and walked inside. Otis's personal security would have identified her vehicle and her as she navigated the driveway long before she ever reached the door.

"Good morning, Ms. Baxter."

Annette nodded to the tall, wide-shouldered man who served as the head of security. "How are you this morning, Blake?"

Blake Dillard had been with Otis for twenty years. He was trained in every manner of hand-to-hand combat and was an expert marksman. Four years in the army's special forces had ensured that his survival instincts were honed to perfection. No one got past Blake.

The big man smiled. "Seeing you always brightens my day."

The genuine sentiment made Annette smile. "Is he in?" He would be. He rarely left home.

"Yes."

Annette didn't have to ask where she would find him. Even Otis possessed one or two predictable traits.

"Thank you, Blake."

Annette's heels clicked on the marble floor as she followed the entry hall to the observatory. When she reached for the door, she prepared for the change in temperature. The instant she opened the door the hot humidity rushed to meet her. A jungle of greenery towered to the second-story glass ceiling. An array of blooming plants served as the undercanopy. Otis had spent years cultivating his hobby. He insisted the gardening provided great stress relief. Annette was certain that maintaining the moisture content and nutritional level of hundreds of plants would do nothing for reducing her stress level. But then, operating at a higher state of arousal had its benefits.

"This is an unexpected pleasure." Otis Fleming did not look up from his scrutiny of the beautiful orchids he tended so meticulously. As casual as his comment might sound to anyone else, Annette understood that he was not pleased, much less pleasured, by her unscheduled appearance.

"We need to discuss my situation." A detailed explanation was not necessary. He was aware of her current circumstances.

He set aside the spray bottle he used to mist the fragile flowers and turned his full attention on her. Despite his age, Otis continued to be a handsome, distinguished man. His hair had grayed to a lustrous white. His blue eyes were sharp and bright. Though not a tall man, his posture remained perfect, his bearing nothing less than refined. The multi-thousand-dollar suits he wore were tailor-made for him. He flew to New York each spring and fall to revitalize his wardrobe.

Most importantly, behind that sophisticated appearance thrived an intelligence bordering on sheer genius.

"I'm certain I've made my position clear on the matter." He reached for a cloth and wiped his hands. "What more is there to say?"

He had no intention of making this easy. She took a breath of the muggy air and reinforced her courage. "My assumption that Wainwright would assign the case to Carson Tanner was correct. He's already begun his investigation."

Otis folded the cloth and placed it on the table next to the lovely pot of orchids. "I would've been immensely surprised had he not chosen Tanner. He is, after all, the very best employed by the District Attorney's Office."

"Then you can understand my reservations."

"Certainly." Otis approached her, his gaze sweeping from her chignon to her stilettos and back. When he had finished his meticulous appraisal, approval glinted in his eyes. "You, my dear, have no reason to be concerned." He stopped one step away and took her hand so that he could cradle it in both of his. "You need only keep your head about you. Unless you crack under the pressure, he will find nothing." He studied her a moment that turned to two, then three before adding, "Unless there is some facet of this situation about which you've failed to make me aware."

Annette tensed before she could stop the reaction. Instantly schooling the response, she placed her free hand atop his and squeezed. "I've told you everything. Of course." She pressed her lips together and gave her head the slightest shake. "But my instincts are screaming at me. There is something more here than we know. This goes deeper than a mere attempt to tie you to certain activities. I can feel it."

Otis released her hand and placed his on her shoulder to gently turn and guide her from the observatory. "There is always that possibility. But you must never allow your instincts to override your logic."

The cooler air in the hall rushed into her hungry lungs. "You're right, as always."

"As always." He ushered her toward his study. "Why don't we have coffee and chat?"

"That would be nice."

The study had a classic design, yet the decor was anything but the usual fare. Exotic woods and art from the deepest, darkest corners of the earth ensured a strikingly alien feel steeped in mystery.

While Otis instructed Blake to prepare their refreshments, she surveyed the room she knew as well as any in her own home. Elegantly bound books, exquisite art, and no shortage of plaques proclaiming his vast philanthropic deeds. But not a single photograph. None of relatives, none of friends. Not one single thing that could connect him to anyone. And yet he knew everyone.

Blake arrived with the tray and served the coffee. Annette accepted the cup and thanked him.

"So." Otis sipped his steaming brew. "Tell me about Mr. Carson Tanner." His gaze settled on hers. "You've done your preliminary work?"

Images of frantic sex attempted to invade her head, but she banished them. "Yes."

She contemplated for a time what she would say next. Otis waited patiently. He preferred a thorough analysis, not some half-baked pitch.

"He's relentless as well as resourceful. He won't give up easily." Her curiosity roused. She told herself the reaction was foolish, certainly uncharacteristic. Carson Tanner was work, self-preservation, nothing more.

"Where would the challenge be if he chose not to do his job to the fullest extent of his capabilities?"

Annette tasted her coffee to cover her irritation that Otis seemed to consider this a game. "Carson Tanner will be a challenge."

"You have what you need. You can turn him around."

Their gazes held for five seconds that lapsed into ten. "Yes." Her pulse rate increased. The stench of blood assailed her nostrils as too-vivid images zoomed across her retinas. She blinked the ugliness away.

"You'll know when the time is right to use that asset."

Her chin lifted in defiance of the uncharacteristic doubt nagging at her. "Yes." She would not hesitate to do whatever was necessary when the time came. Timing was everything.

"You also realize," he qualified, "that in doing so, you will be taking yet another huge risk. Think carefully before each move you make."

"Very carefully," she agreed.

Otis studied her a long moment, again igniting the uneasiness she so rarely felt in his presence. "Despite his hard-earned position and beloved reputation, Carson Tanner is far more expendable than he knows."

Wasn't everyone? But Otis was correct. Maybe that was the part that bothered Annette the most. Carson Tanner was only doing his job . . . he had no idea the price he might very well pay for being too damned good at what he did.

Otis held up his cup for a belated toast. "To the survival of the fittest."

She raised hers. "Survival."

In the end, survival was all that really mattered.

12

11:15 a.m.
1000 18th Street, Birmingham
Federal Bureau of Investigation

Behind her cluttered desk, Special Agent Kim Schaffer turned to a new page in her file. Carson waited patiently. He'd been doing that for an hour now. First to get in for the briefing he'd been invited to attend and now for Agent Schaffer to get down to business.

The lady was not happy with his relentless questions. He wasn't a cop. He wasn't an agent. He was from the DA's Office, which meant he was the guy looking over her shoulder. She had said as much.

Schaffer exhaled a big breath and lifted her gaze to his. "Considering what you've told me, I'm not sure I have anything to share that you'll find relevant, Mr. Tanner."

Bullshit. Judging from the amount of surveillance the Bureau had spent on Fleming and his associates, there had to be more than what she'd given Carson in that flimsy report she'd e-mailed him yesterday.

He pulled a don't-give-me-that-crap expression. "Why don't you let me be the judge of that, Agent Schaffer?" Nothing like playing nice with the feebees.

"Well." She stood, shuffled the reports and surveillance photos back into the folder, and walked around her desk to settle into the chair beside him. "Why don't we go through this one page at a time? If you have any more questions, by all means feel free to speak up."

She couldn't have said that half an hour ago?

"Fine." He sat up a little straighter and prepared to review the contents of the file.

Schaffer propped one booted foot onto the opposite knee and positioned the file in her lap. Carson wasn't aware that cowboy—or cowgirl as the case was—boots were a part of the standard dress code for federal agents. These boots were shocking pink. Her no-nonsense attitude was followed through with a face free of makeup and a practical short hairstyle. No frills, no fuss. Pink boots aside, he would wager that beneath that classic navy business suit she had a pair of brass ones bigger than any of the male agents assigned to the Birmingham field office.

"We've been routinely following the activities of Otis Fleming for the past three years." She tapped the date on the first report in the file. "The distribution of handguns and drugs; stolen vehicles; Acme Landfill"—she glanced up at Carson—"which we have reason to believe is connected to New York organized crime. And yet," she added, shrugging, "we've had zero success in tying him directly to anything other than his philanthropic deeds."

At least she didn't try to sugarcoat the facts. "Finding zero appears to be par for the course," he admitted. "Lots of rumor and innuendo but no concrete evidence connecting the man to anything illegal. He's either brilliant or damned lucky." Could anyone be that lucky? Or did this crafty old bastard have a secret weapon? One fond of stilettos, slinky red dresses, and hot sex?

Schaffer held up a finger. "However." She flipped over a few pages. "We have some usable facts on a number of his underlings. At the top of the heap is this one."

The subject in the photo seemed to stare directly at him.

Annette Baxter.

Carson shifted in his chair. He shouldn't be surprised that *her* name came up first with the Bureau, but somehow he was. Why the hell hadn't he ever heard of her? He'd done his share of keeping up with Otis Fleming and the suspicions regarding what he represented.

But Annette Baxter had been a complete unknown to Carson.

He'd never met her, never seen her face in the news.

Nada.

"This one"—Schaffer indicated the grainy surveillance photo—"keeps the old man covered. For the past three weeks we've been focusing our investigation on her. There appears to be a very close relationship with Fleming, and we feel that she has the goods on him like no other associate in his universe. In fact." Schaffer tapped the photo again. "Very few of his closest associates last long. The faces change regularly, the old ones never to be seen again, except maybe in the morgue." Schaffer looked directly at Carson then. "This one has stuck. She's the key. If we get her, we get him."

Schaffer moved through one report, one surveillance photo, after the other and didn't provide Carson with anything he didn't already have.

Not what he'd been hoping for.

"Did I miss the *usable* facts you mentioned having on this suspect?" To this point Carson had found nothing of any significance in his own research. It seemed the feds hadn't fared any better.

Schaffer took the question exactly the way he'd meant, with a heavy dose of sarcasm. "There's no physical evidence, if that's what you mean. Other than the audiotape. However, we can connect her, time and location-wise, to a number of specific activities."

In other words, they didn't have jack shit. He'd heard the audiotape; it was useless.

"I see." More sarcasm. Baxter didn't strike him as the type to be intimidated by innuendo. It was going to take a hell of a lot more than this to persuade her to turn state's evidence.

Wait.

An abrupt buzz of adrenaline made the hair on the back of Carson's neck stand on end.

"Your people have been keeping close tabs on her for three weeks?" His gut twisted into blistering knots. A blast of new tension roared through his muscles. Shit.

"That's right."

Schaffer's gaze locked with his, and Carson expected her to flip to a new photo showing him and Baxter going into the room at the Tutwiler. Or her coming into his office building.

"Well, most of the time," Schaffer qualified. "There are days, like yesterday, when she somehow slips off our radar. We didn't catch up with her until she showed up at home around ten last night."

Air rushed into Carson's lungs. When he could speak, he asked, "How does she manage to give you the slip?" He saw no reason to pretend that wasn't a major feat. After all, the feds were highly trained. How the hell could someone like Annette Baxter give them the slip *repeatedly*?

Schaffer raised an eyebrow. "You ever pulled surveillance, Tanner?"

Her question should have pissed him off, but he was so damned glad his face wasn't in any of those surveillance shots that he couldn't quite muster the necessary indignation. Besides, in a roundabout way he'd just insulted her.

"Yes." He met that critical gaze head-on. "Many times."

"Then you know." She closed the file. "That sometimes shit happens. The target gets wise to your tactics, gets tipped off, whatever. Once or twice a week she manages to disappear for a few hours. Considering there are seven days in a week and twenty-four hours in each day, that's damned good coverage on our part, if you ask me." Schaffer plopped the thick file onto the edge of her desk. "When she gives us the slip, nobody's happy. But that's the nature of the beast."

Tipped off? That phrase, interjected so offhandedly, stuck out from the others like an empty seat in the jury box. "Is there a possibility that someone in your office has a reason to feed info to Annette Baxter?"

Schaffer didn't look happy that he'd homed in on that part of her assessment—but she'd been the one to go there. He had every right to pursue that avenue.

"No," she said emphatically. "As you can imagine, though, there's always the possibility. Baxter is a very intelligent, cunning piece of work. If she wanted someone inside, she would likely find what she was looking for. I can vouch for the competence and dedication of every agent in this office," Schaffer allowed, "but none of us can see through brick walls or leap tall buildings. We're only human."

Carson's brow furrowed, as much with confusion as interest. "Baxter's that good?" Not that he actually needed to ask. He knew firsthand how damned good the woman was. She'd blindsided him.

Schaffer nodded. "She's that good."

He felt the urge to squirm but squashed it. "What about the others surrounding Fleming? Surely Baxter isn't the sum total of your focus on this case."

Schaffer turned her palms upward. "There are a couple of others fairly high up the food chain, but no one as close to Fleming as Baxter."

Carson needed to know about the others regardless of that deduction. "I'd like to see what you have on them." Schaffer sat back and scrutinized him a long moment. "I'm not sure you fully comprehend what I'm saying."

He started to argue but she kept going.

"Waste all the time you want chasing after these other scumbags, Annette Baxter is the one. She and Fleming have some sort of connection or relationship that transcends business. Get her and you'll get Fleming. It's that simple."

And at the same time, that complicated. Schaffer was the one who didn't fully comprehend the situation.

If Carson could help it, she never would.

Still, there had to be more to the agent's decision than what he'd seen and heard so far. "Call me a stickler for the facts," Carson countered, undeterred, "but there has to be some concrete reason you believe Baxter is your best bet."

Schaffer assessed him a second time. "You just won't be put off, will you, Tanner?"

His gaze narrowed as he searched hers. "Pardon my frankness, Agent Schaffer, but what the hell's that supposed to mean?"

"It means"—she held his gaze in a deep probe—"that I received a tip about Baxter. And if you quote me on this I'll personally spend the rest of my career making yours miserable."

"Let me get this straight." He held up a hand as much in disbelief as in surprise. "You have another source and you were going to keep that from me?" He laughed drily. "Had to be a hell of a tip for you to expend the full thrust of your investigation, not to mention resources, based on that one source."

"And why wouldn't I?" She shrugged. "The tip came from your office. Do you have any reason to believe the district attorney himself would intentionally offer misleading information?"

What the hell? Wainwright had assigned Carson to this investigation. Had given him the entire case file, but failed to declare that he'd provided some additional information to the feds? No way.

"You didn't feel compelled to mention this before?" Carson made no attempt to disguise his skepticism or his annoyance. "What was the nature of this tip?"

"You're asking me?" Schaffer had the look, the one that said she'd given all she intended to. "Look under your own rugs, Tanner, before you come over here telling the Bureau how to sweep their floors. I'd start with your boss. He knows something you don't. I find that quite interesting, don't you?"

As much as he hated to admit it, the ballsy lady was right. He damned sure intended to take her advice. That was the thing about this case: Every time he got answers, twice the number of questions popped up.

If Schaffer had a vendetta against the DA's Office, that would certainly explain Wainwright's disappointment at having her assigned to the case. On the other hand, Carson couldn't fathom Wainwright's motive for not disclosing all relevant facts. Nor could he fully believe that Baxter possessed some damning knowledge against the DA's Office. The concept that these two unknowns could be somehow connected was a viable premise, though the former hardly made sense.

The one thing he knew with absolute certainty at this point was that if he didn't get Annette Baxter first, she would get him. Local law enforcement wanted her, the feds wanted her. It was only a matter of time before she was backed into a corner with no escape. And then she would use Carson for leverage to get a deal.

And he would be screwed for real.

He thought of the close call with the near hit-and-run and then the gas leak . . . that is, if Otis Fleming didn't beat them both to the punch.

Carson rolled through the security gate and into the street, headed to his office. He intended to wait for the right moment to approach Wainwright. Questioning his mentor's ethics or motives wasn't something he intended to explore without due consideration. His cell phone vibrated. He dug it from his pocket. "Tanner."

"Mr. Tanner, this is Sergeant Johnson at the Mountain Brook precinct."

Carson's instincts went on alert. He understood before he asked that this was not going to be a social call. "How can I help you, Sergeant?"

"I'm sorry to bother you, sir, but we have a minor situation."

Carson glanced at his watch. Almost one. Nothing on his schedule that couldn't wait. "What's the trouble?"

"Sir, your uncle, Maxwell West, had . . . an episode at the neighborhood Kroger this morning."

A ripple of a different kind of tension rolled over Carson. "Is he all right?"

"Physically he's fine, sir. I checked his record and found a few other reports indicating that episodes of this nature have happened in the past."

A few other reports. That was putting it kindly. "I appreciate your call, Sergeant Johnson. Are there any charges?" Just what Carson needed. His uncle going off into one of those bizarre worlds of his and acting out his paranoia.

"No, sir. We persuaded the store manager to accept payment for the cleanup and any damages. There'll be no formal charges filed."

Carson exhaled some of the tension. "I'm on my way." He slid the phone into his pocket and set a course for Mountain Brook. This was something Carson failed to value at times. Though he'd lost his family at sixteen, in the years following that tragedy he'd gained an extended family in the law enforcement community. Folks watched one another's backs.

All the more reason the suggestion that Wainwright would purposely leave out vital information just didn't feel right.

Schaffer had to be wrong.

Carson braked at the intersection. When he would have pulled out, he hesitated. A red Mustang parked at the curb on the opposite side of the cross street detained his attention. Or, more accurately, the blond female leaning against the driver's-side door did. His gaze forged a path from the daringly high heels, up long, sexy legs, to the hem of the short, tight black skirt before recognition slammed into his brain.

Annette Baxter.

Dark glasses shielded her eyes, but the irreverent smile on her lips was unmistakable.

Fury tightened in his gut. What the hell was she doing? He glanced in his rearview mirror. He was no more than three blocks from the Bureau office. Yet there she stood, in broad daylight without the first sign of the surveillance the feds had tailing her 24/7.

He turned left, rolling out onto the otherwise deserted cross street, unable to look away from her. As he drove slowly past, she removed those dark glasses and stared directly at him. Challenging him to question her presence. Letting him know she was watching.

So damned cocky. Oh yeah, let her look all she damned well wanted to. He was the last person she was going to see before taking one hell of a fall.

En route to pick up his uncle, Carson exiled his annoyance with Baxter and put in a call to his secretary to arrange payment of damages with the Kroger manager. Once at the Mountain Brook precinct, Carson signed for Max's release then followed Sergeant Johnson to the holding cell.

Maxwell West was a seventy-year-old functioning schizophrenic. As long as he stayed on his medication he was a little on the odd side but fully capable of living a reasonably normal life. But those times when he either forgot or just plain refused to take his meds, *this* happened.

Carson stared at his uncle, who was curled into the fetal position on the floor of the cell. How was it that Carson's mother, a renowned child psychologist, could have had a brother so completely opposite?

"Let's go, Max," Carson said as the sergeant unlocked the door.

Max peeked above the forearms crossed over his face. His eyes were wild with the insanity plaguing his brain. Voices, images, memories—real and imagined—were no doubt whirling in his head like a late-summer tornado. Sweat had dampened his shirt at his armpits and beaded on his face. "They're coming for me this time, Carson. I know it."

Carson tried not to show his frustration. Someone was always coming for Max. Particularly the ambiguous *they*.

The man was a recluse. Lived in a shack in the woods. The same shack where he'd raised Carson until he'd gone off to college. Max had no friends, no living relatives other than Carson. The old man didn't attend social functions. He had nothing of value in his home. He existed. Nothing more. There was no one to fear.

But he'd taken care of Carson as best he could when there had been no one else.

Carson crouched down and offered his hand. "Come on. I'll take you home. We'll get your meds and you'll be fine."

Max sprang up on all fours and glared wildly at Carson. "I can't go back there. I'm telling you"—he swiped at his damp face—"they're gonna get me this time."

Frustration spiked again but Carson tamped it back down. As difficult as moments like this were, not only did he owe the old man, but Max was his only family. Carson had to take care of him.

Who would take care of Carson if this ever happened to him? He'd heard the whispers behind his back fifteen years ago.

The boy could be like his uncle . . . that man's crazy, you know.

Fear trickled. Carson stanched the seeping, creeping flow of it and braced himself. He was not like his uncle. This would not happen to him. It hadn't fifteen years ago, it wouldn't now. "We can do this either the easy way or the hard way," he offered quietly but firmly.

Max blinked, a new brand of fear welling in his eyes. "What does that mean, Carson?"

Guilt nagged at Carson. The man was like a scared kid. Carson couldn't bring himself to be too hard on him, no matter how frustrating these incidents could be. "It means you have to come with me now or there'll be trouble. You don't want any trouble, right?"

Max considered the question a moment then shook his head adamantly. "Take me home." He struggled to his feet. "I'll just have to find a way to fortify my security."

Whatever.

Max refused to wear his seat belt or to sit upright in the car. He hovered down where no one could see him for the twenty-five minutes required to reach his run-down shack deep in the woods that backed up to the prestigious Mountain Brook community.

His uncle had inherited several acres of woodland from the West family. The property abutted the estate where Carson had grown up. Carson's mother ensured that the land was put in trust so that Max couldn't do away with it in one of his frenzies. The old man had built his shack out of recycled materials picked up from wherever he happened to find them. His furnishings were castoffs gathered from curbs. He refused to live anyplace else. Max had made a trail through the woods to Carson's childhood home. Carson remembered vividly how his uncle would sometimes show up in the middle of the night to pillage for food after his monthly allowance ran out. He had refused monetary assistance from his sister, wouldn't take it from Carson now.

He led his uncle into the shack and ushered him down onto the ragged couch. "Don't move."

Max just stared at him, his mania subsiding slightly in the familiar surroundings.

Carson found the prescription bottles and counted the contents. "Dammit." His uncle had been off his meds for six days. And Carson had been so busy screwing up that he'd failed to check on him.

There was no excuse for that kind of neglect.

Annette Baxter elbowed her way into his thoughts. He evicted the image of those long legs and that wicked smile. As soon as he had this situation under control he would come back to that problem. She was going to learn very quickly how he'd earned his reputation as the Avenger.

For just one moment last night he had been certain he'd heard fear in her voice. He'd definitely seen it in her eyes. But like everything else about her, the display had likely been a performance designed to mislead him. To tug at his protective instincts. She shouldn't waste her time.

Carson had no sympathy where Annette Baxter was concerned.

What he did have was a raging desire to take her down.

After prowling through the fridge and cabinets to find something edible, Carson got the meds into Max followed by food. The man was skin and bones. He didn't eat nearly often enough. Something else Carson should have been taking care of.

Instead of fucking Annette Baxter.

Carson stayed with his uncle while the drugs did their work. Soon Max was speaking more slowly and rationally and insisting that he needed to sleep. Time and a few more doses would be necessary to get him back on track.

"You don't need to worry, Car," Max offered as Carson helped him into bed and adjusted the covers about him.

Carson settled on the edge of the lumpy mattress. "Why would I be worried?" Who knew where the old man's random thoughts came from? Carson understood from experience that it was best to give him grace and just play along.

"She knew you didn't mean it."

Tension rippled along Carson's frame. "What're you talking about, Max?"

"Livvy loved you. And she knew you loved her. No matter what happened, she always knew."

The tension turned to a dull ache, one Carson knew all too well. "I know," he said. "I know." He did. Teenagers said stupid things sometimes; their parents forgave them. But Carson had taken it to the next level . . . and he hadn't gotten the chance to make it right.

He had to live with that.

Max drifted off to sleep. Carson sat there watching the old man, the last time he'd spoken to his mother playing over and over in his head.

Carson, you don't understand.

I understand perfectly. I won't let you do this.

Dr. Olivia Tanner had tried to reason with her son, but Carson had refused to listen.

I hate you! Do you hear me, Mother? I hate you!

The fifteen-year-old patient in his mother's office at the time had witnessed the entire scene. Had provided a statement describing Carson's menacing demeanor and the threatening words he'd shouted at his mother—the renowned child psychologist who couldn't control her own son.

For the first twenty-four hours after the murders even the cops on the case had considered Carson guilty. Since he'd made another stupid decision and gotten piss-ass drunk after the fight with his mother, he'd even considered the sickening theory himself. An alcohol-induced blackout. Those unaccounted-for hours had taunted him ever since.

Had he simply passed out in a drunken stupor . . . or had he done what Max often did, gone off the deep end with no recallable memory of the event?

The boy could be like his uncle . . . that man's crazy, you know.

Stop. Carson closed his eyes. *Don't go back there.* That part of his life was over. He opened his eyes and stood. He'd achieved every damned thing he'd set out to accomplish—everything his parents had wanted for him. The law enforcement community respected him. He hadn't failed . . . except that once.

Until recently, he amended.

But it wouldn't happen again.

Restless and damned determined to get his mind off that painful past, Carson checked the house. There were only three rooms. The living, dining, and kitchen areas were all crammed into a twelve-by-fifteen space. There was also a small bedroom where Carson had slept for two years, and a box of a bathroom with nothing but a wall-mounted sink, toilet, and cubicle shower.

Home sweet home.

None of Carson's friends had been allowed to come here. Everyone had known Maxwell West was crazy. Less than half a mile away, the Tanner mansion had sat empty and collecting dust; still did. Max refused to live there. Not that Carson had ever wanted to, either. He hadn't set foot in the place in years. And even then only on those occasions when he needed to refresh his memory of the crime scene.

Only when he had no other choice.

The house remained, other than the initial crime scene cleanup, exactly as it had been fifteen years ago.

Stuck in time . . . just as Carson's personal life had been for so very long. But no more.

The Tanner case was closed, and Stokes was serving a life sentence.

Ask yourself if you'll ever really know what happened.

Maybe not, but the truth was that the past was the least of his worries.

Annette Baxter was the problem of the moment.

But her time was limited.

13

4:45 p.m.
1st Avenue, Birmingham

Jazel Ramirez climbed out of the Lexus. She slammed the door shut and leaned against it to watch her racy red Mustang roar up the street like a mighty beast. Shivers danced over her skin.

God, she loved that car!

The Mustang screeched to a halt, and the driver's-side door opened. Jazel's breath caught as she watched Annette emerge. She was so freakin' beautiful! Jazel wanted to be just like her!

They had the same body build. Lean and toned. Except Annette's tits were huge compared with Jazel's. But shit, that was okay. Jazel was only twenty-two. She had plenty of time to consider implants.

She tugged the blond wig from her head and finger-combed her dark mane, then reached up just in time to catch the keys Annette tossed her way.

"Good catch." Annette leaned against the Lexus. "Any trouble today?"

Jazel propped next to her idol. She shook her head as she exhaled. "It was cool. I went to the park. Drove around in my old neighborhood. Then came here." The black miniskirt and tight-ass camisole looked almost as good on her as it did Annette. Except for the cleavage. Jazel needed those implants.

Annette inclined her head. "You didn't notice a tail at any point?"

A frown tightened Jazel's forehead. "No way. You know I'm too smart for that." Damn. Annette rarely questioned her this way. Had she messed up somehow? She hoped not. The money she earned with this gig was paying for the Mustang. She would never have owned a car that cool without Annette.

Annette nodded. "Good. Payment's in the glove box. I'll probably need you again this week. Is that a problem?"

Jazel grinned. "Absolutely not."

Annette glanced around the empty street like she was nervous or something. "Okay, sweetie. You take care going home."

"I always take care." Jazel pushed off the Lexus and headed for her Mustang. As she slid behind the wheel, Annette drove away in the sleek Lexus. Hell yeah, Jazel wanted to be just like her. Annette had it all. Looks, money, anything she wanted.

Jazel intended to have it all, too. But first she had to finish her nursing degree. Annette insisted. No school, no work. No negotiation.

Burning rubber, Jazel sped away.

A full tank of gas. She grinned. Annette always filled up the tank before returning her car. Jazel tossed the blond wig onto the back seat.

She glanced at the clock on the dash. Damn. She had to get home. Her mother would be heading to work in fifteen minutes. Jazel had babysitting duty tonight. Just one of the many perks of belonging to a huge family.

As she left the city traffic behind she let her inhibitions go and jammed down hard on the accelerator. With the windows down and the wind blowing through her hair she felt as if she owned the road. She pumped up the volume on the radio and belted out the words to one of her favorites on this week's hit list.

Movement in the rearview mirror snagged her attention. She glanced at the mirror. What the hell? A black car was right on her ass.

"Fuck you!" she shouted at the mirror as she stomped the accelerator. Her Mustang rocketed forward. "Hell yeah! Catch me now, asshole!"

The victory high vanished as headlights and a grille loomed large in her rearview mirror.

A frown tugged at her lips. "What in the hell?"

The black car rushed right up on her bumper. Nudged her.

Her Mustang jerked forward even as her right foot instinctively let off the accelerator.

Jazel's heart lunged into her throat. Her fingers tightened on the steering wheel. What was this dick doing?

Stay calm. Focus on the road. Keep it between the ditches. Holding her breath, she glanced at the rearview mirror just to be sure he was gone.

He's . . . coming again!

"Shit." She floored the accelerator. Gripped the steering wheel even tighter and leaned forward. She had to lose this son of a bitch.

He rammed her.

The Mustang lurched forward.

Jazel screamed as she fought to stay on the road.

Where was her cell phone? She dared to glance around the interior. Not in the passenger seat. Not in the floor. Her purse. It was in her purse.

Where was her purse?

Another shove. Hard. The impact caused her to jerk. The right wheels jumped off the edge of the pavement. She wrenched the steering wheel left. Too fast. Shit!

Panic seized her as she fought to get the Mustang back under control and barreling forward.

She looked around, frantic for help.

There was no one.

What the hell was she supposed to do?

Another glimpse at the rearview mirror and terror tore at her heart. Ice filled her veins.

He was coming again.

She braced.

Oh God . . .

14

5:30 p.m.
32nd Street, Birmingham
Sloss Furnaces

Dane Drake hugged himself against the chill that came from deep inside. He couldn't shake it. Felt sick as shit. He wanted . . .

He shuddered. No, he didn't want, he *needed.*

Needed it so bad.

One hit . . . just one line of coke and he'd be okay.

His body shook so hard he could barely stand straight. But she'd be here soon and everything would be all right. She always knew what to do.

The sound of tires crunching on gravel jerked his attention to the Lexus rolling into the area designated as staff parking. Relief rushed through him, making his knees want to give way. Jesus, he thought for sure he'd die before she got here.

He licked his lips as she climbed out of the driver's side of the vehicle. The black skirt she wore was short and tight; the jacket, too. Damn. As sick as he felt, his dick took notice. Made him think about rowdy sex.

Like that was going to happen. This bitch was as cold as ice.

Focus, man. She didn't like it when he got this screwed up. Get it together. *Don't let her see the desperation . . . or the fear.*

He waited for her next to the fence under the overpass. Nobody ever parked this far out of the way. At this time of day the Birmingham landmark was pretty much deserted except for the clerk in the gift shop. Dane didn't have to worry about anybody looking here for him . . . or seeing him with *her.*

"Dane," she said as she approached, designer sunglasses shielding her eyes.

His mouth felt so damned dry. His gut was on fire and all knotted up. He needed something . . . now. Take it slow, talk rationally. Don't piss her off. "I'm sick." He took a deep, deliberate breath. "I need"—he swallowed the taste of bile—"something and I can't go to anybody I know."

She studied him a moment from behind those dark glasses before folding her arms over her chest. "And we both understand the reason you can't go to anyone, don't we?"

Shit. Why was she mad at him? He'd made a mistake. He barely even remembered anything. "It was . . . it just happened. Got out of control," he reminded her. Why did she have to make this hard? Sweat beaded on his skin. His body began to shake again. "What was I supposed to do?"

"I saved your ass, Dane." She moved closer, so close he could smell the faint scent of her perfume. "You know what they'd do to you if they found out."

Shit. He jerked his head up and down. "I know. You can't tell." Panic erupted inside him. "Please." Fury rushed in on the heels of the panic. She had no right making him feel like scum. His jaw hardened. He was Dane Drake, son of a damn US senator! "You'll do what my father pays you to do."

She reached up. He tensed. When she removed her glasses, she stared straight into his eyes, hers arctic-cold. Then she laughed. "You're right." She nodded once in acknowledgment of his puny victory. "Since

I pride myself on guaranteeing that a client gets his money's worth, perhaps I should give him all the details of our most recent transaction."

Dane stiffened with the images that flooded his aching brain. Blood. Everywhere. Digging frantically through pockets. He shuddered. Closed his eyes and drove away the mental pictures.

"That's what I thought."

Anger spewed again, making him shake even harder. "I'm sick," he growled.

She held out her hand. "Give me your cell phone."

His entire body sagged with relief. She was going to help him. He dug his cell from the pocket of his jeans and handed it to her.

After entering a number she handed it back to him. "Make the call. He'll take care of your needs."

Dane tried to conceal the tremor in his hand as he took back his phone. Didn't work.

"Find someplace to lay low for a while." She tucked her sunglasses back into place. "Don't talk to anyone. I'll contact you when it's safe to come out and play again."

He nodded.

"Look at me, Dane."

He stared into those dark lenses.

"Don't screw up. You know what will happen if you do."

He watched her walk back to her car. Yeah, he knew what would happen.

A part of him didn't give a damn. Wanted this to be over. He shut his eyes tight. *Don't look back! Don't think about it.* All that damned blood. His gut seized, doubling him over. He puked. Hard.

The ground tilting around him, he managed to straighten and scrub the back of his hand over his lips. He'd kept his mouth shut for fifteen years, why the hell did they think he'd do any different now?

One mistake in fifteen years. If his family, including Elizabeth, hadn't cut him off financially, he wouldn't have had to take such a drastic measure.

A mistake, that's all it was. He'd fixed it the only way he could. Even that part had been an accident . . . a mistake.

He'd done exactly what he had to do. Things just hadn't gone as planned.

It should have worked.

Whatever. He opened his cell to make the call. Unlike his sister, he didn't give one damn how this all turned out.

Dane just needed to stop the pain . . . and the memories.

15

7:00 p.m.
Birmingham
The Tramont

Annette stepped from the private elevator to the fifteenth floor. Her floor. The entire floor belonged to her. Her private rooms were separated from her offices by a vast entry hall and lobby.

Not classic like the Fleming mansion but every bit as lavish. Annette preferred modern to classic, austere to warm and cozy. Lots of white, glass, and metal; fluid, sparsely furnished spaces.

She was glad to be home and have this day behind her.

"Good evening, Ms. Baxter."

She placed her purse and keys in the hands of her assistant, Daniel Ledger. "I'm not taking any calls or returning any this evening." She was tired. She wanted a glass of wine, maybe two, and a long, hot soak in the tub.

Another unexpected element had cropped up. She now had someone else following her besides the feds. She hadn't recognized the dark sedan, but it didn't take any serious powers of deduction to know what was going on. Someone had decided to end this. Not really surprising. She'd actually wondered why they hadn't chosen that route in the first place.

Killing her would certainly be a lot simpler. But then, knowing those behind this scheme, they would prefer the public humiliation route.

"You have a client standing by via Zoom in your office, ma'am." Daniel looked less than pleased to have to make this announcement.

"A client?" She glanced at the delicate platinum watch on her wrist. Irritation furrowed her brow. She needed to think. The Dane Drake situation was nowhere near under control. And she needed to plan her next move with Carson Tanner. Time was not on her side. "I don't recall having any appointments this evening."

"Dr. Holderfield insisted on standing by until you returned."

Holderfield. Perfect. She rubbed at the ache forming behind her brow. This moment had been inevitable.

"Tea," she instructed Daniel as she headed for her office. She needed tea and then perhaps a martini instead of wine. She cleared her mind, opened the door, and breezed into the room. "Dr. Holderfield."

He glared at her from the large screen mounted above her conference table. The empathetic expression she pulled off did nothing to diminish the fury pulsing behind that hard expression.

"I want the truth. Where is my son?"

Annette ushered sympathy into her tone as she prepared to respond. Considering her knowledge of Zac Holderfield's exploits, doing so didn't come naturally. "I heard the news, Dr. Holderfield. I know this must be a difficult time for you and your family, but I'm sure Zac will turn up or the police will find him."

That simmering fury detonated. "I want you to find him!" He grappled to regain his composure. "This has something to do with Dane Drake. Zac mentioned him the last time we spoke. Something about a meeting or business of some sort." His nostrils flared with a harsh intake of air. "I can only imagine what kind of business."

Hospital administrator Dr. Dwight Holderfield would, of course, never utter aloud the exact nature of his son's dealings with Dane Drake or almost anyone else. The sale of illegal drugs was not exactly what he'd had in mind when he'd sent Zac to Auburn to become a pharmacist. Life often went awry in the best of families.

"If Dane and Zac had any *business* dealings, I'm sure they were carried out with the same finesse as with all Zac's customers." Usually involving covert rendezvous and handguns.

"Fuck you," Holderfield snarled. "I know—"

Daniel arrived with the tea, interrupting whatever he would have said next.

Annette settled into a lush white chair, the delicate china cup and saucer in her hands. As long as she appeared in control, her client would believe she was. At moments like this, the outward show of being collected was crucial.

"Why don't we wait to see what the police discover?" Annette suggested. "You have friends in high places, and I'm certain they're pushing for the speedy resolution of the investigation into Zac's disappearance."

"You know what'll happen," Holderfield charged. "*They'll* cover up the truth. I"—he banged his chest—"have had enough. This is *my* son we're talking about. My only son. They've gone too far this time."

"Dr. Holderfield, *Dwight,*" she reiterated coolly, "you're overwrought. I'm not sure you realize what you're saying." He needed to get a hold of himself before *he* went too far.

"I know exactly what I'm saying," he fired back. "I want you to find my son. I want you," he commanded, "to get to the truth. And if I find out that bastard . . ." He choked on the rest of the words. "I'll—"

"You'll what?" Annette sat her tea aside. Time to defuse this ticking bomb. "I would proceed with extreme caution, Doctor." She met his murderous gaze with lead in her own. "I'm certain you don't want to go there."

Red scaled Holderfield's neck and raced across his cheeks. "Don't you dare threaten me! Whatever they've done—"

"I would suggest," Annette interjected firmly, "that you get things back into perspective and cooperate with the efforts of the police."

Holderfield closed his eyes and heaved a labored breath, visibly struggling with his emotions. "Please." Defeat weighted the lone word. "I just want to find my son."

Annette hesitated. Though history had taught her the prudence in being so, she wasn't completely heartless. "All right. I'll look into the situation."

His gaze flew open and fury abruptly resurrected despite her generous assurance. Holderfield stabbed a finger at her. "And then we're done. I'm pulling my retainer fee and I never want to hear your name again."

Annette didn't flinch. But she did bury the foolish empathy she had allowed to surface. She took a cautious sip of her steaming tea, then just as carefully settled the cup and saucer back on the table. "One step at a time, Dr. Holderfield. I'll see what I can do about learning the circumstances surrounding your son's disappearance, and then we'll talk about our future business relationship."

Holderfield glowered at her. "There will be no future business relationship, Ms. Baxter. Don't doubt my decision. When this is done, we're finished. I'm finished with all of it!"

Annette stood, straightened her jacket, and leveled her most chilling stare in his direction. "Perhaps you've forgotten the conversation we had this time last year."

The color of rage leached from his face, leaving it pale and slack. "I paid you in full for your services."

She executed a firm shake of her head. "The monetary compensation was only half our bargain, Dr. Holderfield. I'm certain you remember our terms. You have an outstanding marker. Until I decide to call it in, you remain in my debt."

"And if I renege on that portion of our agreement?"

The tension thickened in the air. Annette let his insolence go yet again. He was worried about his son. She'd cut him some slack this time.

But business was business. "Then you will suffer the consequences."

The color of rage began its steady creep back up his throat. "You think you're so untouchable. You'll get yours one of these days." He stared at her long and hard. "Maybe sooner than you think."

Annette allowed him to revel in his temporary revolt for a moment, but when he would have ended the meeting, she intervened. "Dr. Holderfield."

He hesitated, his gaze locking with hers. "I have nothing more to say."

"You think you know who I am." She laughed softly, but there was nothing soft or gentle in her manner. "You have no idea. Your concern for your son has you emotional just now. Be that as it may, you threaten me again and you will quickly learn exactly how far I can go to turn that prestigious career of yours into a shambles." She paused so that he might absorb the full implications of her statement. "You have *no* secrets from me, Dr. Holderfield. Don't forget that."

He opened his mouth, no doubt to debate her decree.

She stood. "This conversation is over. Have a nice evening."

Annette tapped the necessary button to end the Zoom connection, and the large screen went black. She walked out, relaxing marginally in the change of setting. She was accustomed to threats. Most were groundless attempts to intimidate. Her position was always covered.

At least until recently.

She'd learned something *they* did not want her to know. Tension coiled inside her. Of all the powerful players on her client list, those unhappy with her right now were the most powerful. And with the darkest secrets. It had taken one glitch, one ripple, to start the tide against her. *They* had banded together overnight. Now everything was falling apart.

If she could stop the momentum in time, she might be able to salvage things.

But that might just be impossible.

At the door to her private rooms, her personal assistant waited patiently for further instructions.

"A martini with two olives," she said as she walked past him. She was too tired for polite conversation.

"Right away."

Lost in her analysis of Holderfield's unexpected defiance, she drifted down the hall leading to her master suite. She needed a good night's sleep. Tomorrow was another day. She would find a way to turn this around.

Shrugging off her jacket, Annette kicked off her shoes, then peeled the camisole from her torso and wiggled out of her narrow skirt.

This day had been far too long without nearly enough accomplished.

She padded to the en suite bath and adjusted the spigots in the tub. As the water flowed and swirled, she freed her hair and let it tumble down her shoulders. She shook it, then massaged her aching scalp. Despite all that had happened, sleep would come easy tonight. She was exhausted.

A tap on the open door drew her attention to Daniel, who had arrived with her drink. Good. Her faithful assistant placed the drink on the rim of the tub.

"Thank you, Daniel." She was more than ready for the escape. "That'll be all tonight."

"Ms. Baxter."

Annette recognized that tone all too well. Another problem. She sighed. Would this day never end? "Yes?"

"You have a private call." He pulled the untraceable cell she reserved for personal communications from his jacket pocket.

Her heart bumped her sternum as she accepted the phone. She didn't have to ask who it would be. She knew. And it would not be good news. "Thank you, Daniel."

When he left her alone, she pressed the necessary button to take the call off hold. "This is Annette."

The hospital.

She listened to the doctor's report, her heart sinking a little more with each word.

"I understand. Thank you." Annette severed the connection and placed the phone on the counter. She closed her eyes and searched for that calm place that had eluded her for days now.

Nothing scared her . . . but this.

Her sister, Paula, had suffered another episode. This one worse than the last. If the outbursts continued, there would be no choice but to isolate her.

The worst possible scenario. Annette remembered all too well the locked rooms . . . and that basement. She shuddered. She couldn't let that happen.

For years her sister had been fine and now, suddenly, everything was spiraling downhill.

Whatever happened, Paula's well-being was her primary concern.

The problem was . . . if everything else fell apart, then Annette couldn't properly take care of her sister.

Filling her lungs with a deep, bolstering breath, Annette opened her eyes and stared at her reflection. She was strong. She could do this.

She had to do this.

Tomorrow she would accomplish more. She dropped her leopard-print bra on the tiled floor, then shimmied out of her panties. The bruises from her interlude with Carson Tanner lured her attention to her naked body. She touched the one on her hip. A frisson of heat lit deep inside her. Startled her. Ridiculous. Tanner roused her curiosity, nothing more. Sex was never enjoyable for her. Never had been and it was highly unlikely it ever would be. Not with her screwed-up history.

What would Carson Tanner think of his precious manhood if he knew she had faked every single orgasm she had supposedly had in her life? Not even he had managed to bring her to that prized place. He had, however, managed to stir a smattering of interest. Most unexpected.

That wasn't supposed to have happened.

Watching him exit the grounds of the revered Federal Bureau of Investigation offices today had been a ploy designed to make him wonder, to make him doubt. To trouble that fiercely analytical mind of his. What she'd succeeded in doing was making herself wonder . . . how would it feel to have a man like that care about her?

All that shiny integrity. Ambition . . . and heart.

Utterly ridiculous. She didn't need a man. Annette Baxter needed no one. Except her sweet, sweet sister.

Stepping gingerly into the deep, hot water, Annette reminded herself that she didn't have sex with men for pleasure. She rarely had sex at all, and then only to accomplish a goal unattainable by any other means. As she had with Carson Tanner. However noble, in the end he was no different from all the others.

Closing her eyes, she blocked the deluge of memories that attempted to flood her.

Don't go back there.

She reclined in her tub and allowed the liquid warmth to envelop her. Reaching for her glass, she considered that she could take her money and disappear. There was more than enough to live on quite comfortably for some time.

But she had other obligations from which she could not so easily walk away. That would not be so readily transitioned. Her sister. There was no quick fix there.

Panic tightened her throat.

Everything Annette did, had ever done, was for one reason. She could not fail now. She had to hold her ground.

A new surge of determination fortified her. Oh, yes, she would do whatever was necessary. She would not lose. She drank deeply of her martini, relished the instant warmth that settled deep inside her.

Annette had been repairing situations for nearly a decade. There wasn't anyone in enough trouble or an act so horrendous that she couldn't turn it around.

She would not . . . could not fail the only person in this world who meant anything to her . . . her sister.

"I'm sorry to trouble you again."

Annette started at the sound of Daniel's voice. He waited at the door. Why hadn't he gone home already?

"What?" She hadn't meant to snap, but she was so tired. Talking, thinking, none of that appealed to her. She needed quiet . . . and maybe a second martini.

"I just heard," he said, regret lining his face, "Jazel Ramirez was killed in a car crash today."

Jazel? How could that be? Annette had rendezvoused with her little more than two hours ago. She'd used Jazel's red Mustang to give the feds the slip and to annoy Carson Tanner. Jazel had been fine when Annette had retrieved her Lexus . . .

She reached for the calm that had deserted her, pushing aside the emotions that would have to wait. "When did this happen?"

"Shortly after five this evening," Daniel explained gently. "The accident is under investigation. According to our favorite reporter, Nadine Goodman, foul play is suspected considering the condition of Jazel's Mustang."

The dark sedan Annette had noticed in her rearview mirror more than once today tugged at her instincts. What color had it been? Navy? Black? Black, she was pretty sure.

An ache pierced her.

Was this merely a warning? Or was she to be terminated in the fullest sense of the word?

"Thank you, Daniel," she said, her voice lacking its usual resolve. Annette summoned her courage. No weakness. No fear. "Thank Nadine for me, too," she said with considerably more potency. "Let me know if you hear anything else." She fought a second onslaught of emotion. "Also, see that Jazel's family has anything they need."

"Of course, Ms. Baxter." Her faithful assistant hesitated before leaving her.

"Is there something else, Daniel?" She needed to be alone. To grieve . . . to regenerate her weary soul.

"You didn't mention putting Mr. Tanner on your calendar for tomorrow." He clasped his hands in front of him. "Does that mean you accomplished your goal during your last meeting?"

Confused and too damned tired to discuss anything at this point, Annette was vaguely aware of shaking her head. "I'm not sure about that yet . . ." She searched Daniel's face, trying without success to decipher what was on his mind. "Is there something on my calendar I've forgotten?" Generally her assistant didn't question her intentions; he simply juggled her appointments and took care of her personal needs. Admittedly, she'd been stressed of late. Perhaps he was merely concerned.

She was concerned.

"You have a meeting with Commissioner Schmale regarding the Festive Fundraiser at ten. Then a two o'clock with Lois Campbell to discuss the October Art Friends auction."

Both those meetings had been scheduled for a while. She had nothing else to add. Nothing Daniel or anyone else needed to know about anyway. "Very well. Thank you, Daniel."

Her assistant left her alone once more.

The steamy water felt abruptly cold. Annette shivered.

If they had decided to get her out of the way in a more timely manner . . . that could only mean one thing . . .

. . . they would want Carson Tanner out of the way as well.

16

9:40 p.m.
Oxmoor Road, Homewood
Homewood Public Library

Dwight watched the Mercedes roll into the secluded parking lot. He couldn't trust that bitch to do as he'd asked. She didn't care about him or his son. She would do whatever was necessary to protect herself. She would do whatever *they* wanted.

He was alone in this endeavor.

The Mercedes came to a stop on the farthest side of the lot where the lighting was its dimmest, where Dwight lurked, like a common criminal. His lips twisted with fury. He was once the finest thoracic surgeon in this region . . . but the lure of power and more money had taken him to another level. Only to be reduced to this. Fear, deception . . . all because of one night fifteen fucking years ago.

He stepped out of the shadows and waited as patiently as possible. He would have some answers now.

District Attorney Donald Wainwright got out of his Mercedes and walked toward Dwight. His every stride highlighted his impatience. The illustrious DA stopped a few steps away, braced his hands on his hips, and glanced around to ensure they were alone. "What're you doing, Dwight?"

His condescension made Dwight all the angrier. "How can you ask me that?" He diminished the distance between them with one bold step. "Where is Zac?"

Wainwright heaved a big breath. "You called me at this hour of the evening, asked me to come here"—he motioned to the empty lot—"to pose a question you know I can't answer." He moved his head slowly from side to side in disappointment, in disgust. "You're losing your grip, Dwight. I know this is a stressful time, but risks like this can't be tolerated. There's too much at stake."

Fifteen years . . . fifteen damned years they had all lived with this secret . . . with one goal: protect *him.* Fear compounding the fury already blasting through his veins, Dwight lost all sense of self-possession. He jabbed a finger in Wainwright's face. "Enough. Enough!" he snarled. "Protecting our own is one thing, but I will not—do you hear me? *I will not* let my son be sacrificed because that bastard can't keep a leash on his own son!"

Wainwright's demeanor shifted—nothing obvious, just the subtlest change in his relaxed posture. Dwight wasn't so over the edge that he no longer owned the good sense to be afraid. *I'm certain you do not want to go there.* The bitch's words reverberated in his skull.

"Your son," Wainwright said quietly, so quietly that only a man who knew him well would understand the malice behind the words, "sold drugs to children. Used his education and every damned other approach available to him to further the corruption in this city. He made his bed, now he'll have to lie in it."

Wainwright adjusted the lapels of his jacket and squared his shoulders. "Let the police handle this matter, Dwight. That's what our tax dollars are for." He started to turn away but reconsidered. The near darkness did not conceal his intentions when he added, "Make no mistake, if you get out of control, I won't be able to protect you."

Wainwright returned to his beloved Mercedes and drove away.

Dwight didn't care that Wainwright was correct about the line he stood on the verge of crossing, just as Annette Baxter had accurately assessed the same. Right now, a single word pounded violently in his brain: *sold.*

Your son sold drugs to children.

Emotion drained out of Dwight like blood sliding down his limbs and pooling on the pavement.

He'd come here, demanded that Wainwright meet him in a safe, secluded place, to get answers, to have the truth.

Dwight had gotten both.

Zachary Dwight Holderfield, his only son, was dead.

17

Friday, September 10, 1:45 p.m.
227 Leonard Avenue, Nashville, Tennessee

Delta Faye Cornelius blew out a big puff of blue smoke.

Carson held his breath until the cloud had passed. When he could breathe again, he guided the lady back to the subject that had brought him here. "You say you considered yourself Annette Baxter's surrogate mother?"

Ms. Cornelius took another drag, closed her eyes while she held the noxious fumes deep in her lungs, then released. When her gaze met his, she said, "That's right. Must've been a dozen years ago. We were thick as thieves."

The case file on Annette Baxter had indicated that her former friend, and alleged pimp, Delta Faye Cornelius, was dead. According to Ms. Cornelius, she'd had to disappear for a while due to a business deal gone sour. She'd only moved back to Nashville three months ago. The feds hadn't reached out to her since she was listed as deceased. In reality, she didn't look far from it. According to her driver's license, which she had used to ID herself when Carson first arrived, she was fifty-six, but she looked every day of eighty. Frail and withered. Her long gray hair had once been coal black. Gold eyes were sunken and heavy-lidded. In the hour since he'd entered her home she'd smoked half a pack of Camels.

Early that morning Carson had run a DMV check on her for no other reason than that her name was on the list of Baxter's past associates. He'd run the whole list. Having a hit come back on Cornelius had piqued his curiosity. He wasn't sure what he had expected to learn from the woman, but since no one else had interviewed her there was always a chance he might discover some usable factoid. So far that hadn't happened. In truth, this was the only lead he'd been able to dig up. Anything was better than nothing.

"To your knowledge Ms. Baxter has no family?" he prodded. Since Baxter had her present secured like Fort Knox, his only avenue of approach was to find something in her past. A single item that might give him leverage.

Delta Faye swung her head from side to side. "Not a soul." She stopped abruptly, cigarette dangling precariously from her thin lips. Her wrinkled features puckered into a deep scowl. "Wait. There was someone she talked about." She pursed her lips and concentrated with visible effort.

Carson's pulse rate escalated.

"Oh, I know," Delta Faye announced. "A sister! She worried about her sister all the time." Her brow furrowed as if puzzling over her own answer. "I didn't remember that at first because I never actually saw the girl."

Caution stalling his optimism, Carson searched the woman's eyes. She had to be mistaken. Annette Baxter had no siblings. Even if she did, there was no guarantee that the link would provide any advantage. "Are you sure about that?"

Delta Faye nodded. "Polly . . . or something like that."

"Did her sister live in Knoxville?" Despite his doubts as to the significance, anticipation had him sitting on the edge of his seat.

Another dramatic shake of her head. "No. I think she was in some institution or something back then. Annette was real sad about it. She missed her sister a lot." Delta Faye lit up another cigarette. "I don't know how I forgot about that. Poor girl. Annette worked so hard to save money. Never could get enough ahead to make a difference I don't reckon."

"What difference did she feel compelled to make?"

Those feeble shoulders moved up and down. "Medical care or some such. She wanted her sister to have some kind of treatment."

"Do you know the nature of the treatment?" That would, at least, give him a starting place.

Delta Faye wagged her head. "Don't have a clue."

Before Carson could thank her for taking the time to talk to him, Delta Faye repeated an earlier question she had posed. "How'd you say she was doing now? I've often wondered about that girl. That's about the only reason I let you in the door."

Since he had no intention of reciprocating in the exchange of information and he'd clearly gotten all he was going to get, he opted not to continue the interview. It was always wise to stop while one was ahead.

Lucky for him, his cell phone vibrated, saving him the trouble of making excuses. He checked the display. Luttrell? "I apologize, Ms. Cornelius, but I have an urgent call." He looked from the phone to the lady. "I'll be back in touch if I have any more questions."

She didn't argue or bother getting up to see him out. "You tell that girl to come see me sometime. We can talk about old times."

Carson promised to relay the message, though he doubted Annette Baxter had any desire to revisit that part of her past. Following up on this lead might very well have proven worth the trouble. The possibility of a sister intrigued him. But he had to substantiate that claim before it would be of any use. If he corroborated the assertion, the real question was: Why had Baxter kept her sister a secret? Could be something significant, could be nothing at all.

Once back in his car he returned Luttrell's call. "What's up?"

Luttrell's initial hesitation set Carson on edge. His friend exhaled a resigned breath. "Wainwright didn't want me to distract you, but you'll hear about it soon enough."

Easing away from the curb, Carson mentally braced. "Sounds like bad news."

"Yeah. It's bad. They found Zac Holderfield's body a couple of hours ago." Luttrell put his hand over the phone and made a comment inaudible to Carson. "Sorry about that, I'm at the scene. Anyway, Bill Lynch is in charge of the investigation. At this point, looks like a botched drug deal. One shot to the upper torso. The body was dumped in a ravine off Highway Thirty-One."

Damn. Disbelief was quickly overridden by the realization that Zac's family would be devastated. "That's a damned shame." Carson didn't bother asking about witnesses or evidence. Too early, particularly since the body had apparently been moved from the primary crime scene and dumped at a secondary site. Unless someone came forward, it would take days or weeks, possibly longer, to piece together a reasonably accurate chain of events, much less pinpoint a suspect.

"Hang on." A male voice in the background informed Luttrell that the ME had arrived. Luttrell thanked the messenger, then said to Carson, "I gotta go, man."

"Yeah, all right." Carson stopped at a traffic light, closed his eyes, and shook his head at the senselessness of the tragedy. "Keep me posted on the progress, would you?"

"Will do," Luttrell agreed. "Since you're tied up, Wainwright wants me to work with Lynch on this one."

Made sense. Lieutenant William Lynch was one of Birmingham's most respected and decorated homicide investigators. Carson exorcised the flashbacks from fifteen years ago. Lynch had worked hard to find the person or persons responsible for the murders of Carson's family. He had remained supportive time and again over the years whenever Carson needed him.

"Lynch is a good man," Carson told his friend. "He's a team player." And he respected the DA's Office, which wasn't always the case.

The investigation of high-profile crimes committed within the Jefferson County jurisdiction automatically included the DA's

Office. That Zac's father was the administrator of Birmingham's premier hospital and was heavily involved in civic matters put his son's murder on that list. Generally, Carson was the DDA assigned to those investigations, but Wainwright wanted him totally focused on bringing about Baxter's cooperation.

Luttrell could be an ass at times but he was a good attorney. He would get the job done.

Carson thanked his friend and tossed the phone onto the passenger seat. Zac. Murdered. Damn. Not his case. Carson had to set personal feelings aside, couldn't allow the distraction. In an attempt to do that, he replayed the interview with Delta Faye Cornelius. Annette Baxter could possibly have a sister.

Was the fact that she'd kept that only living relative a secret significant?

Maybe.

Slim though it might be, it was something. Anything was more than he'd had when he'd awakened that morning.

All he needed was one weakness, one vulnerability he could use for leverage.

The sister could be that vulnerability.

Carson's cell vibrated again. This time it was Anita, the receptionist at the office, with an urgent message. Carson's presence was requested for dinner that evening at the home of Senator Randolph Drake.

Interesting. A man didn't turn down an invitation from Senator Drake. Not even if he were inclined to, and Carson wasn't. The senator's unconditional support was essential to the future of Carson's career.

He thought of how Elizabeth had dropped by his house unannounced the other night. Was this invitation her idea? He couldn't deny a certain curiosity along those lines. That she had invited him to escort her to a major social function intrigued him. Was she contemplating the idea of rekindling what they once had, or was this purely a political move?

Motivation triggered every action. Time would tell what motivated this one.

For now, Carson had a couple of hours to follow up on the "sister" lead. There were a number of resources at his disposal for tracking down an unidentified person of interest, but why not start at the top. He entered the number for Agent Kim Schaffer.

Going that route could serve a dual purpose: confirming the existence of the sister in the speediest of manners *and* providing Schaffer with something the Bureau didn't have—a possible exploitable link to Baxter. Then Schaffer would owe him one.

She had something Carson wanted. If Wainwright had tipped the feds regarding Annette Baxter, Carson needed to understand the nature of the tip and why his boss hadn't chosen to share the information with him. Though he could certainly ask Wainwright, something felt wrong with the whole scenario. Carson wanted Schaffer's version of how this had come about prior to getting the information straight from the horse's mouth, so to speak.

It hardly made sense that Wainwright was keeping a secret that could impede Carson's investigation. Carson had every reason to trust his mentor. On the other hand, he had no reason not to trust Agent Schaffer. Still, prudence was called for in this highly sensitive matter.

The reality that neither Baxter nor Fleming could have kept their business activities so untouchable without inside information wasn't lost on Carson. Whatever, the insider could not be Donald Wainwright. That was the one thing Carson knew with complete certainty. Everything else was up for grabs.

The key was the same as always, *motivation.* Who stood to gain if this investigation, like the ones into Fleming's activities before it, failed?

Glass shattered.

Carson swerved.

He glanced over his shoulder. A rear door window was fractured.

"What the hell?" His right foot went instinctively to the brake.

Another explosion and the windshield ruptured, leaving a web of lines extending out from the hole.

He rammed his foot against the accelerator. Cut the steering wheel hard to the right. The BMW bucked onto the sidewalk. He slammed on the brake and dove onto the floor of the vehicle.

Three more shots in rapid succession punctured the car's body. He jerked with each penetrating sound.

Carson had entered 9-1-1 into his cell phone as the squeal of tires warned a vehicle had sped past.

When the operator responded he dared to peer above the dash. The street was deserted.

"Leonard Avenue," he blurted as he risked sitting upright. "Shots fired."

Surveying the street, the yards, the houses, his shoulders hunched up around his ears, he answered the rest of the operator's questions. After being assured help was on the way, he ended the call and labored to catch his breath.

This was no random drive-by shooting. He stared at the hole in his windshield, on the left side of the rearview mirror. *He* had been the target.

His heart thumped hard against his sternum.

Carson thought of the black sedan from the other morning, then of the gas that had filled his house.

Someone was trying to stop him.

No. He looked at the rear windshield. Cracked lines spread out around a distinct hole. At least five shots were fired directly at his vehicle.

At him.

Someone was trying to kill him.

8:50 p.m.
3202 Fernway Road, Mountain Brook
Drake Estate

"I'm convinced you'll be way out in front of your opponents."

Carson had no reservations as to his ability to beat the competition, but it was nice to hear it from the senator. "I appreciate your confidence, sir."

"Cigar?" Drake opened the ornate wooden box on the desk in his private study.

"No, thank you." Carson had already declined the after-dinner drink he'd been offered. He didn't want to offend the senator, but Carson had met his quota this decade for giving in to temptation. He wasn't deviating from the straight and narrow again anytime soon.

His gut was still in knots from the episode in Nashville. He didn't need a crystal ball to know the police would find nothing. None of the residents had seen or heard anything. Exactly what one would expect in that kind of low-rent neighborhood. His BMW had been towed for additional forensic testing. One of the investigators had given him a ride to a rental agency.

The rental car part was annoying. But he was alive. Had scarcely a scratch. Just one nick on his right cheek from the flying glass. He'd been lucky.

Wainwright wasn't happy about the incident, but he wasn't surprised, either. He wanted to put a security detail on Carson immediately, but Carson had declined for now. He'd just be a hell of a lot more cautious.

"That's right." Drake puffed the imported cigar until the tip glowed, then relished the taste before continuing. "You don't smoke or drink. The way I hear it, you're not a skirt chaser, either." He smiled knowingly. "That's damned admirable, son. The voters are going to love you."

No, Carson wasn't a skirt chaser . . . he'd just made one big-ass mistake with the prime suspect in his latest case. He could kick himself, over and over.

"Work is my top priority, sir." Carson was successful at keeping the guilt out of his tone, but that didn't stop him from feeling a shitload of it. Images of him screwing Annette Baxter all over that ritzy hotel room, then her sprawled across his desk filled his brain.

"Ethical. Focused. Undefeated in the courtroom." The senator settled into one of the leather wingbacks flanking his desk and indicated that Carson should take the other. "Every aspect of who you are was considered at length before the invitation was issued."

Carson understood that, before approaching him, the most powerful men in this city had discussed and debated the idea. His past as well as his present were no doubt scrutinized. Fortunately, until recently, he'd had nothing to hide.

Ask yourself if you'll ever really know what happened. He deported that memory along with the ones involving his recent lapse into stupidity. "I'm glad I passed muster." He relaxed his posture, smiled confidently. Senator Drake had known Carson his entire life. He wasn't about to let the man see the first glimmer of insecurity.

"Personally." Drake studied the cigar perched in his fingers. "I'm glad to see you and Elizabeth working together on this investigation. It's been a long time coming. I'm very proud of both of you."

Carson's instincts stirred. Was this the reason he'd been invited to his first family dinner with the Drakes in more than a decade? As kids, Carson and his little sister had spent nearly as much time at the Drakes' as they had at home. And when they weren't at the Drake home, Elizabeth and her brother Dane were at Carson's house. Before everything had changed.

Elizabeth had been shipped off to boarding school, presumably to keep her away from Carson. Dane, her brother and Carson's best friend, had become a loner, getting into music and then drugs. The senator and his wife had spent the next eight or so years acknowledging Carson's existence only when necessary. Tonight, however, was almost like old times. Yet on some level Carson continued to look for the agenda. Went with the territory in his line of work. *Always look for the motivation behind every action.*

"Elizabeth's doing an amazing job," Carson agreed, pushing the doubts and questions aside for now.

Drake took another long drag, blew out the heavy smoke. "Unlike the situation with my son."

Dane had been a no-show tonight. His mother, Patricia, had used the excuse that her son had an unexpected gig downtown. She'd gone on and on about how much his music meant to him. Elizabeth had chimed in with her own glowing remarks.

"Sometimes following a dream takes an unexpected path," Carson suggested, since there was little else to offer.

The senator shook his head, his expression filled with regret. "Every time I think of Dwight's son I feel ill. I fully expect to receive that same kind of call about Dane."

Unfortunate but true. Carson kept that to himself.

Drake frowned thoughtfully. "Are you sure you don't want that security detail Wainwright offered?" He searched Carson's face as if looking for the doubt. "This case could get dicey, son. We don't want you taking any unnecessary risks."

"I've taken the offer under advisement," Carson allowed. Having someone shadow him night and day wasn't something he looked forward to, but if it came to that he would deal with it.

"Excuse me, gentlemen."

Carson turned his attention toward the door.

Elizabeth was there. "Mother says dessert and coffee are served." She smiled at Carson, the same way she had a thousand times in the past.

The moment made him smile. Felt like old times.

Drake tamped out his cigar. "Let's not keep the ladies waiting." He pushed to his feet; Carson did the same. "I happen to know tonight's dessert is your favorite." The senator winked at Carson.

Chocolate cake. He'd always loved Mrs. Drake's homemade chocolate cake. Carson patted his abdomen. "If I add dessert to that amazing meal, I'll be putting in some extra miles the next few nights."

Drake laughed as he joined his daughter at the door. "I've got a feeling this young man doesn't get home-cooked meals often." He wrapped Elizabeth's arm around his and headed for the dining room. "We'll have to take steps to amend that situation."

Elizabeth peeked back at Carson. "Indeed we will."

Looking elegant in her conservative pink dress, she could be sixteen again, sweet and innocent. His chest tightened. He'd been madly in love with her.

A lifetime ago.

He'd sequestered the notion so many years ago, reflecting on it now felt surreal.

Just like this entire evening.

During dessert the Drakes laughed and talked about old times as if that one day in Carson's history hadn't happened. As if they hadn't pretended he didn't exist for years after the murders. The abrupt turnabout confused him, yes, but he had to confess a certain satisfaction in having come full circle. Regardless of that good feeling, the obsessive region of his brain that constantly analyzed and assessed began to piece together a theory.

Most powerful politicians in Alabama were happily married with a family. Was this part of the package being considered for his future? Political aspirations often required personal sacrifice, that much was true. If the powers-that-be had put their heads together and decided that Carson's success in the political arena required the acquisition of a wife, the question was, who would be sacrificing the most? Him? Or Elizabeth?

Elizabeth hadn't married. No rumor of any engagements or significant boyfriends had filtered to him. He wasn't fool enough to believe she had waited for him all this time.

Maybe he was making too much of this pleasant evening.

"Would you like another slice, Carson?"

His attention turned to Mrs. Drake. She smiled, her hand poised to pare off another portion of the cake she had made expressly for his enjoyment. Patricia Drake had been his mother's best friend. She had treated Carson and his sister like part of the family.

"No, thank you. Though it's seriously tempting."

Patricia smiled, absolutely content to be known for her baking skills and raising the bar for the perfect wife and mother. Guilt pinged Carson for thinking that tonight was anything more than plain old Southern hospitality.

Work really was all he knew anymore. His social skills were rusty. All the more reason to end the night before his imagination got the better of him. He pushed back his chair and stood. "Thank you for having me, but I should be going. I have hours of work ahead of me."

Elizabeth looked crestfallen. "It's still early."

The senator put a hand on his daughter's. "Remember," he glanced at Carson, "he's our next district attorney. He has to stay on top of his game."

Her expression brightened, but a hint of sadness lingered. "Of course." Elizabeth placed her napkin on the table and stood. "Let me walk you out."

Carson hesitated, maybe rustier on etiquette than he'd first thought. "I should help clean up." He started to clear his place setting.

"No. No," Patricia scolded gently. "We'll take care of that."

Carson looked to the senator.

"We've got this under control," he seconded as he rose and reached for Carson's hand. "Keep your social calendar clear, son. We'll do this again soon."

Carson looked from one to the other. "Thank you for the generous invitation." His smile was automatic and completely genuine, despite the persistent questions niggling him.

Elizabeth hooked her arm in his as they made their way to the entry hall. "I've missed times like this."

At the door he turned to her. "Me, too."

A troubled frown marred her smooth brow. "I worry that Father pushes you too hard."

Carson was surprised by her comment. "He has high expectations. But I see that as a good thing."

Elizabeth searched his eyes, hers filled with the same reservations she'd voiced. "Is this really what you want, Carson? To step into Wainwright's shoes?"

Suddenly it was as if they had gone back fifteen years, and Elizabeth was troubled over the insistence of Carson's father that he go away to an Ivy League preparatory school. Or his mother's concern that he and Elizabeth were spending far too much alone time together.

I hate you! Do you hear me, Mother? I hate you! Carson pushed the anguished memory away. "This is what I want," he assured Elizabeth. "The senator extended the invitation, but the decision to accept was entirely mine." Oddly, he liked that she worried about him. No one had done that in a really long time.

"I know how demanding he can be." She sighed. "I just don't want him controlling everything . . ." She looked away a moment. "The way he used to." When her eyes met Carson's once more, there was something else there beyond the worry . . . something hard . . . bitter. "He has a habit of that, you know. Things are different now. We're all grown up. This is your life and my life." Anger flared briefly in her green eyes. "He needs to come to terms with that and back off."

"Everything's fine. Don't worry." Carson gifted her with the most reassuring smile he could manage in view of just how far out of character she'd abruptly stepped. Not once in all the years he'd known her had he witnessed anything other than sheer devotion to her father. Elizabeth was and always had been the epitome of the loving and obedient daughter. "Your father has my best interests at heart. I'm honored that he has such confidence in me."

Another troubled sigh whispered past her lips. "Okay. As long as you're happy." She tiptoed and hugged him. His heart reacted. "That's what matters."

"Then you have nothing to worry about." He squeezed her hand. "Good night."

"Don't forget about the ball on Sunday evening." Her fingers slipped slowly from his as she drew away.

"I couldn't possibly. Good night." Carson looked back one last time as he closed the door behind him. The urge to do a little victory dance at finally having some aspect of his personal life back to the way it once was made him giddy.

But that other, more cynical side of him wanted to dissect the night. Take it apart from every angle and analyze the motives again and again. Especially those final moments with Elizabeth.

The past couldn't be rewritten. There was no option for a do-over. He wished he could have simply enjoyed the familiarity and comfort tonight had offered. But he couldn't. Not without wondering why it hadn't happened before. Why now, all these years later? And what the hell did it all mean? Why would Elizabeth be concerned that her father was pushing Carson into something he didn't want? Did she harbor resentment over the fact that her parents had sent her away when Carson needed her most?

Maybe.

Why not relax and see where this went? He'd waited so long to have that part of his life back.

The feel of Annette Baxter's body hungrily cradling his overwhelmed the fleeting bliss. Every muscle tensed in reaction to the fierce sensation.

And that was precisely why he couldn't let his guard down, couldn't presume anything.

He had to be absolutely certain of everything and everyone.

Including himself.

18

11:40 p.m.

Carson ran long and hard.

He'd tried to work but concentrating had proven impossible. So he'd hit the pavement.

Five miles, six. Then he'd walked another. Every step had been distracted by his need to ensure he wasn't being followed or watched. Whenever a car had idled past on the street, he'd tensed. But he hadn't allowed the fear loitering in the back of his mind to keep him from his usual routine.

No damned way.

Sweat rolled down his face. His T-shirt was plastered to his torso.

Schaffer would get back to him tomorrow with the results of her search into the possibility of Baxter having a sister. The agent thought it was a waste of time, but she had agreed to put aside her doubt and pursue the possibility. Carson had reached out to his contact in adoptive services who would in turn touch base with her contact in Tennessee.

If no evidence or weakness was found, he would have no option but to push for a deal that might appeal to Baxter. Immunity, unfortunately, was generally only a temptation to the criminal with something to lose. At this point it appeared Baxter had absolutely nothing to lose other than the nuisance of being watched 24/7. Unfortunately, she proved so adept at evading surveillance that even that wasn't as frustrating and intimidating as it should be.

There had to be a way to get to her. Annette Baxter couldn't be that good.

No one was.

Not even him.

He was damned lucky the FBI didn't have footage of him going to her hotel room that night . . .. or of her showing up at his office. She'd set him up good. Undoubtedly she'd had a carefully laid-out master plan from the beginning.

Carson wasn't surprised. No one who had survived the life she had would leave anything to chance.

That alone gave him reason to believe there was something that she feared him discovering. Otherwise, why would she care who was on the case? Or bother with acquiring leverage of her own? More importantly, why would she demand his attention to hear her so-called truth? Master plan or no, there was something she was afraid of. Otherwise she would simply use all that information she so blatantly professed to have to stop this investigation dead in its tracks.

He would find what he needed. Carson wouldn't give up until he did. There had to be a way to get to Annette Baxter. To find the fault in her titanium armor.

He stopped in his driveway long enough to stretch out his muscles. Hell yeah. He would nail her so thoroughly she wouldn't dare attempt to blackmail him or to damage the DA's Office.

She'd be spilling her guts before Wainwright had a chance to call his next briefing.

Then Otis Fleming would at last have his long-awaited fall.

Carson scrubbed the sweat from his face with the back of his hand.

The concept that any exploitable information on the DA's Office might have something to do with what Wainwright hadn't shared with him lurked in the back of his mind. He expelled that theory, refused to give it credence in any way.

He trusted Donald Wainwright without reservation. Whatever he'd told Schaffer had to be something Carson was already aware of. There was tension between Schaffer and Wainwright. Maybe Schaffer was the one with a vendetta.

"Feeling the pressure tonight?"

Carson swiveled toward the voice.

Her.

Annette Baxter.

He squinted to see her through the darkness.

She lurked in the shadows at the corner of his house.

A blast of outrage had him striding in her direction. He'd caught her watching him before when he'd left the Bureau, and now this. He had news for Ms. Annette Baxter: She should just save herself the trouble. Nothing she said or did was going to prevent him from doing his job.

"What the hell are you doing here?" he demanded, his pulse rate rushing into the pre-cooldown zone. He glanced toward the street, scanned for her Lexus. Didn't see it.

"Don't worry," she said, "I parked my car a street over. After, of course, I lost my tail."

"I asked what the hell you're doing here." This was stalking at the very least, possibly coupled with the intent to obstruct justice. Until he was prepared to offer her a deal, they had no reason to talk.

"I was lonely. I was hoping you'd changed your mind about hearing me out."

"And why would I do that?" He was always open to a new approach. Why not see where she intended to go with this?

She lifted a shoulder in a negligent shrug, causing one flimsy dress strap to slide down her arm. The silky gold slip of a dress clung to her curves, accentuated every feminine asset. Carson had figured out that she dressed that way on purpose. To distract him. Unfortunately she succeeded every damned time. His overworked muscles reacted as if she weren't the enemy. As if all logic had fled along with his ability to stay on task. That she repeatedly evoked the same reaction confirmed his concern that he was losing his edge.

"Maybe," she suggested, taking a step from the shadows, "because deep down you know I'm right about your beloved boss."

This stopped, here and now. "No more games, Ms. Baxter. I thought I made that clear. I'm not interested in hearing any of your conspiracy theories. This investigation is about you and Fleming. No one else."

She inclined her head, studying him as if strategizing a new avenue of attack. "No games, Mr. Tanner. I'm trying to steer you in the right direction with valuable information. You know, I scratch your back, you scratch mine."

That was exactly what he had surmised. Carson held up his hands. "We have nothing to discuss unless you're prepared to roll over on your friend Otis Fleming. I can offer certain advantages if that's why you're here." The decision to go this route might prove somewhat premature, but no harm in allowing her to understand it was an option. Any forward movement would be better than staggering backward.

"You haven't heard what I have to say yet," she countered. "Do you really want to *call* before the bet is on the table?"

A muscle ticked in his jaw. The lady had guts, he'd give her that. He'd offered her a deal and she still wanted to toy with him. "You could walk away," he clarified. "Start over someplace with a clean slate."

She tossed that blond mane and laughed, the sound at once infuriating and alluring. "Do you really think I've survived this long being stupid? There is no walking away or starting over in my line of work."

His gaze tracked the second dress strap as it slipped slowly down her other shoulder. He gritted his teeth, fought the traitorous response. "We can protect you." Why did he bother? She wasn't going down without a battle. He'd recognized her tenacity that first night they met before he'd even known her identity. He would need serious leverage.

And control of his own reactions.

She strolled right up to him, crowding him with her soft, sweet scent, making him want to reach out and touch those bared shoulders. She stared directly into his eyes. "Sorry to disappoint you, but I was acquainted with two people the feds promised to protect—*was* being the operative word."

Fury blazed deep in his gut. "All the more reason you should do the right thing, Ms. Baxter." He went nose-to-nose with her. "I'm certain you're at least vaguely *acquainted* with that concept."

She pursed those lush lips for a second. "You mean the way all your powerful friends do the right thing?"

The perfect comeback eluded him . . . his attention had stalled on those lips. Full, wet, so close.

"You're so certain your friends are better than mine," she challenged. "Let me tell you a little story, *Mr. Tanner.*"

He almost stopped her . . . but curiosity kept him quiet and motionless. Let her talk. Find out what this so-called damaging knowledge really was.

"Once upon a time," she purred, "there were three boys in college. Donald Wainwright, Randolph Drake, and Craig Tanner. Frat brothers, roommates, buddies." She inclined her head. "You know what I mean. Kind of like you and your good friend Luttrell."

He held his ire in check, not an easy exercise. "Get to the point, assuming there is one." His father's friendship with Wainwright and Drake was no secret. The three went way back. All the way to elementary school.

"There was one girl," Baxter went on. "Lana Kimble. Lana and Randolph were in love. This little detail was the cause of much discord among the three friends since Randolph was already promised to Patricia. Then one night sweet little Lana disappeared. But not to worry—she was found the very next day." Baxter lifted her chin and stared directly at him, as if she suspected before she gave the punch line that he wouldn't get the unfortunate joke. "About three hundred feet below the ledge where she'd waited for her lover the night before. Guess who saw her last?"

Carson shook his head. What could she possibly hope to gain by telling him this fantastic story? "People die young sometimes. They generally have friends. Just because my father and his buddies lost a friend in college doesn't mean they're somehow responsible for the loss." The girl's death would have been investigated. Carson had faith in the justice system. There were times when it failed, but for the most part it worked.

"You didn't answer the question, Tanner," she pressed. "Who do you suppose was the last person to see her alive?"

He threw his hands up in question. "Why don't you tell me? Since you have all the answers."

"The revered Senator Randolph Drake."

The satisfaction in her expression was really starting to piss him off. "But she was alive, according to him, when he left her. His best friends, you know who, backed him up. Lana was perched on that ledge calling his name as young Randolph walked away. Donald and Craig witnessed this from the car—not very far away, of course, and with the aid of the full moon to provide a clear view of the whole event."

What did she expect him to say to that? "Sad story, Ms. Baxter, but somehow I missed your point." She was grasping at straws. He'd been right. She had nothing on Wainwright or anyone else.

Baxter edged a little closer, close enough for him to feel her breath on his face. "Check it out, Tanner. You'll see my point. Lana's death was ruled a suicide, but there were conflicting details. Your powerful friends have some very deep, very dark secrets. This one's only the beginning."

Like Schaffer said, Baxter was one cunning piece of work. "You're accusing three of the most respected men in Birmingham, including my father, of murder." He had to be out of his mind to continue this conversation. "I won't stand here and disrespect those men by listening to your slanderous stories. Put up or shut up, Baxter. You know what I want from you. Think about it and get back to me."

He'd heard more than enough to know she had nothing. Before he could walk away, she countered, "That's right. Take the easy way out.

You're just like the rest of them. You don't really care about the truth. It's all about your reputation. Your prized record in the courtroom." She folded her arms beneath her breasts, purposely emphasizing the cleavage revealed by the skimpy dress. "Go ahead, Mr. Tanner, keep digging until you find whatever evidence they've planted to do me in. Then ask yourself if you'll ever really know what happened."

Ask yourself if you'll ever really know what happened.

How could she use the exact words Stokes had?

Unless she'd been in contact with him.

That was the moment when Carson went over that edge he'd been teetering on for about seventy-two hours now. "While we're on the subject of truth, tell me," he demanded softly, murderously, "how does it feel to crawl into bed with that old man? Does his sagging skin turn you on? How much Viagra does it take for Fleming to get it up?" Carson didn't stop there. Couldn't. "Do you like making your living on your back? Or maybe you do your best work on your knees. What did you do for Stokes to get information out of him?"

The flash of fury in her eyes sent adrenaline charging through him. He'd stooped to her level, but by God he'd gotten to her. Somehow he had instinctively known there was a real human being buried beneath that ice bitch persona.

"You think you know me." The fury cleared from her eyes with one downward sweep of those thick lashes. "You don't know me at all."

Bullshit. He laughed. "I know you fucked me to gain some kind of twisted leverage in this investigation. I also know you'll use that and any other innuendo you can dredge up, like that trumped-up story you just related, to blackmail me, or to try to. It won't work. Unlike you, I do have principles."

"Actually, Tanner"—she looked him up and down then smirked—"all I did was lure you into a compromising position. You stuck your dick in me because you wanted to. Or maybe it was all those principles that compelled you to do it over and over again."

He grabbed her by the chin, unable to restrain the punishing hold. Never in his life had any woman made him feel so out of control. So damned desperate to dominate her. "Take the deal or take the fall. I'm good with either choice." As angry as he was at that moment just being this close, just touching her, even like this, reminded him of hot, graphic sex. Made him want to repeat that insane mistake over and over again.

"You know what gets to you the most?" she whispered, then wet her lips.

That he followed the move with such avid interest enraged him all the more.

"You want me even now," she taunted. "That's why you're so pissed off."

"I don't want you," he snarled. "I despise everything about you."

She grabbed his cock and squeezed. "Yeah, I can tell." That was when he recognized the one glaring difference between them. His whole body pulsed with lust. And she . . . she remained a block of ice . . . of sheer indifference.

"I'll give you that." No point denying it. He wrenched her fingers free of his dick. The feel of her skin burned his hand. He let go of her wrist. "But at least I'm capable of feeling something."

"Now you get the picture." She tugged her chin loose from his cruel grasp and smiled. "Did you really think you could touch me like that? No man, certainly not you, has ever had the power to make me feel anything at all."

It required every ounce of determination he could rally, but he backed off. He was done. "When you're prepared to discuss a deal on my terms," he said, his breath ragged, his tone raw, "you give me a call."

She held her ground as if she was confident she owned this little tête-à-tête. "I'll tell you what, Mr. District-Attorney-to-be, just because we have so much in common I'm going to give you a peek into the future. If my prediction proves accurate, you have to listen to what I have to say." She dared him with her eyes. "Really listen."

Not about to entertain any more of her groundless threats, he went on record. "I think you're bluffing. So don't waste your breath."

A soft laugh quirked her lips, drawing his reluctant attention there yet again. "Why don't you save your deductions for after you've heard me out? Isn't that the standard procedure?"

He crossed his arms over his chest to ensure he didn't do anything else stupid, like haul her ass to the street. "I've made my position abundantly clear."

Undeterred, she spelled it out. "Today Zac Holderfield's body was discovered. His father will be next."

Whoa. Carson searched her eyes, her face. Those instincts he relied on so heavily sounded an alarm, igniting the coals beneath his hibernating reason. "Don't think for a second I won't inform the investigator in charge of the Holderfield case of your remarks." Was she for real? Jesus Christ. "Give due consideration to my offer, Ms. Baxter, before it's too late. Your friend Fleming isn't likely to take our collusion so well. I wouldn't want to be you if he discovers you've been unfaithful."

"Really, Tanner," she argued, not shaken in the least. "Why would I tell you something like this if not to help you? I have nothing to gain by taking this risk."

The lady had missed her calling. She should have been an actress. "I don't operate the way you and your friends do. In my world, we have laws and ethics. Unless you're willing to work within those boundaries"—he pointed to the street—"you can go. *Now.*"

"We operate in the same world, Tanner. On my side of the legal line, we're just a little more up front with our tactics."

The desire to shake the hell out of her was nearly overwhelming. He curled his fingers into his palms, kept his arms tight against his torso to prevent doing exactly that. "You have one chance to save your ass, Ms. Baxter. I'd suggest you take it." Even as he said the words his mind conjured the image of her high, tight ass. His fingers squeezing those firm mounds. Idiot.

"You're the Avenger," she urged fearlessly. "The guy who stands up for the innocent and the defenseless. Don't you want to have truth on your side? To do the justice thing? I'm giving you advance knowledge. The rest is up to you."

He felt sick with disgust at the way his body betrayed him even now. His cock was hard as a rock at just being close to her. Her fearlessness fueled that attraction. Not being able to control this thing between them—knowing she was using him, knowing what she was—made him all the angrier. She represented some kind of challenge he couldn't seem to resist.

"What I want to do," he growled, "is to take you down. What you need to understand is that I *will* make it happen."

Having the last word should have given him one hell of a rush. But it didn't. He'd gotten to her, but she'd gotten to him first . . . and last.

He headed for the house. Enough had been said.

"You really have no idea what you're dealing with, do you?"

He shouldn't have paused. Shouldn't have looked back.

When he did their gazes locked, imprisoned by an intensity he couldn't quite label.

"One last piece of advice, Tanner," she said, her posture every bit as determined as her tone. "Don't trust anyone and watch your back."

Annette Baxter maintained eye contact another dramatic moment before walking away. He stared after her, unable to move or react to her statement, until she was swallowed up by the darkness.

Oh, he intended to watch his back all right. Having his BMW shot up was wake-up call enough. But she needn't have warned him about trust. Trust was something he didn't dole out so cavalierly. Right now, however, the person he trusted the least was himself.

19

Saturday, September 11, 9:00 a.m.
8th Avenue South, Birmingham
Carol's Country Kitchen

"It's difficult to believe the FBI has nothing."

Wainwright wasn't happy. Carson had been so caught up in this travesty of an investigation, he'd failed to keep his boss up to speed. Wainwright had tracked him down that morning and asked for a breakfast meeting.

The DA was restless. He wanted results.

And just maybe Carson had been avoiding him. Schaffer's suggestion regarding the tip she had received from Wainwright was like expert witnesses—as soon as the state refuted one, the defense dragged in another. It just wouldn't go away. Then there was the fiasco with Baxter and her claims about Lana Kimble and her prophecy about Dr. Dwight Holderfield.

The fact of the matter was, he hadn't done one damned thing by the book so far. "Baxter is good," he confessed. "She takes extreme precautions in everything she does. This is going to take a little more time than I anticipated."

But her luck couldn't hold out forever. Carson would hear from Schaffer on the sister lead today. He'd come up empty-handed thus far with his own search. He'd considered tossing the idea at Baxter last night, but he hadn't wanted to tip his hand until he corroborated Ms. Cornelius's claim.

He'd looked into Baxter's story about Lana Kimble for no other reason than to dash the truth back in her face. Kimble's death had been ruled a suicide. There were unresolved questions as Baxter had suggested, but that was the case with all unaccompanied deaths. Drake, Wainwright, and Carson's father had known the woman. But that didn't mean that one or all of them were involved in her demise. The idea was ludicrous. Baxter was doing exactly what he was: searching for something to use to her advantage. And like him, she was coming up empty-handed.

The news wasn't what Wainwright wanted to hear. He toyed with his napkin. "We have to get this done." He stared straight at Carson. "Everything is riding on this one."

"I understand, sir."

He did.

More so every hour that passed.

"Is there anything I should know?"

The DA's question startled Carson. He barely managed to keep the surprise off his face. Baxter's warning about Dwight Holderfield chose that moment to haunt him. He wouldn't bring that up just yet. She hadn't given him anything specific. Could have been an empty threat. Nor would he bring up Schaffer's assertion. Not the time. "I'm not sure what you mean."

"You're up to this, right?" Wainwright squared his shoulders, but even that move didn't disguise his uneasiness. "You generally get straight to the heart of a case. But this one"—he shook his head, his face sober—"seems to have you unnerved. You're a little off your game. As unsettling as yesterday's shooting was, I noticed in our first briefing that you seemed distracted."

Now Carson understood: This impromptu meeting was about him, not the investigation. He looked his boss, his mentor, squarely in the eye. "You have nothing to worry about, sir. I'm on top of it."

"Good. That's what I wanted to hear. Don't hesitate to make use of that security detail. I can't have our future DA being used for target practice."

Maybe it was frustration, maybe it was plain old insecurity, but Carson went momentarily stupid. Otherwise he would not have opened his mouth and stuck his foot squarely inside. "One question. Is there anything the Bureau knows that came from our office that somehow I'm not privy to in this investigation?"

Hell, why hadn't he just asked Wainwright straight out if he'd told Schaffer something he hadn't told Carson? Damn, he *was* off his game.

Wainwright's gaze narrowed. "What kind of question is that? You and I are the only ones on this case. No one else. You know everything I know." He scrutinized Carson closely. "Where the hell did that come from?"

Explain that one, Carson, you idiot. The waitress arrived to take their order, allowing him to drag in what might be his final breath.

Wainwright waved the waitress way. They were waiting for Elizabeth. Wainwright had informed Carson when he'd arrived that Elizabeth would be attending once again as the mayor's representative. She was late. Maybe if she'd been here, Carson wouldn't have stepped so squarely on his dick.

"It's Schaffer, isn't it?" Wainwright charged.

Carson had opened that line of questioning. He couldn't strike it from the record now. Schaffer had warned him to keep this information between them. So much for trust. "It's not actually anything in particular. Just a hunch. A feeling I got from her." *Good job, asshole. Lie to your boss. The man who holds your whole future in his hands.*

Wainwright leaned forward, his face clean of readable emotion. "Don't let her distract you, Carson. Schaffer would like nothing better than to be the one who takes down Fleming. The feds seize the limelight whenever possible. This is our investigation. *Your* investigation. Stay on track and do what you do best." He reclined in his seat and reached for his coffee. "Trust me on this. Schaffer isn't on our side."

Don't trust anyone and watch your back.

Carson exiled Baxter's warning. "Understood, sir."

Behind schedule or not, Elizabeth's timing proved impeccable. As she reached their table, Carson and Wainwright stood. The tension receded as swiftly as a courtroom clearing after the judge recessed for lunch.

"Sorry I'm late. I had an eight o'clock." She smiled, then accepted a hug from Wainwright. "Since the mayor decided to host business until noon on Saturdays, you'd think there'd be more time. Somehow I seem to have less." Her smile widened as she turned to Carson. "Carson."

He gave her a quick hug. As usual, his heart reacted. More of that heavy guilt settled on his shoulders. How could he react to Annette Baxter so fiercely when all he'd ever wanted was Elizabeth? And finally, finally there was hope.

As soon as they took their seats once more the waitress returned, giving Carson yet another momentary reprieve.

"Do we have an update?" Elizabeth looked from Wainwright to Carson when the orders had been given. "The mayor is anxious to hear news that the investigation is progressing."

"Unfortunately, there's nothing new." Carson hated being the reason for the disappointment on Elizabeth's face. "We are," he affirmed, "working diligently to change that. I have a couple of leads that look promising." That was a bit of a stretch, but every good attorney knew how to embellish his case.

She nodded. "Excellent. I'll pass that along."

Carson's cell phone vibrated. "Excuse me." He retrieved it from his pocket and checked the screen. "I'm sorry," he said to Elizabeth before glancing at Wainwright, "I need to take this." Lieutenant Bill Lynch. Lynch had once been involved with the Fleming case, but that had been a long time ago. This call was more likely related to Zac Holderfield. Carson had asked to be kept up to speed. No need to mention that to Wainwright for obvious reasons.

Wainwright and Elizabeth moved into a discussion of whether or not the mayor would run for office again as Carson stepped away from the table.

Once he was clear of the dining room, he accepted the call. "Tanner."

"Mr. Tanner, this is Bill Lynch."

Tension rippled through Carson despite the fact that he'd known it was the lieutenant calling. Not only had Lynch been involved with the Fleming investigation on and off in the past, but he was also the detective who had worked the Tanner investigation. Who had shown compassion for Carson even during those twenty-four hours when everyone besides the senator had considered him a suspect in the slaying of his own family. Hearing the man's voice always resurrected painful memories.

"What can I do for you, Lynch?" Carson braced for news on Zac's murder.

"Well, sir, we have a possible homicide. Dr. Dwight Holderfield's body was discovered in his home early this morning."

Carson's fingers turned to ice, and the phone nearly slipped from his hand. He tightened his grip.

Holderfield? What the hell?

Today Zac Holderfield's body was discovered. His father will be next.

Dread welled in Carson's gut. There had to be some mistake. "Any special circumstances?" Robbery or vengeance. Anything that would explain . . . and had nothing to do with Baxter. Surely she wouldn't go this far to get his attention.

"Not just yet," Lynch said. "We're going to play this thing like it's a murder for now."

Confusion drew Carson's eyebrows together. "For now?"

"We haven't confirmed anything yet, but there's some question as to whether or not the doctor may have committed suicide."

That sickening dread morphed into heart-thumping alarm as the name *Lana Kimble* echoed in his brain.

Before Carson could question that assessment, Lynch went on. "The reason I'm calling you personally, Mr. Tanner, is because we found a notation on his calendar that might interest your office. Luttrell said I should discuss this with you."

Anticipation overrode the alarm. "What kind of notation?"

"According to Holderfield's desk calendar, he had a meeting with an Annette Baxter last evening."

Shit. "What time?" Rage crept into the volatile mix already churning inside him.

"The time wasn't specified. The notation was simply listed on the bottom of the calendar page, after five o'clock."

"Are you at the scene?" Carson needed to be there. *Now.*

"Yes, sir. We've just started collecting evidence."

"Don't move anything," Carson instructed. "I want to see the scene just as it was when you found it."

"Will do, sir."

Carson tucked the phone into his pocket and hurried back to the table. He didn't bother sitting down. "Unfortunately I have to leave." His gaze met Wainwright's and telegraphed the message that he did not want to discuss the details. He hoped like hell that would suffice.

Wainwright grinned broadly. "Now that"—he shook his finger at Carson—"is dedication." He nodded to Elizabeth. "Any man who would leave breakfast with a beautiful young woman to do his job is the real thing."

Elizabeth blushed. "I'm sure we'll have the opportunity again."

Carson sensed that long-awaited possibility vanishing with the mounting evidence that he had completely underestimated Annette Baxter.

She was unpredictable and dangerous.

10:00 a.m.
3348 Sandhurst Road, Birmingham
Holderfield Residence

Carson had donned the shoe covers and gloves.

The media had closed in around the block like vultures waiting to pick the kill.

The family had been sequestered to the kitchen.

Crime scene technicians were standing down until Carson could have a guided tour. En route to the scene he had checked in with Agent Schaffer to get any surveillance info available on Annette Baxter. She'd given the feds the slip last night, as Carson was well aware, but he didn't mention that to Schaffer. This morning Baxter had left her house around half past nine to go the spa. The feds had tailed her there; she was still inside. Until Carson knew more, that told him nothing. Except that Annette Baxter had not come to the Holderfield home unless she'd done so last night after she'd parted ways with Carson.

Schaffer had nothing on the sister search as of yet.

"From what we've been able to ascertain," Lynch was saying, "Holderfield came home late last night and behaved strangely. His wife felt he was extremely agitated. When she asked him what was wrong, he insisted he was fine. Said he'd had a late meeting. Didn't say with whom. She chalked the tension up to their son's recent death."

Carson surveyed the home office where Holderfield's life had ended. Typical paneled walls lined with bookshelves. Framed photos of the family and reference books filled most. The room was tidy and surprisingly unsoiled by the act that was almost certainly suicide.

Holderfield had taken a large black garbage bag, the superior-strength type according to the techs, placed it over his head and torso, then put a bullet from a .38 revolver straight into his brain. The bullet had passed through his head and lodged in the wall adjacent to where he still sat. No blood-spray pattern on the wall, no mess to speak of except what had dripped down the inside of the bag and puddled on the wood floor around his chair.

The weapon had been found on the floor where it had slipped from his lax fingers. There were no signs of intrusion anywhere in the house. But something didn't sit right with the lieutenant. Carson had known Lynch long enough to read him when it came to a crime scene. They had discussed the scene where his family had been murdered many, many times.

"Here's the sticking point," Lynch said quietly as he glanced toward the door leading to the hall. "There's no powder residue on either of his hands."

Carson stepped close to the vic once more, crouched down, and considered the hand dangling at the side of his chair. "The ME will perform additional testing?" Carson pushed to his feet. His heart rate continued to rise steadily. This was real. Baxter's prediction had been real. He swallowed back the bile in his throat.

Why hadn't he told someone?

Lynch nodded in answer to Carson's question. "And the lab will test the weapon to see if there's some reason that might occur, but it would be the first revolver I've run across that didn't leave trace evidence."

A chill settling into his bones, Carson attempted to pursue an appropriate line of questioning. "Any estimate on time of death?"

The ME was on his way. An accident on Interstate 65 had slowed his arrival.

"Couple of hours ago, tops. Rigor's minimal. His wife left at quarter of eight to discuss arrangements for their son at a local flower shop. Her husband was having coffee then." Lynch shrugged. "But don't quote me on the time. That's the ME's call."

If the timing was right, that would have been a full hour or so before Annette Baxter left her penthouse. Did that rule her out or give her opportunity? Considering her skill at evading surveillance, Carson wasn't excluding anything. Uncertainty hammered away at his focus. He kicked it back and examined the calendar on Holderfield's desk. ANNETTE BAXTER was scrawled across the bottom of the page. "Has this been confirmed as his handwriting?"

Lynch nodded. "His wife says it's his. We'll verify it with the lab."

Carson met the detective's gaze, fury starting to override all else. "When are you going to question Annette Baxter?"

"I'm leaving my partner in charge here. I thought I'd head over there now."

Adrenaline sent Carson's heart rate into overdrive. "I'd like to accompany you."

"I figured as much." The detective flared his hands. "You're aware we're conducting a homicide investigation into Holderfield's son?"

Carson nodded.

"There's always the chance that this is a suicide, pure and simple. The man loved his son in spite of"—Lynch glanced at the corpse—"his flaws. His death may have pushed Holderfield over the edge."

Carson forced air into his lungs. No question. But with what he knew and the annotation on the deceased's calendar, interviewing Baxter was the proper course of action. "Of course. But that doesn't change our next move."

"Absolutely not," Lynch agreed.

"Let's do it."

Lynch led the way back through the house, Carson following. His fury lost steam and his gut clenched at the sounds of weeping. He remembered all too well how he had wept at the scene of his own family's slaughter.

Determination swelled inside him. That was why he did what he did. To ensure that justice was served. No one should have to wait fifteen years to know justice.

Or to be left wondering if they'd gotten justice and the horror was really over.

Ask yourself if you'll ever really know what happened.

His questions about his own past would just have to wait.

For the first time in his life there was another truth he wanted more.

And it started with Annette Baxter.

20

11:30 a.m.
Birmingham
The Tramont

Cool, crisp, businesslike.

Annette surveyed her reflection. The white pants and silk blouse that buttoned to her throat paired with the matching jacket were the perfect choice.

Cold, untouchable.

This meeting was asexual. The less distraction, the better.

She knew how to deal with this client. Straight to the point. No room for negotiation.

Three of her wealthiest clients had withdrawn their retainer fees. Two for whom she had not performed services as of yet. Leaving her with no choice but to permit the dissolution of their verbal contracts.

Zac and Dwight Holderfield were dead. No news on either investigation.

Jazel was dead. Annette had checked in with one of her contacts at Birmingham PD. Jazel's death had all the markings of foul play. A single-car accident on a deserted stretch of road. The rear bumper and left rear quarter panel were dented and scraped as if she'd been hit by another vehicle. A black vehicle. Annette shuddered. Jazel's Mustang had left the road at a high rate of speed and promptly plowed into a massive tree. She had been pronounced dead at the scene.

Annette exiled the ache. Not now.

Someone besides the feds was definitely following Annette as well. She'd caught a glimpse of a black sedan twice yesterday.

There was no denying it now: Someone had declared war on her. Jazel's death was either a warning or an attempt on Annette's life. Whenever she and Jazel teamed up to give the feds the slip, Jazel wore Annette's clothes and a blond wig to lead the persistent tail on a wild goose chase while Annette attended to business.

Had Jazel died in Annette's stead? Annette had been driving the Mustang just minutes before her dear friend's death.

Another shudder rocked her.

This game had definitely moved to the next level.

Otis agreed. He had called her as soon as one of his low-level contacts in Homicide had passed along the news about Holderfield. He hadn't mentioned Jazel, though there was certainly no reason for him to. Otis didn't deal with the little people.

Something had to happen fast. But that wasn't going to occur unless she focused.

Blocking all other thoughts from her mind save the coming meeting, Annette stepped into the white sandals with their practical heels and reached for the complementary bag. She was taking an extreme risk confronting this particular client. But those kinds of risks were occasionally necessary. This was one of those times. This morning's deep muscle massage had relaxed her, prepared her for what she must do. Stress undermined control. And that was something she could not lose.

A light rap on her dressing room door preceded Daniel's entrance. "Ms. Baxter, there is a Lieutenant Lynch here requesting to see you. Deputy District Attorney Tanner is with him."

Annette glanced at her watch. Bad timing. But she wasn't at all surprised considering what she had told Tanner last night. She met

Daniel's expectant expression. "Let my twelve o'clock know I might be a few minutes late."

He wouldn't like it, but he wouldn't dare ignore her.

Annette checked her appearance once more. As she spread gloss on her lips, the memory of Carson Tanner's mouth pressed firmly against hers caused a flare of anticipation low in her belly. She frowned at her reflection. What was it about this man that generated such an uncharacteristic reaction? She could not get the recollections and sensations from that one night out of her head.

Her hand stilled, the gloss applicator clenched in her fingers. She would not allow this weakness. No man would ever again hold dominion over her. Otis respected her, had taught her that she, and she alone, possessed the power over her own destiny.

Carson Tanner represented a necessary asset required to salvage this situation. She did not need or want him for any other reason.

There was nothing special about the man. Her only interest in him was his position.

Annette set the lip gloss aside. The media considered him a hero. That was true. He strove diligently to find justice for all. Very honorable. But in her experience, relying on so-called heroes more often than not turned out to be a mistake. She had learned the hard way not to depend upon anyone but herself.

Not even on Birmingham's golden boy. He was a means to an end, nothing more.

Mentally bracing for the confrontation, she headed for her business offices. Daniel would have shown the gentlemen to the conference room by now.

She left her bag on the table in the grand foyer she used as a lobby and separation point between her private rooms and her business offices. Upon seeing to this matter, she would need to leave immediately.

Asking her appointment to wait was unavoidable, but he would grow more agitated with each additional minute that passed. It would be wise not to leave him simmering any longer than absolutely necessary.

"Good morning, gentlemen." She strode into the conference room, her shoulders back, her chin held high. "If you're here about the Policemen's Fund Campaign, I'm afraid you've caught me at a rather bad time." Funny, the police worked diligently to tie her to illegal activities, and she organized literally dozens of fundraising campaigns in support of their work. But then, her allegiances along those lines facilitated certain vital contacts. She learned many, many things from those contacts. Times, locations, personnel involvement. Many things.

Both men stood in the middle of the room. Daniel would have offered them a seat; they had clearly declined.

"I'm Lieutenant Lynch, ma'am." The detective gestured to the brooding man beside him. "This is Deputy District Attorney Tanner. We're not here about the Policemen's Fund."

Obviously neither man was amused by her comment. She glanced at her watch. "I really should be on my way, but I suppose I can spare a few moments." She shifted her attention from the weary detective with his off-the-rack rumpled suit to the golden boy with the elegant silk ensemble. Carson Tanner's suit and shoes likely cost more than Lynch's monthly salary.

Judging by the way Tanner glared at her, he was more than a little pissed off that her prediction had become a reality. She'd warned him. He hadn't listened. She doubted he would take her other advice about looking into Lana Kimble's death or about not trusting anyone. So naive.

This was only the beginning.

"Ms. Baxter," Lynch said, "I have an obligation to inform you of your rights before we begin."

She inclined her head. "I can't imagine what this is about, but I understand you have a certain way you're required to conduct your business. Please proceed."

Annette listened as Lynch warned her that anything she said could be held against her in a court of law. As she did so, she considered Carson Tanner. Unblinking, he held her gaze. For such a hard-ass, totally focused DDA, he certainly had a hell of a time keeping his personal life in control. She supposed that was why he ignored it most of the time. Guys like Carson Tanner were all about work, until the right woman came along and forced them to sit up and pay attention. Then came the march down the aisle and the rug rats. And everything else went to pot.

No thanks.

Some people were simply not intended to be parents. Both she and Carson Tanner fell solidly into that category. Too many demons . . . too many skeletons.

She wondered if he understood that about himself just yet.

In time.

"Ms. Baxter, do you understand the rights I have just recited to you?" Lynch asked.

"Yes, Lieutenant, I do." She glanced at her watch again. "My time is really very short."

"This will take," Carson said, speaking for the first time, "as long as it takes."

Annette held his stare, saw the distaste he harbored for her. And yet—a smile toyed with her lips—he still wanted her. Deep down, where even he dared not go, he longed for intimacy. A paradox. That was what Carson Tanner was. Unstoppable in the courtroom by day, all alone at night . . . with his memories.

Just like her . . .

Lynch opened his notebook and poised his pen. "Ms. Baxter, where were you this morning between the hours of seven and nine thirty?"

That was easy enough. "Why don't you ask Special Agent Schaffer? One of her associates conducted my surveillance this morning. She can tell you exactly where I was."

Lynch jotted on his pad.

"You weren't picked up by surveillance until nine thirty," Tanner disputed. "Until that time you appeared to be at home, but there's no way to confirm that."

Lynch glanced from Tanner to her, obviously picking up on the extra layer of tension.

She raised her eyebrows at Tanner's veiled accusation.

"Appeared to be? I believe the feds have my departure on video."

"Can someone verify you were at home until nine thirty?" Lynch asked, drawing her attention back to him.

"My personal assistant, Daniel." She gestured to the telephone on the table next to her. "If you check my phone records you'll see that I made several business calls before nine thirty."

"Anyone could have made calls from your phone," Tanner argued.

He wanted to spar, did he? "That's true, Mr. Tanner," she allowed graciously, which only pissed him off all the more. "I suppose you and Lieutenant Lynch will simply have to take my word on that one."

"You can rest assured," Lynch cut in, "that we will corroborate all portions of your alibi."

She frowned as if she didn't understand. "Alibi? Why would I need an alibi?"

"Dr. Dwight Holderfield was found dead in his home this morning," Lynch explained.

Dead? The idea that he hadn't used the word murdered struck her as odd considering the context of the discussion thus far. Murder was by far the better choice when paired with alibi. Regardless of who had pulled the trigger, she understood that Holderfield had been murdered. "And you believe he was murdered?"

"We haven't ruled out that possibility," Lynch said, steering clear of a simple yes or no.

"We do know," Tanner pointed out, "that he had an appointment with you last evening after five."

Now, there was something he would never be able to verify. "Actually," she countered, "I had no appointments last evening." She took note of the time once more, further agitating Tanner. "I had drinks with a friend around five-thirty and returned home shortly before seven. I'm certain you can confirm that as well through the FBI's surveillance.

Or perhaps you know something the feds don't." That she spoke so candidly about the surveillance didn't appear to sit well with Tanner or Lynch. Her last remark had the desired effect. Tanner glowered at her but made no further accusations regarding her surveillance.

"You had no business dealings with Dr. Holderfield?" Lynch queried.

"We chatted from time to time regarding various fundraising efforts. As administrator of one of the most celebrated hospitals in this city, he or a member of his staff often called upon my expertise."

Tanner scrutinized her posture, her expression. He was looking for an angle to snare her without exposing himself. She had worked very hard for many years to conquer her emotions and reactions, as she did with all that she sought to learn. Tanner wouldn't find what he was looking for.

"When did you last speak with him?" Lynch prodded.

She gave the impression of mulling over the question. "I can't recall the date." Annette stared directly at Tanner then. "But the last time Dr. Holderfield and I spoke he was very much alive. Although, I will say that he appeared very upset. His son was missing, and he was extremely agitated." She glanced at her watch again. "Really, gentlemen, if you have no more questions, I have a pressing appointment."

Tanner seethed.

Lynch looked from the DDA to her once more. His instincts were no doubt humming. "Be aware, ma'am," he warned, "that we may need to question you again once we've confirmed the information you've given us."

Annette nodded. "I'm happy to cooperate. But now, I really must go." She wondered if half this effort was being expended to solve Jazel Ramirez's death. Of course not. She was no one. Insignificant.

"Thank you for your time." Lynch closed his notepad and led the way to the door.

Tanner followed but not without pausing to look back once. Those dark eyes targeted hers, and she froze. In the five or so seconds that he held her gaze she understood indisputably that he wasn't finished yet.

"In the event charges are filed, Ms. Baxter," he said with a knowing look, "is there anyone we should call? A relative perhaps?"

Alarm flared.

Impossible.

He was guessing. Fishing for a reaction.

Whatever he thought he knew, he would not win this battle.

They were both good at censoring outward displays and manipulating others, but she had far more years of hardcore experience under her belt. He should admit defeat now.

"If the need arises," she responded, "I'll call my attorney."

The corners of Tanner's mouth lifted ever so slightly, and then he walked away.

Uncertainty congealed in her stomach.

He knew something. But how? That was impossible.

If he had discovered her sister . . . he would have used that knowledge already.

Annette could not let that happen.

12:45 p.m.
Birmingham
Jefferson County Courthouse

Mayor Gordon Duke represented Birmingham's old school. He served as mayor for the power and prestige, but he lived lavishly on the money he had inherited from his daddy. Educated at Auburn, he was an Alabama boy through and through. He'd made his share of enemies, but most of Birmingham's citizens looked up to him as if he were the second coming of Christ.

Even at quarter of one on a Saturday his office was bustling with activity. The hallowed halls of the courthouse provided the perfect setting for his ego. Always plenty of attention and no end to the ways to get into other people's business.

"Ms. Baxter."

Annette looked up from her phone as the mayor's secretary approached. Annette had been waiting in the mayor's private lobby for around fifteen minutes. He'd done that on purpose. Made her wait the same as she had been forced to make him.

"Yes." Annette produced the requisite smile.

"The mayor will see you now."

Annette uncrossed her ankles and rose from her chair. She followed the secretary, who matched the decor perfectly: antiquated yet classic.

They approached the mayor's office. His door was open, and he was shaking hands with two gentlemen. His guests wore elegant business suits befitting a visit to this esteemed office. Both looked to be in their late forties to mid-fifties. Their mission was anyone's guess.

"Ms. Baxter," Gordon Duke proclaimed, drawing the attention of his guests to her arrival. "Come on in." He met her in the middle of his vast office and gave her a welcoming but brisk hug. "It's always a pleasure." He drew back but didn't release her shoulders. "Let me introduce you to two movers and shakers who are determined to invest in our fine city."

Introductions were made leaving her less than impressed, and final handshakes were exchanged. Each man nodded politely to Annette as he passed on his way out. The secretary checked to see if Annette needed anything then closed the door.

The bright smile on the mayor's face vanished before the thud of the door stopped echoing in the room. "What the hell do you want?"

Annette lowered her bag onto the closest chair and folded her arms over her chest. When she'd studied the mayor's well-maintained face and glowering eyes for just long enough to infuriate him all the more, she said, "The same thing you want, Gordon. Power, money, respect." She offered her palms in confusion. "It's that last one I seem to be having trouble with lately."

His lips curled into a hateful sneer. "What would a whore like you know about respect?"

She laughed softly. "I know your definition of a whore, Gordon, and I certainly don't fit into that category. That little hottie who serves as your latest intern, now, there's a whore."

"Go to hell," he snarled.

He wished.

For half a lifetime, Gordon Duke had screwed anything that would lie still for him and some that wouldn't. One such encounter had ended rather abruptly and quite badly. But Annette had resolved his problem. That had been five years ago. He'd been in her debt ever since. Now she was about to call in his marker.

"State your business," he snapped. "The sooner you're out of here the happier I'll be."

Predictable. Clients were always eager to please and sucked up to her when they needed her, but after she had fixed their problem and gotten their balls out of the vise, they turned into rude, belligerent assholes. It was a vicious cycle. The trouble was, somehow they—they being men—were never able to stop themselves from fucking up. "I'm calling in your marker, Gordon. Take care of this problem for me and we'll be even."

Suspicion joined the fury clouding his face. "What kind of problem?"

"Someone has grown a backbone. I think you and I both know who that someone is. I need you to find out what his end game is so that I can neutralize the situation before it becomes a problem for certain high-value clients."

Rage glittered in the mayor's too-wide-set eyes. "Is that a threat?" Like all her clients when faced with paying up, his posture went rigid and fire practically blazed from his flaring nostrils.

"Yes, Gordon," she said calmly. "That is a threat."

Then he did the exact opposite of what she expected.

He laughed.

Long and loud.

She kept her surprise as well as her annoyance in check. She would not give him the satisfaction. "What do you find so amusing?"

"You." He laughed some more, had to wipe his eyes. "Take my advice, prepare for a major lifestyle change." All signs of mirth disappeared. "Because you are definitely fucked."

She acknowledged his defiance with a nod. "Then you're no longer concerned with the evidence I have at my disposal."

A vile grin spread across his face. "Not in the least, you loathsome bitch. My back is covered." He tilted his head in disdain. "Can you say the same?"

"Well." She reached for her bag. "I'm glad to see our fearless city leader has finally sprouted some balls." She started to turn away but thought better of it. "Just remember, I know *all* your secrets. *If* I go down, I won't be alone."

She left the office, and oddly the halls had cleared as if everyone present had known that a storm was brewing.

Much to her displeasure, it was. And she was dead center in its path.

As she climbed into her Lexus, her cell buzzed. One look at the display and she knew her life was about to get exponentially more complicated.

21

1:05 p.m.
Birmingham
Jefferson County Courthouse

Elizabeth reread the press release. Each word had to be perfect, had to relay a precise meaning. Mayor Duke's reputation was on the line with each statement, each image provided to the media. Elizabeth wasn't sure anyone understood that quite the way she did.

Otherwise—she glared at the final paragraph—senseless mistakes would not be made on such a regular basis.

She pressed the intercom button. "Michelle, I need a moment of your time."

Michelle Walters was Elizabeth's third assistant in two years. It was ridiculous that good clerical help was so difficult to find. Unfortunately, it appeared that Michelle was no different from the others. Such a shame. She certainly possessed all the other assets Elizabeth had been looking for. Distinguished bearing, well dressed, and well mannered.

But no one was perfect, and this final paragraph certainly hailed that truth.

"Yes, ma'am?" Michelle hurried to Elizabeth's desk. "I was just on my way out the door." Her harried gaze met Elizabeth's. "Remember I mentioned that my eight-year-old has her first dance competition today." She glanced at the clock. "I really need to be out the door already."

Three children. Two years younger than Elizabeth and the woman had three children already. Elizabeth understood how important parenting was and how challenging holding down a full-time job on top of that must be. Still, there was work to be done. And this simply would not wait.

"I really hate to do this to you," Elizabeth said with heavy regret, "but this press release has to be perfect before it goes out." She pointed to the final paragraph. "There's something not quite right with the wording here. The mayor needs to come across as firm, not harsh. Soften the verbiage a bit." She smiled, not wanting to sound overbearing. "Then you can be on your way."

Michelle blinked, her expression somewhere between horrified and frustrated. "But we've changed that paragraph three times already."

Elizabeth tamped down her impatience. "I know and I'm so sorry. But this is extremely important. I'm sure you're aware that *both* our jobs depend upon moments like this."

Her assistant nodded jerkily. "Yes, ma'am."

Elizabeth wasn't particularly fond of making the hard decisions, but someone had to do it. And it was her job to ensure the mayor always looked good. No matter the inconvenience to others. What would happen to those poor patients at the center if Elizabeth failed to follow through with her work when plying money from the wealthy of Birmingham? A large portion of the patients in residence depended upon the contributions of others. Her family had been hefty donors for decades. Ever since Congressman Weller's favorite cousin had been diagnosed as autistic.

One didn't walk away from a challenge until it had been conquered.

Michelle hesitated at the door, then turned back to face Elizabeth. "I'm sorry. I almost forgot. The vet's office called. Gallagher is fine. He'll be ready for pickup around five. No broken bones, just a little banged up."

Relief poured through Elizabeth. "Excellent. Thank you, Michelle."

That was good news indeed. Elizabeth had been so worried about him. Perhaps this time he had learned his lesson about going into the street. Thank God her mother had been there to take care of him when the hit-and-run happened.

Surveying her desk to ensure that all was neatly organized and nothing left undone, Elizabeth considered that tomorrow was her first date with Carson in more than fifteen years. Excitement fizzed in her tummy. She couldn't wait to see him dressed in a tux. He was so handsome. He worked so hard. The evening would be a nice break for the both of them, though it would assuredly be work for her. There was always a good cause in need of funds.

She had waited so long to have her life get back to the way it used to be. The way it was supposed to be.

No one knew how long she had wanted this time to come.

Perhaps she should invite Carson to participate in the telethon for the children's hospital. Last year had been a resounding success. She particularly loved helping the children. One day she hoped to have children of her own.

Probably already would if her parents hadn't ruined everything. She should never have listened to them. Elizabeth should have stayed right here in Birmingham and comforted Carson in his greatest time of need. But she had been a good daughter. She had listened to her father and mother, allowed them to make all the decisions. Even after returning to Birmingham and earning this prestigious position, she had permitted her father to be in control.

No more. She and Carson belonged together. That source of tranquility that was always her saving grace overflowed for her now, filled her completely. It was well past time Elizabeth took charge of her own life.

Tomorrow night was only the beginning.

Nothing would ever get in her way again.

This time she would not fail to protect what she and Carson shared.

22

2:40 p.m.
Montevallo Road, Birmingham
Magnolia Hills Individualized Care Center

Annette sat in her car for several minutes after arriving at the center. She had handled her two o'clock with Campbell by phone. Now Annette had to take care of her sister. There was no way around it. But she dreaded with all her heart the trouble that might lie inside.

She was strong. She would handle whatever fate tossed in her lap.

Hadn't she been doing that her whole life?

In just a few hours she had a historical society fundraiser to attend. No matter that everything was falling apart; she had commitments. She had to hold whatever ground she had left until the bitter end.

Not once had she given up, however bad things were. She wouldn't now.

Annette emerged from her Lexus and walked with determination to the front entrance. After keying in the security code, she entered the nauseatingly quiet building.

The clinical smell immediately assaulted her. Reminded her of the worst times from her past. Visions of blood, sounds of screaming bombarded her. The pruning shears protruding from that bastard's back. Her working with all her might to dislodge the shears. She shuddered, pushed the memories away.

Leave it in the past. Before she could usher the images completely away, more joined the parade. Blood . . . all over her hands, her blouse. She blinked, pushed all of it aside. She had to attend to this issue. Right now, nothing else mattered.

The corridors were deserted since visiting hours ended at two and didn't resume until five. Classical music played softly, banishing the silence and at the same time masking the sterile sounds of treatment. She made her way to the second-floor information desk and identified herself to the nurse on duty. She must be new; Annette hadn't seen her before.

The nurse entered Annette's name and security code into the computer on the desk. "Ah, there you are, Ms. Anderson. You're here to see your sister Paula."

Annette had long ago gotten used to being called Ms. Anderson. The step was necessary to ensure that Paula was never connected to Annette or her work. "Yes." Annette stiffened, steeled herself for bad news.

"Dr. Roland is on duty," the nurse explained. "I'll call her to the desk for you."

"Thank you."

Annette wandered a few steps from the desk to wait for the doctor. Roland wasn't Paula's primary care physician, but Annette had worked with her before.

"Ms. Anderson."

Annette turned toward the gentle voice. "Hello, Dr. Roland. I hope Paula is all right."

"Why don't we step into the lounge so we can talk," Roland suggested.

A scarcely subdued panic clawing at her, Annette followed the doctor to the private lounge and settled into a chair directly across the designed-for-function coffee table from where the doctor took a seat.

Dr. Roland shoved her stethoscope into the pocket of her lab coat before resting her full attention on Annette. "There was a strange incident this afternoon."

"But Paula is all right?" Every incident involving Paula was strange. The doctor's reluctance to share the details had the dread swelling.

"Yes." The doctor nodded. "Paula is fine, physically. But the incident triggered a severe reaction. We were forced to medicate her more heavily than usual."

Annette clasped the arms of her chair to keep in check the emotions roiling inside her. "You keep talking about the *incident.* Can you explain what happened, please?"

"Of course. I apologize," Roland said. "You're aware of our high standard of patient care."

Annette nodded, wishing like hell the woman would get to the point.

"We pride ourselves on safety, first and foremost."

The anxiety pressed against Annette's chest, fisted in her stomach, but she kept quiet. Allowed the woman to get to her point without interruption.

"Somehow, Paula got her hands on a pair of scissors."

"Did she injure another patient?" If Paula was fine physically, doing damage to someone else was an equally disturbing concern.

Roland shook her head. "She cut her hair."

Relief and confusion reigned for a long moment, rendering Annette unable to respond appropriately. Paula had the same blond hair as Annette, only far longer. Paula loved her hair, played with it like a child with a favored toy. Most of the time it stayed in one long braid. She would be devastated at the loss of her hair.

"How did this happen?"

The Magnolia Individualized Care Center was one of the finest in the country. The staff specialized in low-functioning autism. Paula had never been happier.

"Believe me when I say we've investigated every possibility and we're at a complete loss." Roland turned her palms upward. "There simply is no explanation. Regardless, we take full responsibility, of course."

No explanation? *Calm.* Stay calm. "I'm certain every precaution was taken to avoid an incident of this nature." Annette closed her eyes a moment to regain full control of her composure, then met the doctor's relieved gaze. "Things do happen despite our best efforts. Still, I would hope that nothing like this will happen again."

Dr. Roland nodded adamantly. "You can rest assured it will not happen again."

Annette cleared her throat of the rising lump. What Paula could have done with scissors chilled her blood. "Can I see my sister now?"

"Certainly." Roland stood, clearly breathing easier. "But, as I said, she's heavily sedated."

Annette pushed to her feet. She felt so tired suddenly. So very tired. "I understand."

As she walked alongside Dr. Roland, Annette considered the murals on the walls of the corridor. She'd seen them many times before, but she never ceased to be amazed by the detail. Each was designed to lure the minds of the patients who roamed the halls. With autism, most of those like Paula were inclined to retreat to that world in their heads that they alone knew about. The murals and sensory rooms were created specifically to draw them out, to entice them to another place. The whole center was set up in such a way to induce intellectual stimulation or to soothe an outburst in quiet rooms where pale blue was the sole color of walls, floors, and furnishings. Each member of the staff was trained specifically in dealing with the patient's unique needs.

The place was worth every penny of the hundred-plus grand it cost each year. Paula was safe and happy, at least to the degree possible. She received the finest care available, and all new medical discoveries were hastened into trials here.

Annette didn't care what she had to do; she would ensure that her sister received this level of care for the rest of her life.

Roland paused at the door to the room. "Let me know if you need anything or if you have any additional questions."

Annette thanked her before stepping into the room.

Paula lay on her back, arms at her sides, sheet neatly draped over her. Definitely medicated to the max. Paula preferred curling into a ball when she slept.

Annette's eyes burned when she touched her sister's hair, which stood like bristles on a brush. How on earth had this happened? Paula lay absolutely still, breathing deep and steady. Annette kissed her cheek and whispered softly in her ear. "I'm here, baby."

Though her mind was like that of a toddler, sometimes an infant, Paula was three years older than Annette. There were moments when Annette would see recognition in her eyes. Sometimes happiness. But more often than not all Annette saw was that emptiness that left her feeling so utterly desolate and completely inadequate. And alone.

Annette kissed Paula's forehead and settled into the chair next to her bed. The wrist bracelet she wore identified her as Paula Anderson. Annette disliked the deceit when it came to dealing with Paula. No matter, the step was without question essential to her security. Annette would never take chances with her safety.

Scissors. How could such an oversight have happened? The staff were highly trained and meticulous in their work. Not once in all the years Paula had stayed here had anything like this happened.

The notion that it had now, at this particular time, roused Annette's anxiety once more.

Could someone have made the connection?

She never allowed the FBI or anyone else to tail her here. Annette was too good for a careless mistake like that.

No need to overreact. Paula was basically unharmed. If Annette's enemies had wanted to hurt Annette or send her a warning, there were far worse things they could have done.

Like that black sedan that had attempted to follow her when she'd left the courthouse. But she'd given him the slip. And the driver had definitely been male.

Annette shuddered at all the possibilities. She had been protecting Paula since they were little children. Some of the brats in the trailer park where they had lived as kids had liked being mean to Paula. Annette had busted heads. She had grown up tough as nails. At least she had thought she was tough, until, at age twelve, her mother had deserted them at the Walmart. Their father had disappeared years before that. And the only other man in their lives, the bastard who'd lived with them for three long-ass years, had been dead. Murdered. But he'd deserved exactly what he'd gotten.

The foster care system had taken them in. At first Annette had dreamed of a nice home with two loving caregivers. That dream had shattered in a hurry. What she had gotten was shipped from one household to another. No one wanted to bother with Paula, considering the courts had concluded that she had violent tendencies. Guilt assaulted Annette. She couldn't count the times she had come home from school and found Paula tied to the bed they shared or locked in a closet. Finally, the system that was supposed to rescue children had dumped Paula in a state institution. Annette had been placed in a home where rebellion wasn't tolerated on any level. Then another and another after that. The endless stream of so-called caregivers had forced her into one abusive situation after the other. She was fully aware that there were good foster families out there, she had just never been placed with one.

At sixteen Annette had succeeded in running away and staying out of the system's reach. She'd jumped from the frying pan into the fire. Living on the streets had been brutal. She'd learned to survive on her wits and her physical attributes.

Then one day her manager had sent her to a swanky hotel as part of a group of escorts for visiting businessmen, and Otis Fleming had noticed her. He'd taken her in and taught her how to make something of herself. She owed him everything. He had given her the skills to gain considerable wealth, and that wealth had allowed her to find Paula and place her in the perfect environment for her condition.

No one was going to take that away from her. Annette would do whatever she had to do, stop whoever got in her way, to keep Paula safe.

Images of barbaric sex with Carson Tanner intruded but Annette cast them out. Having sex with Tanner had been part of her strategy, not for her physical pleasure. She didn't care for sex. It had been years since she had been forced to use it as a tool. She hated that she had to now. But if that was what it took to keep Carson Tanner off balance, then so be it.

She wasn't afraid of the local authorities. She wasn't afraid of the Federal Bureau of Investigation. But Carson Tanner suddenly scared the hell out of her. She thought of the way he had looked at her today.

If he knew about her sister . . . no, he had to be bluffing.

Annette needed to maintain control as long as possible while divulging the least amount of information. Information was power, but once released it became impotent. The time had to be right.

Timing was everything.

Her cell vibrated. Annette inhaled a deep, bolstering breath before answering. It was Daniel, her assistant. "Yes, Daniel."

"Representative McGrath has requested a consultation with you at three. I told him you were unavailable, but he refused to take no for an answer."

A potential new client. Interesting. At least it wasn't another retainer withdrawal.

Wainwright and Drake were powerful. Dwight Holderfield was dead. Half her client list was pulling out. She had dirt on nearly all of those bastards. Control represented her most valuable asset. Someone was methodically taking it away from her, leaving her powerless.

Were Wainwright and Drake really this influential?

"Shall I tell him you'll get back to him?"

Annette took a moment to gather her composure. "Tell him I'll meet him at five." She gave Daniel the usual protocol and put her phone away.

In the beginning, her work had been more of an intelligence-gathering mission. Otis set her up as a fundraising coordinator. Over time she had developed an in with the most powerful people in Birmingham. Otis gained insight to those he needed to manipulate, and she grew financially secure. As time went by, the services she offered expanded into problem solving. She provided a service no one else could. Kept the ugliness away from those the community trusted and looked up to. Someone had to do it. Otherwise there would be bedlam.

She wasn't a monster.

But the world, her world, considered her just that.

He considered her that.

Carson Tanner thought he was better than her despite the reality that his job dictated he do things far worse than she. He made deals with hardcore criminals. But it was different when he allowed a killer to get less than what he deserved. The law was on Tanner's side. Just as it was on Wainwright's and Drake's.

If the naive citizens of Birmingham only knew.

The fear she inspired in those who knew her, knew what she did, ensured that she would never be anything but evil in the eyes of all those law-abiding citizens.

They just didn't know.

That sense of doom crowded in on her, banded around her chest. She stood, steadied herself. She would get through this.

They would not win.

Annette smoothed her palms over slacks. The look, the attitude. All of it was part of the job. Part of what made her who she was. She would find a way to regain her power.

No man would keep her down for long.

Carson Tanner was hers already, he just didn't know it yet.

—

5:00 p.m.
Terrace Drive, Pelham
Oak Mountain State Park

At least someone still asked "How high?" when Annette said *jump.* State Representative Bryan McGrath had not balked once at the short notice or the change in location. New clients were never given the actual location of the meet until the last possible minute.

McGrath parked his extravagant sedan alongside her Lexus. Annette watched as he got out of his vehicle, removed his jacket and cell phone, and tossed both back into the car. Then he walked to the passenger side of hers. She never met with a client on his terms. Always on her own. And only for the initial meeting so that she could assess his motives and his nature. After that, there was rarely any personal contact.

When he had opened the door and settled into the seat, she placed a jamming device on the console just in case he'd worn any transmitting bugs.

Never trust anyone, that was her motto.

"Nice to see you, Representative McGrath."

"Can we get this over with?"

McGrath was a relatively young man in the political arena; he'd only recently turned thirty. He had a lovely wife and three precious children, as he so often said in the media.

Evidently he also had a dark side. Something for which he needed her expert assistance. This was the part of her work she always found the most fascinating. It never failed to amuse her just how stupid those who had it all could be.

"Of course," she assured him. "Keep in mind that I need all the details. Don't leave anything out."

He swallowed hard. "I have a problem with sex."

She didn't say anything to that. Didn't most powerful men?

"I like," he went on, "having sex with exotic dancers. It's like gambling, I can't resist." He made a sound, like a sob stuck in his throat. "My wife would be devastated if she knew." He rubbed a hand over his face. "I've tried to stop." He closed his eyes and shook his head. "I just can't."

Annette would bet he had tried. Giving him credit, according to what she knew of the man, other than that one dirty little flaw, he was extraordinarily upstanding. Fine husband and father, dedicated churchgoer. The works. It appeared that if he could just keep his cock in his trousers when his wife wasn't around, his life would be perfect.

"I need to know exactly what happened. If you leave out anything, I can't do my job." Annette settled back in her seat and watched the man's profile. He wouldn't want to look at her as he spoke, but she needed to analyze him as he did so.

"I made a mistake. I always go out of town when I . . . I can't bear it any longer."

How thoughtful of him.

He shook his head again as his mouth quivered. "I didn't know she was seventeen. She said she was twenty-one. It was a mistake. Just a mistake."

Annette wanted to laugh, but she didn't. "Forgetting a meeting is a mistake, McGrath. Fucking a seventeen-year-old girl who looks twenty-one is just plain stupid."

He turned to Annette then, his face contorted with fury, but it was the fear in his eyes that kept him seated in her car and taking her shit. "I didn't know. I swear I didn't. She was working at that club." He looked away, shook his head. "I just assumed . . ."

Ah, well. She wouldn't bother telling him what happened more often than not when one made assumptions. "I'll need the name and address of the club and the girl's name."

He gave her the information. She committed it to memory. That was something else she never did. She never, ever wrote down anything she was told or entered it into a database of any sort. Only she had access to the information her clients shared.

"What happens now?" he asked, defeated.

"Now I find her weakness, then I make her a deal she can't refuse."

He moistened his lips. "How much is this going to cost me?"

The bottom line in all her transactions. "Depends upon how much trouble the girl gives me. I'll try to keep it under fifty grand. I'll need half of that deposited into this account." She wrote the number on his hand. "Today." This was an account the feds wouldn't know about. Her business account. Unfortunately, it was only a temporary holding account that automatically transferred all moneys to one or more of her foreign accounts.

He blinked, then nodded.

"Once the situation is resolved, you'll pay the balance. My work is guaranteed. I doubt that she will give you any trouble in the future, but if she does, I'll take care of it at no additional cost."

His gaze collided with Annette's once more. "You won't hurt her? It won't go that far, right?"

Annette smiled. Hardly. "If you're asking me will I do physical harm to her, the answer is no. That's not the way I do business."

"So that's it? I pay you and it's done? That completes our business."

"It's not quite that simple." This was the part no one ever liked. "You will be in my debt. At some point in the future, I may need your assistance. When the time comes, I'll call in the marker. Until then, you should go on with your life as if this incident never happened. As if we never met."

A frown marred the smooth, classic features of his face. "Marker?"

"You needn't concern yourself with that now."

He nodded jerkily.

"But be aware, if you ever discuss this meeting or me with anyone—and I mean anyone—I will ruin you."

Another halting nod. "I understand."

Yes. She was quite certain he did.

"Very well, Mr. McGrath." She arranged another smile into place. "That's all. I'll contact you when the situation is resolved. If possible, I'll take care of it in the next twenty-four hours."

He reached for the door handle but hesitated. He searched her face. "You're that sure you can take care of this?"

Her smile broadened into the genuine article. "Trust me, Mr. McGrath. I have never failed a client."

Strange, she realized as McGrath got out of her car: That was something else she and Carson Tanner had in common.

Neither liked to lose.

23

8:00 p.m.
Birmingham Festive Fundraiser, Birmingham
Historic Richard Erwin House

Annette stood in the background, watching the elite of Birmingham mingle and smile as if they owned the world. Every city commissioner was in attendance, including tonight's host, the distinguished Thomas Schmale, as well as a slew of other honorary event sponsors. The rich and famous gathered in their little cliques based on zip codes and financial portfolios. Gossiping and bragging, partaking of food from the hottest restaurants the city had to offer, and drinking the finest wines imported from around the world.

Not a one paid the slightest attention to her. She was simply another fixture, the woman who had organized and set the stage for tonight's hefty donations to the Birmingham Historical Society's Museum Endowment Fund. The extravagant gown, champagne in color so as to blend in, she'd selected and the sophisticated French twist in which she'd arranged her hair were of no consequence. These people had no desire to know who Annette Baxter was even had she been inclined to offer herself up to such scrutiny. They didn't want to know. She performed with great success the services required, and that was all that mattered. Annette merely orbited their exclusive worlds.

And watched. Absorbed. She knew their secrets and used those secrets to her advantage. Not a one suspected just how vulnerable their inflated existences were until it was too late.

She needed some air. The hypocrisy was stifling and boring.

Annette deposited her glass on the tray of a passing waiter and made her way to the nearest exit, avoiding the clusters of philanthropic patrons. Outside, she crossed the upper terrace and took the steps down to the grand fountain where water misted the night air. White lights adorned the meticulously manicured landscape and glittered in the trees. Sometimes she still wondered at the grit and guts it had taken to claw her way into this ostentatious league.

Hard work.

Most nights she enjoyed her work. But not tonight.

Her world was crumbling around her. Holderfield was dead, just as she had predicted. She had recognized his desperation. Had known he was very close to crossing a line. She had warned Tanner, but her warning had fallen on deaf ears.

Now the man was dead.

Not her responsibility.

Jazel's death, however, was entirely her responsibility.

Collateral damage. Harsh as it sounded, Jazel had known the risks. She had been unconditionally willing considering the exorbitant fee she received each time. But that didn't change how very much Annette regretted her death. Jazel had been like a little sister to her . . . almost. Annette had foolishly let herself care about the girl. Not good.

As for the other, whoever had seen to it that Holderfield took his last breath had ensured she would be a suspect. Her name on the deceased's calendar meant nothing. She and Holderfield had not met in person that last time. Annette never met with a client in person after the initial encounter unless absolutely essential. Video calls were every bit as effective. The police had no physical evidence to connect her to Holderfield on the day of his death or the one prior. Not a single piece of tangible proof.

Yet it wouldn't end so neatly. There would be more. A single item that would tie her to the crime scene was all it would take.

She stilled. Waiting for the other shoe to drop was not her style. Take action, that was her creed. It was time to make those responsible for her current dilemma sweat.

Any action at this point likely would not stop the momentum; all she could hope for was to derail the ultimate goal. She was the target. Not Otis. This was about her, no question. Time and again she had recalled the events of the night that had set this crash sequence in motion and found no fault on her own part. Her actions had been necessary. Rather than appreciate her quick, efficient work, they had decided she was too big a risk. Too great a threat, no matter that taking her down represented an equally dangerous course. She had to wonder how long this decision had been taking shape.

Annette would be the sacrificial lamb, the scapegoat. Any complications would somehow be attributed to her. Guilt placed at her feet. Then it would be done. The sticky mess resolved while concurrently getting her out of the way once and for all.

She had to hand it to them. Collectively those responsible had dredged up far more courage than she would have suspected the whole lot possessed.

Well, she wasn't quite done. Giving up, running, those reactions were not in her character. She had too much to lose. Annette closed her eyes and thought of Paula. Her sister needed her to be strong. No matter how tempting it would be to disappear forever . . . she could not. Not unless there was a way to see that Paula had all that she needed as well.

Stop. She could not allow that seed of doubt to take root.

"How did you know?"

Well, well, she had wondered when he would show up. Annette turned to face Carson Tanner. "I know many things, Mr. DDA. Do you have a specific question? Or are you ready to listen? That was the deal, after all."

He looked harried and rumpled despite the elegant navy suit he wore. Looming on the upper terrace, his hands shoved into his trouser pockets, he glared at her with those dark eyes, his expression equally dark.

Carson Tanner was primed and ready. It had certainly taken him long enough. But then, she'd known that about him. Tanner was a man who assessed a situation carefully before diving in—but once he was committed there was no stopping him.

"You stated"—he descended another step—"that Dwight Holderfield would be next." One more step, then another until he had reached the lower terrace where she waited. "How did you know?"

Seemed Mr. Tanner was a bad sport. She should have expected as much. She took a moment, mainly to set him further on edge, and sized up the man. Several inches taller than her, nice wide shoulders. She'd seen his every asset, sleek, unmarred skin stretched tautly over a muscled frame, sculpted jaw, handsome face. He had it all. Looks, money, and a career on the verge of launching to the next level. Focused, determined, the perfect politician in the making.

But he didn't have the one thing he'd longed for the better part of his life. The truth. No matter how successful his career proved, no matter how hard he worked, he needed the truth to feel complete. Sadly, the truth was only going to turn his vigilantly structured world upside down. Yet he wanted it with every fiber of his being.

Time to give him an answer. She met that livid gaze. "Because he came to me demanding the truth."

"What truth?"

"The truth about his son."

"Why would he suspect you possessed knowledge related to his son's murder?"

Even as he asked the question his gaze slid down the length of her body and back up to tangle with hers. There was something more in his eyes then. Need. Hunger. She smiled. Even knowing, as he did, that she had set him up, worked diligently to distract him from his goal, he still wanted her. Predictable. When she'd done her research on Carson Tanner, she had known his rigid control could be breached if she used the proper tactics. Always understand your opponent's weaknesses as well as his strengths. The need for intimacy hovered just beneath that unstoppable facade he'd constructed. He hadn't trusted anyone on a personal level in more than a decade, yet he wanted desperately to be touched . . . to touch.

He'd lost his family, the girl he loved, his friends, everything in one fatal blow. Everything about who he was testified to his extreme need to fill that void.

"As I said." She watched that desire escalate in his eyes, throb in the hard set of his jaw. "I know many things. It was clear to me after my meeting with Holderfield that he was a desperate man. Desperate people take desperate measures."

With one stride, Tanner invaded her personal space. "All of this is just a game to you." He glared at her, searched her face as if he expected to find something he'd hadn't discovered before. "Right now, right here"—he hitched a thumb toward the historic home behind them—"you mingle with these people like you belong. Like the feds aren't right outside watching every move you make. Like Lynch isn't working diligently to prove you were somehow involved in Holderfield's murder." He shook his head. "Even in the face of those solid facts, you're not afraid. You think you're untouchable."

"I'm sure you have a point," she suggested, undaunted—at least on the surface.

He put his face very close to hers. "You're good, lady." He opened his arms wide as if stumped. "I can't connect a single illegal activity to you. Neither can the feds. All we can do is watch and wait for that first misstep." He lowered his arms to his sides and leaned menacingly close again. "It'll happen. And I'll be waiting, watching every move you make until then. I will get you."

He was right. She knew this. But she also understood something he did not. Time was very short. Her fate had already been decided. How long, she wondered, before his was as well—if not already.

"I had nothing to do with Dwight Holderfield's murder." She refused to look away from the disgust in his eyes. Refused to let him see that the pressure was beginning to get to her. That he was beginning to get to her.

He reined in the fury as well as the disgust, donned that professional mask he wore so well. "The offer I made is still on the table. Give me Fleming and you'll walk away with immunity." He searched her face, obviously attempting to gauge her reaction. "But be forewarned, if murder charges are leveled against you, I won't be able to help you then. It's now or never."

He was right. It was now or never.

"Since you appear to have no intentions of living up to your end of the bargain we made last night—"

"I never agreed to anything you offered," he said, cutting her off cold. "You've heard my offer, take it or leave it."

"How about I sweeten the deal?" She ignored the frustration that wrestled its way past his courtroom face. "Give you something extra. Something immensely personal." Don't let him see your desperation. "Hear me out, Tanner. You'll be glad you did."

He slowly, determinedly shook his head. "Twenty-four hours," he stated flatly. "Make your decision within twenty-four hours or the offer is rescinded permanently."

His insolence was becoming tedious. What was it going to take to get this man to listen? "You do want the truth, don't you?" she argued. "Or is your idea of justice the goal, regardless of the truth?"

His hands went back into his pockets. "Good night, Ms. Baxter." He turned to go.

Just do it! "Your idol Wainwright is playing you."

He hesitated.

"He's using you to get to me." Her heart rammed mercilessly against her rib cage. "He's using me to take the fall for what he's done."

Tanner turned around slowly. His gaze collided with hers, and a shiver washed over her. Fury didn't begin to describe what she saw in his eyes.

"Donald Wainwright's reputation is impeccable. There is nothing you could say to make me believe he has any agenda other than the one he outlined when he assigned me this case."

Breathe. "Then you don't know your mentor quite as well as you think you do."

"Twenty-four hours," he reminded her as he started to go once more.

Say it! "Think about it, Tanner," she appealed, "they're all using you. Making promises, pumping your ego, and pretending the past never happened. Why now? Why you? There's a hidden agenda here and you're just too blind to see it. Or maybe you don't want to." Now she was really pissed off. Annette held her breath, forced her heart to slow. Lose control and you'll lose him.

He moved in, even nearer than before, lowering his voice to a whisper. "Give it up, Baxter. You can't win. I'm not going to stop until I've got you right where I want you."

He smelled like leather and wood, earthy and sexy. She hated herself for noticing . . . she hated herself even more for staring at his lips as he spoke. *Just tell him!*

She wet her lips and shifted her gaze to his. "Did Wainwright tell you about the meetings he arranged with Stokes before you were informed he'd been apprehended?"

Tanner's gaze tapered. That muscle flexing in his jaw temporarily distracted her. "You don't know what you're talking about."

Finish it. Survival. This was about survival. "August eighteenth." She grabbed back self-control and banished the crazy sensations he somehow provoked. "That's when Wainwright first met with Stokes in Mobile. The police picked him up three days later, after an anonymous tip."

One, two, three seconds elapsed with him staring at her before he reacted. "I don't believe you."

"You just don't see it yet." She held that cold stare, didn't flinch. "History never fails to repeat itself. The good old boys run the show. It doesn't matter where you live or what you do, there's always that handful of men who own your world. Wainwright is one of those men."

"What does that have to do with any of this?"

Was he finally going to listen? "Drake, Wainwright, Holderfield, and that's just the beginning," she said quickly. "They own this city. They make things happen. You're a part of their grand plan and you don't even know it."

Fury tightened his features. "Corruption happens wherever there's power. But I"—he banged his chest—"know these people. I trust them implicitly."

She was losing ground again. Fast. "I guess you'll just have to learn the truth too late. The same way you did about Holderfield's death."

"Talk is cheap, Ms. Baxter." His gaze cut straight through her, but she refused to flinch. "You want me to seriously consider this bullshit, give me something real to back it up."

There were so many things she could tell him. But first she had to know with complete certainty that she could trust him to do the right thing with the knowledge. She would give him this one thing . . . something, as she'd told him, so very personal. If he didn't let her down with that, she would give him more.

"Talk to Stokes." She took a breath, ignoring the alarms going off in her head. This was suicide. If he went to Wainwright, she would be dead before daylight. Tanner might be as well. "He'll confirm what I've told you."

Tanner didn't comment. Didn't say a damned word, just stared at her.

"Go see him," she pressed. "Then you'll know. Wainwright isn't who you think he is."

Annette stepped around Carson. Climbed the steps without looking back.

She'd played her trump card. Now it was up to him.

11:30 p.m.
Huntsville, Alabama
The Gentlemen's Club

The Gentlemen's Club was definitely misleading. There wasn't a gentleman in sight.

Annette took a seat at a table in the farthest, darkest corner and watched as the drunken men pawed at the women dancing on the catwalk above them.

Slick, swaying bodies, wearing little or nothing, teased the men. Gyrated and rotated evocatively.

Hungry fingers tucked money into thongs. Bulging eyes leered at the young, toned bodies.

A waitress, also scantily clad, sashayed up to Annette's table for her order.

"Vodka." She met the girl's world-weary gaze. "And a moment with that girl." She pointed to Candi Tate, the one swinging around a pole. Annette passed the waitress a one-hundred-dollar bill. "There'll be another just like that for her."

The girl glanced at the dancer. "It might be five minutes."

Annette nodded. "I can wait that long."

The smoke, the music, the catcalls, all reminded Annette far too much of the past. Her past. The feel of disgusting hands molesting her body . . . rutting cocks stabbing at her.

The memories sickened her.

The waitress returned with her drink, and Annette drank long and deep. To forget. To fortify herself. Something she hadn't needed to do in a long time.

Further proof that this whole mess was getting to her. She needed to reclaim the initiative. To do what she always did. Survive. Dominate. To not feel dirty.

Tanner was her only hope of surviving without a total loss. Hell, at this point she was reasonably certain she would be lucky to wake up each morning. The instant Wainwright got wind of what she'd done, she would be dead.

Tanner would go see Stokes. His own curiosity and that larger-than-life sense of justice would compel him to look into her accusations. She just hoped he would do it without informing his boss.

By the time she had finished her drink, Annette had relaxed a fraction.

A sweat-slickened Candi swayed provocatively over to Annette's table. "You have something for me?" the seventeen-year-old who passed herself off as twenty-one asked. The high of her drug of choice glimmered in her eyes.

"Yes." Annette pulled an envelope from her bag. Inside was twenty thousand dollars. "This is from your friend State Representative McGrath."

Surprise sobered Candi. She stared at the envelope a moment before picking it up. Her lips parted in another show of surprise as she felt its weight. "What's this for?" She carefully placed the envelope back on the table.

Annette leaned across the table. "Silence."

The girl's expression sharpened, turned cunning. "And if I don't want to be silent?"

Annette propped her elbows on the table and relaxed. "Then the authorities back home will learn what you do for a living when you visit your ailing aunt here in Huntsville every weekend."

Fear rounded the girl's eyes.

"The club owner won't be happy about being closed down for hiring a minor." Annette sighed. "The other dancers won't be happy about losing their jobs." She leaned closer still. "And your mother won't be too thrilled when child services comes to take away your three-year-old daughter. They frown on mothers who employ themselves by breaking the law."

Those big eyes blinked. "What I do when I'm away from home won't matter," she insisted in a show of courage.

"Maybe." Annette shrugged. "Maybe not. But I wonder if your mother will be able to retain custody with that drunken father of yours loitering around the house. Men like that pose a risk to small children, especially little girls. But then, you know that, don't you?"

Candi's mouth worked as if she might say something, but no words came out.

"I would suggest"—Annette straightened away from her—"that you forget all about the honorable Mr. McGrath." She tapped the envelope. "Take the money and start a real life for you and your daughter. Get a decent job."

Annette waited for her words to sink past any lingering drug haze, then asked, "Do we have an understanding?"

Candi nodded.

"Good." Annette reached for her bag. Placed a fifty on the table to cover her drink and a generous tip. "One last warning." She met the girl's stunned gaze. "Don't mess this up." She leaned across the table once more and whispered. "We know where you live."

Outside the club, Annette drew in a deep breath, let it out slowly. Some people would consider what she had just done unconscionable—blackmailing a seventeen-year-old girl. But Candi Tate was no typical teenager. Annette had seen the look in her eyes when the subject of money came up. She was no innocent. Not by a long shot.

There were times when diplomacy just didn't work.

"Whatever it takes," Annette mumbled. Live dirty, die dirty.

Those were the rules. Miss Tate might as well learn that lesson now. She had scored a fairly large payoff this time; next time she might not be so lucky.

Annette stalled as she approached her Lexus.

The air evacuated her lungs.

The smashed windshield and bashed-in headlights made her sick to her stomach, but it was the words scrawled in blood-red spray paint that chilled her to the bone.

DIE BITCH!

She spun around, searching the dimly lit parking area for any sign of threat.

No one. Nothing. Just a lot full of cars and trucks whose owners remained inside the low-rent establishment boozing it up and ogling half-naked women.

Annette's pulse raced, sending her heart into a frantic rhythm as her attention swung to her damaged car once more.

Oh, yeah. Time was very, very short.

If she didn't get Tanner on her team soon . . . the game—as he called it—would be over.

And they would both lose.

24

Sunday, September 12, 2:15 p.m.
Atmore, Alabama
Holman Prison

Carson measured the interview room one impatient stride at a time. Back and forth. He'd waited half an hour. Warden Fallon hadn't been too happy to hear from him, particularly on Sunday, but he hadn't dared refuse Carson's request. Having District Attorney Donald Wainwright as his mentor had its perks.

He'd gotten a call en route from Nashville PD. The lab had rushed the ballistics report on the slugs found in the body of his BMW. No matches. No witnesses had come forward. With no leads, there was little chance the incident would be solved.

The black sedan, possibly a vintage Crown Vic, hadn't shown up in his rearview mirror in the last twenty-four hours. Maybe he wasn't being followed.

But the shooting—that was a different story. That had to have been personal. No two ways about it. The BMW would be picked up for the necessary repairs. Meanwhile he was stuck with the rental.

Carson glanced at his watch. There was little if any possibility that he was going to get back to Birmingham in time for escorting Elizabeth to the Newton Ball. She would be disappointed. But he had to do this.

He let out a big breath. He had to prove Baxter was wrong.

The entire night before had been exhausted going over the Tanner case file. Relooking at reports Carson had already analyzed a hundred times. Every crime scene photo. Every lab report. Every damned newspaper clipping related to Stokes. Then he'd reviewed the Baxter/Fleming file again. Nothing. He'd learned absolutely nothing. All he had was her accusations. Accusations from a woman whose record made her an unreliable witness at best.

Carson had to be crazy even to consider her claim.

Agent Schaffer's suggestion that Wainwright wasn't being on the up-and-up with Carson echoed in his brain even now. Wainwright had explained away that allegation. Baxter's bullshit story in no way backed up Schaffer's theory. Carson had only followed through with this ridiculous idea of talking to Stokes to prove to Baxter once and for all that she had one choice. Take the deal.

Ask yourself if you'll ever really know what happened.

As certain as Carson was of his convictions . . . a part of him was absolutely terrified that she might be right to some degree. There were too many loose ends cropping up. Too many questions.

But . . . if he believed even part of what she suggested, then that meant everything he'd ever believed in was wrong.

The interview room door opened with a distinct clang, shattering the troubling thoughts. Two guards guided Joseph Stokes into the room.

"Stand back, Mr. Tanner, while we secure the prisoner."

Carson backed away a couple of steps. Stokes kept his head lowered in feigned humility while the guards seated him and secured his shackles to the eye hook in the concrete floor. The monster looked frail and vulnerable in the baggy prison jumpsuit. But Carson knew better.

"We'll be right outside, sir, if you need us," the same guard who'd first spoken explained.

"Thank you." Carson waited where he stood until the two had vacated the room and closed the door, leaving him alone with Stokes. As he approached the table Stokes raised his gaze to meet Carson's.

He grinned as triumphantly as if he'd just been informed his conviction had been reversed. "I knew you'd come." Laughter rumbled from his vile throat. "You can't stand not knowing everything."

Carson pulled out the chair on the opposite side of the table and lowered into it. "Rule number one," he said, his tone nonnegotiable, "no games. I want straight answers or this interview is over."

Stokes narrowed his gaze. "And what's in it for me?"

Carson had anticipated that reaction. "Warden Fallon has agreed to allow you one hour each week in the recreational activity of your choice."

The sick bastard's suspicion visibly mounted. "Why would he do that? He's sticking strictly to the agenda you sons of bitches requested. Complete isolation. One hour per day outside with no less than four guards shadowing my every step. I can't even look at any of the other inmates."

Carson barely restrained the need to smile. The piece of shit was already feeling the strain of perpetual isolation. According to the psychological profile on Stokes, he craved people. Needed social interaction to fuel his repulsive imagination. Isolation was the worst kind of punishment for him. It would slowly, surely push him over the edge into a place his contemptible ass wouldn't be able to claw out of.

"Let's not worry about the how or why," Carson said. "You cooperate with me and I'll see that you get what I promised."

That sadistic grin appeared again. "You love the power, don'tcha? Feels good. Makes you hungry for more."

Anger started to crowd in on Carson's composure. He pushed it aside, but not without difficulty. "Is that a yes?"

"You want to know what really happened to that fancy family of yours, is that it?"

Carson resisted the impulse to jump at that line of discussion. He had a carefully laid-out agenda. He'd analyzed forward and backward how he should go about this on the way here. He couldn't deviate. If he did, control would be up for grabs. He would not allow Stokes any measure of that control.

"District Attorney Wainwright visited you in Mobile once you were in custody. Do you remember the date?"

The suspicion was back. "I don't know. Maybe. What difference does that make? You could just ask your boss the answer to that one."

Carson ignored Stokes's comments. "You were taken into custody on August twenty-first. Is that when Wainwright visited you?"

Stokes shrugged his hunched shoulders. "Sounds about right. All that should be in the file."

"Are you afraid to answer the question?" Carson leaned forward. "Your deal can't be revoked now. There's nothing to fear."

Stokes leaned back in his seat and eyed Carson. "You think I'm afraid? Fuck, I ain't afraid of nothing." His disgusting laugh reverberated in the room. "Well, maybe I don't like the idea of dying, but you got no power over that. Like you said, the deal's done. You can't go changing your mind now."

"Then tell me the truth, Joseph." Carson swallowed back the bitter taste associated with calling the monster by his first name . . . as if they were friends.

Stokes smirked. "Personally, I don't think you really want to know the truth."

Let the games begin. Carson mimicked his opponent's posture, leaning back in his seat and pretending to be relaxed. Like two old buddies catching up. "If you don't tell me, then there's nothing I can do."

That beady gaze narrowed again. "What would you do?"

Carson shrugged. "I can't answer that without additional information." He placed his palms flat on the table between them and stared long and hard at the other man. "What do you want me to do?"

One corner of Stokes's mouth twitched. "Your big-shot boss is running for governor."

Carson nodded. "That's right."

That disgusting twitch evolved into a curling of lips. "He wants it bad, don't he?"

"He does."

"What if I told you, he's as crooked as a Georgia back road?"

"I wouldn't believe you." Carson paused. "Not without evidence," he qualified, more to see where the bastard was going with this than because he put an ounce of weight in the suggestion. Or Annette Baxter's. The fact that she had made statements word for word like those of Stokes told Carson the two had been in contact at some point since this nightmare started.

Stokes leaned forward another inch or two. "You want Wainwright's job."

Carson tensed. "I do."

Strangely, that answer seemed to appease the bastard. "You don't know for sure what happened that day, do you?"

A muscle in Carson's jaw jerked. He fought the reflex, but it continued. Tick. Tick. Tick. "No. I don't remember much before the police arrived." He'd drunk himself into oblivion with a bottle of Bacardi after the argument with his mother. A total alcohol blackout had never happened before . . . but that day it had.

Stokes chuckled. "Poor bastard. That's a hell of a thing to live with."

One. Two. Three. Four. Five . . . ten. Don't lose it. Stay cool. "It is."

More of the obscene chuckling. "I tell you what. You get me two hours a week with the others and I'll tell you what you've waited fifteen long years to hear."

Carson's tension rocketed to a higher level. "Done."

Stokes hesitated a moment as if he was skeptical. But then he spoke. "You'll make sure there's no backlash from that bastard Wainwright?"

"You have my word."

Stokes bent his head down to rub his nose. "First off," he began, "you weren't nowhere in the house when your people was butchered."

Carson flinched.

"I don't know where you was, mind you. 'Cept what the papers said about you being passed out drunk in your car at some teenage hangout."

A moment of silence . . . then two.

"Go on," Carson urged.

"But I know you didn't kill nobody."

"You confessed," Carson countered, a tight lid on half a dozen emotions whirling inside him. "I believe any question about who committed the murders has already been answered."

Stokes's expression literally beamed with anticipation. "I said what I was told to say."

Adrenaline fired in Carson's veins. "Who told you what to say?"

Stokes harrumphed. "Don't take no rocket scientist to figure that out."

Relax. Don't let him see any reaction. "Just answer the question."

"Your boss told me what to say. Who else?"

"Don't make statements you can't back up," Carson warned. He knew all too well how this guy liked manipulating, playing head games. He wasn't going to blindly believe anything Stokes related without indisputable evidence.

"Three days before the law picked me up on that anonymous tip, Wainwright came to see me."

The statement stunned Carson for about two seconds. The idea that Annette Baxter had told him to say this crossed Carson's mind. But he'd checked the visitors' log. Stokes had not received any visitors or telephone calls since his arrival. That, of course, didn't mean that Baxter hadn't figured out a way to work around the usual means of communication.

"How did Wainwright know where you were?" Not possible. Had to be bullshit. Carson didn't know why he even bothered to listen. He was a fool for even coming here.

"Let's just say he issued me an invitation."

Carson shook his head. "You're going to have to give me more than that."

"You know exactly what I mean. He held a bunch of press conferences and mentioned that I was the primary suspect. He offered that reward. I knew he was talking directly to me. I knew what he wanted. My mama didn't raise no fool."

"Your mother is the one who gave the police that anonymous tip." As difficult as it was to believe, even scum like Stokes had a mother, was once a child.

"She got the reward, too," Stokes reminded. "Wainwright promised she would."

"So you just called up Wainwright and said here I am, come see me?" This grew more ludicrous with each passing moment.

"That's about the size of it."

Carson shook his head. "There's no way you're going to convince me that he came to see you before you were in custody." Even as he said the words, something like dread had started a slow coil in his gut.

"He didn't . . . at first." Stokes reclined in his chair once more. "At first he sent this blond bitch to see me." He shuddered. "Cold as ice, that bitch. But damn, she was a looker. Never seen one so beautiful be so fucking cold."

Annette Baxter.

The dread mounted. "Do you recall her name?"

"Didn't give it to me. Said she was there representing Wainwright."

"And she offered you the deal?" Disbelief hit Carson square in the chest. This just couldn't be. Stokes had to be yanking his chain. But every instinct urged otherwise. Had him second-guessing all he thought he knew.

"She did. Told me what I had to say and how it would go down. Plum down to the part where I'd get to talk to you personally if that's what I wanted." He shrugged. "Wainwright didn't like that part much, but he agreed to it."

Baxter had definitely gotten to this guy somehow no matter what the visitors' log showed. She wanted Carson to believe Wainwright was dirty. Wainwright had protested the idea of Carson talking to Stokes from day one.

This game was over. Carson stood. "I'd say it's been nice, but that would be a lie."

Stokes lunged to his feet. Chains rattled. "You don't believe me."

"You would be right." Carson pushed in his chair. "You're a sick bastard, Stokes. And whatever Annette Baxter is up to, it's not going to work."

"So that's her name?" Stokes raised an eyebrow. "Annette Baxter?"

Carson scoffed. "Like you didn't know."

"I didn't." Stokes growled under his breath. "I'd damned sure like to take that apart, though, one frigid piece at a time."

Carson shook his head. "I'm finished playing games. Tell me the truth now or I'm out of here."

Stokes leaned as far across the table as his shackles would allow. "I'm telling you the truth. The woman came to me, told me what I had to do to get this deal, and then Wainwright showed up and confirmed it. Never saw her before or after and didn't know her name until you just said it."

"You can't substantiate your claim," Carson countered. "Your word isn't good enough." He was wasting time.

"Wainwright told me about the rings," Stokes blurted, his eyes wild with anticipation. "Wedding bands. Gold, I think."

Uncertainty started to tug at Carson's gut. He thought the rings were gold? "You don't remember the rings?"

Stokes looked around, obviously buying time. "I don't know. Wainwright told me but I forgot. Didn't matter. All I had to do was say I did it and sign the paper."

"You really expect me to take your word over Donald Wainwright's?" This was insane.

Stokes rolled his beady eyes. "That's just it. Wainwright ain't afraid of me talking now. He knows nobody'll believe me. Probably just have me killed by one of these other lifers. But you"—Stokes stuck his face as close to Carson's as his restraints would allow—"you know something ain't right. You feel it."

He was telling the truth. Carson's instincts literally hummed with that certainty. But . . . that wasn't possible. No way. "Why, for all intents and purposes, turn yourself in and confess to crimes you didn't commit?" he demanded, disgusted all over again that he was going along with this for even a second. "You'd been tied to all those other murders, but not to my family. No one knew where you were. What you're claiming doesn't make sense."

Fear or something on that order flickered in the maniac's eyes. "I got a problem with my ticker. No insurance, no decent treatment. I knew it was just a matter of time before I was caught anyways. I wanted it on my terms. Nine murders or twelve, what's the difference?" He blew out an indignant puff of air. "The sentence was gonna be the same. This way I got some say-so."

Carson flattened his palms on the table, anger at himself, at this low-life bastard erupting. "Wainwright did you a huge favor to get the truth. To solve two heinous crimes. Why would I put any stock in a word you say?"

The bastard threw back his head and howled that grotesque laugh of his. Then he leveled his gaze on Carson and stared right back. "You wouldn't be here otherwise." Amusement glittered in those beady eyes. "Trust your instincts, boy. That's the only way you'll ever find the truth."

Stokes was right about one thing: His own mother had tipped off the police, and she'd gotten the reward. But the other, the ludicrous claims against Wainwright, couldn't be substantiated.

"You'll see," Stokes hissed, "that I never laid eyes on your family until Wainwright showed me the crime scene photos." He nodded knowingly. "You check it out. You'll find out I'm right."

"So you never had the rings in your possession? Never even saw pictures?" Carson wasn't sure why that mattered, but somehow it did.

"Never saw that shit in no pictures or nothing. I'm telling you," Stokes repeated, "Wainwright told me what to say."

Carson held his spiteful gaze for a beat, then two, his lungs empty of oxygen, his heart stuck somewhere between beats. "I want the truth."

Stokes didn't waiver. "I don't know who killed your people, Tanner. The only thing I can tell you for sure is that I didn't."

25

3:20 p.m.

Carson Tanner had crossed the line.

Lynch watched as Tanner walked calmly to his vehicle, though Lynch felt certain there was nothing calm about the way he felt.

Wainwright would not be happy.

Lynch waited patiently until Tanner had driven through the prison gates. He started his Charger and followed the same route, maintaining a risk-free distance behind the vehicle.

He had known Carson Tanner was up to something more than investigating Annette Baxter.

The visit to Holman pretty much confirmed it.

Tanner was still looking into the murder of his folks.

Even after Stokes had confessed.

Even after he'd been warned.

Not good. Not good at all.

Lynch picked up speed as he turned onto the larger thoroughfare. He liked Carson Tanner, thought he was a good man. But this, this was bad, bad, bad.

This would get him killed.

26

8:45 p.m.
Reverend Abraham Woods Jr Boulevard, Birmingham
Birmingham Museum of Art

Elizabeth kept the requisite smile firmly in place as she moved about the room. She had shaken two hundred hands, exchanged summer vacation stories, and urged the wealthy of Birmingham to be generous.

The night was already a rousing success and it was scarcely half over.

Her parents were here. District Attorney and Mrs. Wainwright. Mayor and Mrs. Duke. The elite had turned out in droves. And she had done what she did best: persuaded them to part with their money.

Yet she was alone.

She paused. Allowed her thoughts to wander to Carson for the first time since her arrival. He'd promised to escort her tonight. But then, at seven, a mere half hour before he should have picked her up, he'd called to cancel. Something urgent related to his investigation had come up. Disappointing to say the least, but she chose to be understanding.

Perhaps this was why her mother took to her sickbed two or three times per week and Mrs. Wainwright took a bottle to bed each night.

The life of a politician's wife was not an easy one.

But it was her calling. Elizabeth smiled. She had loved Carson Tanner since she was five years old.

Their mothers had laughed and said that the two were destined to be together judging from their playground antics.

But that had been before. Everything had changed and her parents had forced her to go away.

Elizabeth's lips pressed together to restrain the fury that to this day arose at the very idea of what her parents had done. They'd had no right to interfere.

She took a deep breath, glanced around the crowded room. But she was over that now. She had her life back. Success belonged to her. The timing was right and nothing or no one would stop her from being with Carson this time. Her family would not stand in her way.

Carson still loved her. She was certain of that. The way he looked at her, held her when they hugged. Oh, yes, she was very certain.

"Elizabeth!"

She turned to greet Congressman Weller and his lovely wife. "Congressman Weller, what an honor to see you and Mrs. Weller here tonight."

Elizabeth and the congressman's wife shared the expected cheek-to-cheek hug; then the congressman took his turn. He always held on a little longer than necessary, crushing her into his chest. Elizabeth hated that about him. But he was a powerful man with deep, deep pockets, so she tolerated his annoying behavior.

"The fundraising work you're doing for the center is astounding," Weller beamed. "I can't tell you how much your efforts mean to us."

"Thank you so much. I'm pleased I can help."

"You look particularly stylish tonight," Mrs. Weller commented, drawing Elizabeth's attention to her and her somewhat dim smile and less-than-pleasant expression.

"Thank you." Elizabeth ignored the obviously insincere compliment. Older women always resented the younger ones. She supposed she would do the same one day. Or maybe the congressman's wife recognized her husband's fetish for young, firm breasts. Poor woman.

Elizabeth did feel especially elegant tonight. She had taken care with her attire. The strapless royal blue cocktail dress fit like a glove. The classic high-heeled, strappy sandals had been meticulously dyed to match. It had taken the cleaners twice to get it right. Too bad Carson wouldn't see her in this outfit.

"It appears the gala is going well," the congressman remarked, moving past his wife's lack of tact and prodding Elizabeth back into the conversation.

"Extremely well," Elizabeth parlayed. "I believe we'll double our expectations."

The congressman waved a finger at her. "Remind me to hire you as my campaign manager next go-round."

Elizabeth beamed but didn't respond to the offer. She liked her job. Already had a plan of her own that did not involve helping someone else attain his goals. "I hope you've already made your generous donation." Might as well get the conversation back on track.

"I'm headed that way now," Weller assured her.

Elizabeth ushered the couple to the table where pledges were being accepted before wandering through the crowd to mingle some more. Basically, that was her job this evening. See and be seen. Ensure everyone pledged a large donation.

She waved to her father, then headed for the bar. Her drink had gone flat. There was little time to indulge herself at these functions, but she kept a glass in hand throughout the night. When she did take the occasional sip she preferred the wine crisp.

Her mother's hasty retreat drew Elizabeth's attention to the other side of the room. What now? Dutifully she followed, leaving her unfinished drink on the nearest tray. Patricia Drake had escaped to the powder room. If her mother did anything to embarrass Elizabeth . . .

No. She wouldn't do that. Patricia Drake, of all people, understood the importance of appearances.

Elizabeth found her mother in the lobby of the ladies' room. When Patricia looked up she immediately tucked her cell phone away.

"What's wrong?" Elizabeth demanded a bit more sharply than she'd intended.

Patricia pushed her lips into a smile. "Why, nothing, dear." She stared into the full-length mirror and pretended to check her makeup and hair.

Who had she been speaking with? "Mother." Patricia didn't look at Elizabeth as she moved up beside her. "What's wrong?"

Patricia dropped her hands to her sides and met her daughter's gaze in the mirror. "I'm just disappointed Carson wasn't able to make it."

No. No. They weren't starting that again. "His work is important," Elizabeth said firmly. "He felt terrible having to let me down at the last minute. But"—she gave her mother a pointed look—"I understand that his obligation to the DA's Office has to come first."

Worry lined her mother's face. "Your father is certain this is a mistake, Elizabeth. There are things . . ." She let her words trail off with a dramatic sigh.

Rage boiled inside Elizabeth. "I don't want to hear it." She took a moment, carefully chose her next words. "Mother, do not allow Father to interfere. This is between me and Carson. I will not pay the price for Dane's mistakes. It's time you made your choice." She let her eyes reflect her determination. "Him or me? What's it going to be?"

Uncertainty flickered in her mother's green eyes before she blinked it away. "You're right, dear. You deserve whatever makes you happy." Patricia took her daughter's hand in hers. "I'll make sure your father does whatever necessary to help make that happen."

"Promise?" Elizabeth prodded.

Her mother smiled. "Promise."

Elizabeth escorted her mother back to where her father was deep into a legislative debate with the congressman. She kissed her mother's cheek before making her way to the bar as she'd intended. She really needed that wine now.

At the bar she waited patiently for her turn. An open bar ensured a line.

"My, my, I do believe you've outdone yourself tonight."

Elizabeth's gaze swung to the woman who had paused at the bar next to her.

Annette Baxter.

Elizabeth watched, appalled, as the woman sidled up next to her. She clamped her jaws together. Calmed the beastly anger that had roared before she could tame it. She prided herself on her ability to find the good in all. But somehow she just couldn't find anything good in Annette Baxter. Even before the investigation had begun, Elizabeth had known there was something inherently evil about the woman.

Baxter faked a smile. "Vodka on ice with lime," she said to the bartender.

Elizabeth blinked, appalled all over again. She had been here first. Holding back her impatience, she smiled for the harried bartender. "Raymond, a fresh Chardonnay when you have time, please."

Raymond gifted Elizabeth with a smile and a nod. She knew how to treat people. Just because someone worked in the service field didn't mean they were any less of a human being. Apparently Annette Baxter had forgotten what it felt like to *service* others. A righteous smile tugged at Elizabeth's mouth, but she held it back. She had manners.

Baxter accepted her drink without so much as a token word of gratitude and savored a long swallow.

Disgusting.

Elizabeth, conversely, said, "Thank you," before accepting hers.

Baxter turned to Elizabeth then and studied her a moment. No doubt noting how elegant Elizabeth looked compared with the skintight, floor-length sheath she wore.

The lavender color was pleasant enough, but the overall effect was tawdry to say the least.

"I see the senator's done a bang-up job of grooming you to replace him."

Elizabeth manufactured a credible smile. "I have no plans to seek a seat in the Senate."

Baxter mirrored that same feigned expression. "According to my sources, that is exactly the plan."

Fury continued to pound at Elizabeth's composure. She prayed Carson was able to send this harlot to prison for a very, very long time. "I'm afraid your sources have failed you this time, *Ms.* Baxter."

The woman had the gall to laugh. "I don't think so."

Elizabeth squared her shoulders and prepared to give her the brush-off. "It's a free country. You can think what you wish. Enjoy your evening."

When Elizabeth would have walked past her, Baxter said for her ears only, "Just remember, *Ms.* Drake, there will come a time when you need me."

Elizabeth glared at her. "I beg your pardon."

Baxter smirked. "I know everything about your family, Elizabeth. *Every little thing.*"

It took the full measure of strength Elizabeth possessed not to dash her wine in the woman's face. "Are you threatening me?"

That was exactly what it sounded like. A threat.

"Oh, no, no, no. I would never do that." Baxter looked directly into Elizabeth's eyes. "I'm in the business of keeping secrets, not divulging them." She dared to lay a hand on Elizabeth's arm. "Trust me, your secrets are safe with me. I would never let the senator down."

27

9:10 p.m.

Dane Drake sat on the edge of the bed. He was so screwed up he couldn't stand if he wanted to.

Not a problem. He wasn't going anywhere.

He would stay right here until the heat died down. Otherwise he'd probably end up dead.

Zac's dad was dead. Dane shuddered. Had to close his mouth to hold back the vomit.

According to the news he'd offed himself. The stupid report insisted it was because he couldn't get over his son's death. But Dane knew better. The old man had been stirring trouble and he'd gotten shut up once and for all.

Just like Dane would if he wasn't careful.

Annette had told him to lay low.

The connection she'd given him had taken care of his needs just like she said.

But he couldn't stay here forever.

He looked around the shabby room.

He couldn't go home.

He was fucked.

Flopping back onto the bed, he stared at the dingy ceiling. His life was shit. Nobody cared about him anymore. He was alone.

He closed his eyes and blocked images of the blood. Blocked the sound of the gun discharging. He'd been scared to death. Hadn't known what to do. So he'd called her, the one person he could count on.

Why the hell couldn't this just be over?

Why'd he have to mess up again?

This was all his fault.

But he could stop it.

Dane sat up. Scrubbed a hand over his face.

He knew how to fix this. All he had to do was make the call and make some long-overdue demands.

Dane fished in the pocket of his jeans for his cell phone. Hell yeah. He should have done this already. There was no reason for this bullshit to drag out. His father was a goddamned US senator. He should stop dicking around and get this taken care of. One call ought to do it.

When his father answered, Dane could hear the noise in the background. A party. His father was always at some fancy function or the other. That was all he cared about.

"I need your help, Dad."

The laughter and chatter on the other end of the line sounded farther and farther away. The senator was moving away from the crowd. Didn't want to talk to his dopehead son in front of people. Anger burned in Dane's belly. He'd always been a disappointment to his father. Always.

"This is not a good time to talk, son."

Of course not. Why the hell did he even bother calling him *son*?

"It's never a good time!" Fury throttled in his chest. "You never have time for me. I'm not good enough, right?" Dane shot to his feet, paced the dinky room. Let the bastard be up front with him for once in his big-deal life.

"We'll talk tomorrow," Randolph Drake insisted.

"No! We'll talk now!" Dane was sick of this shit. The truth was, if it weren't for his big-shot daddy he wouldn't be in this trouble now. His whole life was a direct result of his piece of shit father.

"Are you high?"

"You know what," Dane snarled, "damned straight I'm high. It's the only way I can live with myself." Emotion knotted in his gut. "It's the only way I can live with what you've made me."

The connection ended.

"Bastard!" Dane threw the phone across the room. His father didn't give one shit about him.

The rage he'd held at bay for most of life rocketed through him, shook him hard. Randolph Drake had it all. Everyone bowed to him. While his son paid the price.

Well, Dane had had enough.

He wasn't living with this anymore.

He was putting a stop to it tonight.

28

9:50 p.m.
3200 Fernway Road, Mountain Brook
Tanner Estate

Carson stood on the sidewalk and stared up at the house looming in the darkness.

He hadn't been back here in four years, three months, and two days.

He'd only been in the house three times since that night. October 10. *Fifteen years ago.*

He'd awakened in his car or at least he thought he had. Parts of that evening after the blackout remained sketchy. He had driven from the Mountain Brook Park. As best he could determine the time had been eight or eight thirty. The house had stood in the darkness, as it did now. Staggering up the steps that night, he had dropped his keys twice before reaching the front door.

He retraced those steps now. He was exhausted. He'd left Holman and driven around with no destination for a while. Then he'd come here. The entire trip, scenario after scenario had played out in his head. None made sense. None added up to a logical conclusion.

As he reached the door, he recalled that on October 10 fifteen years ago the front door had been unlocked. Ajar. The realization had confused him at the time, but then he'd still been fairly inebriated. Later, though, he had remembered vividly that the door was unlocked and partially open.

The investigating officers had suggested that he'd wanted to remember it that way.

Maybe he had.

Carson reached into his jacket pocket and removed his cell phone. He entered the number and waited for her to answer. "You know where I am. Meet me."

Tonight he would have the answers he needed. All of them.

From the only source willing to give him the truth, as ironic as it might be.

Annette Baxter.

How screwed up was that?

Carson slid the key that he still carried on his key ring into the lock and opened the door.

The musty odor of disuse filled his lungs. The house no longer smelled like home. New carpet and fresh paint a few months after the murders had stolen the stench of death as well as the scent of his family from the air.

A flip of a switch filled the entry hall with light. A maintenance crew kept the house in good order so that he didn't have to think about it or come here. The furnishings were free of dust, the floors pristine. No one would ever suspect that the worst a man could do had been carried out here against his family.

The sickening sensation that expanded in his chest whenever he thought of that day did so now, tightening his muscles, threatening to explode.

He stood at the bottom of the staircase, his left hand on the newel post. The police had dragged him away that night. For hours he had remained covered in his family's blood . . . until Senator Drake had taken him to his own home and helped him clean up. He'd dressed in Dane's clothes until his own could be salvaged from the wreckage that had been his life.

Carson took the first step upward. His shoes sank into the thick carpeting that lined the treads. His heart pounded. Sweat dampened his skin.

Another step, then another, until he reached the second-story landing.

He halted there. Couldn't force his feet to move.

If he turned to the right, he would find his bedroom and his sister's. Katie had been playing a game on her computer. To the left, at the other end of the hall, was his parents' suite of rooms. His mother had been resting after a particularly stressful day at her office. But her stress hadn't been the usual kind related to her patients. It had been about Carson.

I hate you! Do you hear me, Mother? I hate you!

Just before five that day he'd stormed into Dr. Olivia Tanner's office and confronted her right in front of her patient. He'd demanded to know why she and his father no longer wanted him to see Elizabeth . . . why they wanted to ship him off to a private academy for the next three years. He hadn't gotten any answers . . . only the hurt in his mother's eyes as he'd told her that he hated her.

She'd given so much of herself to her family, to her patients. Children had come from all over Alabama as well as the surrounding states to be treated by the very best child psychologist in the region.

His mother . . . and Carson had hurt her in the most devastating way a child could.

Then she was dead and there was nothing he could do to fix it . . . to make it right.

The pounding in Carson's chest accelerated until he could scarcely draw in a breath.

He turned right. Put one unsteady foot in front of the other until he reached the door to his sister's room. For an eternity he stood there and stared at the brass knob. Told his hand to reach out, take hold, and then turn. He trembled with the effort.

Finally he forced the movement, opened the door, and turned on the light.

For several seconds he kept his eyes shut tight. Knew the room by heart. Pink walls, white canopy bed. Loads of stuffed animals. Dance trophies.

When he opened his eyes he saw none of that.

He saw the blood.

On the bed.

On the floor.

And his sister's slim, pale body sprawled there. Her throat slit and gaping. Her eyes staring unseeing at the ceiling.

He remembered dropping to the floor beside her. Trying to wake her. Trying to stop the blood that had already emptied from her pale body and congealed.

Carson closed his eyes against the images. He tried to set aside the emotion and think of all that he had seen . . . besides the blood and the body. Nothing downstairs had been disturbed. The intruder had walked into the house and gone straight upstairs. The front door had evidently been unlocked since there had been no sign of forced entry.

No murder weapon. No prints. No usable evidence at all.

Fifteen years ago he had left his sister's room and rushed to the other end of the hall.

Carson followed that route slowly. His legs were heavy, his feet reluctant to make the journey. He'd fallen to his hands and knees midway. Puked. Sobbed. Screamed. Then he'd gotten up and run the rest of the way.

He stood at the closed door. Repeated the same ritual he'd gone through at his sister's. Inside the room looked exactly the same as before that horrific day. Then the memories rushed in, filling his vision with the gore that had surrounded his parents' bodies. His mother on the bed . . . his father close by on the floor.

Craig Tanner had been at his weekly poker game with his professional cronies, as Carson's mother had called them. Drake, Wainwright, Holderfield, Roper, the biggest investment banker in Birmingham, and Weller, then a state representative, now a US congressman. The police had concluded that Craig had arrived home in the midst of the killing frenzy. His death had been markedly more violent.

Already hysterical when he'd found his parents' bodies, Carson had moved from one to the other, uncertain how to help. Some part of his mind had known he could do nothing.

The next thing he remembered the police had arrived.

He didn't remember calling, but, according to the 9-1-1 recording, he had. Even now, a decade and a half later, the sound of his own voice haunted him.

Carson slumped against the door frame.

. . . I didn't do it.

If Stokes hadn't done this . . . hadn't killed Carson's family . . . then who?

29

Annette sat in her rented Jaguar. She refused to think about the message someone had left on her Lexus. Instead she stared at the mansion that had been home to Carson Tanner as a kid. His personal life had started and ended here. Last dinner with his family. Last birthday party. Last Christmas.

The end.

She knew enough about psychology to understand that he'd done exactly what she had. Tragedy and trauma had forced him to retreat into himself. Life as he knew it had stopped. Survival had become his focus. Carson Tanner had worked day and night, put all else aside to accomplish his goals. The typical Type A personality. Overachiever, perfectionist, determined to the point of obsession. He had deliberately built a wall between himself and the world. It was easier that way. Annette understood far more about him than he probably understood about himself.

And yet the one thing he craved above all else was someone to love him unconditionally . . . as his parents and sister had. The world had turned its back on him after their murders, and he had been struggling to win someone's—anyone's—approval ever since. The teenage kid who'd lost everything in one fatal blow still waited inside him, needy and vulnerable.

That was the only way in for Annette. The only way to win the man's support was to reach out to that boy. To touch that deeply buried weak spot. That was the thing. Every man had his weak spot, just like the mysterious G-spot for a woman. Some had several. But Carson Tanner had only one and that was physical intimacy.

Annette had found that spot.

Ordinarily she would see that as a success. But this time something had gone wrong. In touching his weakness she had discovered one of her own.

He made her feel things. Things she hadn't felt before. Ever.

That left her only one viable option for luring him to her side. Give him what he wanted above all else. The means to find the truth.

Risky on far too many levels.

But it was done.

Many of her clients called her an ice bitch. A she-devil. And numerous other things that should make her cringe. But none of those labels bothered her at all. She had worked hard to achieve that reputation. The persona was necessary in order to keep her clients in line.

To protect herself.

Yet she'd failed.

Steeling herself for confrontation, she emerged from the car. She reached back inside for the bag she'd brought along, then closed the door. He'd asked her to meet him here. He was probably watching for her arrival.

She eyed the Cadillac parked in front of his house. Where was his BMW? As she walked past the vehicle, she spotted the briefcase on the passenger seat. Definitely Carson Tanner's.

Annette smoothed her silk dress. As usual she had dressed to accomplish her mission. A daring lavender sheath that fit her body as closely as a second layer of skin. The matching stilettos clicked on the steps as she ascended to the front entrance. She took a breath, then rang the bell.

The door opened and Carson Tanner filled the opening. He'd shed his jacket and tie. She unexpectedly enjoyed the bare skin revealed by the three buttons he'd unfastened on his shirt. Stop. This was business.

She held up the bag. "I brought you a birthday gift." It was his birthday, after all. "Is the Cadillac a birthday present to yourself?"

He stared at her, his dark eyes dull. His jaw was set in hard, grim lines. That he hadn't shaved today lent a dangerous air to his brooding good looks. She felt an uncharacteristic stirring of longing. She couldn't remember the last time she'd experienced that sensation. Wished she didn't now.

"Someone used my BMW for target practice," he said flatly. "But never mind that, I want the truth."

"What do you mean target practice?" Someone had shot at him?

"I. Want. The. Truth," he repeated.

She shook off her confusion. *Focus, Annette.* Stokes had obviously told him. Good. Maybe. That Tanner continued to stand there, staring, without saying more or asking her inside made her uneasy. There was nothing in her research that suggested he couldn't handle this. She thought of his uncle and his mental illness. No, Carson Tanner had shown no signs of having any issues—period. He could handle the truth. And then he would owe her. She needed him.

"I take it Stokes confirmed my story."

Tanner drew the door open wider and took a step back, an unspoken invitation for her to come inside.

She crossed the threshold, goose bumps rising on her skin at the idea of the heinous murders that had taken place in this house. Though the thud of the door closing behind her didn't echo, there was an eerie emptiness about the place.

Annette offered the bag again. "Happy birthday."

He ignored the gift. "Let me be clear about this," he said, his voice low, grim. The simmering resignation so uncharacteristic. "I trust Donald Wainwright unconditionally. I have no reason whatsoever to trust you. As far as your claims against Wainwright go, there's just one itty-bitty sticking point. What could he have possibly hoped to gain? Where's his motive?"

Annette stared into that severe expression. "Maybe it's not about him . . . maybe he's covering for a friend. Protecting someone." Secrets were a valuable commodity. She hoped Tanner appreciated what she was giving up.

"No more conjecture. I want the truth. Now."

She settled the bag on the floor. "All right." Shock quaked through her. She'd said the words before her brain had analyzed exactly what she intended to do.

No more pretending she could reach him without going the full distance. She had to give him what he wanted . . . or risk losing everything. If anyone knew about his trip to Holman, she was screwed anyway. Wainwright would know she'd advised him to talk to Stokes. Wainwright was nobody's fool.

No more protecting anyone. But Paula and herself.

Considering the incident with the scissors at the center, being stalked by a black sedan, Jazel's death, the use of Tanner's vehicle for target practice and then the vandalism to her own, there was no denying they were in serious danger.

Annette's gaze locked with his. "Last Sunday evening around six I received a call from Dane."

"Dane Drake?"

She nodded. That he was so surprised told her he knew nothing about what she did for men like Drake. "He had a problem." Deep breath. Just do it. "I've taken care of problems for the senator related to his son before."

"What kind of problems?"

"Dane has a way of getting himself into fixes," she explained. "Usually drug related. He gets involved with the wrong people. Runs up debts he can't pay. Things like that."

"And you do what?"

Tanner's penetrating stare made her uncomfortable. She'd faced far more powerful men than him. That he could make her doubt herself disturbed her.

"I resolve the problem. The fix usually involves paying someone to keep their mouth shut. Simple stuff really." She wet her lips. "Until last Sunday."

"Exactly what happened last Sunday?"

She had his full attention now. His eyes were no longer listless and dull. His gaze was sharp, searching. His posture was different, too. Battle ready.

"Dane called me to pick him up at a friend's."

"Does this friend have a name?"

For the first time in a really long time she hesitated. "Zac Holderfield."

She watched that realization creep over his features. "What're you telling me?" Fury kindled in those dark depths now.

"That Dane killed him." Before he could demand more answers, she added, "But it was self-defense. The gun belonged to Zac. He and Dane had a disagreement over a business deal. There was a struggle, and you can imagine the rest."

"You helped him dispose of the body."

She nodded. Her heart pounded so hard she couldn't draw in a decent breath. What she had to tell him next could go either way, for her or against her.

He closed his eyes. "Jesus Christ." His eyes flew open once more. "Why the hell didn't he just call the police?"

"Think about it. He's Senator Randolph Drake's son. Men like Drake don't abide scandal."

"What did you do with the weapon?"

"Wiped it." She swallowed with difficulty. "Tossed it."

He planted his hands on his hips and started pacing. "You understand that I have to report this."

"There's more."

He glared at her.

"I . . . I have to show you."

"What the hell are you talking about?"

"You're going to have to trust me, Tanner." She was doing all the giving here; the least he could do was cooperate.

His hesitation dragged on a moment or two too long. "This had better be good."

She was fairly certain that nothing about it was good.

"We'll need flashlights and a shovel."

Carson drove. Baxter provided the directions. He wasn't about to let her out of his sight after what she'd told him. Dammit. Dane had monumentally screwed up this time. The senator would be devastated by this turn for the worst.

Dane's actions had actually killed two people. The idea that Dwight Holderfield had committed suicide because of his son's death . . . and Dane was responsible. Damn.

"Turn here."

He took the right. It wasn't that far from the house where he'd grown up. A side road that as best he recalled was a dead end only a couple hundred feet into the woods. Deeper into those woods was a path that led from his house to Elizabeth's. A slight detour from that same path ended at his uncle's shack. They'd used those paths all the time when Carson was a kid.

Where the hell was Baxter taking him? Were there more skeletons he hadn't heard about yet?

He wasn't sure he wanted the answer to that question.

They emerged from the car and gathered the flashlights and shovel.

"It's this way."

He followed her through the dense underbrush until they found the mostly overgrown path of his childhood adventures in these woods. He didn't ask any questions. She didn't offer any information. Something about coming here made him uneasy and, for the first time since the night his family was murdered, he felt afraid.

Baxter stopped suddenly. "Give me a minute."

While he watched, she walked in circles scanning the ground with the aid of the flashlight. Eventually she appeared to find what she was looking for. Essentially, a spot like a hundred others.

Baxter dropped to her knees and brushed the leaves away. He crouched beside her. Using the shovel he'd brought along, she dug fiercely for a minute or so until he heard the sound of metal on metal. Then she pushed aside the dirt to uncover what she was looking for.

A Beanee Weenee can. What the hell?

She tossed the shovel aside, squeezed the end of the can open, then looked up at him. "Hold out your hands."

A smart man would have declined, but instinct urged him to do as she said. He cupped his hands, and she poured the contents of the can into them.

It wasn't until she aimed the beam of her flashlight on the items that he realized what he was holding.

Wedding bands.

Some instinct he wouldn't name had him searching the inside of one for an inscription . . . *Forever, Olivia.*

The missing wedding bands . . . the symbols of his parents' commitment to each other.

Stokes had been telling the truth . . . he wasn't the one.

The drive back to Tanner's childhood home was made in silence. Annette wanted to explain but she couldn't find the words.

When he parked next to her rental, he finally spoke. "How did Dane come into possession of these items?"

"That I can't answer. But I can tell you that once he'd realized what he'd done, trading the rings for drugs, he was frantic to get them back. He and Zac argued, and Zac ended up dead." God, she was suddenly so tired. "You have to remember he was pretty messed up when I got to him."

"So he told you nothing."

She stared at him through the darkness of the car's interior. "He kept mumbling something about keeping secrets too long. That it needed to be over."

Tanner stared forward. "Go home. We'll talk about this tomorrow."

That icy monotone was back. She didn't like it. "What're you going to do?"

He turned to her then. "I honestly don't know."

She'd given him what she had in the hope of winning his support, but that was all she could do. The rest he had to come to terms with himself.

"You know what they'll do to me if they find out what I've told you. Someone shot at you and trashed my Lexus. I'm reasonably sure we're both already on someone's kill list." She didn't mention Jazel or the black sedan.

"Go home," he said without looking at her. "Stay there."

Annette got out of the Cadillac and climbed into the Jaguar. Tomorrow. She had lived with this for days now. She'd done all she could. Running out on Paula was out of the question. There was only one choice: Trust Carson Tanner.

She drove away. Carson Tanner was a victim of the same people his family had been. Whatever had happened, whoever had ultimately been responsible, she hoped he realized that he was now in the same dangerous situation she was. The questions he wanted answers to had not changed. But he did have physical evidence now. He could get to the truth. Like her, it was going to cost him everything.

At this rate, she was dead anyway. If she could ensure Paula's safety, maybe Annette could finish this without Tanner. She could go to the feds, spill her guts on Wainwright and the others. Could she trust the feds to protect her sister?

If she went that route, maybe Tanner could still salvage his life.

Her fingers tightened on the steering wheel. She had no business feeling sorry for him. Yet she did.

Was there even a way to stop this lunge toward disaster without additional risk to him?

She needed to think. There was one other route she could try. One man powerful enough to end this. After all . . . it began with him. But *he* wasn't the kind of man to whom one could pay an unannounced visit. She had to be absolutely certain she wanted to make this move. It was a no-turning-back decision. Once she crossed that line it was done.

Frankly, it was the only feasible strategy she had left outside trusting the feds. Considering the feds were two-and-zero when it came to protecting their witnesses, that option would definitely be a last resort.

Annette dug around in her bag for her cell phone, then put through the call to the private line *he* used for business of this nature.

"We have to talk," she said without preamble. He needed to understand she wasn't taking no for an answer. "Face-to-face."

"We have nothing to talk about."

His response was exactly what she had anticipated.

"You know better than that," she argued. He could pretend all he wanted, just not with her.

He then explained all the risks involved with such a meeting. Risks to her.

"I know the risks." Did he think her a fool? "I also know the risk to you if you refuse to see me." She paused for effect. "Is now a good time?"

Checkmate. She had threatened the most powerful man in Birmingham. The silence that followed warned that he was not pleased by her defiance.

All her past experience combined could not have prepared her for what he said next.

"It's over. I know what you've done."

What did she do now? She tossed the phone onto the passenger seat.

Fear tightened like a noose around her neck. If *he* knew what she'd done . . . there was little chance she or Tanner would survive the night, much less the day to come. Allowing the two of them to live with this knowledge, no matter how incomplete, would be too risky.

Did she dare go to the feds? If she confronted him in person, would it change things?

Headlights appeared in her rearview mirror, seizing her attention.

Her breath caught. *Stay calm.* Could be nobody, just another car on the road. She should have just gone home like Tanner said. Stayed there and waited for his decision.

Her fingers tightened on the steering wheel. Focus. Drive.

The twin beams behind her grew larger, loomed closer in the mirror.

Go faster. Her foot flexed, pressed harder on the accelerator. The Jaguar zoomed forward. She took the curves way faster than she should, struggled to keep the vehicle on the crooked road.

When she dared to glance in her mirror again the headlights were gone.

Her heart seemingly stilled in her chest.

Where . . . ?

Panic shot through her veins.

Right on her bumper. So close the headlights were no longer visible in her rearview mirror.

Her right foot rammed harder against the accelerator. *Shit!*

The first nudge against her rear bumper propelled her forward, sent the Jaguar careening into the other lane. Annette fought the momentum, wrestled the vehicle back under control and into the proper side of the yellow line.

She couldn't risk taking a hand off the wheel to reach for her cell phone. Why the hell hadn't she allowed her cell to connect with the damned car? *Shit!* She had to go faster. Had to lose him.

She thought of Jazel . . . was this what she'd . . .

Annette's breath stalled in her lungs.

A second set of headlights appeared in her side mirror.

What the hell?

The car right on her bumper backed off, but not far.

The new arrival roared up right next to the car following her. Moved in so close she couldn't believe the two didn't collide.

Her attention snapped forward. Adrenaline burned through her limbs as she barely made the next dangerously sharp bend in the road. By the time she could breathe again and risk another lingering look in her rearview mirror the road behind her was black.

Both cars had disappeared.

30

He brought the Charger to a screeching halt.

Bill Lynch bailed out the driver's side door and raced around the hood. He peered through the darkness, could see the headlamps of the black sedan deep in the ravine below. He'd forced the car off the road at eighty miles per hour. The larger trees had stopped its momentum.

Flashlight in hand, he cautiously picked his way downward. He considered that this particular Mountain Brook road could be treacherous. If a vehicle left the pavement and plunged into the wooded hillside, it might not be found for days. It had happened before. Several larger saplings had lost the battle with this particular vehicle.

He'd seen this same vehicle lurking around Carson Tanner's location once or twice before. Bill had run the license plate, which was assigned to a local car dealership. The dealership claimed the sedan didn't belong to them and had no idea until the manager looked that the license plate in question was missing.

Palming his service weapon, Bill slowly approached the vehicle. The headlights still blared into the darkness of the woods. Too bad the driver evidently hadn't been wearing his seat belt, since his head and upper torso protruded through the windshield. The air bag had done its job as the vehicle plowed down a couple of smaller trees, but the final impact had come after it deflated. Too much blood to ID the victim visually.

Bill put his unneeded weapon away before kicking in the driver's side window. He reached inside, shut off the headlamps; then fished the wallet from the driver's hip pocket. Took a look at the man's driver's license beneath the flashlight's beam.

Well, that was a surprise.

He knew the guy all right.

Bill pocketed the wallet. He would dispose of it later. Might as well buy some time before the driver was ID'd. The fewer complications at this point, the better.

The whole situation was escalating out of control far too fast.

Bill took one last look at the victim. If he wasn't dead already, he would be soon considering the visible injuries. Oh well, he deserved to die.

You just couldn't get reliable help anymore.

31

11:59 p.m.
3202 Fernway Road, Mountain Brook
Drake Estate

Senator Randolph Drake dropped the receiver back into its cradle. She would never let it go with a simple phone call. She would demand that face-to-face showdown.

He should have anticipated that. He had not.

She was far more resourceful than he had realized.

Far more determined.

Deep down he had known she would never cooperate, even when faced with her own downfall.

No, she was made of sturdier stuff than that.

Forged in fire, that one.

He had hoped she would disappear. Take her money and run.

But she had surprised him.

He reached for a cigar, clipped it, then lit the tip. He savored the taste, considered a nice Scotch or perhaps bourbon.

Not now. He would need to attend to this fully before allowing the indulgence. Things were getting too out of hand. Steps had to be taken to end this once and for all. The knob on the door of his study turned.

That hadn't taken long. She must have been very close when she had called.

Damned ballsy of her to come to his home and walk in uninvited. Thankfully, he was alone. He had dismissed the household staff early tonight and his wife had gone to bed as soon as they arrived home from the Newton Ball.

Very well. The sooner this business was finished, the better.

The door opened and he looked up. The identity of his visitor startled him.

"I want this to end."

He blinked, confused. What in the world? His gaze dropped from hers to the gun in her hand. *A gun?*

"What are you doing?" He started to push out of his chair, but the weapon waved threateningly. He frowned, couldn't quite wrap his mind around the reality of what his eyes were seeing. Then he understood. *She knows.* "You understand what has to be done," he explained patiently. "It's the only way."

"You swore you wouldn't let this happen again." The business end of the weapon leveled on him. "But you lied."

He shook his head, held out his hands imploringly. "You mustn't interfere. You have to trust me."

"No."

He saw the movement—a ruthless finger depressed the trigger. He felt the impact of the bullet as it tore into the center of his chest.

He stared down at the round hole in the starched white shirt he wore. Watched the blood pulsing forth.

Funny, he hadn't heard the explosion of the bullet bursting from the barrel. What was that old saying from his military days?

If you don't hear the shot, you're dead already.

32

Monday, September 13, 2:10 a.m.
2402 Altadena Road, Vestavia
Tanner Residence

His cell phone buzzed.

Carson roused slowly.

He sat up, scrubbed a hand over his face. He glanced around his living room half expecting to see Annette Baxter. Then he remembered that he'd sent her home.

His bleary gaze settled on the items lying on the coffee table right in front of him. His gut tightened.

The wedding rings . . . golden bands his parents had never taken off.

Images of Annette Baxter on her knees digging frantically in the dirt rushed one after the other through his head.

Dane must have murdered his family. That was the only way he could have had the rings in his possession. He had definitely murdered Zac Holderfield. Carson closed his eyes, rubbed the images away. Was it possible Wainwright had known? Had covered for Dane? Flashbacks from his visit to Stokes had bile churning in Carson's gut.

His cell buzzed again.

He squinted at the digital clock on the cable box next to the television: 2:15 a.m.

Where the hell was his cell phone? He felt in his pockets. Didn't find it. Shit.

Another buzz.

He found it between the couch cushions. "Tanner."

"Carson."

"Elizabeth?" He blinked, considered the quavering sound of her voice. "What's wrong?" Panic seized him. If something had happened to Dane . . . Carson might never get to the truth.

"It's Daddy." A low keening sound echoed across the line. "He's dead, Carson. Somebody killed him." Elizabeth lapsed into sobs.

Carson shot to his feet, stumbled slightly. "Where are you?"

"Home. We're home. Daddy's in his study."

"I'll be right there." He shoved the cell into his trouser pocket. Rubbed his eyes again. What the hell?

Senator Drake was dead? Murdered?

Why hadn't Wainwright or someone called him?

Shit!

Carson lurched around the room until he found his jacket. Searched the pockets to ensure the fob to the Cadillac was there, then headed for the garage.

Drake was a powerful man. He no doubt had numerous enemies. A man didn't get that high up the food chain without stepping on a few heads and over a few bodies along the way.

Was it possible the bodies of Carson's slain family had been among them?

The mere thought made his stomach churn.

3:05 a.m.
3202 Fernway Road, Mountain Brook
Drake Estate

There was no strobe of blue lights at the scene.

Out of respect for the family, the police as well as the ME had left their vehicles dark.

The first person to approach Carson as he emerged from his rented car was Special Agent Kim Schaffer. She held a large cup of coffee in her hand.

"I'm surprised you weren't the first one here," she said bluntly.

At the moment Carson didn't give one damn what she meant by that remark. "Just got the call or I would have been. Have you been inside?" He slammed the car door shut and headed in the direction of the house.

Schaffer followed, nodding. "It's pretty straightforward. One shot to the chest."

"Anyone else at home at the time of the shooting?"

"The wife. The gunshot woke her out of a dead sleep."

An eerie sensation of déjà vu enveloped him as he considered that just down the road, around the curve and beyond the woods, his childhood home stood in the darkness. Fifteen years ago a too-similar scene had played out there. Only the lights announcing that a crime had taken place had been blazing. Shock and pain had radiated through the community whose worst fear at the time had been break-ins. Murder had never happened in the elite hilltop neighborhood. People who lived here had been above that sort of viciousness.

Until then.

And now. The other questions reeled through his mind, but he couldn't think about that right now. Right now Elizabeth and Patricia needed him. When he was through here, he would find Dane and have some answers.

The Baxter/Fleming case would just have to wait. That his never-fail reputation was on the line no longer mattered. All that mattered was the truth.

When did you stop caring about the truth?

The words rang all too true. He'd been so focused on finding justice for so long; was it possible that he had started overlooking the truth? Settling for something else?

Winning? Building his career?

He shook off the disturbing thoughts. Now wasn't the time.

Yellow crime scene tape had been draped around the perimeter of the property, reminding all who arrived that their presence was welcome by invitation only.

He couldn't get right with the idea that no one from the office or from the local police had called him to the scene.

Senator Drake's murder scene.

Unbelievable.

Drake had protected him when there had been no one else.

His family and the Drake family had been like extensions of each other until the night of the murders.

Before everything changed.

Before murder had altered the landscape of this exclusive area where the rich and powerful lived.

He would find Dane. He would have the truth.

Carson ID'd himself for the officers maintaining the security of the scene. Both knew him, but he showed his identification as a matter of procedure. At the front door he slipped on shoe covers and latex gloves, as did Schaffer.

Inside, Schaffer led him to Drake's study, as if Carson didn't know the way. He let her. Truth was, a fog had descended and wrapped itself around his brain. The same questions kept churning inside that haze.

Who would murder the senator? Had Drake known that his son had the wedding bands belonging to Carson's parents? Had he used his position to cover up whatever Dane had done?

Did his murder have anything to do with keeping that truth a secret?

The door to the study was open and evidence technicians flowed in and out doing their business. Carson stopped at the door and allowed his gaze to travel over the scene.

Drake sat slumped back in the chair behind his desk. Blood had soaked his shirtfront, splattered on the papers on his desk. Definitely hadn't been suicide. Whoever had fired the shot had clearly done so from across the desk.

Carson pushed away the emotion of seeing the man he had admired most of life dead . . . murdered. Banished the other questions. Focused on the details. Nothing in the study appeared to be disturbed. Two evidence technicians were going over the room; another was taking the necessary photographs. The ME and his assistants were preparing to take possession of the body.

"First officer on the scene said there was no sign of forced entry."

Carson glanced at Schaffer. "Any witnesses come forward?" If they were lucky, one of the neighbors had seen or heard something.

"Nope. Officers are canvassing the neighborhood but there's nothing yet."

Damn.

Not exactly surprising on second thought since the homes were spaced generously apart, the smallest of the properties being approximately five acres. Most of the estates were densely wooded, the only clearings the lawns surrounding the enormous homes.

"What about security?" Though the neighborhood wasn't gated, there was a roaming security guard on duty at all times. The guard on duty fifteen years ago had been the one to arrive on the scene first. Carson had questioned him time and again over the past five years, even after he'd gone into the assisted living facility. He hadn't seen or heard anything prior to discovering Carson at the scene with his slaughtered family.

Schaffer pulled a pad from her jacket pocket and consulted her notes. "The security guard on duty saw no unfamiliar vehicles tonight, none at all in fact. Heard no gunshot or other out-of-place noises."

Carson heaved a weary sigh. Just like fifteen years ago. The only thing the guard on duty at that time had eventually heard was Carson screaming. According to that guard, he'd heard the screaming as he'd driven past the property that night; then, as he'd turned into the drive, he'd gotten a glimpse of a bloody Caucasian male running into the house. Though Carson had no recall, traumatic amnesia aggravated by intoxication, the detectives assigned to the case had assumed that he had run out to his car with the idea of going for help but then been unable to find his keys. Those keys had been found on the floor in his sister's room. The interior of the car had been bloody where it appeared he had searched for them: the ignition, the seats, the console.

This was going to be fifteen years ago all over again.

Carson could feel it in his gut. No usable evidence. No witnesses. Nothing. Except questions.

He needed to find Elizabeth and her mother. They would need his support. He had to be there for them the same way the senator had been there for him, even if only for that short little while until he was cleared of suspicion. Had the senator known even then that his own son might be involved?

Carson cleared his mind again and walked out of the study, headed for the family room. Two police officers loitered there but no one else.

"You looking for the family, Mr. Tanner?"

Carson didn't recognize the officer who spoke. "Yes."

The cop jerked his head to the left. "Kitchen."

"Thanks." Carson headed that way.

He braced for the devastation. Though Elizabeth was far older than he had been when he'd lost his family, her grief would be profound. He couldn't imagine what Patricia would do now. She did everything with her husband. Was always at his side.

"Carson!"

Elizabeth ran into his arms. Carson hugged her until her sobs against his shoulder subsided. Guilt that he could feel the lust he did for Annette Baxter assaulted him. He had no right to hold a woman like Elizabeth in his arms, to wish for things to be the way they used to be . . . when he had given in to his lust with Annette Baxter.

"I'm so sorry," he murmured. Sorry for far more than she knew.

She peered up at him. "Who would do this?"

Determination charged through him. "I'm damned sure going to find out."

Elizabeth hugged him again, hugged with all her might. "I know you will, Carson."

It wasn't until he looked up from Elizabeth to check on her mother sitting at the table that he took note of all those present in the room. Wainwright he had fully expected to see. He sat next to Patricia, one arm around her shoulders. The next face stopped him cold.

Keller Luttrell.

What the hell was he doing here? Having him step in for Carson on the Holderfield case was one thing, but this was Senator Drake. No one but Carson should be on this case.

"Carson."

His attention swung to Wainwright, who had vacated his seat next to Patricia. Elizabeth pulled out of Carson's arms and hurried to take that empty place. The two women fell into each other's arms, sobbing and whispering softly.

Why hadn't Wainwright called him?

"Let's step into the family room," Wainwright suggested quietly.

Carson pushed aside his frustration with his mentor. "I need a moment." He walked to where Patricia and Elizabeth sat, knelt next to the woman who had just lost her husband, and took her hand. "If there is anything at all I can do, please just say the word."

Patricia smiled vacantly, her expression frozen with pain. "Thank you for coming, Carson. The senator loved you like a son." Her lips quivered. "He would want you to take care of Elizabeth and me."

Could Carson be wrong about the senator? There was always the possibility he had known nothing about his son's illegal activities. Someone else could have been covering for Dane. The thought hardened inside Carson. "You can count on it." He hugged Patricia, let her feel his determination, then, knowing Wainwright was waiting, made his excuses and followed his mentor to the family room. Wainwright asked the two officers there to give them some privacy.

Carson asked the question twisting in his chest. "Why didn't you call me?" He was in charge of investigating high-profile cases. "What else have you been keeping from me?" he tacked on before good sense could override his frustration.

"This case—"

"Don't even think about using the it's-too-personal excuse," Carson warned. "Yes, it's personal. But that won't stop me from getting the job done. You"—he glared at the man he had admired for so very long—"haven't been straightforward with me and I deserve to know why."

It was during the moment of silence that followed that Carson recognized the cool fury on his boss's face. Carson wasn't the only one pissed off.

"I'm going to let that one go," Wainwright said, "but you'd better watch yourself and listen up. No, you won't be conducting this investigation or prosecuting the case. In fact, as of right now you're on administrative leave."

Shock radiated through Carson. That was the last thing he had expected to hear.

"What're you talking about? What administrative leave?" That action was reserved for staff members suspected of wrongdoing. Unethical behavior and the like.

Cold, clinical dread dropped like a rock in his gut even before Wainwright spoke.

"Warden Fallon finally reached me after church last night. He wanted to know why you were questioning Stokes and requesting special privileges for that monster. I can't imagine what possessed you to go down there, much less any of the rest. But I can tell you that this action was the final straw as far as I'm concerned. Since I turned the Baxter case over to you, your behavior has become erratic and completely unacceptable."

"Wait." No way. He didn't understand. "I—"

Wainwright held up a hand to stop his protests. "Until I can conduct a thorough investigation into your activities during the past few days, you will remain on administrative leave. If I discover that you have, in fact, conducted yourself in any unbecoming manner that could jeopardize the case, your career in my office will be over."

Carson felt as if he were in a tunnel, in the dark, watching this scene play out far, far away in the light at the very end. This could not be happening. He was the one who had unanswered questions.

"There's been some misunderstanding," Carson offered. He needed to explain, but the words eluded him. Images of him and Annette Baxter in any one of a dozen compromising positions kept bombarding his brain. But that didn't matter . . . what mattered was the truth. What Stokes had told him. Carson had the rings taken from his family's murder scene. There were reasons he'd acted irrationally.

"There is no misunderstanding," Wainwright countered. "I know about your personal involvement with Annette Baxter." He shook his head, his expression heavy with regret. "That was the last thing I expected from you, Carson."

Carson wanted to argue, but he had no case. He couldn't excuse that one. He had royally screwed up. But there was more. Didn't matter. Nothing he said to Wainwright now would matter. Carson had to have a rock-solid case. Innuendo and theory weren't enough.

"I don't know what's going on inside your head," Wainwright went on, "but you are systematically destroying everything you've worked for."

The man Carson had admired, had striven to be like, walked out. Left him standing alone with nothing but the echo of his disapproval and disappointment.

The worst part was that Carson couldn't deny a single one of his charges.

Two days ago this moment would have devastated him. Right now it just pissed him off. If Wainwright had anything to do with the cover-up of his family's real killer, the self-righteous DA would be eating his words.

Until Carson had a case, at least a credible scenario to build on, he would take this crap from his boss.

Still, if the feds hadn't picked up his lapses into stupidity with Baxter in their surveillance, how the hell had Wainwright figured it out?

Luttrell walked past the door, didn't so much as spare Carson a glance.

Fury discharged inside Carson. He stormed after his so-called friend. He caught up with him right before he entered the primary crime scene.

"We need to talk." Carson manacled his arm and dragged him toward the front parlor.

"Hey. Hey!" Luttrell jerked free of his hold. "What the hell is with you, man?"

Carson shoved the door closed and rounded on his colleague. "Why don't you tell me?"

Luttrell shrugged. "Wainwright's pissed."

"No shit." Carson raked a hand through his hair. "What the hell happened?"

Luttrell clapped him on the shoulder. "I'd love to hold your hand and talk you through this, bro, but I have a homicide to investigate." He started to walk past Carson but hesitated. "Take my advice, Carson."

Carson turned his head to look his old friend in the eye.

"Next time you get the highest profile case in Birmingham history handed to you on a silver platter, don't fuck the prime suspect."

Luttrell left him standing there with that profound truth echoing around him. *Don't trust anyone.*

Carson was a fool. Problem was, he was the only one who hadn't seen it until now.

He stormed outside, ripped the shoe covers off. He was through being a fool. Whatever the hell was going on, he would get to the bottom of it. To hell with the consequences.

"Glad I caught you before you got away."

Carson stopped halfway down the steps and whipped around. "What do you want?" He didn't give a damn about appearances any longer. He couldn't trust Schaffer any more than he could anyone else.

She inclined her head and studied him quizzically. "Sounds like you've got one hell of a burr under your saddle."

He took a breath. Told himself to calm down. This wasn't the way to get the job done. He had to be cool to out-manipulate the people he now recognized as his enemies. "What's up, Agent Schaffer?"

The agent stopped on the step above him. "You asked me to look into that lead about the sister."

Carson's instincts stood at attention. "Did you find something?" He wasn't sure how relevant that was at this point, but what the hell?

"Annette Baxter doesn't have a sister." Schaffer sat down on the step and tugged the shoe covers off her colorful boots. "No known siblings."

That just meant Delta Faye Cornelius had made a mistake. Carson no longer gave a shit. He had other leads to explore. And he wasn't sharing any of it with Schaffer or anyone else.

"But," Schaffer said when her gaze met his once more, "Baxter's mother had a sister who died. She had a daughter, one Paula Aldridge. Thirty-four years old. She ended up in an institution when she was a kid. Autistic."

Anticipation revved Carson's determination. This could be the relative Cornelius remembered. "Where is she now?"

"Aldridge fell off the radar about nine years ago." Schaffer smiled. "Now this," she went on, "is the interesting part. Before she disappeared she was signed out of the state institution by someone we both know and despise."

Carson smiled back. "Annette Baxter."

"You got it." Schaffer pushed to her feet. "Question is, what'd she do with Aldridge? If she cares enough about the woman to provide care for her, sounds like we might have an angle to develop. If Baxter wants to protect her cousin by hanging onto her freedom, she might just be willing to make a deal."

"Yeah." Carson's tone lacked the enthusiasm Schaffer had expected judging by the way her expression changed from victorious to questioning.

He shouldn't have second thoughts about using Baxter. The idea that she was a victim . . . had been her whole life . . . didn't excuse who she was now.

He kicked aside the soft emotions that would interfere in what he had to do. Baxter, Dane, none of them would get in his way. Whatever the cost, he was going to find the truth.

"I have to get to the office," he said to Schaffer to escape any more questions.

"Same here." She started down the steps, then hesitated. "I couldn't help overhearing what went down between you and Wainwright."

Anger flared. Yeah, he'd bet she couldn't have helped it. "Don't worry about it. We'll work it out."

He took the final step, headed for his car.

"I'm not worried about Wainwright," Schaffer called after him.

Carson paused, looked back at her.

"It's you I'm worried about," she said frankly. "I'm pretty sure you should watch your back."

33

4:30 a.m.
Birmingham
The Tramont

At this point Carson didn't care if the FBI noted his activities in its surveillance. He was fucked anyway.

He pushed the button for the penthouse once, twice, three times before she answered.

"Yes?"

"Open the door." He didn't give a damn about etiquette or any damned thing else right now. His career was in the toilet and he wanted answers.

He wanted whatever she knew about his family and Dane. He wanted the truth and by God she was going to help him find it.

A distinct buzz sounded, and he opened the door. He strode to the elevator and selected the top floor. The slight delay in the car's upward movement told him her approval had been necessary. During the ride to the penthouse he worked to slow his breathing and regain some of his composure. Didn't help. He only got angrier.

Drake had lied to him. Wainwright had used him.

He couldn't trust any damned body. But her. And that was the most unfortunate part of all. He had absolutely no reason to trust anything she said.

Yet she was his only chance at solving this screwed-up mess.

The doors slid open. Annette Baxter stood in the marble-floored entry hall waiting, a rose-colored robe hugging her body. Her posture and resolute expression told him she was prepared for battle.

"You finally understand what you're up against. That's why you're back here. Wainwright's dirty. And you need my help." She held his furious gaze without so much as a blink. "You need *me*."

"Senator Drake is dead."

Several seconds lapsed before she schooled her expression to the one of aloof indifference she usually wore. Just enough time for him to see the shock and confusion. Maybe the ice bitch wasn't so untouchable after all. The guilt that pricked him was immediately overridden by his fury.

"When did this happen?" She tightened the sash on her robe. Shivered visibly . . . maybe purposely to garner his sympathy. Didn't work.

"Around midnight." A new sense of determination and outrage kindled inside him. "Did you kill him?" He actually hadn't considered that until this moment. But they had parted ways hours ago. She could have gone to Drake and . . . he had to be out of his mind. He was grasping at straws.

"What?" Her horror looked genuine enough. "I drove straight here like you said. I've been here ever since." She took a breath, looked away a moment as if she had something to hide. "How was he murdered?"

Carson shrugged. Tried to calm his raging fury. Whether he was mad solely at her or at Wainwright or both, Carson couldn't say. But she was right about one thing, he needed her. "How would I know specifics? I've been put on administrative leave."

More of that atypical emotion flashed across her face before the mask of apathy resumed. "Answer the damned question! Shot? Stabbed? What?"

Carson set his hands on his hips to keep from reaching out and shaking the hell out of her. Besides Stokes, she was the only person who had ever made him want to resort to violence. She was the bane of his existence. Had launched his whole world into chaos. He forced himself to calm down enough to speak rationally. "Someone shot him in the chest."

She blinked. "In his home?"

The fury burst into uncontrollable flames. "Ding. Ding. Ding. Give the girl a prize." Why the hell was he standing here answering her questions? He had questions! He had an agenda, and wasting time wasn't on it.

"Wait." A frown marred that smooth, flawless complexion. "I don't understand. Why are you on administrative leave?"

He charged forward the three steps that stood between them. "For fucking you."

A sound somewhere deeper in the residence reverberated. A cell phone?

She looked startled by the interruption. "I have to take that."

He started to argue but didn't. Instead, he trailed after her like a freaking lost puppy, standing outside the door of her bedroom while she took the call. A "yes" then an "I'll be right there" punctuated the lengthy pauses.

She hit the disconnect button and turned to him. "I have to get dressed."

"Just so you know," he said as she attempted to close the door in his face, "wherever you're going, I'm going with you. I'm not—"

"Look," she shouted, "you're not the only one in danger here. Some . . ." She shook her head, threw up her hands. "Somebody has been following me. Tried to run me off the road after I left your house."

"What're you talking about?" He absolutely refused to acknowledge the protective instincts that immediately surfaced.

"I have to get dressed." She slammed the door in his face.

Goddammit! He wasn't letting her out of his sight until he had some answers. Until he got what he wanted. Fleming. Dane. And the truth about Wainwright and Stokes. And any damned thing else she was hiding.

6:00 a.m.
Montevallo Road, Birmingham
Magnolia Hills Individualized Care Center

At least now he knew where Paula Aldridge had vanished to.

She used the name *Paula Anderson.* Both the nurse and the doctor who had spoken to Annette had called her Ms. Anderson.

Again he had to admit that Baxter was good. Too damned good. But as good as she was, he felt confident that she couldn't have faked her surprise about Drake's murder.

She wasn't the one . . .

He had to have answers. Carson would not stop until he knew who had murdered his family. Why Holderfield and Drake were dead. And why, apparently, the same black sedan that had been tailing him was tailing Annette, too. It would seem they both had stepped into something over their heads.

The position of Jefferson County District Attorney was likely out the window along with his position as DDA, but he no longer cared. The truth was all that mattered.

Paula Anderson sat in her bed, her knees curled against her chest, and rocked back and forth. The doctor had said that the outburst was so violent, heavy tranquilizers were required. Paula would slip into unconsciousness anytime now. Neither the doctor nor the nurse seemed able to explain what had set off the outburst. One minute she was watching television in her room, the next she was attempting to tear it apart.

Annette cradled her cousin, whom she referred to as her sister, against her breast now as the woman lost the battle with the drugs. The emotion on Annette's face startled Carson. Love, fear, desperation. She stroked her sister's stubby hair, whispered softly to her. There was no question just how much she loved Paula.

How was it possible for a woman so cold to feel that depth of emotion?

Carson surveyed the well-appointed room. Individualized care like this wasn't cheap. He imagined it cost Annette a sizable fortune to keep her sister in this facility.

Objectivity, no sympathy. He had to keep that in mind.

When Paula had settled into that drug-induced coma, Annette kissed her forehead one last time then led the way out of the room. She closed the door and sagged against it.

"Twice in one week." She closed her eyes. "Why are they hurting her like this?"

Before Carson could ask her whom she meant by *they,* the doctor and nurse approached, both wearing solemn faces.

"Ms. Anderson," the doctor began, "I'm not sure how to explain this . . ."

Annette straightened from the door. "What? You said you had no idea what prompted the outburst."

The nurse and the doctor exchanged a look.

Carson tensed. There was definitely something amiss here.

But it wasn't his problem. Baxter was his problem. The whole fucking world outside this ritzy institution was his problem right now.

He didn't give one shit about her sister or cousin or whatever. He and Annette weren't friends. They were enemies.

And he wasn't backing off until he had her right where he wanted her—in an interview room spilling her guts.

Carson stopped himself. What the hell was happening to him? He was losing it completely. Since when did he blow off basic human compassion?

"Ma'am," the nurse said, her hands wrung together in front of her, "when the episode began, Gage, one of the attendants, and I were the first to get to the room."

"Go on," Baxter urged.

"We managed to get Paula back into bed and restrained." The nurse swallowed hard. "That's when I saw them."

"Saw who?" Baxter looked from the nurse to the doctor and back.

"Little white mice." The nurse cleared her throat. "The kind you buy at the pet store."

Stark confusion and something very much like fear claimed Baxter's face. "There were mice in Paula's room?"

The doctor looked mortified. "We don't know how it happened. It's simply unbelievable. This is one of the cleanest, most tightly run centers in the country. I simply have no explanation for how this happened."

Baxter's expression went from confused to resigned. "I'm sure you do all you can to prevent any sort of incident like this."

The doctor tucked the file she held beneath her arm. "Considering this is the second incident in the past week involving your sister, I believe we can safely say there is a problem."

"What kind of problem?" Baxter asked cautiously, uncertainty in her tone as well as her eyes.

The doctor sent the nurse back to her station and kept her voice discreetly low. "We operate a fine institution here. As you know, we pride ourselves on the safety and excellent care we can provide for our patients. But no one who isn't authorized to be here gets in. And certainly no one but authorized personnel is allowed to view a patient's file. That leaves me with only one plausible explanation. Someone on staff. I can assure you there will be an in-depth investigation."

"In the meanwhile," Baxter suggested as the uncertainty in her eyes solidified into determination, "I would appreciate it if you added a round-the-clock security detail to her room. I'm extremely worried about her safety."

"Of course." The doctor gave a firm nod. "We've already discussed that step. Paula will be monitored twenty-four seven. At no additional expense to you, of course, until we've cleared up this . . . situation."

Baxter thanked the doctor, then led the way out of the building and back to where they had parked. It wasn't until they were off the property and barreling down the road in her rented car that her ice bitch persona fell back into place. "Paula has had the occasional episode related to her autism. She would be uncooperative or mildly violent . . . but this is different." She shook her head. "There's no question in my mind now."

"What does that mean?" Carson prodded. He was completely lost here.

"It's Wainwright," she said. "I know it's him."

Although Carson was doubting his mentor for the first time, he couldn't deny that, but this—he didn't see how Wainwright could have anything to do with this. "We didn't know you had any living relatives."

She slammed on the brakes, sending the car skidding to a sidelong halt in the middle of the road. "I'm telling you," she shouted, "he's dirty. He's behind this, Tanner. Accept it."

Carson twisted to stare directly at her. Any softer emotions he'd stupidly felt vanished. "Why the hell would he or anyone else do *this?* How is putting mice in some poor woman's bed relevant to anything?"

Long pulse-pounding seconds of silence elapsed. Baxter moistened her lips, then met his gaze. "Because the last foster home we shared had rats. Hundreds. They'd come out at night after we went to bed. We woke up dozens of times with one or more crawling around in bed with us. They terrorized Paula. Somehow he found out." She exhaled a weary breath. "All her worst fears are annotated in her file, along with any allergies and medications." Her eyes searched Carson's. "Don't you see? All these years, there's never been a staff member who wanted to hurt Paula. And now, suddenly, someone is out to get her. Think! Where's the motive?"

Carson hardened his heart. Refused to feel that pang of sympathy stabbing at his gut. "Life sucks sometimes. Having to share a home with a few rats isn't the worst that could have happened to either of you." As soon as the words were out of his mouth he wanted to take them back. He knew that wasn't the worst . . . what the hell was wrong with him?

Annette stared coldly at him. "You're right. It wasn't. The worst was the sexual abuse." She let off the brake and maneuvered the car back into its proper lane.

"That's"—he took a breath—"unfortunate." No sympathy. No goddamned sympathy. This couldn't be about how devastating her life had been. It had to be about the truth. They were wasting time.

"Like you said," she snapped without taking her gaze off the road, "life sucks sometimes."

It took every ounce of willpower he possessed not to reach out to her on some level. No one deserved to be treated as she and Paula had been. Whatever Annette Baxter had done, she hadn't deserved that. But he couldn't let her see sympathy, not even for a second. If she suspected he was sympathetic, he would lose the upper hand. He had to be in charge here.

Stick with the facts.

"How long have you been taking care of her?" He hadn't meant to ask that question. He'd intended to shift the conversation back to Wainwright and Dane. But sitting here in the dark with her, her fear and desperation palpable, he couldn't not ask. The dim lighting from the dash allowed him to see more than he needed to see of her pain.

She stared off into that darkness that enveloped them like a blanket. "Since we were kids."

"I'm sure it's been difficult." Dammit. He had to get back on track . . . but then maybe he could use this moment to get what he needed. He rolled that idea over. Catching Annette Baxter in a vulnerable place had so far been impossible. He had the perfect opportunity now.

Dear God.

Was he really that desperate?

Yes.

"Sometimes it's hard," she murmured, almost to herself, "sometimes it's harder. But it's what I have to do."

He rested his head against the seat. He understood that all too well. Memories of dozens of incidents with his uncle invaded. *Don't get distracted. Focus.* "I need answers. Or things are going to get a hell of a lot harder for both of us." He squashed the persistent sympathy.

She glanced at him, allowed him to see the full depth of the desperation in her eyes. "I'll tell you what I'm going to give you, Mr. Hotshot DDA."

Anticipation had him sitting up straighter. Now maybe they were going to get somewhere that would make a difference. He studied her profile, noted the rigid set of those delicate muscles. "What's that?"

She glanced at him again. "Everything you need to nail those bastards." Her full attention returned to the street. "Every damned one of them."

34

8:30 a.m.
Birmingham
The Tramont

Annette dropped her keys and purse on the table as she passed through her entry hall but didn't slow her pace until she'd reached the gallery. Her favorite room. She surveyed the elegant pieces of sculpture and the edgy contemporary works of art. This was her trophy room. The room that said she had reached that prestigious place she had fought tooth and nail to attain.

Under normal circumstances she felt safe here. Calm. But not today.

The emotions roiling inside her wouldn't slow down, wouldn't allow her to think logically.

Fury whipped, stinging, raging, joining the frenzy. There was absolutely no question now. Someone knew about Paula. Annette had to protect her. Even if it meant throwing away everything she had achieved. Even if it meant taking her sister and running.

She had money tucked away for emergencies. Not as much as she would like, but it would just have to be enough. On the drive back from the center she'd made up her mind. She would give Carson Tanner everything he needed to make them all pay. And then she and Paula would disappear.

It was the only way.

Annette was out of options. It was only a matter of time before Drake's murder, as well as Zac Holderfield's, was blamed on her. She understood this with complete certainty.

Carson deserved to know the truth. He would just have to deal with taking down the men he'd thought were his friends. He needed to know they would sacrifice him in a heartbeat. Coping with the knowledge was his problem, not hers.

And for some completely foolish reason, she wanted him to have closure. She wanted him to win.

She turned to face the man who lingered near the door. "Where do you want me to begin?"

His gaze held hers, and she didn't miss the tiniest hint of vulnerability there.

She couldn't say when she'd decided to think of him by his first name. Not something she did on a routine basis. Too familiar. Nor had she consciously made the decision to give him the answers he so wanted at any particular point before now. But after seeing Paula, helpless and innocent, tortured, Annette understood that the decision was made. This had to be done.

The game was over.

"The beginning is usually the best place." He strode to the sleek white sofa and settled there, his attention fixed fully on her. He looked tired. Tired and damaged. Just as she was damaged. Funny, he had no idea how much they had in common.

The beginning. Wow. That was a place she didn't visit often. Too painful. Too scary. She almost laughed at herself. She was thirty years old; how could the past still frighten her? Maybe because she knew the only difference between being there and being here was money.

Lots and lots of money.

And a safe place for Paula.

That would be the hardest part to fix.

But Annette would get the job done. Somehow.

Her gaze locked on the man once more. His beard shadowed jaw distracted her. Shouldn't have. But did. His hair was tousled from running his fingers through it too many times. Made hers twitch with the need to do the same. Not normal for her. And definitely not smart. Not smart at all.

"I was born in Knoxville." She folded her arms over her chest. More something to do with her hands than anything else. "Katrina, Kat Baxter, my mother—"

"Was a prostitute," Carson interrupted. "I already know that part."

She shook her head. He had no idea. "You know what's in your file. You don't have the whole story."

He waved a hand for her to continue.

A good stiff drink would be nice about now but she resisted. She needed her head clear for this. In her profession, giving up a secret, even one, was career suicide. If not personal suicide. There were people who would kill to uncover what she knew . . . and many more who would do the same to ensure it stayed buried.

"My mother had a sister. Her name was Margaret. She died of cancer when I was five. My mother took in her only child, a girl three years older than me."

"Paula," he guessed. "The feds figured out that part after I tracked down Delta Faye Cornelius."

Fear snaked around Annette's heart. "They know about Paula?" God, she had to move quickly.

He held up a hand. "They know she exists. They don't know where she is. Delta Faye couldn't even remember her name."

Annette relaxed a little. At least that was something. But someone damned sure knew.

Then a frown worried her brow. "You located Delta Faye?" Annette hadn't thought of her in years. Was surprised the woman was still alive. Annette wasn't particularly worried about whom she might have talked to besides Carson. The one thing Delta Faye had always been especially good at was keeping secrets. If she'd decided to talk to Carson, she had trusted him on some level. That was the first rule of the street. You didn't talk to anyone you didn't trust, and you trusted almost no one.

"She sends her regards," Carson offered.

Annette nodded. It felt weird hearing about someone from that time in her life. Back to her story. "There was never any official documentation. Paula, being low-functioning autistic, wouldn't have really benefited from school, so that was pointless. Mainly, Kat was afraid they would take both of us away from her if she was . . . investigated."

So long ago. Feelings Annette would rather not have felt again in this lifetime flooded her. She hated her past.

"For a few years things were okay. I took care of Paula while Kat worked at night. In the daytime I went to school and Paula stayed locked in our room." That alone should have been a red flag regarding Kat's mothering skills, but Annette had been a kid. Seemed normal to her. "Then Reggie came into the picture."

Carson's eyebrows raised. "Reggie?"

"A new boyfriend." Annette walked to the wall of windows that overlooked what the city called progress to the natural beauty beyond. She loved this view; nature's struggle against progress reminded her of her own struggle to survive. "My father abandoned us when I was four. Kat had managed a boyfriend here and there but nothing that lasted more than a week or so. But"—Annette forced back the worst of the memories—"Reggie was different. He liked the idea of having Kat and two other sources of entertainment."

"You were what by this time? Eight? Nine?" His tone oozed with disgust.

"Ten, but that didn't matter." The burn in her eyes infuriated her all the more. She hardened her heart in defiance of her own emotions. "It was what he did to Paula that killed me, inch by inch. When I turned twelve and worked up the nerve to fight him, he started to beat me. And Paula. He knew I'd do anything to keep him from hurting her." Annette hugged herself tightly. She had never told anyone this part.

"Our neighbor was a big gardener. She left her pruning shears outside one day and I took them. Hid them under my pillow."

Judging by Carson's expression, he knew where this was going.

"One night . . . I couldn't take it anymore. So I pulled out the pruning shears with the intention of killing him but he knocked them out of my hand." She closed her eyes, shuddered at the memories. "Paula picked them up and . . ." Annette swallowed the bitter taste of misery. "While he was fucking me, she buried them in his back."

But it was her mother's reaction that finished destroying any emotion Annette had still possessed. "Kat came into the room, saw what we'd done, and took us to the Walmart and left us there. We never saw her again."

"That's when you went into the foster care system."

She nodded. Annette would never forget that day. "At first they put Paula and me together, but the family couldn't handle her autism and the idea that she could be violent. The police had ruled Reggie's death self-defense, but still, Paula wasn't wanted. So they moved us to another family." She made a sound; it wasn't pleasant. "The man of the house took up right where Reggie had left off."

"Damn."

Annette kept her gaze focused out the window. She didn't want to see the sympathy in his eyes. Hearing it overtake his voice was bad enough. She didn't need any damned body's sympathy.

"Eventually Paula became a burden once more and she was taken away. Only this time, I was forced to stay. They put my sister in a state mental hospital." She turned to face Carson then. "Have you ever had the occasion to visit one of those lovely places?"

He nodded, his expression grave.

"I was thirteen. There was nothing I could do." She stared out the window once more. "But time passed and I grew up. Grew wiser and braver. Finally, the day I turned sixteen, I left for good. I'd run away several times, but I'd gotten caught and dragged back each time. No one believed my rape accusations. A little mock investigation would be carried out and I'd end up back with the same family or someplace new that was just as bad or worse. But they didn't find me that last time. I'd learned all the right tricks. I headed for Nashville and all the glamour Music City had to offer."

"You turned tricks on the street to survive."

She flinched, didn't mean to. He would have known that part. At eighteen she'd gotten busted. Twice. "Yes."

Then she'd gotten lucky.

"When I was nineteen I hooked up with a more high-class operation." She'd been one of the lucky ones. She had stayed clear of drugs and worked hard to keep herself in shape. "I was working a private party at a hotel and I caught the eye of Otis Fleming."

"The perfect alliance," Carson said, sarcasm squeezing out the sympathy. "You kept his sex life interesting and he taught you how to utilize your assets."

Fury crammed against her sternum. She pivoted on her heel and glared at him. "You don't know anything about our relationship."

Another of those condescending waves of his hand. "Enlighten me."

"Otis is like a father to me. He took me in, taught me how to play with the big boys. How to make myself invaluable. He showed me how to save Paula and myself." She owed him everything.

Annette worked at calming her emotions before continuing. Emotions worked against one at a time like this. She had to be cool, in control.

"I'm curious." Carson propped his right ankle on his left knee. "What exactly did he teach you?"

"How to glean and use knowledge." She faced him now. "How to take a problem and solve it and gain money and markers doing so. He introduced me to Birmingham society, helped me become indispensable to those whose most valuable asset is reputation. I am particularly adept at reversing a situation with the utmost discretion."

He scrutinized her as if she were a bug he intended to squash beneath his shoe with his next move.

"Give me an example."

"Dr. Dwight Holderfield." His name came to mind first considering recent events. "If you recall, a couple of years ago there was a situation at his hospital. A patient died and the family sued the hospital and the physician involved; they even threatened to sue Holderfield personally."

"The suit as well as the investigation were dropped," he acknowledged. "The hospital evidently settled. Keller Luttrell was involved on some level with the investigation."

Oh, yes, Keller Luttrell. A man she despised, but who easily gave in to temptation when it came to money and glory. "Yes. Holderfield's career was on the line. Apparently, he altered the records to cover the physician's mistake. He was terrified that the tampering would be discovered."

The look on Carson's face told her he found the whole scenario disgusting. "You bribed the family into dropping the allegations."

She shook her head. "Not exactly."

His gaze narrowed. "How *exactly* did you make that happen?"

"Simple." She returned that unmerciful stare. "I dug up the deceased's one skeleton in the closet and threatened to expose his drug use, which could have contributed to his unexpected demise considering he hadn't given the hospital that information."

"So you dug up all this dirt and used it to manipulate the grieving family."

The renewed disgust in his tone kick-started her defense mode. "Your sins always find you out." One of her foster mothers had loved spouting Bible verses. Made her feel superior.

"Nice."

Annette knew that tone. To him she was plain white trash, evil, capable of anything. Who was he to throw stones? He and his kind helped killers get away with murder all the time. All in the name of the law. Screw him.

She walked over to the chair facing the sofa, facing him, and took a seat. She smoothed a hand over her navy skirt. She'd chosen it because it was short and sexy yet still gave off a professional air. The white blouse was skintight and buttoned to the throat. She had needed that facade. If it kept him off balance, all the better. "I do what I have to do. We're alike in that way, I believe."

The comment hit its mark. His expression darkened. "Fundraising is your cover."

"Yes. But, as you are well aware, I'm very, very good at ferreting money from the most unlikely places." Knowledge was power. Her clients never failed to give generously. Elizabeth Drake had nothing on her.

"You apparently have some powerful clients."

"Name any powerful man in this city and I can put a checkmark on my client list." She looked Carson dead in the eye. "Including Drake and Wainwright."

He still didn't completely believe her; that was obvious. But he would. Very soon now.

"What did you mean, money and *markers*?"

That part had been her idea. Otis had praised her for her resourcefulness. A man like Otis Fleming didn't offer praise often. "I never complete a service for cash only. There's always a marker held in reserve. If I ever need a favor, the marker is called in."

She lifted her chin in defiance of what he no doubt thought of that. "I never fail a client and a client never fails me," she explained. "We have an unwritten contract, and we never meet in person after the initial contact. There is never any link between us. I take clients by personal recommendation only." Any meetings after the first one were accomplished by videoconference via a secure link. The link bounced all over the internet. No one could trace it back to her.

"What exactly," Carson ventured, "is the nature of your business relationship with Fleming?"

That one was simple. "I provide him with secrets he can use to manipulate the cooperation of those who might otherwise block his efforts. Occasionally I resolve a problem with someone who isn't cooperating, but that doesn't happen often. I don't have direct access to his business dealings, but I've made it a point to know what he does."

"And what does he do?"

"He facilitates the needs of anyone who offers the right price." Her pulse sped up at the idea of what she was about to say. "If someone in, say, New York needs something to happen in Birmingham, Otis arranges it. If a drug cartel needs to extend territory, he buys the real estate, if you know what I mean. Men like Wainwright and Drake protect him." Protected her until recently.

Carson sat forward, bracing his forearms on his knees. "I'm not saying I believe Drake and Wainwright are or were involved with you or Fleming, but we'll set that aside for the moment. Right now, I need the whole truth about what happened to my family. And how Dane plays into it." He leveled a look at her that related just how serious he was. Dead serious. "If you lie to me on any part, no matter how insignificant, I will see that you spend the rest of your life in prison—your mentor, too."

Poor Carson. He still thought truth and justice would prevail. *Not a snowball's chance in hell.* No matter. She had made her decision. Let him believe what he would.

"Fair enough." She crossed one leg over the other and, to her dismay, savored the way his gaze followed the movement. "As I told you, August fifteenth Wainwright hired me to carry a proposition to Stokes. I was to inform him of the deal and then ensure that he was persuaded. Not that it was difficult. Stokes knew he would get caught sooner rather than later and that he would most likely be facing a death sentence. Under the circumstances, my job was simple. He added only one addendum to the proposal."

"Five minutes alone with me."

She nodded.

Carson considered that a moment then said, "But you can't prove Wainwright hired you to go to Stokes."

"Other than Stokes's word," she admitted, "which you heard for yourself. Then on the eighteenth, Wainwright visited him personally. There is, of course, no proof of that, either."

"You suggested that Wainwright went to these lengths to cover up the identity of the real murderer?"

"He wanted to help Senator Drake. Dane is his only son, after all, and the senator has taken extreme and numerous measures to keep him out of trouble. I can vouch for that."

Carson shot to his feet. "That's certainly convenient." He threaded his fingers through that thick dark hair. Her fingers curled into balls of resistance. "The man is dead. He can't exactly defend himself."

"What it is," she said, "is damned lucky for you that I'm willing to give you this information at all." Fury tightened her lips. She forced it back. "This is what I do. It's all I have, and the steps I've taken in the past twenty-four hours end it. I'll have nothing."

He braced his hands on his hips and turned another of those fierce glares on her. "All right, for the sake of argument, let's go with that. Why would Dane murder my family?"

"I can't answer that question. I can't even guarantee that he did. I only know that he had the rings in his possession and was frantic to get them back. He kept going on about some secret."

That muscle that always ticked in Carson's jaw when his tension rose had started its rhythmic flexing.

"But Dane knows something about it," she considered aloud. "And if he didn't kill them, someone he knows did, otherwise he wouldn't have had the rings."

Carson lowered back onto the sofa.

Annette concentrated hard to remember all Dane had said that night. She'd been focused on hiding the rings and getting rid of the murder weapon and the body. "He mentioned something about all the blood and how he hadn't wanted to hurt anyone."

Yeah, that was right. He kept repeating the same things over and over.

"But . . . that doesn't mean he killed anyone," Carson argued. "There was a lot of talk and media pandemonium about the . . . scene. The drugs probably skewed his memory." The low monotone of Carson's voice told her he was fighting a serious case of denial.

"There were things"—Annette hesitated, trying to think exactly how Dane had worded his delirious ranting—"he knew that no one except someone who'd been on the scene could have known."

"Such as."

"Something about placement of the bodies." Annette shook her head. "That's about all he said that was in any way sensible."

Carson closed his eyes against the images no doubt evoked in his mind.

"You know he had a drug problem even then," she suggested, hoping to lessen the blow somewhat.

Those dark eyes opened and his pained gaze fixed on hers. "Drugs or not, I cannot believe that Dane would have hurt my family. That's simply too far outside the realm of reality. He wouldn't do that. He . . . loved my family."

Annette exhaled a heavy breath. "You have to be realistic. I didn't just make all this up."

Carson moved his head firmly from side to side. "What you're alleging is impossible."

"One thing is relatively certain," she felt compelled to mention. "Dane is the only person who knows what really happened. If we can get him to talk, you'll finally have that truth you've been searching for and the men who covered it up will have to pay."

Carson continued staring at her as if his reasoning hadn't caught up with hers just yet.

The phone on the table next to her rang. It wasn't until then that she considered the time. Daniel should have been here by now. She could definitely use a healthy shot of caffeine.

"Excuse me," she said to Carson as she lifted the cordless receiver. "Annette Baxter."

"Ms. Baxter, we have a situation."

Building security. Annette rose and crossed the room. "What situation?"

"The authorities are here. They're requesting access to your penthouse."

Not exactly surprising. Since she'd learned of Drake's murder she had fully expected to be questioned. Wainwright would pin it on her if there was any way possible.

"I understand. I'll be waiting here for their arrival."

She ended the call and turned to Carson. "The authorities are here requesting to see me. You may want to leave by the back entrance."

He stood. "Back entrance?"

"There's a rear elevator in my suite. It goes down to the basement garage. You're welcome to use my rental."

"No. I'll stay."

That surprised her. She wasn't foolish enough to misunderstand his motives, but it was somehow comforting to know he would be there. He'd at least heard her out. Even if he didn't believe her, she had deposited the necessary doubt as to the integrity of his mentor.

A frown tightened her brow. Where was Daniel? He was never late.

Special Agent Kim Schaffer led the parade of cops, including Special Agent Boyd Davis, one of her colleagues, and Lieutenant William Lynch, into the room. Annette gathered her wits and braced for battle. "To what do I owe this unexpected pleasure?"

"Annette Baxter," Schaffer announced, "We'll be executing a search warrant of these premises. And you're to come with me for questioning as a person of interest in the murders of Senator Randolph Drake and Zachary Holderfield."

Annette squared her shoulders. "Of course. I'm always happy to cooperate."

Carson stepped forward, shocking Annette again. "Agent Schaffer, I'd like to observe the interview."

Lynch looked from Schaffer to Carson. "Son, I don't think that's a good idea under the circumstances."

Before Carson could argue, Schaffer held up a hand. "Mr. Tanner will be assisting me as an adviser in this interview."

Annette had never cared much for the feds, but this was one time she was damned glad they were here.

35

9:50 a.m.
1000 18th Street, Birmingham
Federal Bureau of Investigation

The interview room was more spacious than the ones used by the local police, but still austere.

Annette took the chair Agent Schaffer indicated. The one in the center of the room. No table, just a chair. Agents Schaffer and Davis, along with Detective Lynch, sat behind a long table, nearer the observation window, their backs to those inside that booth. Those observing only needed to see the body language of the suspect or, as in Annette's case, the person of interest, and to hear the interview.

"Would you like water or coffee, Ms. Baxter?" Davis asked.

"No thank you."

"Let's get started then," Schaffer suggested.

Annette relaxed more fully in her chair and cleared all thought from her mind. She was a master at the art of outwitting a polygraph. Preventing these cops from reading her face or her body language would be a snap.

"Where were you between ten and midnight last night?"

With Carson. But that was none of their business.

Annette pursed her lips as if giving the question due consideration. "I was home," Annette lied. "Fucking my assistant. I believe you've met him."

Davis scribbled a note on his pad. He looked up when he'd finished, taking a moment to drag his gaze from her legs to her eyes. "We'll need to confirm that."

"Be my guest."

"Since your assistant is in your employ," Schaffer countered, "and is therefore obligated to you on some level, is there anyone else who can confirm your whereabouts?"

"Your team generally keeps tabs on my movements. I'm sure you can follow up with them on that as well." But then, she'd given them the slip last night as she did on numerous occasions. It was all too easy. Annette had several sources at her disposal. For the exorbitant fees she paid, any one of them would gladly take her place and lead the feds on a wild goose chase. Funny thing was, it always worked.

An ache tugged at her chest. Except for Jazel . . . she was dead. Annette thought of the car that had tried running her off the road last night. Was that what had happened to Jazel? She shuddered inwardly but worked fast to check her emotions. She couldn't let them see any weakness.

Schaffer moved on. "Did you have any personal or professional contact with the senator?"

Focus, Annette. "None."

There wasn't a single verifiable link between her and the senator. At any time.

"Did you have any reason to want the senator dead?"

Annette hesitated only a moment. "Not unless you count his lack of judgment in the way he cast his votes in recent Senate sessions."

Davis smirked.

Lynch glared.

Schaffer rolled her eyes. "We have all day, Ms. Baxter. Take your time with your answers."

Agent Schaffer was growing frustrated. Good. She had nothing on Annette. She did, however, have a rather bland pair of boots on today. Brown. Just plain brown. Maybe the fed was depressed. Perhaps the death of a high-profile politician in her jurisdiction had something to do with her current disposition.

"I'm waiting, Ms. Baxter," Schaffer prompted.

Annette would be out of here in no time. And they would still have nothing.

She couldn't prove her suspicions about who killed Senator Drake, but the one person who could give Carson the truth and prove Annette was on the up-and-up was Dane Drake.

She and Carson had to find him.

Before anyone else did.

"While you consider your answer to that question," Schaffer said, moving on, "let's talk about Zac Holderfield. Where were you on Sunday, September fifth, between eight and eleven p.m.?"

Annette shifted her position; the men in the room followed the move with considerable interest. "I was home." She looked directly at Schaffer then. "You had me under surveillance. You should have that answer on record."

"Did you," Schaffer asked, undeterred by her attitude, "have any personal or professional dealings with Zachary Holderfield?"

"You'll recall," Lynch added, "that your name was written on his father's appointment calendar."

Time to finish this. "I was not acquainted with Zachary Holderfield. My only contact with Dr. Holderfield and Senator Drake was in my capacity as a fundraising coordinator. We attended a few of the same social functions." She shrugged. "That's where it begins and ends. There's nothing else to tell."

The door to the interview room opened and another player, one Annette didn't know, rushed in and handed a document to Lynch.

This could be trouble. In Annette's experience, a last-minute addition to the agenda always meant trouble.

Lynch passed the document to Schaffer, who studied it a moment before leveling her gaze on Annette once more. "Ms. Baxter, do you own a thirty-eight-caliber revolver?"

An alarm sounded deep inside Annette. "No. I'm anti-gun." There were far better and simpler ways to manipulate a result than violence.

Schaffer glanced at the document once more. "Have you ever used the alias Annette Anderson?"

Panic banded around Annette's chest. "Excuse me?" How the hell had this happened? No one knew.

"The thirty-eight registered to that name has been confirmed as the murder weapon in Zachary Holderfield's murder."

Impossible. Annette had disposed of that weapon.

"Confirming this alias will be a simple matter, Ms. Baxter," Schaffer pressed. "Your cooperation would make matters far better for you. Have you"—she looked directly, bluntly at Annette—"ever used the alias Annette Anderson?"

The panic mounted, pulsed inside Annette as her gaze swung to the mirrored glass shielding the observation booth . . . to where she knew Carson Tanner watched.

He was the only one who had known.

Had he changed sides since they arrived?

For that matter, had he ever been on her side?

"Since you appear disinclined to answer that question," Schaffer pressed on, "perhaps you'll answer this one."

Annette fixed her attention back on the tenacious agent. *Get this over with and get out of here. Stay calm.*

"What time last night did you finish your *business* with your assistant, Daniel Ledger?"

Annette shrugged. "Around midnight. Daniel was—"

"Daniel *was*," Schaffer contended, "your alibi."

Dread bloomed in Annette's chest. "Daniel is my alibi."

"Daniel Ledger was killed in an automobile accident."

Denial and then remorse flooded Annette. Daniel had been her faithful employee for six years. God. First Jazel . . . now Daniel. "When?" The one word was tainted with far more anguish than she would have liked Schaffer to hear.

"I can't give you a specific time. The accident occurred in the Mountain Brook area. According to the ME, probably in the last twelve hours." Schaffer considered Annette a moment before continuing. "The strange thing is, he was driving a stolen Crown Vic, black in color, with a stolen dealer's license plate. Were you aware your assistant was a thief?"

Thief? Daniel wasn't a thief . . . he was . . .

Annette went cold as memories from last night's close encounter on the road in the Mountain Brook area swarmed her head. Black sedan. She'd seen it before. The driver had been able to stay on her tail when the feds couldn't.

But . . . Daniel wouldn't have tried to run her off the road . . .

. . . would he?

36

By the time Schaffer was finished questioning Annette, Carson had started to sweat. Each time she crossed or uncrossed her legs his entire body tensed when he should have been completely focused on the questions.

It didn't help that Wainwright and Luttrell, along with Schaffer's boss, had been in this booth with him for nearly two hours. Neither wanted him there, but Schaffer had overridden their protests.

Carson owed the lady big time. He was, frankly, a little stunned. Why would she protect him when her butt was on the line?

Special Agent in Charge Talley had kept his thoughts to himself. Carson was relatively certain the man had decided there was enough tension in the room without his interference.

Luttrell reached for the door at the same time as Carson.

The glare-off lasted a full five seconds.

"I suppose," Luttrell mocked, "you'll post her bail when she's arraigned."

Carson chuckled. "You'll have to find enough evidence to charge her first."

He walked out of the room. Didn't spare any of the three men another glance. Maybe his career was over, but he wasn't backing off until he had the truth.

The whole truth.

To do that he needed Annette Baxter. And Dane Drake.

Wainwright, sans Luttrell, caught up with Carson halfway to the elevators. "You're throwing away everything," he cautioned.

Carson stared for several seconds at the man he had trusted, had admired, before he responded. For one of those seconds he considered that Wainwright was correct . . . maybe Carson was throwing away all that he'd worked so hard to achieve. "All I want is the truth." He searched his mentor's guarded gaze. Until a few hours ago, Carson had never doubted this man . . . but that had changed now. "Doesn't that put us both on the same team?"

Wainwright moved his head from side to side, that fatherly worry cluttering his expression. "You're the last person on earth that I thought would fall for her ludicrous story."

There had been a time when a part of Carson had desperately needed a father figure . . . he'd prized that aspect of his and Wainwright's relationship. Not anymore. "What story is that?"

Wariness instantly replaced the worry. "Whatever that woman has told you is nothing but fabricated nonsense to cloud your perspective. You've read her file, you know what she's capable of. I don't think I need to spell it out."

That was the moment Carson understood just how deep the lies went. Schaffer had been correct. Wainwright was hiding something. "You're right. You don't need to spell it out." He clapped the man he'd once respected above all others on the shoulder. "When I'm done, I'll have the whole truth."

Carson walked away, didn't look back until he'd reached the elevators where Annette waited. He glanced back once, long enough to see Luttrell and Wainwright huddled with Talley.

Annette didn't speak until she and Carson were outside the building and headed for her car. She wheeled on him. "You told them, didn't you?"

Carson was confused for a moment; the conversation with Wainwright was still reverberating in his head. Then he understood. "About the Anderson name?"

Fury radiated from her blue eyes. "No one knew! Only you."

She got into her rented Jag before he could answer. Shaking his head, he rounded the hood and climbed behind the wheel. Apparently she was too angry to drive. He started the vehicle and turned to her. "I didn't tell them. I don't know how they discovered your connection to that alias, but I had nothing to do with it. Remember, I just found out. At the center. Clearly, someone already knew, or your sister wouldn't be a target."

That reminder seemed to calm her down or, at least, to shift her anger in another direction.

Carson considered the issue of the murder weapon. "You said you disposed of the weapon Dane used."

"I did." She stared forward. Wouldn't look at him.

"And if the thirty-eight isn't yours, that will come out."

She turned and stared directly at him. "If they want it to be mine, it will be."

She was right. There were ways. They would use slugs from the weapon in their possession and claim they had been retrieved from the victim. Almost anything was possible.

"I'm . . . sorry about your assistant," he offered.

Annette closed her eyes for one long moment. "I don't want to talk about that."

He felt like a heel for asking, but the insanity surrounding this whole mess wouldn't allow for too much tact. "Do you know anything about the stolen car?"

She moved her head slowly from side to side. "All I know is that I was in the Mountain Brook area last night and a dark sedan attempted to run me off the road." Her gaze collided with his. "Then it disappeared."

Carson considered the sedan that had nearly run him over and the one, possibly the same one, that had been following him. Black. Maybe a Crown Vic.

"Do you have any reason to believe your assistant would want to stop what we're doing?" Jesus, could no one be trusted in this?

"All I know," Annette said somberly, "is that we have one chance to prove the truth. We have to find Dane Drake before anyone else does."

Carson agreed completely. "Where do we start?" His first thought would be to call Elizabeth. But that would only give away their intentions.

"With his friends," Annette said. "In places you've never been."

Annette provided the directions to Dane's most recent address, the SoHo Building in Homewood. The guy moved around like a gypsy. Six months ago his father had leased him an apartment in one of the better high-rises in downtown Birmingham. According to Annette, Dane preferred the gutter to his daddy's gift.

"If he's not here," Carson noted aloud, "I'll talk to Elizabeth to see if she's heard from him." That Dane had been missing from the scene of his father's murder that morning nagged at Carson. Why the hell wouldn't the guy show up for his mother's sake? For his sister's? Then again, he was likely terrified that his link to Zac's murder would be discovered.

Carson damned sure intended to ask him the instant he found the bum.

But Carson knew Dane. No matter what Dane said under the influence, Carson couldn't believe that he would hurt his family. Or his own family.

No way.

There had to be another explanation of how he came into possession of the wedding bands. And that explanation could be the first real lead in the case.

Once on the property, Annette led the way into and through the elegant lobby as if she'd been here many times before. Considering Dane was one of her repeat clients, she likely had. She paused at the elevator and pressed the call button. When the doors slid open, they stepped inside and she selected floor four.

When Carson leaned against the far wall, Annette joined him there. Her subtle scent tugged at his senses. Made him want to lean in her direction.

His body reacted. All his powers of concentration were required to maintain a steady respiration rate. The way she'd uncrossed and then crossed her legs during the interrogation kept rewinding and playing in his head. The woman knew how to get to a man. Knew how to make him want her in a way he'd never wanted anyone before. Despite the insanity going on all around him. Despite the slow, steady destruction of his whole life.

He told himself that letting this thing between them get any further out of control would be a mistake . . . and still his body hardened at just being near her.

Bad idea.

The instant the elevator doors opened, he was out of there. At Dane's door on the fourth floor, Carson banged repeatedly. Called the guy's name. Nothing.

Annette tried the door. Locked.

Then she surprised Carson all over again. She removed a lockpick kit from her purse. Less than a minute later they were inside.

"Clever," he commented drily. That was something he'd never taken the time to learn. Mainly because it was illegal.

"One of the perks of growing up with perverts and assholes. You learn many escape maneuvers."

That she had been sexually abused as a child twisted in his gut. Made him wish there had been someone there to protect her.

Did she need protecting now?

There was a hell of a crazy notion. He'd never known a woman more capable of protecting herself.

But then, evading a homicide charge was a little more complicated. He expected Drake's murder to be pinned on her as well.

Concentrate on the matter at hand, Carson. Everything was on the line right now.

Dane's apartment was empty. They checked each room twice.

"Doesn't look as if he's been here in a few days." Carson checked the fridge. The milk had gone out of date several days before.

"He disappears all the time," Annette reminded him. "The last time we talked I told him to lay low for a while."

Carson and Dane hadn't kept in touch. He had no idea what the guy was up to or even where he lived.

If this was home, he didn't eat or sleep here on a regular basis.

The place was a mess. Clothes tossed here and there on the floor. The walls were bare as were the shelves. Carson had checked the closet: more haphazardly stored clothing items. A couple of crumpled dollars on the dresser. And not much else.

"I have a few contacts I can reach out to," Annette offered as they prepared to exit the apartment.

"I'll give Elizabeth a call." He hated to bother her with this on a day like today, but he needed to check on her and Patricia. It was the right thing to do. And finding Dane was their only hope of finding some answers.

"Be careful what you say to her," Annette suggested. "I'm not so sure you should trust her."

The woman had to be kidding. "Elizabeth would never do anything to hurt anyone." He glanced at Annette as they entered the elevator once more. "Not even to protect her brother."

Annette said nothing to that. Carson selected the first floor. As the doors glided closed he watched the woman waiting on the opposite side of the car. A paradox. Definitely.

"How do you do it?" He had no business asking the question, but there it was. With all that was going on, with his career—his entire future—in the toilet, *this* should be the last thing on his mind.

"How do I do what?" Her steady gaze rested on his.

"Be so distant and cold, like in the interview today." He studied her closely, too closely for his own comfort. "That night at the Tutwiler, you were hot and wild. Was that night just an act?"

She reached out and pressed the stop button on the control panel. The elevator car jolted to a halt between the third and second floors, but the doors remained closed.

She reclined against the wall and analyzed him a moment. "I play the part that's called for in any given situation."

Well, he'd asked for that one. "So you're saying that when we had sex, you didn't really want to, you just played the part. Didn't feel a thing, like you suggested." This was not the time for his bruised ego to enter the picture. Or maybe he just needed a break from the escalating tension. Either way, this was just one more indication of how out of control he was.

"That's right." Her frank tone left no room for speculation. "Don't beat yourself up, Tanner. No man has ever given me an orgasm."

He tamped down the incensed protest that was automatic. "And the lack of panties in today's interrogation, was that part of getting into character?"

A ghost of a smile haunted her lips. "You should have recognized that one. It was a distraction tactic. Don't you use a similar technique in the courtroom when you're out of forthright options?"

Before good sense could stop him, he'd crossed to her side of the elevator. "That's one I haven't used." He braced a hand on either side of her, trapping her with his body. As ludicrous as it was just now, there was one thing he had to know. "So you felt nothing when we were together that night? Nothing at all."

She tilted her head back and stared directly into his eyes. "You mean, when we fucked?"

"Yes, when we *fucked*."

"Nothing, Mr. Deputy District Attorney. I turned that off a very long time ago."

"Maybe," he allowed. "And maybe you're just protecting yourself." He leaned in closer. "Maybe you're afraid to feel something that personal."

She laughed softly. "I'm not afraid of anything."

He didn't believe her. "I think you're scared to death."

She searched his eyes, his face. "I think you have something to prove."

How the hell could she read him so well? "I have nothing to prove," he lied.

She laughed. "You're pissed because you couldn't make me come. Get over it, better men have tried."

"Why would I care? I did. That's all that matters, right?"

"Then why are we wasting time discussing the issue?"

She was right. He had something to prove. The epiphany might not have been so profound had it not occurred to him in the middle of his entire life being turned inside out.

The bottom line was, he needed to get past this. And there was only one way to do it.

Before good sense could kick in, he reached down and hiked up the hem of her skirt. Hoisted her up against his chest and wrapped her legs around his waist. Need rushed through him, making his heart pound, making his breath ragged. "I've wanted to do this again since the first time you crossed your legs in that interview room."

"Then why don't you shut up and do it. For the good it'll do you."

He kissed her hard. "Oh, you'll feel me." His fingers jerked at his fly. He rammed into her. Her body tensed. Oh yeah. She felt that. He thrust deeper.

Desire erupted inside him. He resisted. He would not come before her. By God, not this time.

Harder, deeper, faster. He ground his pelvis into hers. Her breath caught. "Felt that, didn't you?"

"Felt what?" She looked straight into his eyes and smiled. "Give it up, Tanner. You're going to fail. As difficult as that concept is for you to comprehend, there's a first time for everything."

"Come, damn you," he growled, pumping harder, deeper.

She made a sound, not quite a whimper. "Not going . . . to happen," she stammered.

Her halting words urged him on. "Oh, yeah, you're going to come this time."

"Dream on." She gasped.

He watched her face. That cold mask had slipped just a little, revealing the struggle her mind fought with her body. He was winning.

He reached between them and massaged that sweet spot. She squirmed in his arms. His mouth closed over hers and he kissed her long and deep, sucked on her lips, all the while keeping up the rhythmic pumping, the rubbing of that hot button.

She tried to push him away. "Damn you!"

He didn't let up. Her eyes opened wide in surprise. He slowed down the pace, wanted her to enjoy the charge of sensations.

"Noooo!" She pounded his back. "Faster."

He flexed his hips. Gave her what she wanted.

She came with the same fervor that she did everything else. The scream muffled between their kisses sent him over the edge. The release left him weak in the knees and suffering from a vulnerability he had never before experienced.

What the hell was wrong with him?

She trembled as she pushed at his chest, lowered her feet to the floor, and shoved her skirt back down.

He tugged at his own clothes, the air raging in and out of his lungs, his pulse pounding as if he'd run ten miles.

When he looked up, she would not meet his gaze.

The ice bitch had thawed.

He looked away . . . couldn't bear to see the result.

The elevator car jerked into motion.

By the time it stopped on the lobby level they both faced the doors, ready to escape the scene of the crime.

They walked silently to her car, her one step ahead. Got in simultaneously.

He wanted to say something. Wanted to revel in his victory.

But he couldn't bring himself to do either. He'd beaten her at her own game.

There was just one sticking point . . . at what cost to her?

To him?

His cell buzzed, breaking the choking tension.

He dragged it from his jacket pocket. "Tanner."

It was Elizabeth. She wanted him to come over right away. She was frantically worried about her mother. The pain and grief in her voice tortured him.

There was no question now . . . he was crazy. Stark raving.

"I'll be right there."

He backed out of the parking slot and rolled toward the street. "That was Elizabeth. She needs me. I can ask about Dane while I'm there."

Annette didn't respond.

She didn't have to. He understood. He'd stripped away the tough veneer that protected the fragile woman beneath. A picture of her as a twelve-year-old child left alone and defenseless, beaten and abused, consumed him. Annette Baxter had been fighting her way through life ever since. Had been fighting for survival, most of the time against men.

He stopped at a red light. His mind did the same.

What did that make him?

37

5:30 p.m.
3202 Fernway Road, Mountain Brook
Drake Estate

Carson held Elizabeth for a long while. Her mother was sleeping now, but she'd been a wreck when he had first arrived.

At least Elizabeth and Patricia had each other. He'd had no one when his family was murdered.

Except his uncle Max. He didn't count on so many levels that it didn't seem appropriate to bother the attempt. But he'd been there as best he could.

"What can I do?" Carson asked, certain there was something. Luttrell might be assigned to the case and Carson might be on administrative leave, but that wasn't going to stop him from doing what he could. Luttrell wasn't nearly as good as him. And Carson intended to prove it.

Somehow, all of this was tied together. Carson was determined to get to the truth.

Elizabeth shook her head. "Thank you. Just being here is enough." She cuddled deeper into his arms.

Guilt poked him at the idea of what he and Baxter had done in that elevator. It felt almost as if he'd cheated on Elizabeth. More crazy notions. "Have you notified the rest of your family?"

"There really isn't anyone. Dane is never home. Who knows what's going on with him?"

If Elizabeth only knew.

Time to broach the question. "Where is Dane?"

Elizabeth lifted her gaze to Carson's. "I don't know. He disappears like this all the time. And I just can't deal with it right now." She squeezed her eyes shut and made a desperate sound. "It's been all over the news. Hundreds of our good friends have called. Surely Dane has heard by now that Father is . . . dead." She rubbed at her temples. "For all I know my irresponsible brother could be drugged out somewhere unaware he's even in this world."

"I'll find him." That would serve more than one purpose. Carson needed the truth. And Elizabeth needed her brother. Then again, with what Carson knew, Dane was only going to bring more heartache to his family.

"Will you bring him home when you do?" She dabbed at her nose with a tissue. "Mother needs him as badly as I do."

The fresh wave of tears in her eyes tugged at Carson's heart. "You have my word."

She placed a chaste kiss on Carson's cheek. Hugged him tightly. "I know you will, Carson. You're the one person I can depend on right now."

Self-disgust churned in his gut, made him sick. "Your father was there for me when I needed him most." The possibility that Drake had concealed the truth about that night to protect his son twisted in Carson's gut. But he didn't know that for sure. Not yet.

Elizabeth blinked at the emotion brimming past her lashes. "But I wasn't." She wiped at her eyes. "They sent me away." She closed her eyes and shook her head again. "I shouldn't even be asking you to help me."

"Of course you should. We're like family." He swallowed back the bitter taste of deceit. "I won't let you down, Elizabeth." Even as he said the words snippets of those moments in the elevator with Baxter flashed in his brain. Good God, the information he was keeping from Elizabeth now . . . what had he turned into? Where were his ethics? His vow to defend justice?

Elizabeth's tearful farewell as he left ripped his heart to shreds. When had he become such a consummate liar?

It was one thing to distort the facts in the courtroom to win a case.

But this was Elizabeth.

He should have told her the truth.

But he couldn't.

He couldn't talk to anyone, couldn't trust anyone . . .

Not until he had all the facts.

And maybe truth wasn't always found by doing the right thing. Maybe sometimes you had to break the very laws you were supposed to uphold to ensure justice was served.

38

Carson would find Dane.

Elizabeth watched him drive away.

She had smelled Annette Baxter's distasteful scent on him.

Elizabeth told herself not to worry about that. He had been investigating the woman. Just because Wainwright had put Carson on administrative leave didn't mean he would give up.

Carson never gave up.

He would win and Annette Baxter would be history.

It couldn't happen quickly enough for Elizabeth.

Baxter and Fleming were scourges on the face of this city. They both needed to be sent to prison for the rest of their despicable lives.

If anyone could do it, Carson could.

Elizabeth knew he wouldn't let her down.

If her parents hadn't sent her away, she and Carson would be married by now. Perhaps have children.

She thought of the way he'd hugged her before he left. It wasn't too late.

Elizabeth sighed. She should check on her mother. This was so difficult for her. Patricia tried so hard to be the perfect wife, the perfect mother. At times she failed, made mistakes, but didn't everyone?

Elizabeth would take care of her, as she had so many times taken care of Elizabeth.

Considering the tranquilizers her mother had consumed, she should be sleeping soundly by now.

Elizabeth trudged up the stairs. She was so tired. Her mother would be disappointed that Dane wasn't there. But Carson would find him. Telling her so would be reassurance enough.

Outside her mother's bedroom door, Elizabeth hesitated. Her mother was speaking to someone.

Had someone called? Elizabeth hadn't heard the phone.

The door wasn't closed completely so she eased it open just a crack more so she could hear more clearly. Was there news of her brother?

"You have to listen to me," her mother whispered sternly to whomever was on the other end of the line. "You have to do as I say. Now. Tonight. There's no time to discuss the details."

Her mother paused for a long moment. Elizabeth frowned. No wonder she hadn't heard the phone—her mother was using her cell.

"Please," Patricia pleaded, "trust me. You have to trust me. Do as I say and everything will be fine. You know I would never let anything happen to you. Tell me the truth and I'll take care of everything."

She had to be speaking to Dane.

Poor Mother. She worried so much. Dane had hurt them all far more than he realized. Now Father was dead and Dane wasn't even here to support Elizabeth and their mother. What kind of brother failed to be here at a moment like this?

One who couldn't be counted on.

For anything.

"Don't worry," her mother urged, "this is not beyond salvaging." Another long pause. "You know I will. I'll take care of everything the way I always do."

Elizabeth started to ease away from the door. The conversation made her uneasy. What was going on? If her mother was keeping things from her . . .

Patricia's rush to enter another number into her cell caused Elizabeth to hesitate. Who was she calling now?

"It didn't work," Patricia muttered vehemently into the phone. "What am I supposed to do now? She isn't going away . . . and he's helping her. This has to stop. Do you hear me? Otherwise . . ."

Her mother's face contorted with anger as she listened to a response she clearly did not appreciate.

"I don't care," she snapped. "Do whatever you have to. Just fix this mess!"

Had to be about Dane. Elizabeth could only imagine what Dane was up to. Heaven's sake, what had he done that would keep him away from home with their father murdered? And have their mother so overwrought?

There was only one thing Elizabeth knew for certain would strike such terror into her family.

Verifying her conclusion wouldn't be simple. Lieutenant Lynch and District Attorney Wainwright had insisted that a security detail be left at the house.

Elizabeth would need to escape their careful watch.

She waited the hour or so until it was dark. Then she slipped out of the house the way she used to as a teenager. Usually to creep through the woods to meet Carson. Into the garage and out the side door nearest the woods.

With the flashlight gripped firmly in her hand, she sneaked into the dense cover of trees. The underbrush was thicker now. She and Dane had kept it trampled down when they were kids. A trail had led through the woods to the Tanner home. But that wasn't her destination.

Once she was deep enough into the woods she turned on the flashlight and veered off the path just a bit. She was close. Very close. Then she saw it, the makeshift cross she'd fashioned from leftover craft supplies. It was brown and dirty now from exposure to the rain and winter weather. It had stood there, looking more like an *x* than a *t,* for twelve or thirteen years—since the last family pet had passed.

Her breath caught. She hadn't brought a shovel because she hadn't expected to have to get her hands dirty.

But now—she stared at the disturbed ground—good Lord.

Elizabeth dropped to her knees. She clawed at the already loosened earth. Someone had been here.

What the hell had Dane done?

Her fingernails scraped something hard. She wiggled it loose. Grabbed the flashlight and directed its beam there.

She sucked in a ragged breath before the tranquility she counted on so very much cloaked her. "Pepper," she whispered wistfully as she tilted the skull so that she could trace the fracture line with the light. "Poor thing." He'd simply been too large for a family pet. He'd always made such a mess. A German shepherd could be such a nuisance. Her mother had suffered tremendously attempting to endure the big, sloppy animal.

Elizabeth tossed the damaged skull aside and kept digging with one hand, holding the light with the other. The bones glistened in the light, gleamed so white. Each one told a story from Elizabeth's childhood.

"Digger." She cradled the much smaller skull in her free hand. Such a sweetheart. A dachshund. Far smaller than the German shepherd but so pesky. The animal had dug holes all in the yard. Dane had loved this one so much. Too bad. Mother's flowers were too delicate for the little beast. Elizabeth lobbed the skull aside.

Bones, bones, bones.

She dropped the flashlight, dug faster.

Where was the little tin box?

She smiled as her fingers curled around the cool metal. There it was. Not bothering with the light, she opened the little box and fingered the interior.

Empty.

Her smiled faded and her heart pounded. *He wouldn't have done this!* Surely not.

She sat back on her haunches and directed the light into the box. Nothing. She surveyed the mess she had made.

They were missing.

Fury welled up inside her so fast she could hardly sit still.

She had to find Dane.

If he ruined everything . . . he would be so, so, so sorry.

39

7:00 p.m.
31st Street, Birmingham
Fleming Estate

Annette waited in the observatory.

Her hands were still shaking.

Inside, she trembled like a newly hatched bird who couldn't see or stand, much less fly.

How had this happened?

She had set out to solicit Carson Tanner as an ally. She had been in charge. She had made the rules, set the pace.

Her eyes closed as she relived that moment when he'd made her reach a physical climax. No one had ever been able to do that. Not even once.

She had gone months, sometimes more than a year without sex, and even then her chosen victim had not given her an orgasm.

What made Carson Tanner so damned special?

Yes, she was between a rock and a hard place. Yes, she was admittedly feeling vulnerable. But those conditions had never induced such a physical bonding before.

She couldn't possibly be in lust with him, much less love. She wasn't capable of either emotion. The only other human she had ever loved was Paula. Her sister by choice. Annette supposed that she had loved her mother, but her betrayal had left the memory foggy.

The really frustrating part was that Carson left Annette feeling exactly like that little girl who'd awakened one morning to find her mother still hadn't returned. Was gone for good. Annette and Paula had walked home from the Walmart. Annette remembered sitting by the window and watching for hours, hoping her mother would come back. Paula had moaned and called out over and over again from the other room. But Annette had ignored her. She had been certain if she watched long enough, eventually she would see her mother coming.

But she hadn't.

No one came until three days later when a nosy neighbor had reported the children being left alone for an extended period.

Annette had tried to hide herself and Paula when those people had arrived. But Paula wouldn't stop making sounds. Even when Annette put her hand over her mouth, she kept moaning and crying out.

Then the police had found Reggie's decomposing body under the back porch.

Years later when Annette had finally escaped, she had promised herself she would never be afraid again.

Never.

She was afraid now.

The realization sent another tremor quaking through her.

Afraid for Paula. Afraid of the . . . unknown. Maybe afraid of Carson Tanner and what he could make her feel. Her body melted each time she thought of him. The sensations, the heat. All of it was new to her, all of it prompted by him. Only him.

Control had been essential to her life for more than a decade. Now it was gone. She was in a reactive state. She hated that place. Hated it. Hated it.

Fury burned away some of the more fragile emotions, and she was glad for it. She wanted to be angry. She wanted to feel anything but this weakness. This need.

The door opened and Otis appeared, looking regal as always.

Annette rearranged her expression into one he would expect. Courage, determination. "Good afternoon, Otis."

When he came close enough, she kissed his cheek.

He stepped back, surveyed her closely. Uncertainty broke out on her skin as tiny beads of perspiration. He never missed anything. He would know something was wrong.

This was the first time in all the years they had been together that she had hidden anything from him. He didn't know about the rings. And he couldn't know what she had done for Carson Tanner.

Never, never, never.

"You look a little flustered," he noted. "Things are not as they should be." That wise gaze met hers.

She flashed a pathetic attempt at a smile. "Things are . . . complicated."

"Yes." He stroked his chin and seemed to reflect. "Things are very complicated."

"Daniel is dead."

"I hadn't heard that."

Who was he kidding? He heard everything. Otis Fleming generally knew a man was dead even before the dead man recognized it. Annette resisted the urge to knot her hands together. "I need your help, Otis." She hated the feeling of not being able to handle her own affairs. But this was way beyond anything she could hope to turn around.

"I understand you're concerned for Paula," he announced. "I've been looking into centers of the same caliber as the one here. There is one in the Caymans that I would recommend."

The chill that had been hovering around Annette settled deep into her bones. "That's probably a prudent move." The American authorities couldn't touch her there. Both murders would be pinned on her. She didn't need to be able to see the future to speculate. She knew.

His gaze locked on hers once more. "As dear as you are to me, Annette. The time has come for you to go."

She'd known this was so, but she hadn't wanted to face that reality. "Yes. I'm aware that I'm fighting a losing battle."

"They have formed an alliance against you. They will do whatever it takes to bring you down in order to protect themselves. As we speak they are working to tie Zachary Holderfield's murder to you. As well as Senator Drake's."

A frown worried her brow. "I'm aware of their proposed strategy." All too aware.

Otis moved his head side to side in regret. "I'm guessing evidence was planted pointing to you. They're far too cocky just now not to have at least one ace up their sleeves."

She wanted to ask him if there was anything he could do to help, but she knew better. Otis Fleming had been like a father to her. Loved her, she felt certain. But he would not sacrifice his standing to save her.

That she understood with complete certainty.

She was on her own. Just as she had been most of her life.

"Well, I should make arrangements to go before it's too late." She blinked back the burn of tears. Dammit.

"That would be the judicious choice."

She started to end the conversation there, but she had to ask, "Why have they done this? I've been keeping the powerful in Birmingham out of trouble for ten years. Doesn't that count for anything?"

A rare smile touched the older man's lips. "You have indeed. I'm very proud of how far you've come. I have no doubt you will build an even more esteemed clientele elsewhere. However, power is a very dangerous thing. It can be your best friend or your worst enemy. You possess a great deal of power, Annette. It has become toxic to those in your debt. They will take you down, no matter how many of them must be sacrificed in the effort."

They. The elusive they that no one could ever know about. Only Annette and Otis knew the names on her client list. Most didn't even know about one another. But a handful of the most powerful who had given and received personal recommendations to acquire her services had come together, formed that alliance Otis spoke of. Wanted her gone. She could thank Dane Drake and his self-indulgence for that.

A moment of sentimentality struck her hard. "Will I ever see you again?" Her chest tightened. For nearly eleven years he had been her closest friend, her family.

"Perhaps." Another of those rare smiles. "I'm an old man, Annette. I don't travel as much as I used to. But not to worry, we'll keep in touch."

That was her cue. It was time for her to go. There was nothing else to discuss. Except . . .

"There's one thing I have to do before I go." She dredged up her courage. She would not leave until this was done.

Otis studied her at length. "This thing is something you would risk your own freedom for?"

As outlandish as it sounded. "Yes."

Finding Dane Drake and proving what really happened to Carson's family wouldn't exactly help her at this point. But she had to do it for Carson. It was completely irrational. Yet she could not leave him in this position. He stood on the verge of losing everything . . . because of her.

"Ah." Otis nodded. "I see. You've developed an attachment to this young man."

"No." Her first instinct was to deny the accusation, but deep down she knew Otis was right. He always was. "Perhaps."

"Be warned," Otis cautioned, "his glory days are over as well. He will not recover."

That was exactly what she was afraid of.

"Before I can go." She took a deep breath for courage. "I have to help him."

Surprise twinkled in Otis's eyes. "You wish to help him? Still? When I have warned you of the risk?"

She nodded. "I have to."

When this whole thing had started it was about saving her ass, but now . . . it was about saving his.

Annette had no idea how that had happened, but it had. It wasn't as if it wouldn't benefit her to some degree. So the decision didn't quite qualify her for martyrdom.

"I see."

She hadn't expected otherwise.

Otis could help her; whether or not he would, she couldn't say. But she had to ask. "I need to find Dane Drake. It's imperative. He's the only one left who can help."

Otis inclined his head and contemplated her request for a time that prompted more of that sweat to secrete from her pores.

"I'll nudge my contacts," Otis offered finally. "He could be dead considering his consorts."

She prayed that was not the case.

"Or he could be in hiding considering his father's murder." He gave a wave of his hand as if the decision was made. "I'll see what I can do. If I learn anything, I'll let you know."

"Thank you so much, Otis." She looked into those familiar eyes. "I wish there was some way I could repay you for all you've done for me."

"My dear." He took her hand. "Watching you bloom has been repayment enough."

Annette hugged him closely. "I'll miss you."

"As I will you," he murmured.

Time to go. He would call if he learned anything useful.

As she reached the door, she hesitated, looking back at the man who had been more of a father to her than anyone else in her life, biological or otherwise. "Will *you* be all right?" She had been so wrapped up in her own troubles she hadn't taken a moment to consider how things would turn out for Otis when the dust had cleared.

Strangely, he didn't answer right away, just stared at her with a look she had not seen before. "There was never any question as to my survival. There was only the matter of the price."

A stretch of silence elapsed between them. She didn't have to ask the price. She feared she knew all too well. Annette wasn't sure she could bear the answer.

She saw herself out of the observatory. She worked hard to focus on what she must do next. Any emotion she allowed would only get in the way. She had already set up transportation arrangements for the search. All she had to do now was hook up with Carson. And evade the FBI's prying eyes.

Oddly enough, Carson appeared to be the only person she could count on at this point.

Images of their physical coupling just a few hours ago had her heart racing.

Don't think . . . find Dane Drake. He was the one chance Carson had of turning his life around.

Blake, the houseman, nodded to Annette as they passed in the long hall. He carried a tea tray.

Two cups.

She stalled, turned to watch the man move toward his destination.

Did Otis have company? There hadn't been any other cars in the drive when she'd arrived.

Blake entered the study . . . not the observatory.

Her heart pounding, Annette eased back in that direction. She slipped into the room directly across the hall, leaving the door cracked so that she might get a glimpse of whoever was waiting in the room.

What the hell was wrong with her?

Otis had guests frequently. Usually business associates. She had no right spying on him like this. He would be very displeased if he learned of her behavior.

As if the troubling thoughts had summoned him, he entered her line of sight. Opened the door to the study to go inside. His guest rose from his chair and extended his hand.

Donald Wainwright.

Otis's archenemy.

What could those two possibly have to discuss?

The answer was simple. If she'd had any doubts, there was her confirmation.

She was the price of Otis's survival.

When Blake had left the two men alone and the door was closed, she counted to ten, giving Blake time to clear the hall, then made her exit.

She had to find Carson.

Not only was she his only hope, he was hers as well.

Enemies or not, there was one thing Annette had to keep in mind. There wasn't a man in power in this city who had not achieved his position without help of some sort from Otis. Even Carson's invitation to run for the office of Jefferson County District Attorney would have been a part of the good old boys' strategy. He just didn't see it yet. Drake and Wainwright may have extended the invitation, but she would lay odds that the approval had come from Otis Fleming.

Despite the differences he had with men like Wainwright and the occasional all-out war, Otis owned this city, lock, stock, and barrel.

And all of it was negotiable.

Outside, Annette climbed into the Tahoe she'd used to lose her federal tail. She had arranged several vehicles in as many locations around the city in the event they were spotted. Time was clearly running out. As soon as forensics had additional evidence that the .38 belonged to her, though it most certainly did not, she would be arrested for double murders. She had to get this done and be out of here before that happened.

She still couldn't shake the unthinkable—the only man she had ever trusted had sold her out.

Why was she surprised? It wasn't personal, it was simply business.

As Otis had said, she knew too much. *They* wanted her out of their lives for good. To maintain his untouchable position, he would facilitate that effort.

As much as she considered her current dilemma to be about ousting her from power, some part of her was dead certain that there was more involved. A deeper cover-up about which she only had snatches of knowledge.

So what if Dane had gone apeshit and murdered Carson's family? Wouldn't it be easier just to off the little son of a bitch? No matter how she looked at it, she was nearly positive that all of this was connected to something bigger than Dane's screwup. The decision to take her down, Stokes, Carson's sudden fall from grace. It all revolved around one central motivation.

The question was, what?

Better yet, why?

Frankly, after fifteen years, why did anyone care?

There had to be some part she couldn't see.

Her cell rang; she dug it from her purse. "Yes."

"Where should we meet?"

Carson.

She gave him the location of the black Range Rover. They would rendezvous there and take the Rover until the need to change vehicles arose again.

When he didn't say more, she asked, "Did you learn anything from Elizabeth?" For some reason she despised the woman. Maybe it was the whole wholesome, Little Miss Goody Two-Shoes persona that gagged Annette.

"She doesn't know where Dane is," Carson said, frustrated. "But I promised her I would find him."

How sweet.

"I forgot the two of you once had a thing." Annette snapped her mouth shut. Hadn't meant to say that. The idea that it smacked of jealousy irked her to no end.

"Yes, we once had a *thing.*"

Her mouth went bone dry. "Do you still have a *thing?*"

Shit. Shit. Shit. What was wrong with her? That she had asked a second idiotic question made her furious. And yet she sat on an emotional ledge awaiting his answer.

"I don't think so . . . maybe."

"I'll see you in ten minutes." Annette disconnected. She didn't want to hear any more of that tender emotion in his voice. She was stupid.

Of course a man like Carson Tanner would end up with Little Miss Princess, the pride of Birmingham's elite. He wasn't going to feel anything for Annette. Other than the urge for sex perhaps. And she cared nothing for him. Men couldn't be trusted. Not even the so-called good ones.

She had learned that the hard way.

But then, what did she need with a man? She'd never really cared about sex either way until recently.

Such bad timing.

That was the thing. The whole world, every little detail of every little thing that took place was all about timing. Made the difference between life and death . . . and everything in between.

Her life was over and she was philosophizing. Oh, yes, she was totally, totally screwed.

She sat up a little straighter behind the wheel. But the best thing to do when being screwed was to screw right back. Those rich, powerful bastards had better watch out.

She wasn't done yet.

Not by a long shot.

40

8:30 p.m.

Dane opened his eyes and stared at the water-stained ceiling.

He tried to raise up but his head was spinning so hard he had to lay back down. Damn. He was messed up big time.

Why the hell had he snorted that last line of coke?

Bile rushed into his throat. He rolled to his side and puked until there was nothing left to come up.

Dane spit out the bitter taste and tried again to push himself into an upright position.

"Damn." The room tilted.

He needed to go to the bathroom, but the room wouldn't stop moving.

What time was it? Maybe food would help.

He struggled to focus his fuzzy gaze on the clock on the bedside table. He frowned. What was that?

His hand wobbled as he reached out to pick up the bottle. He turned it around in his hand. Prescription bottle?

Where had that come from?

Maybe it was the medicine he needed to feel better. That would be good.

On the floor next to the table was another bottle. This one bigger. He picked it up. Tequila. Now he was really confused. When did he buy that?

"Dane."

His head whipped around. What the hell?

He blinked. The image split into two.

"Dane, you have to listen to me."

What was *she* doing here?

"It's time for you to do the right thing."

"What?" Damn. He wished she would be still. She kept turning into two people. Shit. That would be bad. One was hell on earth.

"Now, Dane," she urged. "You know what you have to do."

He stared at the prescription bottle in his hand.

You know what you have to do.

"Take the medicine and you'll feel much better."

He scrubbed his face to try to clear the haze fogging his brain.

"Take all of it, Dane."

Did he say that? Maybe she did.

Whatever. She was right.

She always was.

He knew what he had to do.

41

Tuesday, September 14, midnight
Highway 11, Midfield

Dane Drake was nowhere to be found.

Carson wanted to beat the hell out of something . . . or someone.

Annette had visited nearly every damned contact she had who knew Dane. No one had seen him in three days.

Dane was either hiding out or dead.

Carson needed him to be alive. Though they no longer socialized in the same circles, they had known each other since they were kids. Used to be best buds. Elizabeth and her mother couldn't take losing him, too.

And, dammit all to hell, Carson needed answers. He had to find Dane.

Carson still refused to believe that his old friend would have hurt his family, but then he wouldn't have thought Wainwright would just turn his back on him, either. Or manipulate a confession for crimes not committed. That was way, way out of character for the man who had been his mentor and friend for more than five years.

He was hiding something.

Or maybe Carson had never really known him.

Nothing added up to the bottom line Carson had expected to find. There were no clear-cut answers. No plain truths.

Senator Drake was dead.

Wainwright had kicked Carson to the curb.

When Elizabeth and Patricia learned the news, Carson doubted they would still think so highly of him. Whatever had Elizabeth coming to him would stop on a dime.

That left Carson with no one. Again.

He glanced at his passenger.

Except for Annette Baxter.

His jaw clenched.

An unholy union to say the least.

But he needed help. Obviously he couldn't do this alone.

He needed *her.*

She was the only person who seemed to want the whole truth as badly as he did. The idea that she had known things about the slaughter of his family and hadn't told him up front should have him on the defensive. He should still despise her. But somehow he couldn't. She'd done what she had to in order to survive, and on some level he understood that seemingly selfish concept. Besides, she hadn't owed him anything. For all intents and purposes they had been enemies until as recently as twenty-four hours ago.

But there were other people who had known . . . who had deliberately set out to prevent him from finding the truth.

Luttrell. Fire raged in Carson's gut. That son of a bitch had stabbed him in the back. Carson couldn't fathom just yet the extent of his former friend's treachery.

Not that anything excused Carson's own behavior because it didn't. He'd screwed up. Royally. But Luttrell was supposed to be his friend. As was Wainwright.

Yeah, right.

What Carson really felt right now was the burning desire to find the truth and see that justice was served. No matter who was destroyed in the process.

If Wainwright had been part of a cover-up surrounding his family's murder, Carson would see that he paid. Yet it didn't make sense. Wainwright had been a friend to his father. So had the senator. Poker buddies. The whole country club routine. Special advisers to the city council. They were the very men who had helped make Birmingham the thriving metropolis it was today.

The whole scenario was mind boggling, surreal.

But Carson had to know for sure. Too many little things nagged at him. Like Wainwright's sudden about-face. The obvious fact that he was hiding something. Drake's abrupt supposed interest in reuniting Carson and Elizabeth. Carson may have read entirely too much into that, but he was pretty sure that had been the man's intent. Had it been for his daughter and Carson? Or had Drake had other motive for wanting them together again?

Putting all that aside, Carson understood with complete certainty that he and Annette were in danger. Apparently, her own assistant had tried to kill her. If Carson's conclusions were correct, Daniel Ledger had made at least one attempt on his life . . . perhaps two, taking into account the gas allowed to leak into his house. At the very least, the man was the prime suspect, in Carson's opinion.

"There it is."

Annette pointed out the road, and Carson slowed for the turn.

"You're sure?" He didn't see a sign, and this was the first intersecting road they had seen since they'd hit this long stretch of deserted highway.

"That's it. I've been here before."

He couldn't help staring at her. The dim interior lighting didn't allow for him to read her expression fully, but she looked dead serious and damned determined.

"Don't ask," she said before he could.

A couple of houses on either side of the narrow road were dark, but it was the one at the very end they wanted.

Small frame house on the verge of falling in on its occupants. Weeds and knee-high grass had overtaken the clearing around the structure.

The woods crowded in on the property as if they planned to take over next. The moon's light filtered down over the property, but it was the dim porch light that provided the meager visual on the place.

Three cars—one as dilapidated as the house, two SUVs, both more valuable than the real estate they were parked on—sat in the yard at the end of the road.

For the first time in his life Carson wondered why he'd never gotten a permit to carry a weapon. Now would be the perfect time to be armed.

"You should probably stay in the car."

A laugh burst out of Carson's throat. "Like I'm going to let you go to that door alone." He gave his head a firm shake. "I don't think so."

"I know this guy. LeBron McGaha. He and I have crossed paths before."

Well now, that explained everything.

He put the Rover in park and shut off the engine. "I'm still going with you." Chivalry might be dead these days as far as most men were concerned, but not for Carson. He wasn't about to let the lady go it alone.

Clips of him screwing her in a dozen different positions flashed in his head.

Lady. Elizabeth was a lady. Proper, sweet, churchgoing. But did Annette's desperation and the actions she'd taken as a result make her less than a lady?

Maybe. Maybe not.

"Suit yourself." She got out.

He did the same.

Annette marched right up to the door and knocked loud.

Carson cringed each time she pounded her fist there. He doubted that whoever was inside was going to be happy to find unexpected company on their porch.

A few more heavy knocks and the door opened. "What?" a scraggly-looking weasel demanded. He stood about five ten, with long greasy hair and a mug taken right off the most wanted bulletin at the post office. But he couldn't have been over nineteen. Just a kid.

"We're looking for Dane Drake." Annette's voice was strong, fearless.

The guy stared at her for three beats then glared at Carson for about one. "What the hell do you want with Dane?"

Annette moved in closer to the guy. Carson tensed.

She put her face in the weasel's and said, "I owe him a blow job. You got a problem with that, LeBron?"

The bastard's gaze narrowed. "I know you. You're that bitch that got Dane and me out of trouble one time."

Talk about friends in low places.

"You got that assault charge off my back." He nodded, grinned. "Yeah, I remember you."

"That's right," Annette shot back. "Now I need your help."

She had gotten an assault charge dismissed to keep this guy in line.

Carson wanted to be indignant, but, if it benefited their cases, lawyers did what she'd done all the time.

"Name it," the long-haired creep said.

"I need to find Dane Drake now. Do you or any of your friends have any idea where he is?"

LeBron got that deer-caught-in-the-headlights look on his face. "I'm not too sure—"

"Yes, you are," Annette argued. "You know exactly where he is. Now tell me."

"Okay, okay." Lebron glanced at Carson.

"It's all right," Annette assured him. "You can talk in front of him."

No way this guy was going to roll over on his friend. "Take Highway Eleven until you hit Three. He's hiding out in the Holiday Inn Express in Fultondale. Says somebody's after him."

Dread pooled in Carson's gut. If anyone else got to Dane first . . .

"Thanks, LeBron," Annette said. "Now we're even."

As they hustled back out to the Rover, LeBron shouted, "Hey, if Dane don't want that blow job, I'll sure as hell take it."

Annette didn't respond. She jumped into the passenger seat and ordered, "Drive. Fast."

1:15 a.m.
Fultondale
Holiday Inn Express

"He won't be registered under his own name." Carson surveyed the vehicles in the parking lot. "There's no way to know which room he's in."

"That's where you come in."

He turned to Annette. "What do you mean?"

"The clerk's a woman." She shrugged. "Go in there and pour on the charm, then flash that officer-of-the-court ID you've got and see if you can't get the room number and the key."

He'd never considered the ID as a means to prod information. He might as well go for it. He reached for the door handle. "I'll be right back."

Carson heard the power lock click into place after he exited the vehicle. He didn't blame her. She had reason to be afraid . . . even if she refused to say it out loud.

He opened the door to the lobby and scanned for other patrons. None. Good.

At the counter he waited for the clerk—young, pretty—to finish the call on her cell phone. Then he smiled for her. "Hey."

Interest stirred in her eyes. "You need a room?"

"In a way." He laid a one-hundred-dollar bill on the counter. Her mouth dropped open. "I'm Investigator Tanner." He flashed his badge. "I'm looking for a person of interest in one of my cases."

She looked from him to the bill and licked her lips. "Who?"

"Well, I'm sure he's not using his real name. He's tall, thin, dark hair and eyes. About thirty-one. His real name is Dane Drake, but he might be going by something else."

Her eyes narrowed as she concentrated on the people and faces she'd likely seen pass through this shift. "I don't know." Another period of contemplation. "We definitely don't have a Dane Drake. Wait. There was this one dude." She raised her eyebrows. "Kind of grungy looking. He came in here to get coffee early in my shift." She shuddered. "Gave me the creeps."

Carson placed another hundred-dollar bill next to the first. "I need a room number and the key."

She bit her bottom lip, then asked, "Is he under arrest?"

"I need him for questioning. It's extremely important. He could be in danger."

She looked around quickly. "Are there people after him?"

Carson nodded. "Unfortunately. I need to find him first."

"Gotcha." She checked her computer, then swiped a key. "Room two fourteen. It's on the back side, second floor."

"Thank you." Carson winked. She blushed.

He jogged back to the car. "Room two fourteen. Other side of the hotel."

"Do you think it's him?"

Carson started the Rover. "I gave his description. The clerk seemed to think so."

"I guess we'll know in a minute."

Carson drove to the back of the hotel. He and Annette were out of the car and headed for the stairs to the second floor before the vehicle rocked to a complete stop.

Outside room 214, Carson hesitated. He'd never known Dane to carry weapons. But if he were scared and desperate, he might be capable of anything. Zac Holderfield's death was testament to that.

"We need to consider how we're going to do this," Carson suggested.

Annette snatched the key from his hand. "Stand back, I'll show you."

Before he could stop her, she'd inserted the key and was pushing the door inward.

"Dane, it's Carson," he shouted over her head, in the hope of preventing a physical altercation.

The room was dark save for one bedside table lamp. Dane Drake lay sprawled on the bed. An empty tequila bottle lay on the floor. Alongside it was what looked like a prescription bottle. And a drying puddle of puke.

Annette rushed to the bed while Carson examined the prescription bottle. Patricia Drake. Tranquilizers. The bottle was empty. Shit. His attention shifted to the bed and the motionless man lying there.

"Dane." Annette shook him. He didn't respond. She drew her hand away. "He's cold."

"Dane." Carson put his face close to his old friend's. "He's not breathing." Carson checked his carotid pulse. Dread settled in his gut. "Call nine-one-one."

As he assessed Dane more closely, he recognized that it wouldn't matter how fast help arrived.

Dane was already dead.

"Wait," Carson said, desperation fueling him, "don't make that call."

Annette stared at him in disbelief and no small amount of horror.

"Just . . . don't," Carson reiterated.

42

1:50 a.m.

"It's over."

Carson turned in his seat at the sound of Annette's voice. They sat in the Rover, in the dark, in the hotel parking lot. They'd been doing that for about fifteen minutes. He still couldn't believe what he was about to propose. But he was out of options.

Dane was dead.

There was no place to go from here. No way to find any answers, much less the whole story.

He stared beyond the windshield, into the night. He'd risked everything, and he'd gotten nothing in return.

He'd failed.

"I have to move Paula. Tonight."

Carson's attention shifted back to the woman in the passenger seat. She had lost everything as well. Her sister's safety was in jeopardy. She was on the verge of being charged with two high profile murders. The citizens would demand justice. Annette Baxter would be painted as a cunning, manipulative harlot in the media. Then the witch trial would begin.

He and Annette didn't have a shred of evidence to support their theories. Hell, he didn't actually have a fleshed-out theory. He was still reeling with all that she had told him. With the visit to Stokes. With all that he suspected.

Frustration coiled inside him. How the hell had he allowed himself to be backed into a corner like this? He never lost a case. Never got so caught up he couldn't properly assess a motive or a suspect.

Never gave up.

His gaze dropped to the steering wheel, where his hands were clenched as if he were racing along a winding road. He could not give up like this.

Fury tightened in his gut.

Hell no. He wasn't giving up.

They had one opportunity here.

"I have a plan."

"You're wasting time. We can't beat them." Annette leaned against the headrest. "They've already won."

Anticipation roared through Carson. "They've only won if we give up."

She looked at him. Though he couldn't make out the emotion in her eyes, he could feel the intensity there. "There's a time when you cut your losses, counselor. Or didn't they teach that technique in law school?"

He started the Rover. "I must've been absent the day they discussed that technique." He shot her a look, wanting her to see the determination on his face even in the dim lighting. "We don't have any solid evidence, that's true. But"—he shifted into drive—"we do have a witness."

"Dane is dead!"

Carson pulled out of the parking slot and headed for the street. "But *they* don't know that."

As he yielded for traffic, he watched that realization strike the worry from her face.

She smiled. "This is true."

He eased into the street and considered the plan already formulating in his head. "We have to implement this strategy very carefully." He glanced at her. "We only have one shot."

"And only a few hours before the maid service at the hotel discovers Dane's body."

"You're right." Carson rolled into the left lane and made a U-turn.

"Where're you going?"

"To buy us some more time."

3:50 a.m.
2201 Lime Rock Road, Vestavia
Schaffer Residence

Carson had hung the Do Not Disturb sign on the door to Dane's room. If they were lucky, that would give them the rest of the day to get this done.

If Special Agent Schaffer would cooperate.

Clad in sweatpants and a T-shirt, she had allowed them into her home at this ungodly hour. That hadn't actually been surprising considering her surveillance team had been attempting to locate Annette for the better part of the night. Persuading her to listen to their story without calling in to report their arrival had been slightly more difficult.

Schaffer propped her feet on the coffee table of her family room, then took her time assessing first Annette and then Carson. "You want me to believe," she said to Carson, "that Wainwright, along with his deceased friend Senator Drake, is manipulating all that's happened in order to facilitate some massive cover-up?"

Carson didn't blame her for being skeptical. Their story sounded crazy at best. But he was sticking to it. Hell, it was the only one they had. "Yes."

"Then why would Wainwright have come to me," Schaffer insisted, "with that video?"

The video? That was the tip Wainwright had given her. "There wasn't anything particularly earth shattering on that video," he reminded her.

Schaffer snorted. "That's because you got the edited version. I wasn't about to trust you with the real thing. When you didn't appear to know about it, I wasn't sure what was going on in the DA's Office."

Carson looked from Annette who shrugged back to Schaffer. "What was on the tape?"

"Your friend here was assuring Fleming that she could take care of the senator. Two weeks later he's murdered."

Carson and Annette stared at each other. She shook her head. "It wasn't like that." She turned to Schaffer. "His son was in trouble again. Senator Drake wasn't sure I could make it go away to his satisfaction. He played that card every time. He refused to come to me. He always went to Otis. Or had Wainwright take care of it."

"There you go," Carson urged. "Wainwright used that conversation out of context."

Schaffer turned to Annette then. "Him"—she hitched her thumb in Carson's direction—"I can halfway believe. Though I'm not saying I do. But you." Schaffer folded her arms over her chest. "Why would I put any faith in a single word you say?"

Carson felt a twinge of sympathy for Annette. Even as a child, no one had believed her when she'd told the truth. No wonder she'd stopped trying and had chosen another path to survive. He studied her profile, noting again the delicate features that so belied the tough-as-nails woman beneath.

"I have no reason to lie."

Judging by Schaffer's expression, that wasn't the answer she was looking for. "I can think of one or two." She relaxed into the thick sofa cushions. "Holderfield. Drake. Ring any bells?"

"I didn't kill anyone," Annette fired back. "Those murders—"

"The murder weapon used on Zac Holderfield," Schaffer interrupted, "has been linked to an alias of yours. My people, as well as the Jefferson County Sheriff's Department, are working overtime to confirm that link. That same weapon we now know was used to murder Drake." She lifted an eyebrow at Annette. "How do you explain that?"

"Those murders," Annette began again, seemingly unfazed, "are part of the setup. I know too much. They want to discredit me so that nothing I claim against them is reliable, and then they want me on death row. Or dead."

"Correct me if I'm wrong," Schaffer said to Carson, "but this entire investigation has been about bringing down Fleming." She rested her gaze on Annette once more. "We were, still are for that matter, perfectly happy to offer you a deal including immunity. All you have to do is provide the evidence we need. I might even be able to make the murders go away. We might not work as hard as we need to in order to prove the gun was yours."

Before Carson could respond, Annette countered, "That may be the way it started for you, but that was never the goal for Wainwright and Drake. They want *me,* not Otis Fleming. And the gun isn't mine."

"I don't have any doubts," Carson said to Schaffer, "that they want to nail Annette, but"—he turned to Annette then—"I'm certain at least the secondary goal is to bring down Fleming."

"There are things you don't know," Annette explained. It wasn't until then that he noticed how tired she looked. Even her voice lacked the usual commanding air. "I went to see Otis just before we started our search for Dane. He told me he had negotiated a deal for himself."

When had she gone to see Fleming? The only time Carson couldn't account for Annette's activities was while he had been with Elizabeth. No matter what Fleming said, Carson knew just how badly Wainwright wanted to bring him down. "What could Fleming have possibly offered in exchange for himself?"

Annette moistened her lips. "Me."

Carson choked out a laugh. Unbelievable. "And Fleming told you this?"

"Yes."

"How can you be sure," Schaffer interjected, "that he was telling the truth?"

Annette looked straight at Schaffer then. "Because Wainwright was there."

The disbelief drained out of Carson, only to be replaced by an equally startling emotion he couldn't quite label. "In Fleming's house?"

"Having tea," Annette confirmed.

A prolonged moment of stunned silence followed.

"The bottom line," Schaffer announced, shattering the tension-filled quiet, "is you don't have any evidence to back up your accusations. As much as I like you, Tanner"—her gaze connected with his—"I can't go on hearsay or conjecture. I need something tangible to make this leap."

"We have a witness." Carson's gut knotted. He hoped like hell the agent wouldn't see the lie in his eyes.

"Who?" Schaffer didn't bother keeping the doubt out of her tone.

"Dane Drake," Annette answered for Carson. "He was there when Carson's family was murdered. He knows what happened as well as the steps that were taken to cover up the truth."

Again Carson was blown away by the woman's ability to lie without the slightest flinch. How could he trust anything she told him? Panic trickled in his chest. He was basing his entire theory, risking everything, on what she had told him . . . on *her*.

"I need to question this witness," Schaffer said without preamble. "Where is he?"

"He's in hiding." Carson wondered how many laws he would have to break before this was over. "As you can well imagine, considering that his father has been murdered, if Dane shows his face he's a dead man." The image of Dane sprawled on that bed flashed in Carson's head. He clenched his teeth to hold back the grimace.

"So what exactly is it that you're proposing?" Schaffer wanted to know. "What's your strategy? And what do you expect to gain?"

Carson felt some amount of relief at the idea that the agent was even willing to hear him out. Now if she would just suspend logic and go with his plan.

At this point, Carson had nothing to lose.

"I put in a call to Aidan Moore, the attorney who represented Stokes," he explained. "I tell Moore that I have new evidence indicating that Stokes and Wainwright made a deal that included this massive cover-up. That's just the trigger. Wainwright's reaction will provide the rest of what we need." Slim, very slim. Who the hell was Carson kidding? The whole plan was damned anorexic.

Schaffer's eyebrows shot upward. "Do you possess actual evidence?"

Carson opened his mouth to say not exactly but Annette beat him to the punch.

"Yes, we have the wedding bands taken from the victims."

He nodded. "That's right." The wedding bands most likely couldn't be linked to a perpetrator, but they did have them.

"You call Moore," Schaffer said, drawing Carson's attention back to her, "and he calls Wainwright. Then what?"

"Wainwright calls me. I agree to meet him with the rings," Carson glanced at Annette wondering just how she would take this next part. "Your people monitor the meeting, during which I'll manipulate the confession."

Schaffer lowered her feet to the floor and leaned forward. "I know you're good, Tanner, but do you really expect to be able to outmaneuver the man who taught you everything you know?"

Annette as well as Schaffer stared at him as they awaited his answer.

Was he crazy to think he could do this? Maybe. Probably. But he was desperate at this point. And, as he'd already recognized, he had nothing else to lose.

"Yes," he said at last.

When Schaffer hesitated, he tacked on, "I'll take full responsibility for everything if this goes wrong. I'll swear that I presented false evidence to you, causing you to misuse resources. Whatever I have to do, I'll do it, if you'll help me make this happen." To some degree he was doing exactly that.

Now it was Annette who was startled and staring at him.

Schaffer shrugged. "What the hell? It's your career on the line. And if we break this case, we'll both be elevated to legend status."

Carson took his first deep breath since calling Schaffer to ask for this meeting.

"Let's do it," he said, determination rocketing inside him. He might not win but he damned sure wasn't going down without a fight.

"I can have my people in place within the hour," Schaffer said, entering a number into her cell phone as she spoke.

Carson pulled his cell from his pocket. "I'll make the call to Moore."

Before he could select the attorney's name from his electronic address book, his cell rang. His uncle Max's name appeared on the screen. Shit. Not now. He didn't need this now. But he couldn't not answer.

The instant he pressed the button to accept the call he could hear his uncle's frantic shouts. "They're after me, Carson! Help me! I'm hiding in my shack . . . but they're breaking through the door!" Each sentence was punctuated by shattering and crashing.

The connection ended.

Dammit. Dammit.

Maybe he could send a patrol unit over there.

"Is something wrong?"

Carson glanced up at Annette's question. "It's my uncle. He's evidently gone off his meds again. Sounded like he's tearing the place apart." Carson stood. "I'll have to get someone over there. He could hurt himself." *Or someone else,* Carson didn't add.

"I'll go."

His gaze collided with Annette's.

"I can't help you with Wainwright," she explained. "There's nothing I can really do right now except wait."

"My team is making preparations," Schaffer said.

"I'm calling Moore now." Carson focused on his phone, selected the name and number. He still had to do something about his uncle. Annette's offer was damned generous. "Okay," he said to her before Moore answered. "You go take care of Max. I'll do this."

"You'd better use my car. No one will pay any attention to it," Schaffer offered to Annette. "A warrant could be issued for you any minute now. You'd be no help to us behind bars."

Moore answered as Schaffer scrounged up her car keys for Annette. Carson didn't get a chance to say anything to Annette before she was gone.

He hoped like hell she didn't get spooked and run.

Right now, everything pretty much depended upon her being able to back him up.

That and their dead witness.

43

5:00 a.m.
Mountain Brook

Annette parked the sedan she'd borrowed from Kim Schaffer along the side of the deserted road. She stared through the darkness. Light glowed from the two windows on the front of the shack where Maxwell West resided. His old pickup truck stood to one side of the shack. She didn't see any sign of Max.

With her cell phone tucked into her pocket, she opened the car door and got out. She listened for several seconds. Too quiet. Where were the rants of a mentally ill man? No sounds of things being tossed around inside his house though half an hour ago he had been in a desperate rage, according to Carson.

He could have injured himself. Could be dead.

Fear snaked along the column of her spine.

Walking quickly, she made her way along the gravel drive. Her heels crunched, jarring the silence pressing in around her. She glanced back to the car twice, three times, her fingers wrapped tightly around the cell phone in her pocket.

Annette wasn't usually so jumpy. But this could very well be a setup. She wasn't sure Carson had considered that possibility, but she sure as hell had. Even if it weren't, it was unfamiliar territory.

She understood how to handle her sister's outbursts, but this was a man with an entirely different problem set. He would be far stronger than Paula. Once Annette reached the small porch, she moved a bit more stealthily. If he had worn himself down, fallen asleep, she didn't want to startle him.

At the door she tried the knob. Not locked. Annette braced herself and slowly, noiselessly turned the knob. The locking mechanism clicked as it moved to the open position. She flinched. Stay calm. Be ready. Then she opened the door.

The room was well lit.

The Spartan furnishings were turned upside down. Items had been ripped from their shelves, cabinets, and drawers. Photographs had been torn into pieces. But no sign of the man who had carried out such destruction.

She listened a few moments more. Nothing. "Max?"

Silence.

Her nerves jangled. She squeezed the phone in her pocket tighter. "Max! Carson sent me to see if you needed any help cleaning up."

"Shhh!"

Annette whirled toward the door.

Max West grabbed her, held her close to his body. "Shhh," he hissed in her ear. "They'll hear you."

Her heart thudding against her chest wall, Annette nodded. He must have been hiding behind the door.

"They're gonna get me this time," he muttered. "I know it."

Annette turned her face up to his. That was about the only part of her body she could move at the moment. "What do they want?" Instinct told her to play along. If the man was delusional, arguing wouldn't work.

He stared down at her, his face a mask of confusion and frustration. "Me, of course!"

She nodded. "We should make a run for it." The idea gained momentum quickly. "I have a car. Should we go get help?"

Max moved his head from side to side in a slow, resolute manner. "If we go out there, they'll get us for sure."

"I understand." She glanced around the room. "We should find ourselves weapons." She looked back up at him. "Maybe prepare something to hide behind. Like that couch over there."

He seemed to consider her suggestion, then shook his head adamantly. "We can't touch anything. It's all evil. That's why I had to fight it."

"Carson is worried about you." She didn't know what else to say. "He wants me to—"

"Where is that boy?" Max demanded, his tone loud and gruff. "He should've been home by now. The last time he did this . . ."

Annette's insides froze. Was he referring to the night Carson's family was murdered? Or some other night that had suddenly flashed through his muddled gray matter? "What happened last time?"

Max shook his head hard. "I can't say."

Annette lowered her voice to a more soothing tone. "You can tell me anything, Max. I'm Carson's friend. He trusts me."

He looked away from her as if he'd heard someone else speaking to him. "She's not Carson. I can't tell her," he said to the voice only he could hear.

"No," he screamed. "I won't tell her!"

"It's okay, Max," she urged. "You don't have to tell me anything. Let's just stay calm and be quiet so they won't hear us."

He snapped his mouth shut, surveying the room as if he fully expected to see someone else standing nearby.

"I can't tell her," he growled.

His arms tightened around her, and Annette felt the first glimmer of panic.

"Where's your medicine, Max?" she asked tentatively.

He lowered his mouth close to her ear. "It's evil. I can't take it."

She was going to have to disable him. There appeared no way around it.

"I WILL NOT TELL HER!"

Annette cringed at the words screamed so close to her ear.

When her ears had stopped ringing, she studied the man's face. Whatever was going through his head, he was scared to death. "Max, can you show me what you're afraid of?"

If she could distract him from the voice, that might be helpful.

He stared at her a moment, then started ushering her deeper into the shack. Bedroom. The panic bloomed larger. Images and voices from her past whispered in her whirling thoughts.

She forced the memories away. This was Max . . . not her mother's boyfriend or one of her foster fathers.

The coppery odor of blood yanked her full attention back to the moment a split second before the crimson trailing up the tousled bedcovers registered. As her sluggish brain grappled to wrap around what it all meant, her gaze locked on what was lying in the center of the bed.

Blood. Something gray or black. Long tail.

A raccoon.

Her stomach roiled. The raccoon had been mutilated. Had bled out in Max's bed. Judging by the odor it had been there a day or two.

She swallowed back a gag. "Max, is that your raccoon?" Damn, anyone who would kill a helpless animal had to be seriously twisted.

"It was in my trash can," a female voice announced calmly.

Before Annette could crane her neck around and see beyond Max's shoulder, to see who'd spoken, he started to howl and cry. He pushed Annette away and ran to the corner. He huddled there with his knees to his chest, his arms wrapped around his legs.

Annette faced the woman who had appeared seemingly out of nowhere.

Patricia Drake.

The gun in her hand was the next thing Annette became aware of. Well now, this was certainly an unexpected development. The senator's wife definitely wasn't anyone Annette would have considered a threat.

"I couldn't tell her!" Max cried. "She's not Carson!"

Patricia sent a glare in the old man's direction. "Shut up! I need to think."

Annette mentally shook off the surprise and evaluated her situation. This woman intended to kill her. The certainty with which she understood that reality made her pulse react.

Annette's mouth went dry.

Could Patricia Drake be responsible for Dr. Holderfield's death? For the senator's? Surely she wouldn't have killed her own husband.

The way the two had doted on each other in public. Patricia was always so meek and mild. An uncharacteristic tremor of fear rattled Annette. But . . . if she had killed her husband, she damned sure wouldn't have any qualms about killing Annette.

For the first time in over a decade Annette had no idea how to fix a situation.

She was screwed.

"Carson's dear uncle Max has a message for his nephew," Patricia explained in a haughty voice. "He was in his sister's house that night. *He* committed the murders. Carson needs to hear that so this nuisance can be put to rest once and for all. That's the way it should've been handled from the beginning." Patricia inclined her head and glowered at Annette. "But Carson isn't here. Where is he?"

There had to be a way to turn this around. "He's with the FBI." Annette looked the other woman straight in the eyes and went for broke. "He's telling them his suspicions about you and your son. We found Dane. He told us everything."

Patricia laughed. "Don't be foolish, you ridiculous whore. Carson has no idea what really happened to his parents. Dane would never tell. Never. He loves his sister too much. Besides, I don't think Dane has been *talking* to anyone."

"You," Annette argued, fury bursting inside her at what those cruel words undoubtedly meant, "should have gone to the police about Dane years ago. Why did you let Carson live in hell all those years?" *What kind of person could do that to another human being?*

The front door flew open. Annette hoped it would be help. But her hope was short lived.

"Mother! What're you doing?"

Elizabeth.

Well if she hadn't been screwed already, Annette certainly was now. This was what happened when she tried to do something nice.

Patricia pointed a disapproving look at her daughter. "Stay out of this, Elizabeth. I have everything under control."

Elizabeth ignored her mother, unleashed her fury on Annette. "You're a fool. You should have left town while you had the chance." Then she wheeled on her mother once more. "Answer me, Mother. What are you doing?"

Annette considered her chances of survival if she took a dive at Elizabeth right now. Too risky. Patricia Drake might not hesitate to shoot—even in the direction of her daughter.

"I told you," Patricia snarled, "I have this under control. All will be exactly as it should be very soon."

Elizabeth's face puckered into an expression of disgust. "What is that smell?"

"I used the raccoon to scare him," her mother explained impatiently. "Max is going to confess to Carson. That story makes far more sense than that ridiculous Stokes scheme. It should have been done this way years ago. Wainwright's an idiot."

Patricia killed the raccoon? What a sick bitch. Hearing Wainwright's name was no surprise. Annette had known Wainwright was in this up to his eyeballs. The bastard. She hoped he got his. If she were lucky maybe she would live to see it.

"Why did you do that?" Elizabeth demanded, her voice small and high-pitched, like a child whining over a lost toy. "You do it every time! I was making a pet out of the raccoon. You had no right!"

Patricia scoffed. "Don't be foolish. He was a wild animal. You've never properly taken care of a pet. The only things you need to be focused on are work and Carson."

"You never listened to what we wanted," Elizabeth snapped. "Never, never, never! Every time Father got us a dog you found something wrong with it. Wanted it out of the way. I think you were just jealous, Mother. Jealous of how much Dane and I loved those dogs."

"Don't be ridiculous, Elizabeth," Patricia patronized. "It was for the best. I know what's best for *you.*"

This just got more and more twisted. Annette had to make a move. "What about Carson?" She directed her appeal to Elizabeth. "Hasn't he been hurt enough? Does your mother have to drag his uncle into this nightmare, too?"

The princess of Birmingham morphed instantly from helpless little girl to psychotic bitch. "Don't pretend you know Carson. He only slept with you because he couldn't have me."

Okay, so Elizabeth wasn't a potential ally. "Or maybe," Annette tossed back, "it was because I was helping him find the truth."

"Liar." Elizabeth snatched the gun from her mother's hand and moved in a step closer to Annette. "You don't know the truth any more than he does."

Annette wasn't sure whether Elizabeth was less of a threat than her mother or not. Might as well take a stab at throwing her off balance. "Were you going to kill Carson when he came here? The way you did your father?"

"How dare you even suggest such a thing!" Elizabeth leveled the barrel of the weapon on Annette. "I loved my father. And no one's going to hurt Carson. We're going to be married. Father would have come around in time. He loved Carson. My father was only worried that Carson would cause trouble with all this digging into the past."

"That's why we have to do this now," Patricia urged. She looked from her daughter to the gun in her hand and back. "We can't take any more risks."

Annette had to keep them distracted and divided until she had a plan. "Maybe your mother killed your father for you."

Patricia Drake's chin jutted out. "He went too far."

Elizabeth watched her mother as she spoke. Her lips quivered. "He did," she agreed, her voice low, grim. "But he didn't have to die. You could have talked to him. You always kill everything!"

"He wasn't listening." Patricia's cold expression melted as she peered lovingly at her daughter, brushing a strand of dark hair from her cheek. "I couldn't let him hurt you all over again. He wanted Carson dead."

When Elizabeth would have argued, Patricia implored, "I heard your father give the order, Elizabeth. I had no choice. He had to be stopped."

Annette shuddered. A part of her had wondered if Wainwright and Drake would really go to that extreme. Killing her was one thing, but Carson? For all intents and purposes, he was one of them. Now she knew. If she didn't get out of here alive to warn him . . . it could still happen.

Say something! Anything! "The way you stopped Lana Kimble when you were afraid Randolph might choose her over you," Annette insinuated. More conjecture, but it was worth a try.

Patricia's face darkened with renewed rage, but there was no mistaking the flicker of surprise in her eyes. "I didn't kill her. She fell. It was an accident. We were arguing. Besides, Randolph never really loved that pathetic little slut. It was me he needed. She would have ruined him."

Jesus. Annette had guessed right. "So you were just protecting the man you loved?"

"Of course," Patricia insisted. "He would never have achieved all that he has without me. I've always made sure my family was protected."

No shit. Like a bear protecting her cubs. Annette fought the quaking that had started in her limbs. She needed more time. *Think!* The prescription bottle in Dane's room. It had belonged to his mother. "The way you protected Dane?"

"He wouldn't stop causing trouble!" Patricia's voice grew higher and thinner as she spoke. "I told him to stop, but he refused. Trading the rings for drugs was the last straw. He left me no choice."

Elizabeth stared at Patricia. "What did you do, Mother?"

Patricia glanced around the room as if buying time while she came up with an excuse. "I . . . I gave him something to help him sleep, dear. That's all. Maybe he'll do better after he's had some rest."

"Doesn't matter now," Annette blurted, hoping to keep the tension mounting between mother and daughter. Both glared at her. "Like I said," Annette improvised, "Dane told us everything. *I know what you did.*"

"Dane's an idiot," Elizabeth contended. "Drugs have ruined him. But he would never do anything to hurt me."

What now? Annette had just one genuine ace up her sleeve. "Dane is dead, Elizabeth."

Elizabeth's mouth went slack. Her eyes widened for a moment before the fury resurrected. "I don't believe you."

"He took those tranquilizers your mother gave him, rented himself a hotel room, and checked out." Annette needed Elizabeth confused, emotional. Anything but determined.

"You're lying."

Annette shrugged. "Call the Holiday Inn Express in Fultondale. Ask them to check room two fourteen. Your brother's there, he's dead." She glanced at the older woman. "Why don't you ask your mother exactly what she did?"

The weapon in Elizabeth's hand shook. "I don't believe you." She jerked out her cell phone, entered a number, and waited for an answer.

"Don't listen to her," Patricia scolded.

Elizabeth ignored her mother. "Dane! Call me as soon as you get this message. I need to hear your voice."

"He won't get your message," Annette warned. "He's dead. She killed him."

Elizabeth stared at her phone as if willing it to ring.

"Elizabeth, baby," Patricia pleaded. "I had to do it. It was the only way to protect you. Dane just kept getting worse and worse. It was time to give up on him and put him out of his misery for all our sakes."

Elizabeth's demeanor went abruptly and eerily calm. "You didn't have to do that, Mother," she said placidly. "I could have talked to him." She backed a step or two away from Patricia. "You always overreact. You kill everything I love. I can't even have a pet because of you! You'll probably kill Carson, too, if he makes a single mistake."

Annette felt sick at the idea of what these two had done. What they would continue to do if someone didn't stop them.

"I've always protected you," Patricia reminded her as she reached out to her daughter. "I won't ever let anyone hurt you."

The sound of the weapon discharging exploded in the room. Annette's breath trapped in her lungs.

Patricia stared at her daughter for one long beat before looking down at her chest. Blood gurgled from the small hole near her heart, spilled down her pink blouse. Patricia opened her mouth to speak but crumpled to the floor in a lifeless heap instead. Her eyes remained open as if even in death she wanted to see how this ended.

"Max, come here!" Elizabeth commanded.

Annette's body shook with equal measures of fear and shock. She tried to rationalize what she'd just witnessed. Elizabeth Drake had killed her mother. Annette's muscles quivered once more then turned to lead. She told herself to breathe. She had to make a move or stand here and let this bitch kill her, too.

"Noooo!" Max wailed. "Don't make me!"

"Come here," Elizabeth ordered, "or *they'll* come for you and I'll let them."

The old man struggled onto all fours and crawled unsteadily to where Elizabeth stood.

"Please," he begged, "I don't want them to come."

"They brought you that dead animal as a warning," Elizabeth told him. "Don't make me call them back."

Max began to moan and weep.

What the hell kind of power did Elizabeth have over that poor man? Who the hell were they?

"No one's coming, Max," Annette promised, anger mounting inside her, overtaking the fear. By God, she wasn't going down without a fight. "You don't need to be afraid. Elizabeth is lying to you. Patricia brought the raccoon."

Elizabeth's gaze collided with Annette's. "Shut up!"

"What's the matter?" Annette smiled as if victory already belonged to her. "You afraid he'll realize you have no power over him?"

"I said, shut up!" Elizabeth pointed the weapon at Max. "Shut up or I'll shoot him."

Max howled in agony, curled into a ball of pure terror.

Annette refused to let go of her courage. "You can't shoot us both at the same time. Who're you going for first? Him or me?" She eased one foot in front of the other as if bracing to make a move.

The gun's barrel swung back in Annette's direction. "Maybe I'll just shoot you and blame it on Max. After all, you're a stranger. No one would question it. You showed up and he shot you. Everyone knows he's crazy."

"Does Max own a weapon?" If Annette could keep her talking a little longer, she might just be able to come up with a plan.

Elizabeth smirked. "That can always be arranged after the fact, as you well know."

Determination fired in Annette's veins. No way was she letting this spoiled brat win. "You're not that smart, *Miss Deputy Mayor.*"

"I was smart enough to figure out how to make you squirm." She smiled sweetly. "*Ms. Anderson.*"

Murder roared in Annette's chest. "It was you."

"The whole plan was so easy," Elizabeth taunted. "I was touring the center with a group of potential donors and I saw you there. Finding out about your *sister,* Paula, was simple after that. The staff adores me. My family and I help keep them fully funded. They have to love me."

Annette wanted to kill her for what she'd done to Paula. But not yet. Dane was dead. Patricia was dead. She needed Elizabeth alive.

She needed the whole truth. "Did your plan include murdering Dr. Holderfield, too?"

Elizabeth shook her head. "I'm not telling you anything else."

"Wainwright probably gave the order," Annette goaded. "Did he make you do it?"

"Please." Elizabeth rolled her eyes. "Wainwright doesn't give the orders. My father was the one in charge. The others did what he told them." Elizabeth straightened her jacket with her free hand and smoothed her hair. "No matter the mess, the cleanup is always quite civilized. Lynch makes sure every last detail is taken care of. Just like he'll do here."

Annette wasn't surprised that Lieutenant Lynch was involved. He would know exactly how to ensure that the evidence, if any, pointed in the right direction. "I guess he screwed up on the gun that's supposed to be registered to my alias."

Elizabeth laughed drily. "Don't you worry. That minor issue will be resolved, and you'll be charged." She sighed. "Posthumously, it seems. Now put your hands up, away from your body. Make any sudden moves and I will shoot you."

Slowly, Annette raised her hands in a gesture of surrender. "So, you're going to kill me and pin it on Max," she wondered aloud. "But then there's Dane's admission to having killed Carson's family. Who's going to fix that? Carson's not going to forgive you for keeping Dane's secret."

"Please," Elizabeth rebuffed, "my brother couldn't have admitted all that. He doesn't have the guts to say it, much less go through with it."

Well, well. If Dane didn't do it . . . "I suppose you had the guts, *Princess.*" The sweet, wholesome image the media played up made Annette want to puke. If they only knew . . .

"Don't call me that!" Elizabeth waved the gun. "You have no idea what I can or cannot do much less what I've done."

"I wouldn't even believe you killed your mother," Annette countered, "if I hadn't seen it with my own eyes."

Elizabeth cocked her head, stared down the length of the barrel. "Maybe I will kill you just to shut you up. Then Carson and I can finally be happy."

Annette kicked back the panic that threatened her cool. "If you really loved Carson, why murder his family? What did they do to you?"

"Shut up!" Elizabeth crowded in on her, jammed the barrel of the weapon into Annette's chest. "You don't know anything about me!"

Renewed terror held Annette mute for a pulse-pounding instant. Elizabeth's eyes danced with something that looked exactly like insanity. An epiphany hit Annette. Like mother, like daughter. No matter that the business end of a weapon poked her sternum, Annette pushed a knowing smile into place. "Genetics can be a bitch sometimes."

Fury claimed Elizabeth's face. "I am not like my mother!" she screamed. "She was the one, not me." A moment passed as she visibly struggled to regain her composure. "She did it, so they wouldn't know."

Annette had to keep her talking. She needed every last detail. "Wouldn't know what? That you loved Carson and his family? Your mother must not have understood or she wouldn't have killed his family."

"Are you stupid? Of course, she knew I loved Carson. That's why she had to do it."

What the hell? Keep it together, Annette. Get all the facts. If you survive, you'll need them . . . for Carson. "I think maybe you're just as nuts as your mother."

"I *am not* like her!" Elizabeth screamed. "I never did anything *that* bad." She shook her head adamantly. "It's not like I killed the stupid girl. She fell down the stairs and broke her shoulder. It was an accident. She was clumsy. Just because she was a cheerleader didn't mean she wasn't clumsy. But then she wouldn't come back to our house anymore and Father blew it all out of proportion."

Annette felt cold with certainty. Though she didn't know this story, she could easily imagine what really happened. "You pushed her." It wasn't until she saw the rabid look on Elizabeth's face that Annette realized she'd said the words out loud.

Silence thickened between them for one endless second.

"It. Was. An. Accident." Elizabeth's lips quivered with rage. "But *he* wouldn't believe me so he forced me to be evaluated. To endure therapy sessions."

Annette's heart thumped hard with her next realization. *Carson's mother.* The renowned child psychologist. Annette suddenly knew where this was going. "Dr. Tanner was your therapist."

"That stupid woman wanted to send me away." Elizabeth jeered at the idea. "She said there were indicators that I might have uncontrollable violent tendencies. Father was going to do it, too! He thought it would be best for me. He would tell everyone I was away at a prestigious school. No one would ever know. And when I came back I'd be well."

Annette now knew the truth that Carson Tanner had searched for all those years. "Patricia killed Carson's mother to keep the truth from coming out. About *you.*"

"She was only protecting me." Elizabeth tilted her chin in challenge. "There was no other choice."

What next? What next? "You probably tried to stop her." *Good idea. Act like you're on her side.* "You knew it would hurt Carson, so you tried to stop your mother."

Elizabeth stared at her, those green eyes glittering wildly. Her respiration still ragged. But at least she wasn't screaming or poking the gun deeper into Annette's ribs. "I was with Carson that night. He'd had too much to drink because of the fight with his mother. Mother said the timing was perfect. We couldn't wait."

Annette remembered Carson saying he'd blacked out, didn't remember anything. It wasn't impossible that the alcohol alone had done that, but considering the rest of the story, Annette wasn't convinced. "He was upset." She lowered her hands a little, braced to tackle the other woman. "You had to be there for him. Calm him down."

Elizabeth sighed as if she were weary of the subject. "The pills calmed him down."

Annette restrained the outrage that burned in her chest at what these evil bitches had done to Carson. "Sure." She nodded agreeably. "He needed the pills."

"That's what Mother said." Elizabeth stared right through Annette as if recalling some faraway memory. "Put two in his drink and he'll rest. Everything will be all right after that."

Somehow Annette had to make sure Carson learned the truth. All of it. She had to keep Elizabeth calm. Had to figure a way out of this damned shack without a bullet in her chest. "But you didn't hurt his family," she reminded the woman with the gun. "You were with Carson. Dane and your mother were the ones."

"She made Dane help her." Elizabeth still had that distant look in her eyes. "He didn't want to."

"You and Dane were victims," Annette urged with all the sympathy she could fake. "None of this was your fault."

Elizabeth blinked for the first time since she'd stopped shouting. "I don't want to talk about this anymore." All signs of vulnerability disappeared as she firmed her grip on the weapon. "I have to decide what to do with you."

So much for reverse psychology. Make a move. Any move. Now or never. Now!

"Max, they're coming!" Annette shouted.

Max clambered to his feet. "Huh?"

Elizabeth jerked her attention in his direction.

Annette rammed her. They hit the floor in a tangle.

A bullet discharged, the sound exploding in the air.

Annette bit the other woman's cheek. Elizabeth screamed.

Using all her strength, Annette wrenched the weapon out of Elizabeth's hand. It spun across the floor.

"Whore!" Elizabeth grabbed Annette by the hair with both hands. "You have to die!"

"Stop!" Max screamed.

Annette fought like a wildcat to pin Elizabeth down.

"Stop!"

In her peripheral vision Annette got a look at Max. He had the gun. Shit.

"He's got the gun," she warned.

Elizabeth released Annette's hair. They pulled apart, scrambled to get up, both very much aware that anything could happen with the weapon in the hands of a mentally unstable man currently off his meds.

"Give me the gun, Max," Elizabeth ordered.

"Don't listen to her, Max," Annette urged. "*They* came with her."

Max blinked, focused the weapon on Elizabeth. "It's you." He nodded. "You're the one who hurt them."

Oh hell. "Max," Annette pleaded, "let me have the gun." If he killed Elizabeth . . .

"Drop the weapon, Mr. West."

Annette's attention veered toward the intrusion.

Lieutenant Lynch loomed in the open doorway, a lethal bead on Max. "I said," he repeated, "drop the weapon."

Max hesitated only a second, then he let go of the weapon as if it had burned his hands. It plopped to the floor.

"Thank God you're here," Elizabeth said, her posture sagging with relief. "She killed Mother!" Then the sobs began.

Damn. Just Annette's luck that a dirty cop would come to the rescue. Had Schaffer called in backup? If this was Annette's backup, she might as well kiss her ass goodbye.

She wondered if Carson would ever know the whole story. The idea that he might end up with this twisted bitch made Annette's chest ache. "Detective, you don't—"

"Don't say a word, Ms. Baxter," Lynch ordered. "Anything you say can and will be held against you."

Fucking perfect.

Elizabeth sidled away from Annette, moving toward the door and the man who was her ally. "I don't know what I would have done if you hadn't gotten here when you did, Lieutenant. She would have killed me, too."

"Turn around," Lynch said to Elizabeth. "Put your hands behind your back."

Birmingham's princess stared at him in shock. "What did you say?"

"Do it! Now!" he commanded. "Or I'll have no choice but to use force."

Annette watched, bewildered, as the detective cuffed Elizabeth.

"You're next," he said to Annette. "Turn around and put your hands behind your back."

Then Annette knew. When she turned her back he would shoot. She would be out of the way without a lengthy, media-hyped trial. Damn.

"Do it," Lynch demanded. "Turn around now!"

Annette had no choice.

She summoned the image of Carson Tanner, wished him well, and turned her back to the man with the gun.

44

5:40 a.m.
Birmingham
Criminal Justice Center

Carson sat down behind his desk. He surveyed the files and notes he'd left yesterday . . . or had it been the day before that? Damn, he was so tired he couldn't remember.

"Let's do a sound check."

"Loud and clear," Carson said, answering Schaffer's voice coming across the tiny communication piece in his ear.

The clear device stuck to his lapel would pick up his voice as well as any sound in the room. Schaffer and Davis were monitoring the communication link from the Bureau's van down the block from the Criminal Justice Center.

"Heads up, Tanner," Davis said, "Wainwright has entered the parking garage."

Carson prepared for the confrontation. He'd spent five years admiring Donald Wainwright. Wanting to be just like the man. Wainwright had been like a father to him. Far more than a mentor and boss.

The idea that Wainwright had anything to do with this cover-up tore at Carson's insides. How could he do that to Carson? He'd watched

Carson go through hell all those years. How could he have done it to Carson's family?

And Drake. How the hell could he have known what he apparently knew and look Carson in the eye? Have him to dinner?

The idea that Dane had been involved felt wrong. Dane had never been a fighter. Never a bully. He'd been harmless. That part just didn't make sense.

Carson's office door flew open. Wainwright barged in. Maybe now Carson would know the whole truth.

"What the hell do you think you're doing, Carson?"

The DA's face was rage red, the veins in his neck bulging with fury. Otherwise he looked exactly as he did every day. Classic suit, crisp shirt, and red power tie.

"You might want to have a seat," Carson suggested, working hard to keep his tone calm.

Wainwright loomed over Carson's desk, refused to take a seat. "Where is this evidence you've supposedly discovered?" He leaned down, braced his fists on the desktop. "I hope you know this is going to cost you everything. I'll have you up before the bar by week's end." He moved his head firmly from side to side. "No one threatens me, and this feels exactly like a threat."

Carson opened the small box he'd placed on his desk and slid it toward Wainwright, then gestured to a chair. "As I said, you might want to have a seat."

Wainwright glanced at the contents of the box, then leveled a glower on Carson. "You called Aidan Moore, you called me, for *this?*" He pointed at the evidence. "So what, you found the missing rings. What does that prove? Nothing. What the hell did you think you were doing turning this into some kind of goddamned conspiracy?"

"It's not just the wedding bands." Carson closed the box, met that enraged glare without so much as a blink. "It's the statement given to me by Stokes."

"Fuck Stokes." Wainwright laughed outright. "Who's going to believe him?"

Carson kept his cool, not an easy feat considering he wanted to make this man pay more than he wanted to take his next breath. "There's also the statement from Dane Drake about the night my family was murdered."

Surprise flared in Wainwright's eyes. He recovered quickly and shrugged. "Dane's a drug addict. You can't believe anything he says."

Carson shook his head. "No. He was quite specific about details." He allowed Wainwright to see the victory in his eyes. No way was Carson going to be beaten, not even by the man who had mentored him. "He told me everything. He's willing to testify against everyone involved."

Wainwright straightened, his unrelenting gaze proof that he did not intend to give an inch despite the mounting evidence against him. "You don't really think you can get away with this, do you?"

Oh the man was good. He was choosing his words so very carefully. Manipulating him into incriminating himself wasn't going to be easy.

"Get away with what? Exposing that you worked a deal with Stokes to get him to say what you wanted him to say before he'd even been arrested for anything." Carson stood, matching the older man's stance. "You lied to me and everyone involved in the investigation of this case. You concealed information relevant to a triple homicide. I think you're the one who's not going to get away with it."

"Sometimes we do what we have to, Carson," Wainwright argued without the slightest remorse. "We're lawyers. We lie, skirt the boundaries of the rules. Whatever we have to do to get the job done. I've watched you do it in the courtroom. So don't hand me that holier-than-thou bullshit." He adjusted his tie. "Clean out your desk. You're finished."

"Tell him I've interviewed your witness," Schaffer whispered in Carson's earpiece.

Schaffer was turning out to be a real team player. "There's just one other thing," Carson said when Wainwright would have turned away.

Wainwright rested his smoldering fury on Carson once more.

"Dane Drake has confessed to his part in the murder of my family. He insists you were involved in the cover-up."

Okay, he was really reaching now. "Agent Schaffer is going over his statement, as we speak."

The color of outrage drained away, leaving Wainwright looking a little pale. "Why would Schaffer believe anything that pathetic piece of shit says?"

"I guess you'll have to ask her."

Wainwright leaned over the desk once more, going nose-to-nose with Carson. "Stokes is in prison. Let it go, Carson. Nothing you do now is going to change the fact that your family is dead. Stop now before it's too late." This time Wainwright turned around and walked all the way to the door before Carson decided on his next move.

"I just can't get the images out of my head," he said, stopping Wainwright in his departing tracks. Now he was going out on a real limb. "He kept going over and over how the whole plan had been your idea."

Wainwright spun around. "That's a lie. It was Drake's idea. He called Lynch and Holderfield . . ."

That was the moment. Carson saw it on his mentor's face. Wainwright realized he'd been had.

Carson held on to the final vestiges of his composure. "You, Holderfield, and Drake. You helped cover up what Dane had done." Fury bellowed inside him, made him want to jump across his desk and kill the man he had admired and respected for so damned long.

Wainwright shook his head. "I have nothing else to say." He turned toward the door but hesitated. His gaze connected with Carson's once more. "I will tell you, since it'll probably come out anyway as soon as Dane gets it right in that scrambled brain of his, he wasn't the one."

Tension vibrated inside Carson, had his heart thundering. "It was Patricia. She dragged Dane into the whole mess. She knew Drake would protect his children no matter what." Wainwright shrugged, defeated. "Drake had been protecting Patricia since college. He just didn't comprehend back then what he was getting himself into. His mistake"—Wainwright strained out a pathetic attempt at a laugh—"destroyed him and everything else he cared about. No one can control her. God knows I've tried."

"Why my family?" Carson heard himself ask. He'd wanted the answer to that question for so long. The problem was, he'd asked the wrong man last time.

Wainwright shook his head. "That's the most pathetic part." He made another of those defeated sounds that couldn't be called a laugh. "Drake discovered that his daughter had some of the same psychotic tendencies as her mother. Sick, Carson." Wainwright pressed Carson with a look of desperation. "Those two women are seriously sick. When Elizabeth pushed one of her classmates down the stairs, Drake knew he had to do something."

Carson vaguely remembered the incident but didn't recall any talk about it being anything other than an accident. The girl, Suzy or Cindy something or other, and her family had moved away the next year.

When Carson started to question Wainwright, he held up a hand to indicate he wasn't finished yet. "Drake thought with the right treatment his daughter could be helped since she was so young, but the plan backfired. Your mother, Olivia, promised to do what she could to help Elizabeth. Of course Drake didn't tell her the whole story, just little things he'd noticed about his daughter's behavior when no one else was looking. Your mother started seeing Elizabeth privately, completely off the record. When Olivia realized the extent of the problem, she urged Drake to send Elizabeth to a specialized clinic for intensive, long-term treatment."

Carson was the one holding up his hands this time. He'd heard enough of this. It didn't make sense. "What the hell are you talking about? Elizabeth is"—he shook his head, uncertain how to explain—"sweet and kind. You know that. Look at all she does for the community." This was insane. Moments he'd put completely out of his mind abruptly intruded. Little things Elizabeth had said or done that seemed out of character or odd at the time. But that wasn't enough evidence to point to the sort of disorder Wainwright was alleging.

Wainwright shook his head again, his expression resigned. "Poor Carson. You always want to believe the best in people. You have no idea."

Fury bolted through Carson. "How the hell did Elizabeth's so-called mental illness get my family murdered?" Just like before, twice the number of questions arose.

"Patricia learned of Olivia's plan so she took matters into her own hands. She wasn't about to let anyone send her daughter away." Wainwright's gaze bored into Carson's with a certainty that couldn't be feigned. "She wasn't about to let Olivia take you away from Elizabeth, either. So she eliminated the threat. She dragged us all into the cover-up." Wainwright shook his head. "Ultimately it was all about Elizabeth and *you.*"

That said, Wainwright opened the door to walk out. Two Jefferson County Sheriff's Department deputies were waiting.

Carson's heart bumped erratically against his sternum. The truth was all he'd ever wanted. Now he knew. Agony swelled inside him.

. . . it was all about Elizabeth and you.

"Tanner," Schaffer said via the communication link.

Carson jerked at the sound of the agent's voice. "Yeah."

"We have to get you to Eighth Avenue. Your uncle is there."

Carson blinked. Had to pull himself together. Wait. Annette had gone to help Max. "Where's Annette?" The irregular thudding in Carson's chest slowed to a near stop as he waited for a response.

"She's there. Elizabeth Drake, too. Lieutenant Lynch is singing like the proverbial canary. Looks like we've got a wrap, Tanner."

As painful as it was, as ugly as it was, Carson could finally put the past to rest.

45

Wednesday, September 29, 8:30 p.m.
3rd Avenue, Birmingham
Tanner Law Firm

Carson closed the case file and leaned back in his chair.

Man, he was tired.

His first week in his new law office and he'd put in more than eighty hours.

He surveyed the small office with its view of the alley. There was an even smaller lobby fronting his office with scarcely enough space for a receptionist's desk. It wasn't like his former home in the Criminal Justice Center, but it was where he wanted to be.

The offer to take over as acting district attorney had been on the table after Wainwright's arrest, but Carson hadn't been interested. He'd decided he didn't care for the political side of that position.

This was what he wanted to do with the rest of his life. Work for the people. Champion the little guy. Already he had a sizable client list. There would be no lack of cases.

He doubted he'd be making the papers or the news again anytime soon—but that was okay, too. He'd had enough of the spotlight to last him a lifetime. The first week after the story broke on Wainwright and his cronies, Carson had been inundated with interview requests and even a small cluster of paparazzi.

Justice had been served. He was finally at peace with the past. Stokes was still serving a life sentence. Wainwright had been arraigned and was awaiting trial. Lynch had turned state's evidence, narrowly dodging first-degree murder charges for his part in this nightmare. Lynch had come up with the idea of making the Tanner murders resemble those of a then-active serial killer—who turned out to be Stokes. Wainwright, Drake, and Holderfield had all cooperated. There was still some discrepancy as to whether Lynch had killed Dwight Holderfield, or Wainwright had. Each insisted the other had done it. According to Wainwright, Fleming had given Daniel Ledger, Annette's assistant, the order to terminate both Annette and Carson. Ledger hadn't worked up the wherewithal to do anything more than utilize scare tactics, though he had murdered Jazel Ramirez. Seemed he'd harbored some loyalty to Annette after all.

Carson still found it incredible that the people he had known and trusted could commit such horrific crimes against his family and him—people who they supposedly cared about.

Holderfield, Patricia, and the senator were dead already, so they had gotten theirs. As had Dane, though his had been undeserving to a large extent. Carson had concluded that his uncle had witnessed some part of the horror and that the people who had used his property to access the Tanner home the night of the murders were likely the *"they"* he so often spoke of during his episodes.

Carson would never in a million years have believed Patricia Drake capable of that kind of violence. All to ensure that her beloved daughter wasn't treated for her own mental illness and that she got what she wanted—Carson. Patricia had been one sick bitch who hadn't received the appropriate treatment for her multifaceted disorder. According to the experts she had likely suffered from borderline personality disorder with a hefty dose of narcissism and paranoia thrown in.

Carson couldn't help feeling some amount of guilt. If he hadn't foolishly fallen in love with Elizabeth, maybe his family would still be alive.

He couldn't change that now. He'd had no idea there were issues back then. In his mother's attempt to help Elizabeth while protecting Carson, she had sentenced herself and those she loved to death. But she hadn't known the full extent of what she was up against: a twisted daughter with a psychopath for a mother. Elizabeth was undergoing psychiatric evaluation to determine her fitness for trial.

And all that time Carson had worried about *his* genes.

Annette was cooperating with the FBI, and Otis Fleming was going down. The old bastard had been denied bail since he was considered a flight risk. The whole city was enthralled with the evolving events around the case.

Agent Schaffer had been offered a position at Quantico, a promotion. She hadn't decided yet if she would accept the offer.

Carson stood and stretched. He was exhausted, but it felt good. For the first time in his adult life he didn't have a cloud hanging over his head.

He had found the truth. Strangely enough, he owed that accomplishment to a woman who had operated outside the law for most of her life. A smile slid across his face. Her past had been put to rest as well.

The bell jingled, indicating someone had entered his office. He frowned. Hadn't he locked the door at six?

Carson rounded his desk just in time to run into Annette at the door between his office and the lobby.

"You should learn to lock up after hours, counselor." She leaned against the door frame. "A guy could get mugged or . . . *worse.*"

His gaze roamed from those beautiful eyes and those lush lips all the way down to the sleek black stilettos. The short black dress in between showcased slender curves and toned legs. He wet his lips, could taste her already.

"How was your visit with Paula?" Annette had called at six to let him know she planned to see her sister. He'd opted to work late instead of going home alone.

"Good." Annette straightened from the door and moved toward him, forcing him to back up. "Very good. Did you get a lot done?" She glanced at the mass of folders and notes on his desk.

"I did."

"Excellent." She grabbed him by the tie and pulled his face down to hers. "Because I'm going to take you home and do all kinds of things to you."

He tugged at a strand of her hair. "What's wrong with right here?"

She smiled. "Nothing, counselor." She wrenched open his belt and then his fly before pushing him back onto his desk and scaling his body. "Not one damned thing."

This thing between them could go anywhere or nowhere but the ride . . . was all that mattered for now.

ACKNOWLEDGMENTS

Birmingham, Alabama, is one of the largest cities in the state of Alabama. According to the official website for Birmingham, the city is nestled at the foothills of the Appalachian Mountains at the cross-section of two major railroads. Once the primary industrial center of the southern United States, Birmingham grew so fast in population it was called the "Magic City." In recent decades, Birmingham has become one of the foremost medical centers of the south. That fact is why, for me, Birmingham is the Magic City for a much more personal reason.

At age eighteen I had my first child, Erica. Erica was born with a rare and permanently debilitating congenital defect called arthrogryposis multiplex congenita. Few doctors had ever even seen a child with arthrogryposis, much less had the daunting task of caring for one. Fortunately for me, my obstetrician, Dr. Lewis Letson, rushed my sweet baby girl to Birmingham's Children's Hospital, where she was eventually placed in the capable hands of Dr. Kurt Neimann. Dr. Neimann, willingly and for very little pay, embraced that daunting task. He and his team of orthopedic residents worked with Erica through serial casting, numerous surgeries, hideous braces, and endless hours of physical therapy until her precious arms and legs were no longer useless, gnarled limbs. It was Dr. Neimann who urged me to treat Erica like a normal little girl; otherwise she would certainly never be normal. Dr. Neimann and his team never gave up and provided an endless source of hope and encouragement when other doctors informed me that I was looking for a miracle that I would not find.

For eighteen years Erica received the finest treatment available, allowing her to grow into a happy young woman with a bright future. For this, I owe the city of Birmingham and its brilliant physicians and medical facilities a tremendous debt of gratitude.

Birmingham is the Magic City, and I thank you with all my heart.

ABOUT THE AUTHOR

Photo © 2019 Jenni M Photography LLC

Debra Webb is a *USA Today* bestselling author of more than 175 novels. She is the recipient of the prestigious *Romantic Times* Career Achievement Award for Romantic Suspense, as well as numerous Reviewers' Choice Awards. In 2012, Debra was honored as the first recipient of the esteemed L. A. Banks Warrior Woman Award for her courage, strength, and grace in the face of adversity. She was also awarded the distinguished RWA Centennial Award for having published her hundredth novel. Debra has sold more than ten million books in many languages and countries. The author's love of storytelling goes back to her childhood, when her mother bought her an old typewriter at a tag sale. Born in Alabama, Debra grew up on a farm and spent every available hour exploring the world around her and creating stories. For more information, visit www.debrawebb.com.